THE PA

MW01715357

Jeffrey M. Houska, R.N., C., F.N.P.

It is the early 1970's. An old and powerful cardinal at the Vatican has somberly observed the decadence of the '60s — drugs, extramarital sex, the hippie movement's anarchy, riots, protest marches, broken marriages and families, and the general population's disillusionment with religion and authority. His thinking has progressively degenerated. Finally he breaks when his perceived hidden aberrancy of nature, the homosexual movement, rides the wave of satanism and makes public its demands for "Gay Liberation."

The twisted old man enlists the aid of two world-class biogeneticists who share in his extremism. Together they conclude that they have been divinely "chosen" to return mankind to a God-fearing morality. They conspire to plant a plague amongst the sinners, not unlike God's own plagues upon the sinners in Biblical times. It is hoped that this disease will be regarded as a warning from God for all of mankind to stop its self-destructive behavior and return to the "fold."

A handful of thrilleresque subplots develop as the story weaves through the next two decades, with avarice and power brokers carrying the central theme to its unexpected finale.

❦ ❦ ❦

About The Author

Mr. Houska is a nationally certified family nurse practitioner in private practice and holds a medical school faculty appointment. He is also a patented inventor and sculptor.

He was raised in the Black Hills of South Dakota where he developed his forthright and iconoclastic "emperor has no clothes" outlook on the human condition.

His first love, however, is writing, hence *The Pandora Factor,* his first novel.

❦ ❦ ❦

The Pandora Factor

by

Jeffrey M. Houska
R.N., C., F.N.P.

Notice: This novel is entirely fiction. Any words, thoughts, or deeds expressed by any of the characters herein are purely imaginary, generated in the author's whimsical mind.

Babylon Publishing Company
Albuquerque, New Mexico

Babylon Publishing Company books are available at quantity discounts when used to promote products or services. For information, please write to Babylon Publishing Company, PO Box 35819, Dept.H, Albuquerque,, New Mexico 87176-5819.

Published by:
Babylon Publishing Company
PO Box 35819
Albuquerque, New Mexico 87176-5819
U.S.A.

THE PANDORA FACTOR

Library of Congress Catalog Card Number: 89-81754
ISBN 0-9625646-0-5 - Limited Edition Hardcover
ISBN 0-9625646-2-1 - Quality Trade Edition

First Printing, January 1991

9 8 7 6 5 4 3 2 1

Printed in New Mexico, the United States of America

Dedication

This, my first novel, The Pandora Factor, is dedicated to my mother, for her instilling in me, since childhood, the ability to accomplish personal goals through freedom of thought and expression, and for her continued emotional and inspirational support toward the completion of this undertaking.

Thanks, Mom!

Acknowledgement

I wish to thank my editor for her patience and tenacity. Thanks also to Western Publisher's Consortium for assistance and technical advisement, and to K.W. for her ability to calm the savage beast within!

Part One
The
Conspiracy

Prologue

"Desmond? *Desmond?*" Cardinal Saffioti tugged on the pleat of Cardinal Wentworth's scarlet-trimmed black cassock as he repeated his name.

Wentworth swayed, off balance, then turned to Saffioti. "*What?*"

"Er . . . excuse me for being so forward, but take this from a friend, as it's intended. Don't you think you've had enough?" asked Saffioti, his long time friend and confidante. "You've been doing so very well for such a long time. I hate to see —"

A string quartet interrupted, its whimsical muses rose softly and reverberated through the background in the ancient granite and marble hall, intermixing with idle social chatter and the tinkling of crystal stemware.

Wentworth ignored his friend. "Isn't that 6/8 time? Hmm . . . The dominance of the cello . . . Yes, of course. It's Beethoven's Second Movement of 'Razumovsky!'" He turned abruptly away from Saffioti, immersed in the music for a moment. He drummed his fingers in the air in time with the music, and then, unexpectedly, whirled back around. "Thank you for your concern, my old friend, but this is a *grand event*, correct? And how do *you* propose to know when *I've* had enough?"

"Oh, *come now*, Desmond."

Wentworth sneered, tightening his grip on the stem of the fifty year old, classic Fostoria glassware. The crystal snapped, sending both the glass and its twelve year old contents tumbling down over his black cassock. "Now, see what you've done!" he said indignantly. "You *know* how upset your harping can make me!" He haphazardly jabbed his napkin at the liquid dripping down the front of his formal cassock.

"Desmond, don't be so abrasive," his friend admonished. "It's perfectly obvious that you've had enough. You can't hide it. The corner of your eye is jumping like crazy." Saffioti began wiping the splatter from his own garb.

"Sor - ry," Wentworth half apologized, half defended. "The *tic* . . . Am I doing it again . . . now?"

"Yes, you are. You haven't been bothered for two or three years, and it's now only when you've had too much to drink."

"Thank you." Desmond stared at Saffioti. "I'll try to control it. But it isn't related to the drink, you know. It's just a little nervous quirk. I mean, we *all* have our little . . . problems . . . Don't we now?" He thought for a moment, then, "Saffioti, you're such a boor!"

"Ah, Cardinal Saffioti," the tuxedo-clad, gray haired man said as he stepped forward to take the cardinal's hand, "and how are you? It's been years!"

"I'm quite well, Dr. Thomas," Saffioti said, facing the gentleman and shaking his hand. "It's very good to see you. According to the newspapers, you're becoming a man of note. Biogenetic experiments, is that it?"

"That's right, Cardinal," Dr. Thomas said. "You keep up well."

"Why, thank you, Doctor. If I'm not mistaken, you might possibly be close to finding a cancer cure."

"Exciting stuff, isn't it?"

"God's work always is. But, I think you'd better get a new tux to suit your new status. That batik pattern hasn't been in style since—"

"To say *nothing* of your cassock, Cardinal! How long has *that* been the style . . . getting on two thousand years?" Noah Thomas laughed.

"But *I'm* not a man of note, Doctor. Take my advice. Get rid of the batik."

"Man of note is a bit grandiose, isn't it?" Noah said, blushing slightly.

"Not at all. You've become a true pioneer. Besides, modesty doesn't suit you."

"The work is exhilarating, but my attempts at biological engineering could only be classified as infantile. The field is so new."

"There you go again. Modesty just isn't— Oh, dear. Oh, I'm so sorry, Desmond." Saffioti proceeded to correct his social blunder with a thinly disguised laugh. "Dr. Noah Thomas, I'd like you to meet an old and dear friend, Cardinal Desmond Wentworth."

"Pleased to meet you, Cardinal Wentworth."

"The pleasure is mine, I'm s-sure." Wentworth, now well conscious of his twitching eye, tried to overcome the embarrassing effects of the alcohol by making several erratic hand gestures which he hoped would distract the doctor's attention. "I know much about you, Dr. Thomas. You're one of the principals in getting this art project off the ground, which is the reason for this extraordinary gala. I'm thoroughly enjoying myself."

"So happy to hear it," Noah said dryly.

Wentworth swung his arm dramatically, indicating the party in the large hall. "How many attendees, perhaps three hundred? And how much did each contribute? They're all well-heeled, no?"

Noah looked at Saffioti and saw a look of tolerant impatience. Noah lowered his voice to a whisper. "Please, Cardinal Wentworth, your forthrightness is humorous, but somewhat improper in here. Someone might overhear you! Our large contributors are rather quiet types."

"Cardinal Saffioti. Cardinal Saffioti." The page boy eased his way through the crowd, then spotted the man he was looking for. "Cardinal, you're wanted in the lobby."

"Thank you, young man. Oh, and since you're here, could you please have someone clean up this mess?" He pointed at the broken crystal on the floor.

"Yes, Your Eminence, right away." The page disappeared into the crowd.

"Well, excuse me, gentlemen, but I'd better go see who's

demanding my presence. Enjoy yourselves. And remember our little talk, Cardinal." Saffioti sat his drink on the table nearby and vanished into the horde of socialites.

"How 'bout another cocktail, Dr. Thomas?" Wentworth asked.

"I believe I will, thank you. Let's go that direction, I think there's a bar set up over there. And, please, call me Noah."

"By all means, Noah, and you call me Desmond." They crossed the great, well lit room, single file, passing in front of the quartet, and approached the bar.

"What's your pleasure, Noah?"

"White wine, please. Oh, I don't know, it seems I've had more than my share this afternoon. Maybe I'll just have water."

"Noah, Noah. It's such an historic event! You, as one of the principal 'shakers,' are entitled to a congratulatory toddy! How many others in this world can claim that they helped convince the conservatives of the *Vatican*, for God's sake, to admit modern art into its galleries? You are a walking *enigma*! And to accomplish this so quickly. When will the new works be open to the public?"

"Thank you for the flattery, Desmond. In '73, just two years away. And *you* have an innate ability to influence people's decisions yourself! Sure I'll have another. I like you, Desmond."

Wentworth smiled to himself. Someone to drink with who wouldn't harp on his background. "Bartender, sir, a double Glenfiddich straight up, and your best white wine," he called out. "And leave the bottles, too," he commanded. The barman fixed their drinks, then plunked the two open bottles on the bar. "Come with me, Noah, let's go where we can talk intelligently." He handed the full glasses to Noah, then picked up the bottles. "There's a quiet, comfortable lounge area off the lobby. I think we're going to become good friends."

Wentworth felt something about this charming, intelligent man. Possibly he had found someone with whom he could really, *truly* relate, releasing all of his pent up emotions over the years. He had grown weary of single-handedly carrying the emotional burden.

Wentworth held the door open for the doctor. "In here."

"My, this is very nice," commented Noah. "How did you know of it?" It was a sparkling, modern room, compared to the great hall. The sun shone through the southern windows.

"This is where I come to read and meditate. It's my refuge . . .. believe it or not, this wonderful room is used very rarely. Most people overlook it as some kind of a formal living room. Please, sit over there on the divan. It's very comfortable." The doctor did as suggested.

Desmond Wentworth was more and more amazed as the time passed. What might have been simply a brief exchange between new acquaintances turned into a long and satisfying conversation. They shared so many similar opinions and were mutually amused by their common ideologies on the human condition. Politics, religion, society, world events, crime, hunger, greed, and the shared perception of the stupidity of world leaders throughout history. They laughed at the same sarcasms and cynicisms, each trying to outdo the other in black humor. The liquor flowed freely and the men became drunker. The sun had died away hours earlier, and the lively conversation waned. They became serious.

"Desmond, sorry to interrupt you, but, if I may be so bold. Do you have some kind of a neurologic disorder? Your facial tic, it must drive you crazy. You know, there are surgical options."

Wentworth looked up, somberly. "No, no, something I've learned to live with. It's nothing, really. When I get on a topic that causes me stress, it just happens." Wentworth's inhibitions were now fully anesthetized, and he didn't give a whit about the tic. "It started when I was a boy," he rambled, slurring as he spoke. "My father abandoned us, and my mother needed money. When I'd see my mother with all those men. . ." And what I let them do to *me*, he quickly thought to himself.

"Excuse me? I didn't hear, you were mumbling."

Wentworth became irritated. "I *said*," loudly, "my mother was a *whore*!"

Thomas, stunned at first, finally realized the man's advanced state of drunkenness, then chose not to comment. What could be said in a situation like this? He tried to be soothing and supportive. "We all have things in our past we'd rather forget, Desmond."

"Let's change the subject."

"Well, then, let's *do* change the subject." Noah immediately smiled, trying to be more upbeat. He was relieved that the cardinal, not wanting to dwell on his past, had allowed a smooth transition into another topic, *any* topic. "I believe we've more than buried the topic of sin and the human race's spiritual degeneration over recent history. Alas, like politics and the weather, there's nothing to be done about it anyway, except for some lip service."

"I suppose," Wentworth said sullenly.

"And as for the coming out of the homosexual movement, well . . . What can be said, much less *done*, about that? Er . . .we talked about it earlier."

"Not a thing." Wentworth stared blankly.

"I guess we'll simply have to wait until God decides it's time for another plague." Noah laughed.

"Unless . . . "

"Unless what, Desmond?"

Wentworth sat up straight. "A plague . . . " He tapped his fingers against his nearly empty glass. "I suppose man could take things into his own hands."

"Man? What man?"

"Some brilliant scientist. An intervention of sorts . . . To 'respiritualize' society . . . You understand." Desmond laughed.

"Pretty far-fetched."

"Perhaps."

1973

VATICAN CITY, MAY

It was particularly warm for early May, Monsignor Brian O'Casey observed that morning as he leisurely strolled toward the New Gardens. The lilacs were in full-colored brilliance, the air was heavy with their overpowering fragrance.

Brian passed an old Yugoslavian bishop whose name he didn't remember, only the story of his escape from political imprisonment. He bid, "Good morning, sir."

The bishop nodded, "Off to anoder meeting vid da cardinal and dat tveed-suited gentleman, Monsignor?" he asked in his barely understandable dialect. "Vat's going on vid you folks, anyvay? Wery secretive . . . Your meetings used to be so much more frequent. It seems like a year ago ven you used to meet so often."

"Why do you feel that my speaking with these men is so mysterious?" Brian tried not to show his discomfort with the bishop's observation. *How does this old man know anything? Have we been that obvious?*

"I have noticed, over time, dat you and da cardinal never come to da garden to meditate, singly, dat is. If von of you shows up here, da odder shortly follows, and den da tveeded fellow joins you. Vat are you doing, vorking on a plan to save da vorld?" the bishop laughed.

Brian laughed nervously. He hoped his expression was

controlled. "Sure, that's it, we're out to save the world! Good day to you, Bishop." He continued his uneasy laugh, trying to sound sincere, as he walked briskly away.

Brian was a young man, for a monsignor, anyway, in the eyes of the church. He was ruggedly handsome, square jawed, with large blue eyes, and a shock of reddish-blond hair that swooped laterally across his forehead, a style remnant from the early Beatles era.

Continuing in his gait, he took some deep breaths in order to regain his composure. *Nah, the bishop didn't know anything, he was just making light talk. Nosey old thing, didn't have anything better to do than sit and spy on people.* He felt better with this resolve and returned to admiring the garden. It was beautiful.

Some of the citizens at the Vatican, mostly old and retired church figures of international importance, were forced to stay in their apartments this time of year because of their pollen allergies. How unfortunate for them, Brian thought, being unable to enjoy one of God's great endeavors, this annual glorious arrival of spring. He stopped several times along the way to fully appreciate the tantalizing bouquet swelling in his nostrils.

Something was different this morning, he noticed, as he looked skyward. The air was delightfully clean in contrast to the normal grayish appearance he knew so well. There had been a slight moist breeze through the city during the night, he remembered, clearing the air of yesterday's essence of Rome.

The lilac's lavender blossoms were incredible, none like he had seen in the States. Perhaps they were of a different strain, or possibly it was that he had never seen so many, and clustered into a particular area such as these most beautiful gardens. The dew still clung to their downy flowers, magnifying their beauty and color by radiant solar reflection.

Brian was pleased that he'd been called out to the gardens for this meeting. It made the anticipated company and subject matter more tolerable. He glanced at his watch, then hurried his pace, knowing how his superior, the cardinal, disliked tardiness for any reason.

Cardinal Desmond Wentworth was a very powerful man, holding the title of Prefect for the Congregation for the Doctrine of the Faith. He held the power to make or break a lesser's career; for this reason Brian was attentive to the grisly old man's demands.

He strode down the worn flagstone pathway, awed by the tremendous cypress trees that towered overhead. They were huge, ancient spires, undoubtedly having been witness to the sculpting of world events, events that had been shaped in these very, historic gardens. So perfect they were, in thin vertical elliptical shapes, that one would think they were manicured weekly, but that idea was impossible on their sheer height alone. The well-planned assortment of other conifers and sculptured greenery added to the serenity.

Wentworth, an Englishman who had been at the Vatican for thirty-eight of his sixty-eight years, was seated on a bench in the far northeast corner of the gardens as the monsignor rounded the last row of cypress trees. Even though he was still quite far away, there was no mistaking the old man's hooked nose and goiter profile, appearing as an earth-bound vulture who had somehow lost the gift of flight.

The old man had both elbows on the stone table in front of him, as if in prayer, but his eyes were fixed eerily on Brian, as the younger man closed the last fifty yards. Wentworth yearned for his youth whenever he saw this idealistic young man, this man full of life, and hope, and dedication to the vocation of serving God through humanity.

Wentworth knew that Monsignor O'Casey was an Irish-American, another non-Italian rarity like himself at the Vatican City. The young man had attended seminary school somewhere in the state of Illinois, and was ordained at the age of twenty-five, just five years earlier. He held a master's degree in international relations, and his father was well connected in the political world as the U.S. ambassador to Sweden. He was trilingual by necessity, due to his family's foreign travel, speaking Swedish and Spanish almost as well as English.

"Damn," the cardinal muttered to himself. The bothersome facial tic that too often now claimed possession of his left eye always became apparent when he mentally delved into the many deep annoyances of his usually dull, placid existence. "It must be due to our mission."

Wentworth's tic exacerbated, predictably, as he sunk once again into thoughts of his hatred for homosexuals, the entire focus of this meeting. *Why couldn't they just shut up and keep their sick behavior out of the public eye? Seven years. Seven long years of torturous self-guilt resolution and aversion therapy!* He had finally, after enduring these years of personal pain, lost his desire for sex with young men. Anxiety and guilt over his sinful behavior had almost caused his suicide. *I hate them!*

Wisely, he had outwardly avoided this personal hatred when he involved the other men in this project. *"It's not the homosexuals in particular, but all of humankind, who must interpret this plague as a warning from God to return to His way,"* he remembered telling the men at the original planning meeting.

He tried diligently, but unsuccessfully, to control the worsening twitch, oblivious to the young monsignor closing the last few yards. He must regain control of himself! He massaged his eye, and the tic abated.

Brian cleared his throat. "I said *good morning*, Your Eminence. It is truly a beautiful morning, don't you think?" Monsignor O'Casey was now standing over the cardinal, his head quizzically cocked to the side. "Are you all right, sir?"

"How long have you been standing there, Monsignor?"

"For just a few moments, but you seemed so absorbed in thought, I thought I'd wait." Brian continued to stand, watching the facial twitch of the old man. He momentarily reflected on his disdain for the frail old wretch.

The man had a sallow, sunken face, with protruding gray eyeballs that stared through outdated wire rimmed, dirty glasses. Brian wondered how the old man could see through the filthy lenses. The old man's twitch continued, one that Brian had seen many times before, which seemed to worsen when the man went into one of his tirades about the deteriorating condition of man's relationship with God.

It would just be a short time, Brian hoped, before he would receive another promotion and wouldn't have to put up with the old man's rantings. He waited to be asked to be seated.

"Er, yes . . . That I was, er, deep in thought, meditation." The old man squirmed for a moment as he regained his composure. "Yes, yes . . . it's a beautiful day, Monsignor. How was your recent trip?" The cardinal was not really interested in a response, but pleasantries somehow seemed in order before undertaking the matter at hand. "Please, be seated," he added with a commanding wave toward the bench opposite him. He thought he could avoid a long response by this interruption of his own question.

"Thank you," Brian said as he slipped sideways onto the cool, hard bench. His cassock made any other approach impossible. "Washington was beautiful, and the cherry blossoms were more picturesque than ever this year. I've got some slides to show that are wonderful. Perhaps you'd like to see them tonight."

"Yes, that would be nice," the cardinal replied indifferently. "I'm sure they're lovely. Now, have you seen Dr. Thomas yet?"

"No, Your Eminence, I had thought he'd be with you. I know he knows to meet us here about now, however."

"Well, I guess we can talk a little, then. Monsignor, I get the feeling that you are not totally committed to this project." His penetrating eyes burned through Brian.

"I, uh, *do* have some reservations, but as time goes on, I certainly understand the rationale, and I *am* in agreement, in principal, anyway."

Brian knew he was in for another long diatribe on the cardinal's motives for the project. It was strange, Brian thought, how *all* of the men were so easily influenced by this old man. Brian agreed, though, that humankind must return to a moralistic state in order to sustain itself.

The cardinal cleared his throat, then subconciously contorted his mouth to the left, trying earnestly to stop the spasm. Brian had seen him do this often, and ignored the urge to comment.

"My naive young friend," the cardinal began, "you have not been on this planet long enough to know what life *used* to be like. True, there were wars and other atrocities, but *nothing* like we are experiencing in these trying times. In fact, wars may have even been beneficial. They bonded people together for a common cause, and usually the *good* side won, and almost always claimed the win for God. The *bad* element, the *evil*, almost always lost, and with their loss God sent a great number of sinners to hell!"

Brian was taken aback. He knew of the cardinal's ultra-conservatism, but *this* statement was the most sanctimonious of all! He continued to listen, distasteful as it was.

"Anyway, people were basically simple and good, and felt a bonding with God in earlier times," the cardinal continued. Brian was becoming uneasy, being forced to sit and listen, feeling unable to say anything contrary.

A young priest, whistling absent-mindedly, slowly ambled past, then stopped to smell the blossoms on the bush next to them.

Unaware, the cardinal carried on. "Yes, there were truly bad, sinful people, too . . . *prostitutes* and such, who never accepted God and therefore went, quite righteously, to *hell*. But man has slipped ever deeper into the quagmire of sin. Now we are faced with divorce . . . birth control . . . extra-marital sex . . . abortion . . . drugs . . . violence . . . homosexuals.

"Now, I'm a forgiving man, mind you, and when an evil person comes forth and makes amends with God, confessing his sinful desires and acts, I can find it in my heart to forgive that person. Believe me, Monsignor, I know of what I say . . . *I* was once a sinner, but through the grace of God I have found inner peace."

His tic returned as he rambled. Brian sat with his eyes cast downward at the stone table top, wishing, somewhat fiendishly, how he could ask the old man about his "sins."

"Beneath all of this decadence," the cardinal droned on, "Satan is at work, eroding the discipline of the soul and replacing it with wanton hedonism."

The young priest nearby was now turned toward the cardinal, listening intently.

"Would you like to join us, Father?" asked Brian.

He looked sheepishly away, then turned back. "I—I'm very sorry

. . . I didn't mean to pry. But Cardinal Wentworth, sir, I've always admired your philosophies, and I couldn't help myself . . . I wanted to listen." His face glowed with the rosiness of a child caught stealing candy. "If you *really* wouldn't mind, I'd *love* to join you!"

"Please, then, sit down," pleaded Brian, with the cardinal's obvious pleasure. Brian was happy to share his boredom. The old man would have another diversion to stare at through his dirty glasses. The young man sat.

"Now, where was I . . . " the old man beamed. "Oh, yes . . .
As I have long felt, the church has been remiss in dealing with the new liberalism, too tolerant of waywardness. Particularly in the U.S., where trends, like "Gay Liberation," seem to conceptualize, germinate, grow, and finally spread throughout the world with explosivity.

"I lay much of the blame squarely on the Vatican Council II of the early sixties. I feel the council members, in spite of their well-intended modernization of the religion, opened Pandora's box. Tell me, my young friends, can the learned wisdom of two thousand years of canon law be dramatically altered such as it was without consequence? I think not." He answered his own question again.

Brian had learned to overlook this idiosyncracy while the cardinal was in a rambling mode. He smiled to himself, trying not to let his sparkling eyes give him away.

"And now, the newest dilemma to attack and threaten the sovereignty of the church, the homosexual movement. Again, the sexual revolution and new demands regarding personal rights and preferences above the will of God in sexual gratification has struck. Homosexuality, in the past regarded as a sociopathic illness and a wretched aberrancy of nature, is being openly discussed as a "me too" issue in the new hedonism. Now they call themselves 'gay' for Pete's sake! I *used* to have such a fondness for that word . . . its pleasant connotation of light-hearted happiness! "

"But, Your Eminence, don't you think God created homosexuals for *some* purpose?" the enthralled young priest queried. "Does God have *anything* on His earth without purpose?"

"What is your name, Father?" growled the cardinal, glaring at him like Brian had never seen him look at anyone before.

"Antonio, Eminence, please just call me Antonio." The young man shrunk, his voice became meek. He wisely didn't offer his surname.

"Please don't interrupt me *again*, Father Antonio!" the old man barked. Brian successfully contained his belly laugh, and his compassion for the young man. "Tell me, wise young man, is there a purpose to crime, or hunger, or *flies* and *ants*, for that matter, other than to test our resolve while we occupy our physical life on this planet?"

"Uh . . . uh . . . " the frightened young priest's voice crackled. "I'm sorry, sir . . . perhaps I should be going." He stood and hastened away.

The cardinal finished his tirade, ever louder to insure that the quickly fading young man could hear. "And now, homosexuals are openly admitting their sexuality, and openly *flaunting* their unnatural, bizarre lifestyles, in the streets!"

The cardinal's face subtly changed. At first, grisled and mean, then his taught lips separated slightly, then a little more, and eventually widened to a large grin. He suddenly broke into a deep, throaty roar of laughter, with Brian carelessly joining in.

"The poor, frightened little rabbit. It was such an obvious attempt at brown-nosing. He'll never make it past assistant pastor," the cardinal cajoled. "But, you, Brian, on the other hand, have what it takes. Be loyal to me, and great things may come your way. I know why you were selected as pronuncio to the U.S. Your archbishop over there recommended you to my good friend, Cardinal Safiotti. Do you know Cardinal Saffioti?"

"Certainly. He's a wise and greatly respected man. He told me that I was given the position, which I realize is highly desirable, to replace Cardinal Libio when he got sick and retired."

"Yes, that's true. You know, at first, before I came to know you, I was annoyed that Saffioti promoted you so quickly, and just to fill the position. I was somewhat, shall I say, envious. I had to *work* up to my position the old way, through dedication and hard work."

"And you don't feel I'm dedicated?" Brian was offended by the inference. He looked down and flicked a small twig away that had fallen on his lap.

"Oh, you are *very* dedicated, I know that. And Cardinal Saffioti provided me with many of his reasons for promoting you so quickly. You see, the hierarchical powers of the U.S. church would be indignant if they were forced to accept a common working priest as their official ambassador from the Holy See. But, quite honestly, your youth was held against you at the time, by myself and some of the other conservatives here.

"However," he paused, tapping his finger tips together, "how shall I put this? You were *promoted* simply to fill the pronuncio's role, because in the political arena, credentials are everything. Safiotti had actually wanted to elevate you to the position of *cardinal*, as are the other pronuncios! Can you imagine," he laughed at Brian, "a thirty-some-odd year old *cardinal*?"

Brian hid his frustration. *Why couldn't there be a young cardinal?* He held his tongue. "Yes, I can see where that would be *much* too radical," he lied.

"You know, Cardinal Saffioti harbors great plans for you. You *may* end up the youngest cardinal in church history, after all! But be patient, young man."

"Yes, patience . . . I *do* feel as though I've made great strides within the U.S. I feel as though they are finally accepting me, in spite of my youth, and knowing I've only had this position for two years. I'm quite confident of my capabilities. I'm careful to use a liberally conservative approach, trying to maintain a balance. I try to travel frequently back and forth to keep the lines of communication open between the Vatican and the U.S. church."

"You know, then, that there is great concern here over the Americans. That's another reason you were named pronuncio. Their priests seem to be more liberal in translating church law, and you, with your youthful outlook, appeal to them more than an older, hard-liner might."

"I sort of reckoned that. *Too* liberal over there for the old goats, huh?"

"Monsignor O'Casey! Please use some *decorum.* You must understand the problem . . . American Catholics are making their own moral decisions, with the seeming approval of U.S. priests, by making personal amends with God. Many have forsaken the will of the Pope, and the teachings of the church, when these principles don't meet their own needs. 'Free love' . . . birth control . . . optional abortion. The news media has even dubbed this 'free love' movement to be 'teenagers exploring their sexuality.'"

"Well, possibly—"

"Don't interrupt, Monsignor!" The cardinal's mood quickly changed, and the tic was once again obvious. Brian knew he was in for another verbal onslaught. *"How preposterous! Damned fools!* The Pope's infallibility in interpreting God's will, and the wisdom of canon law of the past two millennia . . . all threatened by this self-righteous rebellion.

"It seems to have started with the social upheaval of the sixties. And now, the homosexuals are demanding political influence, and, worse yet, want acceptance within the *church!*"

Brian cast his eyes downward, trying to mentally shut out the old man's drone by thinking of the cherry blossoms in Washington. He felt a welcome bolt of relief when he caught sight of the approaching doctor, Noah Thomas, in his peripheral vision. "Ah, here comes Dr. Thomas." The old man shifted his position to watch the doctor approach.

Dr. Thomas walked up at a brisk pace, apologizing as he approached. "I'm sorry, gentlemen, but I had one phone call to wait upon before I could give you any information. It looks strongly as though we can proceed," he panted as he sat at the stone table. "These old bones aren't what they used to be," he grunted, raising his leg over the bench manually. "Much better, yes."

"Not even a 'hello?'" Brian smiled. "How are you, Dr. Thomas?"

"Oh, I guess I'm just absent-minded and too harried in my old age," he smiled. "Hello!"

"So . . . continue, Doctor. I'm anxious to get on with it," the cardinal interjected.

"Everything is going satisfactorily. We may have a small problem, however, as some of the research students don't understand the goal of this project. They are asking questions, even though they have been told that our research lab has been contracted by a Swiss pharmaceutical company to do a small facet of testing for a new live biologic pharmaceutical. The students want to know why we are involved in primate testing. I don't know, just don't know . . .

"When I was a student, many years ago, mind you, we didn't dare question whatever research we were working on. We respected those in control of the project as brilliant scientists, and felt fortunate to be involved in the improvement of world health through our meager efforts, to work as an international team, you know. I'm happy we only have two students to concern ourselves with. It seems *nothing* is sacred. Uh . . . beg your pardons, sirs. I must be more cognizant of figures of speech, I guess."

"Yes, yes," Cardinal Wentworth replied, intolerant of the doctor's rambling. "Were the students sufficiently satisfied with your explanation for the research?"

"I believe so. They've been told they're involved in a virology research project that may open some new pathways in cancer research by extracting naturally occurring viruses from these green monkeys. These animals carry an odd, self-destructive viral complex, but at the same time they've developed viral antibodies to protect themselves."

"Well, what are the students *supposed* to believe?" Brian didn't like the deceit.

"They've been told that we're trying to duplicate this process in hopes of applying it to human cancer forms. They're amazed, as we all are, with the physiologic adaptation of this species, and are following orders very well. We must be very careful, as they're very bright and seem to be piqued at some of the research data we ask for."

"Be *careful*," the cardinal warned. "We don't need any extraneous interference from those young, fool hardy, bleeding-heart rebels. It amazes me how one single whistle blower can destroy a worthwhile project, in its infancy, on a personal, subjective opinion. There seems to be no regard for the societal common good anymore, its *me!*, *me!*, *me!*"

"I agree whole-heartedly, Your Eminence," Dr. Thomas responded, "and hence my participation and commitment to this endeavor."

The monsignor, whom to this point had been pensively gazing and massaging his chin, nodded his head in what seemed to be a consensus. "Well, so . . . what has transpired through your research, Doctor?"

"Ah, yes. As I mentioned, I was awaiting a phone call from Stockholm to confirm our theory, which I received only an hour ago. It seems that we're on the right track."

The cardinal smiled. "It's possible, then, that natural occurrences can still manipulate the self-indulgent destruction of society, albeit aided by a handful of mortals like ourselves. I feel deeply that it is His will, this act of divinity that we are intent upon."

"But, Your Eminence, what if our project has greater repercussions than we've considered?" Brian interjected. "I realize that we've been quite diligent in our approach so far, but, for example, what if—"

"Please, Monsignor, I believe we have hypothesized all of the possible scenarios already," Cardinal Wentworth interrupted. "By creating further delay through self-doubt, we gain nothing more than to compound our already difficult mission. *Through* self-doubt, we create schisms in our devotion to this singular ideology for salvation from man's self-destruction. Isn't the fact that everything has progressed so favorably to this point reassuring? You must remember, we've been *chosen* for this mission of salvation, yes?"

"You know full-well that I support the purpose of this intervention, Your Eminence, but we are, obviously, working with somewhat limited data."

"Are you questioning the abilities of Dr. Thomas and his associates, Monsignor?"

"Gentlemen, gentlemen, please . . . I, too, have moments of personal concern. But we *have* done repeated computer simulations of any potential catastrophic downturns. All can be avoided or controlled by using our master plan. Now, all we need is the agent and the vehicle confirmations. The agent prospect is fairly well documented. Hans, er . . . Doctor Bjorgstad—"

"Who is Dr. Bjorgstad?" Brian cut in.

"Er, he is the 'silent' partner who shares our beliefs. He's a *brilliant* researcher. Anyway, he has determined that the virus from the primates can probably be introduced into the human species. We, Hans and I, feel that the world scientific community would be caught off guard with this new disease suddenly manifesting itself in humans. Eventually they would track it to the monkey. At the onset, they'd have a great deal of difficulty determining the transmission route into man, but, being of primate origin, it would be conceived as quite possible. Much better than to introduce the synthetic biologic agent we'd considered. That could be tracked to *us*, eventually. The synthetic agent would cause immediate alarm, as it has no possible natural occurrence.

"Dr. Bjorgstad felt, and I agree, that it's much wiser to use a viral agent than a bacterial agent, as antiviral pharmaceuticals and vaccines would take modern science years to develop. I feel certain that it'll take some length of time just to isolate the causative agent for this bizarre disease, and only then could research be started to establish possible cures or vaccines."

Both the cardinal and monsignor were awestruck, hanging on every word that monotonously flowed from the mouth of the garrulous Dr. Thomas.

Monsignor O'Casey had uneasily shifted position twice during the outpouring of new information. "You people don't dally, I must say!"

"All this has occurred only within the past year. I find that amazing," said the cardinal.

"Well, Sir, when a professional team is working within its scope of knowledge, and well capitalized, I might add, thanks to your generosity, great things can be accomplished in relatively short periods of time. It's when politics, professional jealousies, and egos come into play in the scientific community that projects seemingly go on forever and then often times fizzle.

"And, incidentally, we are *relying* on these self-propagated research blocks to further delay the isolation of the causative agent and possible cure by world health researchers. I project that isolation will take maybe five years, but a curative agent may never be identified." Noah stood to stretch his legs. "I'm sorry if I seem to get carried away with my nonstop talk, but as a research scientist, this project is the high point of my career!"

"Bravo, Noah Thomas!" cheered Wentworth. "Please, carry on!"

"Well, then, thank you, Cardinal. Dr. Bjorgstad, in his Stockholm lab, and I here in my lab, each researched different aspects of these biologic agents, thereby reducing the time factor. We were able to choose the most suitable agent in the least amount of time."

"I find it all somewhat frightening, Dr. Thomas," the young monsignor said. "How do we insure that the virus will only be passed through the homosexual community? What if, for some reason, it goes beyond that and becomes a pestilence in the non-targeted population at large? How would we stop it? *Could* we stop it? These are grave questions I feel must be answered prior to initiating the disease process."

"Monsignor, your concerns are well-taken. First, in order to limit the disease to homosexuals, we are now working on mutating the virus so that it spreads rapidly only through the colonic mucus membranes, which means that sodomy would be the mode of transmission."

"Sick, animal behavior, you mean," the cardinal shook his head. "Excuse me, please continue."

"Uh, yes . . . There are proteins in most bodily fluids that stop viruses, but the virus we have genetically mutated from the naturally occurring ape virus would, in effect, pass through the protective proteins of the bowel and slowly replicate itself in the tissues. The colon's close proximity to the prostate gland would allow the virus to invade that tissue easily. If you are unfamiliar with the prostate gland, it's just anterior to the distal colon and serves as a male sex organ."

"What purpose does that gland serve, Doctor? Several of my colleagues are incessantly speaking of troubles with their 'prostates.'"

Wentworth's unbending interest grew with each new bit of data.

"From it comes the bulk of seminal fluid, which acts as the sperm carrier during normal ejaculation." He glanced at the cardinal.

He continued again. "Now, using this theory, the virus would spread from the infected person to the recipient through anal intercourse. It would then proceed to the recipient's prostate, and so forth into the next victim. Using this transmission technique, we could contain the disease in the homosexual population, with the process slow and certain. Most people will be protected inherently in their genetic structure, and will not contract the lethal effects of the virus, even over time. In the extremely rare case of a fatality, death would occur in possibly one to five years, maybe longer."

"Er, excuse me, Doctor," Brian interjected, "but I don't understand, what is this 'lethal' talk? I thought we had planned to cause illness severe enough to frighten them, not *kill* them, just to stop their behavior. And what of the talk of covert propagandizing into the fundamentalist religious groups . . . that this was a plague of condemnation, a warning from God to stop homosexualism? What has happened to our original intent?"

"Uh, er," the doctor was glancing rapidly between the monsignor and the cardinal, caught off guard. "Aren't you aware of what has happened, didn't Cardinal Wentworth speak with you about the change in plans?"

"Not at all! Cardinal, what is this? Do you know of this?"

"Brian, Brian, young man. I made the sole decision to pursue this track after I spoke with Dr. Bjorgstad and Dr. Thomas four months ago. At that early time, even, the projection was that in order to engineer a specific virus that could cause a significant negative effect on health, but guaranteed not to result in death, was very futuristic. The doctors told me that the primate virus they're working with could probably be brought to the point we are at now, but further specializing and refinement, to the non-lethal level, could take many more years of research, years we don't have. If we're to stop this homosexual liberation movement, and all the other decadence that this sick behavior symbolizes, *we must act now!*"

"But, Sir—"

"You *know*, Monsignor, we've *agreed* that someone should have stopped all this sin many years earlier than now. The decision is something we'll abide by. It is the will of God," Wentworth intoned, "an act of 'weeding His garden.'"

"But what if—"

"Please, Monsignor O'Casey, all this banal discussion is counterproductive. As Dr. Thomas just stated, most people will have the proper genetic protection. They will not contract the lethal phase of the illness. Who knows, maybe none will, and just the ill-health effects will be noted. And if they do contract the lethal stage . . . so be it, God's will be done." Wentworth closed his eyes for a moment, then opened them to glare squarely at O'Casey. "Homosexuals are unnatural in God's plan. They cannot bear children to further God's will. Lord help us if those abominations of the human race *ever* manage to come into any significant social power, as well they *might* in the liberal and misguided thinking of today's world."

Brian was disconcerted. "Before I conspire with you any further, I need my questions answered. What about spread into the heterosexual community, say, by means of sexual behavior. Could the female pick this up, then, through anal sex?"

Dr. Thomas, agitated, looked at him squarely. "Nothing suggests that possibility in our primate research thus far. And your high school anatomy has slipped you," he added sarcastically. "The female of the species has no prostate gland. Therefore it would not spread." He smirked, took off his glasses, and smugly cleaned them with his handkerchief.

Unremitting, Brian said, "I am aware of that, Dr. Thomas. My final question: What does the terminal stage of this disease consist of, say it did progress to that level?"

"This virus attacks the body's immune system, hence the name we have given it, ISV-1, for Immuno Suppressive Virus number one. The ultimate intent is chronic illness for the affected person. Always miserable, poor health, frail. However, if the recipient should have other significant health problems, possibly, or genetically was susceptible, this virus could become nasty enough to cause oddball illnesses . . . otherwise common illnesses that the normal body could fight off. And," he hesitated, "possibly forms of cancer. In the end, death might result due to the ineptness of the immune system. Actually, if it makes you more at ease, the virus itself won't cause death; rather the failure of the recipient's physical adaptability. But let me reiterate. None of our controlled studies to date has resulted in death of the hosts."

"Meaning the apes without the natural protection, in this instance?" O'Casey asked. Dr. Thomas nodded. "I'll need some time to digest this. It's very distressing, Dr. Thomas. In the past, we've discussed a possible vaccine. Where does that stand at this point? Have you abandoned that, too, without my knowledge?" asked Brian.

"No, sir, that's still on track. *That* is the final research obstacle prior to the release of the virus into humans. We *must* have the ability to exercise a bail-out option at all times. We've been extremely fortunate in our discovery of the disorder in the monkeys. They've given us basic molecular structures for both the disease-producing virus and the specific antiviral protein that protects them from the effects of the virus. All we've had to do was to biologically mutate the virus and corresponding antiviral protein to match, engineering them so neither would disturb the human immune system too dramatically at the onset. It's possible that it might trigger the immune system enough to form its own antibodies, or, on the other hand, cause such a rapid onset of symptoms of the disease that the scientific community might get alarmed and suspicious of foul play. We're working slowly on the vaccine, and it's doing well, right on schedule. It may take us, reasonably, another three months to complete. Then we'll be ready to introduce the ISV-1 into the homosexual community."

"How will that be done . . . you know . . . introducing it into the gays?" Brian asked. He was still overwhelmed with disbelief that this 'little scare from God' had so quickly and dramatically mushroomed to this possibly lethal level. It was frightening.

"*That* phase, you and I have to discuss, Monsignor," said the cardinal. "Do you have anything else for us at this point, Dr.

Thomas?"

"That's the current status, and I'll keep you both informed of new information. I prefer these intermittent tete-a-tetes, as questions can be openly dealt with. Not like phone calls—too great a risk of misinterpretation."

"Fine, fine," said the cardinal. I believe it's time for a light breakfast. Let's find a nice cafe for croissants and tea." He moved, for the first time in a long time, slowly getting up from the bench with a grunt. "Ugh, are you ready, gentlemen?"

"That sounds delightful, Eminence," the doctor chirped. "I know of a nice little place within walking distance on Via Leone IV where they have the best homemade preserves and espresso . . . Are you coming, Monsignor?" They had started to walk away when the doctor noticed that Brian was still seated, staring blankly toward the dome of St. Peter's Basilica.

"Er, oh, I'm sorry, I was just thinking . . . No, I believe I'll stay for awhile, it's so peaceful here in the morning." He stood slightly and nodded farewell.

"All right then, I'll see you next time we have significant developments," returned Dr. Thomas. "Good-by for now." The two of them walked away, chatting lightly about the various species of spring flora about to blossom in the Vatican.

O'Casey sat back down, images of pestilence and doom floating in his head. How could the men, who had just left his presence, be discussing such a trivial topic as flowers! *My God, we've just finished planning a plague on the world!* He breathed a deep sigh, "Oh, Lord, guide us, in Your omnipotent wisdom, in our endeavors on this insignificant little planet. May Your will prevail above all else, and please grant us all, on this planet, salvation, as we know not what we do, for You alone are Holy. In the name of the Father, the Son, and the Holy Spirit, Amen." He made the sign of the cross and remained at the stone table, hands folded in reverence for his morning meditation. It was a beautiful day, after all.

• • •

The next day Brian was in the chapel early, asking God for

guidance in the undertaking before him, asking himself questions whose answers kept alluding him. How had he become so deeply involved; so quickly involved? Was it out of personal gain, perhaps, thinking that taking part in this strange plan would somehow give rise to his escalation within the church? Was he in it because he subconsciously thought that the cardinal could assist him in faster hierarchical promotions? Did the old cardinal have enough influence with His Holiness to arrange such things? He didn't know, but after all, the man *was* the prefect for the Doctrine of the Faith, and must have some kind of power by title alone.

No, that couldn't be it! It was true enough that ascending the hierarchy was a primary personal goal, but surely he couldn't be a party to human disaster as a means. Was it because he was convinced that this eccentric scheme would truly benefit man, to return the lost sheep to the fold, as Christ would put it? He had to confront himself with the fact that he wasn't fully convinced of this rationale, either, but only in part. Yes, mankind had strayed too far from God's plan by volition. And, yes, something . . . something had to be done to turn the tide from evil and self-destruction.

Unfortunate for the poor lost souls, homosexuals happened to be at the crux of the issue because of their own flagrancy, thumbing their noses at morality, daring damnation from God himself. And then there was the final issue to resolve along that same line of thought. Believing this about the homosexuals and God . . . *am I really chosen?* . . . along with the rest of the small group, to intervene and crush this newest outrage?

Couldn't their blasphemous behavior be compared with that which took place in the Book of Exodus at the base of Mt. Sinai, while Moses was on the mountain awaiting His commandments? The wild orgy and the idolization of the golden calf were followed by the stern condemnation from God.

Yes! That analogy seemed to fill the missing gap in his search for justification of his involvement! The current homosexual movement was analogous to the blasphemy of the orgy, and Brian was chosen to help right their wrongdoing in the eyes of God.

As with a blinding flash of insight, he knew with a certainty. He must continue as one of the chosen group, but he must maintain a cautious vigilance of the others; they seemed too unrestrained in their fervor. He prayed, thanking God for this new insight. After a few moments of peaceful inner solitude, he made the sign of the cross, rose to his feet and genuflected, then exited the chapel.

• • •

Cardinal Wentworth called Brian to his office, later in the week.

"Good morning, Eminence," Brian said, in an upbeat tone. "You wanted to see me?"

"Ah, yes, good morning, Monsignor. You've resolved your uncertainty, I hope?"

"Yes, sir, I am much more comfortable with our purpose than I had been."

"That is good news, Brian. I'm happy to hear it. Oh, by the way, I enjoyed your slides of the cherry blossoms the other night after dinner. Very beautiful."

"Thank you, Eminence. I tried to capture the richness of their beauty."

"Why don't you sit, please. I need to discuss our next task. You asked how we would initiate the viral infection. Actually, it's quite simple. Monsignor, I picked you to help us for many reasons; foremost, your loyalty to others. You are also dedicated to a given task, and you possess the tenacity to see its completion. The final reason, in a more practical sense, is your position in the Holy See. You, as a pronuncio, can travel fairly easily without suspicion. You have contacts in both Europe and the U.S. You are young and handsome, and these attributes open doors for you that are not open to older men."

Brian sat, watching his every move, trying to understand where all of this flattery was headed. "Thank you for the compliments, Eminence, but don't you feel that you and the distinguished doctors possess much more influence than I?"

"In certain capacities, yes. With this specific goal, no."

"And what might that be?"

"It will be your assignment to travel to major cities where homosexuals gather, playing the role of a wealthy jet-set homosexual yourself. You must return with the names, and any other personal information you can obtain, of the most sexually active and well-travelled gay men you can find."

"How do I go about this? Do you have any suggestions?"

"Again, quite simple. Go to known homosexual meccas—New York City, Los Angeles, Chicago, London, and Paris, for examples—and go into the wealthy gay hangouts. Simply observe behaviors, become friendly with them, ask questions about who's who . . . discreetly, of course. It should be an easy, and interesting, assignment. Record as much information as you can on how to locate these men, then bring the information back to me. I'll make arrangements for you to go to New York and get started next week, under the guise of church business. You will be supplied with more than adequate money to travel freely from there, spending about three weeks gathering information. Then you will return here for a week before leaving for Paris. With Paris as a base, you can travel to the German, British, Dutch, and Scandinavian cities with the same mission, collecting names and information. When we have sufficient information we'll sit down and choose the seven recipients."

"Not very scientific, is it?" Brian smiled. "Then what happens next?"

"Then, with our list compiled, we await the final go ahead signal from the doctors. I'm in complete agreement with you as to not starting until we have a proven vaccine to abort the project if needed. Oh, you do realize, Monsignor, that this vaccine is not a curative agent, but only gives protection to those not yet infected, and so we must have plenty on hand to vaccinate those at risk in case we abort the mission. Those already infected, well, it would be too late for them, whatever happened." Wentworth waited patiently for Brian's response.

"I see now where this plan will, in the end, benefit the soul of mankind," Brian said, with complete assurance. And as calloused as it may sound, for those infected, I must engage the attitude of 'Que sera!'"

"I admire your change of heart, Monsignor. I've had my doubts these past few days, and I must say, I'm relieved.
Do you have any further questions?"

"Yes, one more. Once everything is ready, and we've received the go ahead and the viral agent, how do we implant it in the subjects?"

"That arrangement is tentative, for the moment. I think we should address one hurdle at a time . . . to keep from confusing our ultimate goal. When the time is right, you'll be involved in that planning."

Brian became noticeably uneasy, as though he expected he would have to carry out that task. His inquisitive look at the cardinal was unmistakable.

"Don't look so alarmed, Monsignor, *you* will not do the implanting," the cardinal said emphatically, slightly grinning. "Now, carry on with your usual daily routine and don't raise any suspicions. You'll receive the travel plans in your mail, along with the tickets and money orders for cash. Oh, yes, Monsignor, please don't try to spend *all* of the money, but do show a certain amount of flash."

"Yes, Eminence," he smiled. "You can count on me completely."

1974

VATICAN CITY, MARCH

Dr. Noah Thomas searched through the hordes of crick-necked tourists, as they followed the bellowing tour guides down the pathway toward the Borgia Apartment. He was to meet Cardinal Wentworth and Monsignor O'Casey on one of the benches in the area. All of them he'd seen so far were occupied by foot-weary tourists who were there to see the world famous Vatican art collections. He caught a glimpse of someone waving at him, squinted into the sun, shading his eyes with a newspaper, and saw the men on a distant bench. "Aha, there you are!" He walked hastily toward them, slightly panting as he arrived. "Nice to see you both again after such a long time."

The men greeted him. It had been over a year since they'd last met in person, communicating by telephone in the interim, with updates and questions. "This is a bad place to talk. Let's walk over to the library where it's quieter," said the cardinal.

Doctor Thomas reached down to retrieve the thick, heavy briefcase he'd just placed on the grass next to the bench. "I'll get it," said Brian, seeing that the old man was showing his age. He bent over and picked it up. It was much heavier than it looked. No wonder the old man was panting.

They proceeded to the greenway in front of the library, now

hearing the bellowing of the guides and the occasional screams of misbehaving children in the distance.

"This will do," the cardinal said as he sat down on a bench. The doctor sat next to him and Brian seated himself on the grass.

"I'm very pleased to tell you gentlemen that we're finally ready to proceed," Noah began. "As I told you on the phone, we've stabilized the virus as best we could in this time frame. It's time to begin. In accord with our desire to have a vaccine available, in case we have to abort the plan for some reason, we've produced enough preventive vaccine to take care of a half million people. I daresay I cannot foresee a need for that great an amount, however."

"I'm glad to hear it," Brian said, then saw Noah's frown and felt as if he'd interrupted. "Sorry."

"Based on computer simulations," Noah went on, "we feel that, if this plan is successful, homosexualism will cease to be practiced within a decade. Not that the disease will change the individual's sexual preference, but the fear of contracting this unpleasant disease will cause the individual to restrain himself from homosexual activity."

"Amen," Wentworth sighed.

"If everything goes as planned, we won't need the vaccine. On the downside, God forbid, Dr. Bjorgstad and myself know the vaccine's formulation and could produce more. We agreed, for security reasons, to never divulge it to anyone else. Now, your turn. Have you finished the selection of the original subjects for infection?"

"Yes, Doctor, we have," Brian replied. "I've visited several cities in the U.S. and Europe and obtained information on many potential candidates. The cardinal and I have gleaned through all the possibilities and come up with what we consider the best seven. We had many, many more than we needed, so we have an ample pool of alternates, in case one or more can't be located."

"And what kind of people did you select?"

The cardinal spoke. "We decided on only the more affluent and world travelled. Earlier on, we considered infecting two commoners, with the logic that they would interact more with street people who may tend to spread it faster. You know, by male prostitution."

"That sounds reasonable. Why didn't you?"

"After talking with a number of homosexuals, in bars and such places, during my search," Brian said, "I learned that many of them, even the affluent, go for occasional thrills by hiring young male street prostitutes anyway. We decided we could get better coverage by using the well-moneyed traveler."

"Excellent! Hand me my briefcase please, Monsignor." Noah took it from Brian and opened the lid slightly. "I don't want to expose these bottles where someone may see them, so look at them in the case if you will."

As casually as possible, Brian and the cardinal glanced into the case. There was a row of seven disposable plastic enema bottles, each having had its original commercial label replaced by a plain white label with a number on it.

"These bottles contain very high doses of the ISV-1 virus. Each will be injected into the colon of one subject and the empty bottle returned to us through the mail. The person doing the injecting must also send a Polaroid picture of the subject, with an acceptable personal form of ID, as proof of completion of the task." He closed the briefcase.

"That simple," Brian stated. "There's a lot of power in that little case, Doctor."

"Absolutely! Actually, there's enough virus in each of these bottles to infect two dozen men."

Brian was surprised. "Why so much?"

"We want to be absolutely sure. Don't we?"

"Of course, but—"

Noah turned abruptly to the Cardinal. This was no time for a discussion of side effects, lethal or otherwise. "Have you arranged for the deployment of the virus into the subjects yet, Cardinal?"

"Yes, Dr. Thomas. I've contracted the services of a man whom I understand does unpleasant tasks for money. He's kind of a maverick, according to himself, and takes jobs that others won't do. You know, with an element of danger, like acting as courier for business documents, jewels, that sort of thing. He also acts as a debt collector. He was quick to point out, however, that he charges appropriately for his services."

"How much does he charge?" Brian asked.

The cardinal cleared his throat. "Well, uh, he assures me that his work is totally confidential and that he doesn't fail his employers. He is also discreet." He shifted nervously. "He will charge one hundred thousand U.S. dollars for each subject."

The others gasped.

Wentworth continued. "But that includes expenses, as he pointed out, and those will be quite substantial. After all, he'll need to travel the world and spend large amounts of money to gain the confidence and interest of the subjects."

"Yes, I suppose that's true," Noah said. "Where will the money come from, if I may?"

"The money issue is best left to me. I know it's a tremendous amount, but so has been the cost of the development of the virus. We can't stop here. There are certain discretionary funds available to me for my official work in the Doctrine of the Faith. Don't you both agree that probably nothing approaches the goal of this office *more* than this attempt at the return to morality? I have no qualms about using the money on this project."

Both men hemmed a little, then agreed. "I suppose you're right, Cardinal, but I don't like it." The doctor looked down at his briefcase. "When will you meet with this . . . this employee?"

"He'll be here this afternoon to meet us. You can give him instructions on the proper handling technique and administration of the enema bottles."

Dr. Thomas was startled. "What? I don't want to meet him. I was under the impression that the only people aware of my involvement would be Dr. Bjorgstad and yourselves! My anonymity was to be protected, if you will remember."

"Please, Doctor . . . I first spoke with him three months ago to see if he would be interested, knowing that your research and development was finally coming to fruition. I feel we can trust him, from what I know of him. Think about it . . . Is he going to admit, to anyone, his own involvement in this conspiracy? Never, I should think."

"Maybe you're right, but—"

"In my own defense, doctor, I never intended his meeting you, but he started to waver in his agreement, when I was too vague about the principals involved. He said he would only take high risk work if he was fully aware of the risk involved. He demanded a complete exaction of the details. I had to furnish them, I'm afraid. He did, finally, express empathy for our cause, and said he would take the work, if he could meet all of us."

"All right, all right . . . I suppose it was necessary. How did you meet this fellow? Hopefully he's not a stranger to you!"

"No, no, I've known him for a long time. He came to me several years ago, imploring my help in obtaining an annulment of his marriage within the church. He's from Palermo. Poor man . . . It seems his wife was cheating on him, but he couldn't prove it, nor could he remain married to an unfaithful woman. The church wouldn't grant an annulment without proof of her infidelity. Being a devout Catholic, he came to me for help. I arranged an annulment, on other grounds, out of sympathy for him. I remember when I told him it had been approved. He cried and thanked me profusely, over and over, telling me that if there was anything I ever needed done to call on him. He did, I might add, have the air about him of sort of a ruffian, but I liked him. I thought of him for this project well over a year ago, and was finally able to track him down through his parish in Palermo."

"At the very least, it's comforting to know that you have some type of personal history with him. Where did you plan to meet?" Noah asked.

"How about right here at two o'clock this afternoon? Any objections?" Both men indicated agreement. "Fine, then. And now, if you'll excuse me, I believe I'll take a stroll." He stood and slowly ambled down the walkway.

• • •

Two o'clock came quickly. Dr. Thomas and Monsignor O'Casey were already present when the cardinal and a stranger approached. The stranger was nattily dressed in expensive tweed clothing, very handsome, and solidly built. He exuded an air of confidence. Probably thirty-five years old or so, Brian thought.

"Good afternoon, gentlemen," Brian said as they approached.

The stranger smiled warmly and nodded, and Cardinal Wentworth replied, "Good afternoon to you. Enjoy your lunch?"

"Yes, we ate in an American restaurant . . . Hamburgers, don't you know," the doctor laughed.

"Let me introduce Mr. Salvadore Danella, the gentleman from Palermo I was telling you about," said the cardinal.

"Pleased to meet you," Sal smiled, as he extended his hand, first to Brian, then to the doctor. He was very charming, Brian thought.

"This is quite an undertaking, if I fully comprehend what it is you've started," Sal said, as he sat down on a bench facing the other three. "Cardinal Wentworth briefed me on your plans. I wouldn't have agreed to work with you on blind terms. As I told him, my work is treacherous enough *knowing* what I'm dealing with! I've found myself in some awkward situations in the past through ignorance of purpose. Let me parrot what I know, for clarification. Now . . . You gentlemen, men in high places, I might add, have agreed that the world's spiritual health has deteriorated to an abominable level, and, even though this is common knowledge throughout the scrupulous world, nothing has been done. The downward spiral persists."

"Sad, but true," Wentworth said.

"Therefore, you've taken the responsibility upon yourselves to return morality and Godliness to humankind by imposing a pestilence amongst the most flagrant recent abomination, homosexualism. To this end you've created a virus that will plague them with illness. The illness will be transmitted venereally among their own kind, yet preserve the rest of society intact to bear witness. And, finally, you plan to leak the information to the world, through the fundamentalist sects, that this is a plague of warning from God, so that all others who practice immoral deeds and thoughts will take heed and return to uprighteousness. Have I expressed my understanding satisfactorily?"

"Bravo!" The cardinal was beaming, the others amazed. "I couldn't have worded it more effectively, Mr. Danella!"

"Good, then, because I agree with your very noble intent. Perhaps there's a place for each of you in Heaven! Now, what do you expect of me? I am at your disposal, and I understand you've accepted my terms."

"We did discuss your fee, and quite honestly, I feel it's exorbitant. But you have the trust of Cardinal Wentworth, and that's good enough for me." Doctor Thomas had never been one to go unheard, and the price really did eat at him, especially from someone who had just stated what a noble cause it was! If Danella really felt that strongly, one would think he'd work for a more reasonable price! But the haggling was over. Why waste precious time discussing it? Noah put on a smile.

"In this briefcase, Mr. Danella, there are seven enema bottles, the kind you can buy in any drugstore," Noah continued. "Each contains enough ISV-1, the virus we engineered, to infect several men. We overloaded them intentionally, to insure infection, especially with *your* fee," he chided, adding one last jab. "We couldn't afford to have to do a repeat, even if we knew one had failed!"

"Please, Doctor . . . " The cardinal scowled.

Noah glanced at him, then back at Sal. "I simply want Mr. Danella to know exactly how I feel." He handed him a sheet of paper listing seven sequentially numbered names and addresses, along with several traits and habits peculiar to each individual. "Your job, sir, is to locate each man on this list. You will somehow, at your own discretion, gain each man's confidence, possibly pretending to be an interested lover." He took a small brown pill bottle from his case and handed it as he spoke. "When the timing is right, you'll use this chloral hydrate, in an alcoholic beverage, as a Mickey Finn to knock out the victim. Then, using the correct bottle, with each man's number, corresponding to each name on your list, you will insert the tip of the enema into his rectum and squeeze out the entire contents." He reached into his case for other items. "Here are some rubber gloves. I strongly advise you to wear these to prevent the possibility of self-infection."

"Whoa. Hold on there." Danella glared at the Cardinal. "Nobody said anything about that kind of risk. How about let's just—"

"The good doctor takes caution to the extreme, I'm afraid," Wentworth interrupted. "There's actually no danger to you at all. Is there, Dr. Thomas?"

Noah swallowed hard and understood exactly what his reply had to be. "None at all," he said confidently, then patted one of the plastic containers. "You could probably *drink* this stuff with no ill effects at all. You see, it's designed to—"

"I think we should make this job worth an even million," Danella said.

"But, Mr.—"

"Up front."

"Out of the question," Cardinal Wentworth said quickly. "Seven hundred thousand is as high as we intend to go." Danella creased his pretty face into a frown. "Think about it."

Danella thought. Work had been a little slow lately. Goddamned dollar. Seemed like every time real estate took a turn for the better in the United States, his own value went down. And the villa he kept, just outside Paris, was in need of some redecorating in the master bedroom. Goddamned women. It was always something.

"Well?" Cardinal Wentworth asked.

"I'll do it."

Brian looked at Noah and breathed a sigh of relief.

"If I may continue," Noah said sternly. Danella nodded. "Finally then, when the injection is complete, you must show us proof of your completed work by taking the subject's valid identification, such as a driver's license, and place it on his chest along with the empty bottle. Use the enclosed instant camera to take a snapshot of his face and the paraphernalia on his chest. To collect your money, you simply insert the empty bottle and picture into one of the provided mailing envelopes and drop it in the mail."

Danella abruptly stood up. "Hold it right there, Doctor," he said, pointing an accusing finger. "Are you saying I get paid only *after* each job is completed?"

Noah looked up at him. "How else can we be sure that—"

"You can't."

Wentworth got to his feet. "Gentlemen, let's be calm about this. Mr. Danella, we assumed, rightly or wrongly, that, in your line of work, some proof of a mission completed would be required, before payment, by whatever entity had hired you. Isn't that usually the case?"

Danella laced his arms across his chest. "Half up front, or it's no deal."

Wentworth looked at a glaring Noah, then back at Danella. "I have no problem with that."

"But it's—" Noah began.

"I have no problem with that," Wentworth repeated. "Please sit down, Mr. Danella . . . and *do* go on, Dr. Thomas."

Noah cringed at the reprimand, but managed to control his anger. "Upon receipt of each envelope, you will receive a deposit of one hundred thousand U.S. dollars . . . ah . . . that will be one hundred and fifty thousand after the first job, to the Swiss account of your specification. Please put your account number in the first mailer only, we'll destroy it then. Do you have any questions?"

Sal had been attentive through the rest of the instructions. It seemed straightforward enough now. "No, no questions. Do you have a specific completion date in mind? I'd hate to be rushed, especially if some of them are difficult to find or approach once I've found them. I can probably have them done within a year."

"I think that would be satisfactory," said the cardinal. "Now, finally, Sal, you must be made aware of the gravity of this undertaking. If ever we were to be discovered, by anyone, we would all be severely punished, legally, and every other way you can imagine. But let's think nothing of ourselves in comparison with the church. The church must never be conceived as being involved. Its two thousand years of good standing must never be compromised. The church knows *nothing* of this plan. It was conceived entirely by myself and these other men before you, who joined me in securing its reality. You must swear that you'll never reveal any of this to anyone. You must take this knowledge to the grave. Do you swear to this?"

"Sure, Cardinal. I'd never place the reputation of the church in jeopardy." Sal's serious expression disguised the smile behind it, as he laughed inside about the potential legal prosecution. Big deal, injecting a few enemas to make people get the flu! If they only knew!

"We're in agreement then," the doctor said. He closed the briefcase and handed it to Sal, tapping it. "This is everything you need. Never let it leave your sight. I believe we're finished?" he asked, looking at the others.

1975

PHOENIX, NOVEMBER

The handsome young man sat watching people in the concourse coffee shop, sipping iced tea. George had strategically positioned himself so he could see his airline's television schedule monitor. Flight 337 to L.A. started flashing again, as he watched. DELAY.... DELAY.... DELAY.... flashed, and the time changed to forty-seven minutes later, from its already delayed time of 7:30 p.m. "Damn," he mumbled under his breath. He hated being scheduled to work, then showing up and encountering these delays. *Airports are so boring.* He wondered why more customers didn't complain to the airports and the FAA about scheduling screw ups. Enough people complain and something might get done.

And he was wilted. His uniform clung to him uncomfortably. *Why don't they fix the air conditioner on this concourse?* It had been down the last time he'd been through here three weeks ago.

"Hey, Mister. Got change for a dollar?"

George looked left at a pretty young girl; about eight-years-old, he guessed, and dressed in bright red. He smiled. "Well, let's just have a look." He dug into his pocket.

"You a pilot?" she asked.

"Uh . . . "

"My daddy's a pilot. In the Air Force. Pilots are the greatest."

The one I had last night wasn't all that great, George wanted to say. "I'll bet your daddy's the best pilot of them all," he said instead.

"Sure is." The girl beamed with pride. "But I bet you're pretty good, too," she added quickly.

Depends on where I'm 'flying' and who I'm 'flying' with. "That's very nice of you to say. Look here. Four quarters. Will that be okay?" George asked.

She thought a minute. "Just right. Four quarters." She took the change, then pressed a crumpled dollar bill into George's hand. "Thanks, mister."

George smiled at her, then frowned, as she turned to leave. Without even knowing him, she'd touched the one sensitive chord that always put him into a depressed state. As a boy, he'd wanted to be a pilot more than anything. He'd taken all the right courses in high school, gone to college, studied hard. With no help from his parents, he'd paid his way and saved enough money to get into pilot training. Then he'd washed out. Couldn't take the stress. The old anxiety crept back into his skull. Emergencies. Even in the simulator he'd panic, lose control of his rational thinking. An ulcer took the blame. *No shame in that,* he told himself for the thousandth time.

His focus returned to people-watching. If nothing else, Phoenix was an interesting place to furlough and hang around the airport. People here wore all kinds of upbeat clothing, all the latest styles, Hawaiian shirts, cowboy boots, and some dressed in downright rags. It was odd, he observed, that one could tell the nouveau riche from the old rich by their personal clothing style. The nouveau flaunted their wealth by wearing expensive stylish clothing and hairdos and jewelry — lots of obnoxious jewelry. The old, established rich wore subtle but classy clothing, more of a continental vintage motif. People who knew fine clothing could pick them out readily, and he congratulated himself for his upper crust taste. Then he caught a glimpse of a very handsome man who walked through the entrance and stood, momentarily, assessing the room.

He *was* classy, darkly tanned, and very well dressed. *This* man had money! George was turned on! The man was probably in his early thirties, and very fit.

The man glanced straight at the young flight attendant, seeming to recognize him, then proceeded to the counter and ordered a scotch over. George returned the look, studying the man, casting his eyes away when the man looked at him. After a few minutes of this body language banter, the man left the bar and came straight toward him. A lump formed in George's throat.

"Mind if I sit?" the stranger asked.

"Not at all, please do."

"Don't I know you from somewhere? You're very familiar looking."

"I don't believe I recognize you. Do you fly a lot?" George asked. He loved the man's bass-pitched voice. It had a certain crooning quality.

"Yes, frequently. I'm a free lancer in the power-broker world."

"What does that mean?"

"Oh, I do a little of this, a little of that. I contract out my services as a courier of documents, gems, whatever."

"Sounds like interesting work. My name's George Williams." He extended his hand.

Danella reached out. "Phillip Ash, nice to meet you." He took George's hand and held it slightly longer than a routine handshake required. A final, firm little squeeze, direct eye contact, a slight smirk, and they both knew. "So you're a flight steward, I gather," he said, looking down at the uniform.

"Very perceptive," George said lightheartedly. They both laughed easily, knowing that they were simply engaged in small talk. The best was yet to come. "Yes, been doing it for a little over a year, and I love it. I get to travel, get furloughs in all the fun places. Then, on my off time, I get to fly any airline, anywhere, for pennies! But you probably know that already if you fly a lot."

"Yes, Uh-huh. I still think I know you from somewhere. Do you ever go to bath houses, like maybe the Blue Moon?"

"As often as I can. If I have the money at the time, of course. It's an expensive kind of place. Maybe you've seen me there?" George was overwhelmed by the man's charisma, searching for intelligent sounding conversation.

"It's one of my favorite haunts, too. I'm fortunate enough not to have to worry about the money end of it, so every time I'm in the area I make it a point to go spend a day there."

"Lucky fellow," he said sincerely. "Where are you headed now?" George was hooked.

"L.A., for an overnight trip."

"Really? That's *my* final destination . . . but it's delayed until about 8:15."

"Flight 337?" Phillip asked.

"You're on it too? I was thinking, a little while ago, about how people ought to complain more about the sloppy operation of the airline companies since deregulation. All the lost luggage, too. I work in the industry and I know that, with a little whip cracking, things could improve overnight. Do you know why we attendants carry on our luggage? Other than changing flights quickly, the number one reason is loss prevention!"

"You chatter a lot, George. Do I make you uncomfortable or something?" He reached under the table and squeezed George's hand, then left his hand on George's thigh.

"Um, no, not *too* much."

Phillip leaned back in the chair. "Relax, relax . . . I find you to be a very attractive young man and I'd like to get to know you better. Where will you stay in L.A.?"

"With a friend, I guess. I'm never sure until I get there. I've got a key to his house. Where are you staying?"

"I'm not sure either. I may rent a car, drive down to San Diego, and stay at the del Coronado." Phillip awaited a response.

"*Very* nice. I've always wanted to go there, but I hear it's really expensive."

"Well, if you'd like, I'd enjoy your company. You can come with me. We'll dine at the restaurant there, then get a room."

"Sure, Phillip. Sounds delightful."

All was set.

By midnight they were seated in the dining room of the hotel, starting the entree of cordon bleu, which had been preceded by calamari and oysters on the half shell. A drink at the bar, then a bottle of Pouilly Fuisse with dinner, followed by a bottle of Dom Perignon after dinner, and George was beginning to feel the effects of too much alcohol.

"What time is it?

"Two a.m. Why?"

George was used to late hours, but he didn't want anything to interfere with the pleasure he'd envisioned in the arms of this dark-skinned beauty. "Past my bedtime," he quipped, hoping to steer his companion toward the piéce de résistance.

"Then I say we get out of here," Phillip said. He left cash for the dinner check. George glanced at the total. Two hundred ninety-three dollars and some cents. *Wow!*

They started for the elevator through the lavishly appointed lobby. It was quiet, certainly because of the hour, with the quiet augmenting the splendor of the decor. Off on the third floor and down the hall twenty yards to the right they found room 328. George felt a little light-headed from the wine, and took the opportunity to sway closer to Phillip, taking his arm as if for balance. "Wine makes me tired."

"Not too tired, I hope," Phillip said, as he pushed the key into the lock.

"Never too tired . . . for you." George fully expected to turn into Phillip's arms as soon as the door was closed behind them, but Phillip surprised him and walked directly to the credenza across the room.

George eased himself down on the bed and decided on a different tactic. "Do you want me, macho man?" He started to unzip his pants, when Phillip turned around from leaning over the credenza.

"What are you doing?" Phillip asked in a gruff voice, then softened his tone. "Wouldn't you prefer to 'savor the moment,' so to speak? Let's have another glass of this wonderful nectar of the gods first." He turned back around and bent over the credenza once again.

George was crushed. He had *never* experienced such aloofness from a lover! He zipped his pants up again, somewhat embarrassed by this man, the only man he had never immediately controlled. But, he would end up having him, conquering him like all the rest. He decided he could manipulate him through the patronizing approach. "Sure, let's share another glass."

Phillip had been busily handling the wine bottle and glasses. "I'll be right there; I'm having trouble getting the cork out." He concealed his real activity, by standing with his back to George, and squeezed the contents from the green capsule into one of the wine glasses, then continued to jockey the glasses and bottle. George was reclining on the bed, unaware of the inordinate delay. "Aha, got it!" Phillip turned around and walked to the bed, handing George a glass. "Salud!" he said, raising his glass. "And good night, my beauty," he mumbled inaudibly, as George hurriedly gulped the hundred and fifty dollar champagne.

Even though George gently protested, they talked for another fifteen minutes, then George began to slur terribly. He was dead-out five minutes later. Phillip went to the closet and took out his light overnight bag. He carried it to the bed and pulled out the disposable enema bottle marked with George's number. Five. With some difficulty, he pulled George's pants down to his knees, donned the rubber gloves, and picked up the enema. Spreading George's buttocks apart, Phillip inserted the enema tip deep into the exposed rectum, squeezing out the liquid contents.

"Five down." It was getting easier and easier.

Phillip took George's wallet from his rear pocket, found his airline ID card and driver's license, and rolled him over on his back, laying the ID on his chest. He then went to his bag for the Polaroid flash camera and took a close-up of the unconscious victim, being careful to get the face and ID. The crushed enema container and picture he placed in the pre-addressed, padded 9x12 mailing envelope and sealed it, then replaced it in his bag to mail the next day.

"And two to go." Thinking about the next hundred thousand that would be deposited as soon as the envelope arrived at its destination, Phillip almost forgot something. The capsule. "Damn." He'd actually been rattled by this particular queer; he'd actually found this handsome blond quite sensuous and attractive. His touch, that feigned move in the hallway, had given Phillip a jolt of passionate trembling he hadn't experienced since . . . . "My God, what am I thinking about?"

George slept peacefully now. "Get hold of yourself, man," Sal reminded himself, as he looked down at the supine body, so casually draped across the wide bed, and began putting things to rights. When the man awoke, some time tomorrow, he probably wouldn't even suspect what had happened to him. Sal looked around for the capsule and found it on the floor near the credenza. "Still the best Mickey in the world," he said, as he held it to the light. "And to think that some people waste it as a sleeping pill," he laughed sarcastically, then went into the bathroom and flushed the empty gelatin shell.

By the time he'd finished checking the room,Sal was back in his usual assured frame of mind. He hated queers with a passion. They were disgusting animals, aberrant freaks of nature.

"Number five down, two to go," he smiled to himself. "You sick queer faggot sap," he said sarcastically to the drugged body on the bed. "You really thought you had me, didn't you? Ha!" He wouldn't mind killing a few of these sickos just for fun, for free, yet! Sal hummed a little ditty to himself, smiling as he pulled off the gloves and threw them into the bag. Then he looked at George and started talking as if he could hear him. "Pretty easy work, and actually kind of enjoyable, flitting around the world, sticking disease in queer's butts. And the meals and lifestyle I'm enjoying ain't too bad, either!" he laughed. "It's too bad there were only seven of you guys. I could retire if I had another half dozen or so of you faggots. Oh, well."

He left the room and walked down the hallway, pondering his remaining two victims. Clancy Pfizer and Enrique Sosa, yes . . . He knew he could catch these remaining flighty ones with a little more time. First he would go to Texas and see his old 'friend,' Walter LeBeau, to get Clancy. Then off to Madrid for Enrique, if he could find him. That guy was always off screwing around somewhere in the world. But Phillip had notified the cardinal that he was running behind his completion date of one year, and that it might take an extended period to get Enrique, possibly another year.

The cardinal had O.K.'d his extension, telling him that Enrique *must* be infected because he was one of the best candidates they'd found. "Take as much time as you need, Mr. Donella," the cardinal had said. Sal had other jobs he could do in the interim. There was a forty thousand dollar contract job on a small-time hood who had played around too many times with the Kansas City heavies that he needed to take care of soon. "Damn!" he muttered. That was such messy work, having to dispose of bodies and everything. Why couldn't there have been more of these queers?

1976

DALLAS, JANUARY

"The Lord giveth and the Lord taketh away. Get my drift?" Phil said, pulling a power play.

"Well, if you put it that way, what can I say? Give me a week to find him. He's always flitting around the world, quite the playboy. For a queer, anyway. He goes both ways, from what I hear. I'll have to go through my old pile of wholesale magazines to find his ad so I can locate him. If I didn't owe you a favor, I wouldn't do this, you know. I hate the guy. He gives me the heebie-jeebies. You just remember this, down the road, in case I may ever need anything." Walt LeBeau was seated in the back room of his mall jewelry store, speaking with Phillip Ash on the phone.

"Sure, Walt, sure. We scratch your back, you scratch ours. An excellent business principle, for a *healthy* business, you know. Make sure and get the right guy, Clancy Pfizer. Make an appointment for him to come to your place to show some pieces to us. I'll bring cash to pay for them, because I want to impress the little turd. I'll play the customer bit when he comes in, and I want you to introduce us."

"What did this guy do, anyway? I know I owe you guys a lot for your help, but I don't want to be involved in any foul play. You're not going to snuff him or anything, right?"

"Aw, come on, Walter," Phil laughed. "You watch too much television! That method of enforcing the rules died long ago. I just want to talk with him about something that doesn't concern you, O.K.? I'll check back with you in a week to see when he'll be coming in." Phil hung up the phone and smiled to himself.

Walt hadn't heard from Phillip Ash for a long time. Maybe not since Phil had helped him to get his second start. LeBeau's Jewelry was one of those rags to riches success stories. Walt LeBeau had been a jewelry salesman for years, then decided to open his own discount store. His first attempt on a side street downtown failed, and the Small Business Administration denied him more money. He'd been to all the local banks for loans but was refused, one of the credit review committees making the well-worn statement about 'not chasing bad money with good.' That was probably their most commonly used line in turning somebody down, Walt had scoffed. What ever happened to personal knowledge and character, potential, all of that? Take a gamble on a good guy? Not these days. You had to have a half million in the bank to take out a fifty thousand dollar loan. "Hell, if I had the half million, I wouldn't need the loan, right?" he told them. "Sorry, sir," their stock answer. The SBA was on the verge of foreclosing on him when he responded to a newspaper ad offering venture capital. He was desperate for money; he would do anything. The lenders said they were very impressed with his potential but felt he needed a nicer location. He met Phillip Ash at the second meeting with the lenders. Phil was introduced as a friend of one of them, and he happened to be in town for a few days. Phil later became the man who insured that payments were made in a timely fashion, and represented the lenders for their other business needs.

Within two weeks Walt's SBA loan had been paid in full. It was arranged that he would relocate his store to the most opulent mall in the Dallas area at the end of the month. He'd been provided with investment capital enough to keep afloat for three years. He did, at first, need to draw more money, but now he was doing well on his own, and repaying the business loans at the high interest rate. He was also required to alter some of the records on his cash flow, and exchange larger bills in amounts of up to twenty thousand dollars at a time. A jewelry store met the lender's needs perfectly. Wealthy adulterers would come in with cash and buy expensive pieces for their concubines in order to avoid records of the sale. The store could record the value of the piece at whatever price it wished to explain the large cash flow. Mr. LeBeau simply didn't ask questions, enabling him to maintain a clear conscience.

"Phillip, your wish is my command," Walt said aloud, as he stood up from his desk.

Phil called the next week to confirm the appointment time for Clancy. "So, you set it up?"

"Sure. It took me two days to find his ad in the old magazines. It's hard to get him because he keeps two numbers, one in San Francisco and one in Miami. Anyway, he's going to Europe for a week, then he'll be back here in the States. The appointment is set for three o'clock on the nineteenth of this month."

"Perfect. Is he bringing the—?"

"He's coming in with some of his better pieces to show me, just like you asked. If you can get in here by two, you can play the customer bit, looking at the more expensive stuff in the back. I'll introduce you as a special customer. Then, if you would, please get him out of my store as soon as you can. I don't like having the creep around."

"Thanks, Walt, you're a pal. See you soon." Phil hung up the phone and smiled his twisted little sneer. "All set, only one more after this one. Maybe a little time in Rio . . . I've been working awfully hard lately."

Phil showed up at LeBeau's at two o'clock on the nineteenth. "Walter, my friend, how are you? This place looks great! It's truly amazing what a little money will do for a guy, huh?"

"O.K., rub it in. Come on in the back. Coffee?" He led him around the counter to the private viewing area in the back.

"Sure, black. Say, this is nice back here. Leather chairs, plush carpet. Hey, have you got an eye loupe I can use for a minute? I want to look at this rock a friend gave me who owed me some money." He sat in one of the chairs by the table with the flexible arm magnifying lamp.

"Of course I have a loupe, this is a diamond store! I'll get it when I bring your coffee." He left for a few minutes, then returned. "Here, catch," he said, throwing the loupe.

Phil looked at the small print on the side, 5X. "No, no, Walt, I want the one *you* use. Come on, Walter. When you're selling, the *customer* gets to use the five power, and if you're buying or trading, *you* use the fifteen power. It's an old game, Walt."

Walt took the fifteen power loupe from his pocket and his face flushed red. He handed it to Phil. "Here . . . "

Phil smiled and took it, placed it in his eye, and looked at the gem. "You see, Walt, I was born at night, but not *last* night." He laughed. "Not too bad, probably a four-four-seven," he rated the diamond. "I guess the price was right. Head's up." He threw the loupe back to Walt. "Thanks."

"Mr. LeBeau, there's a Mr. Pfizer here to see you." It was one of his counter help talking.

"Please show him in, Larry."

"Hey, long time no see, Walter," said Clancy, as he came in the door. "How've you been?"

"Fine, Clancy, fine." There was no hand offered on Walt's part. "Oh, I'm sorry, this is Phillip Ash, an excellent customer of mine. He likes the nicer items, and would like to see what you have. Got some nice stones to show?"

"That's why I'm here. Pleasure to meet you, Phillip."

"Likewise, I'm sure." Phillip gave Clancy's hand a little squeeze.

"I was just in Tel Aviv with our bearded friends. They had some exceptional South African stones, so I bought half a dozen, each over a carat. Here." He took a paper wrapper from his pocket and unfolded it on the brightly lit table. There were several smaller tissue papers within the larger one, each containing a cut diamond. "I'll show them to you. Then, Mr. Ash, if you're interested, I'll leave your business dealings in the hands of Walter."

"That would be fine. Your loupe, please?" Walter again retrieved his eyepiece and handed it to Phil. "Yes, very, very nice indeed." He studied them for a few minutes, then placed four in a separate pile. "I'd like these. How much?"

Walter cleared his throat. He examined the diamonds with the loupe and did some figuring on the desk with a calculator. "I can let you have those four pieces for thirty-seven large ones. I'll make it right with you, Clancy, after Mr. Ash leaves."

Clancy was flabbergasted when Phillip went to his briefcase and started counting thousand dollar bills. "I'll give you twenty-five and no more," Phillip said.

Walter and Clancy looked at each other for a moment, each nodding approval.

"Done, then," said Phil. He handed the wad of bills to Walter.

"Want a receipt, Mr. Ash?" Walter asked.

"No, I'd prefer to keep this off the record. I have to leave now, back to the hotel. Clancy, I understand you're at a hotel, also."

"Yes, I'm over at the Classic."

"How coincidental, so am I. Would you join me for dinner, tonight, perhaps?" Phil established firm eye contact.

"By all means . . . call me . . . room 630, at about seven." Clancy was smiling.

"Done," Phil said again. "I'll speak with you then. And good day to you, Walt, and thank you." He closed his briefcase and stuffed the gems in his pocket, then left. He needed to hurry over and get a room at the Classic.

"I like his style!" said Clancy.

"Yeah, smooth guy." Walt said. Clancy was unaware of the meaning.

Clancy showered and primped, checking himself in the mirror, as he lightly dabbed on his expensive cologne. I wonder what he's like, what he's *really* like? He's so intriguing and, at the same time, so forthright, he turns me on! And so-o-o handsome. And money? Oo-la-la! The phone rang in the other room. Clancy let it ring two or three times. Don't want to appear too anxious. "Hello, Mr. Pfizer speaking."

"Hello, Mr. Pfizer, this is Mr. Ash. Are you ready for dinner? I made reservations at the Grapevine down the street. It's French continental, and they have a wonderful wine list." Phil was a social chameleon. He could become whatever or whoever he needed to be. It helped him more than any other asset in his line of work. The term con man didn't appeal to him. He preferred to think of himself as socially adept, and he'd turn on the charm for this one.

"Oh, yes, I know of it. Sounds ravishing. I'll meet you in the lobby in ten minutes, all right?"

"I'll see you there, sir." Phil hung up the phone. Count this one done. This work was just too easy. He wished there were more than just the seven assignments—and the pay was great.

"Hello, Mr. Ash," Clancy smiled as he sauntered up. "Good to see you again."

Phil was always careful not to make the opening address with people he was trying to impress. It was a psychological tool he'd learned to use. "Yes, good to see you again." He took Clancy's hand, and repeated the little squeeze from their first introduction. "Shall we be off? I'd prefer to walk. It's a short distance, and the winter evening chill pleases me."

"I have no objection. I think that would be nice." The doorman opened the door, and they walked down the street making small talk about the city, gourmet dining, and so on.

They dined on duck l'orange and drank Dom Perignon, Phillip's favorite. He was careful to insure that Clancy was drinking more than his share. More wine, then aperitifs and toasting each other's styles. Clancy became frivolously silly. Phil decided it was time to leave, before Clancy drew too much undesired attention to themselves. "Clancy, I find myself extremely attracted to you. I like you a lot." He tried not to show his actual disgust with the flaming faggot.

"Oh, you do-o-o?" Clancy giggled. "I hoped you would, because I find you very sexy."

Phil was nauseated. "Let's go dancing. Do you know of any clubs nearby?"

"I certainly do-o-o! The Club North isn't far. Have the maitre d' call a cab!" He giggled again.

"Please allow me to get the check," Phillip said. He turned it over and made certain that Clancy caught the two hundred and twenty-four dollar total.

"O-o-oh, you're so sweet!"

The Club North was full of gays, some dancing to the pounding music, some seated quietly alone, waiting for some action, others making out in the corner booths. The atmosphere was carefree and happy. Phillip and Clancy sat in a dark booth, Phillip hoping that no one would happen to recognize him. *What the hell, why should I worry about that? If I see someone in here that knows me, I could turn it against him if I ever needed to.* He made certain that Clancy's drink was freshened regularly. They danced twice, and Phillip had had it. Clancy was sufficiently drunk. "Are you ready, my friend?"

"Sure. Let's go back to the hotel." He smiled his most seductive smile.

When they entered the hotel lobby and walked toward the concierge's desk, Phillip was trying not to let the man hang on him too openly. "Would you send a bottle of Dom Perignon to the Presidential Suite, please, and bill it."

"Yes, right away, sir." The concierge picked up the phone and placed the order.

They boarded the elevator. "You *are* coming to my suite for a nightcap, are you not?" Phillip asked.

"I wouldn't have it any other way," Clancy cooed.

The bottle arrived within minutes of their entering the over-sized double doors of the suite. "My, you go firr-sht class!" Clancy slurred. The main sitting room was classically decorated in French Provincial, with large crystal chandeliers hanging from each end of the ceiling.

There was a completely furnished wet bar in the corner, and a bedroom opened to each side of the large sitting room.

"Yes, I like to be comfortable," Phillip replied. "Let me go in the rest room to open this bottle, so I don't spill it in here on this lovely carpet. You make yourself comfortable. Turn on the television, if you like."

Phil took two glasses from the bar and the bottle and entered the bathroom, turning on the vent fan to cover any suspicious noises. He popped open the bottle and poured two glasses, then reached in his pocket and pulled out a green capsule. Poking a hole in the end, he squeezed the contents into one of the drinks, then replaced the empty capsule in his pocket. Perfect. He was careful to carry the one with the chloral hydrate in it in his right hand. "Here you are, my lovely." He handed Clancy the proper glass.

"O-oh, thank you, kind sir," Clancy giggled again.

Stop that damned giggling, Phillip thought to himself. "To your health!" He raised his glass to Clancy.

"Hear, hear!" Then more giggling. Clancy drank his wine quickly, as he had been doing with his liquor all evening. "So, I wanna know all 'bout you. Exactly wha d' ya do?"

Phillip obliged him with a long story of crap. When he finished, he looked over at Clancy, who was snoring by now. Phil rolled him down onto the floor and took off his clothes, then went through the procedure with the enema bottle and the photograph. Smiling, he wrote a note and left it next to Clancy's unconscious form. "Thanks, sweetie, I hope you enjoyed it as much as I did. I had to catch a plane. Love, Phillip."

He repacked his bag, threw the room key on the desk, and left, whistling, down the hallway. He smiled as he wondered what the suite was going to cost Clancy.

CHICAGO, DECEMBER

O'Hare was packed as usual during the bustle of the holidays, with thousands of people scurrying about like confused cattle at a feedlot. Christmas music played through the speaker system interspersed with pages for a whole array of foreign and domestic name calling to, "Please pick up the white paging telephone."

"Mr. Williams, Mr. George Williams, please pick up the white paging telephone," directed the alto-pitched female voice. George had heard that voice several thousand times in airports throughout the world and the only difference he could discern anymore was the foreign dialect of the particular country he was in. He sometimes, half subconsciously, wondered if there was a central paging office for all of the airports of the world.

Hurriedly forcing his way through the crowded concourse to the phone bank along the wall at Gate 26, he considered himself fortunate that he was garbed in his uniform. It was a trick he'd picked up over the two years he'd been in the business, walking briskly and pulling his suitcase through the cattle herd, throwing out frequent "Excuse me, pleases," as the sea of human forms opened magically before him. Flight attendants somehow commanded fast passage through the herd. He smiled to himself, thinking that he would do as well with a vigorous "Moo!" He knew he couldn't make such smooth passage based on his physique, like he'd witnessed travelling athletes do, and he was not recognized, other than to himself and his lovers, as a celebrity that people would gladly make way for.

He was, however, aware of his striking "California beach boy" good looks and sinewy but well-muscled medium frame. He was ogled by beautiful women everywhere he went, but they went unnoticed in favor of the frequent glances of beautiful men, which he acknowledged subtly but regularly. He smugly thought about how the world bowed to him due to his physical attributes, let alone his ability to conscientiously manipulate his world to obtain personal gratification. He was, at age twenty-three, at the height of his sexual prowess, and he understood well the tremendous power he possessed over others because of his sexual desirability. The only source of power stronger than his was money, he thought, and he could have that, too, through his genetic gift of good looks.

George had known of his attraction to men since he was in the ninth grade, and acted upon it with four different classmates before he finished his first year at the private academy in Toronto. He thought it abnormal and harbored severe guilt for two or three years, but his guilt waned with the more open tolerance of gays in the early seventies. He justified his lack of a need for women by considering that there really was no need for them in his life. He wanted power, self gratification, and money, and men freely met all these needs.

He picked up the paging phone and waited for the operator. "Yes, hello. This is Mr. George Williams."

"One moment, sir." It was not the same woman who did the paging, he noted.

"Hello, George?" the quavering deep voice asked.

"Hi, Tom, how the hell are you, anyway? I'm sorry I'm late but we were delayed at LaGuardia. I only have three hours before my next flight to L.A. I still want to see you, though. Can you meet me at the Hilton here at the airport in twenty minutes?"

"Sure, George. You know I couldn't let you blow through here without seeing you. By the way, I've got a little high-quality nose candy for you, too. Is there anything else I can pick up for you on the way?"

"No, just hurry. Oh, Tom, I'm a little short. I could use some cash."

"No problem. Is five hundred enough?"

"Super! Thanks, Tom." George hung up the phone and started for the ground transportation area. Again he smiled to himself, as he thought about how many hundreds, or was it a thousand now, times he had done one of these "quickies" on a layover. Tom was one of the few lovers with whom he maintained an ongoing relationship. He actually admired Tom and envied his status; however, he couldn't help but sense a certain amount of power over him which he relished.

Tom picked up the intercom to his secretary. "Jeri?"

"Yes, Mr. Pillen?"

"Please fill out a personal voucher for me in the amount of five hundred dollars, then run it down to the teller and cash it. Meet me at the first floor north exit. Oh, and if Mrs. Pillen should happen to call, tell her I was called out to a meeting and I may be home a little late."

"Yes sir. I'll meet you downstairs in ten minutes."

Tom hung up the phone and pensively stared out the window across the street at his competition, the "other" bank. He wondered if perhaps there was an executive of theirs, sitting in his nice plush office on the twenty-second floor, looking back at him with the same thoughts. Not that it had any more profound importance than a single grain of sand on a deserted beach somewhere; moreso, it was his coping mechanism to deal with times of guilt and stress. It eased his burdened conscience to think that he was not the only man in this world to lead such a double life, a life filled with doubt and turmoil.

What would Peggy, his wife, do if she ever found out about his "other" life, trying to arrange liaisons with hopefully discreet males like George, or, uglier yet, his lost battles with other sexual desires of a worse nature?

His therapist had attempted, many times, to make him accept his double life. He was told that he was not alone, that many men were in a similar situation. They had no choice but to learn to accept their existence and remain discreet. The therapist had recommended group therapy with other professional men, but Tom couldn't accept that approach. What if someone, anyone, learned of his bizarre lifestyle? He shuddered when his thinking soured to memories of picking up boys, younger than his youngest son . . . "God, please help me," he quietly uttered to himself.

George was waiting in the lounge when Tom arrived at the hotel. It took a few moments for Tom's eyes to adjust to the darkened corners of the bar, and then he saw George at the round corner booth, his right hand raised slightly to discreetly catch Tom's attention. Tom acknowledged with a quick wave and proceeded to the booth. "So how are you, George?" he stammered.

"Fine, fine. It's been awhile. Three months, maybe?"

Tom slid into the booth. "At least. Too long. You know I look forward to being with you. I miss talking with someone on an intelligent level, with someone who understands me, and the physical closeness, too. I'm still having chronic problems with accepting my hidden life, and I surely can't let on at home. I just feel like such an outcast. But, on the humorous side, if I were to divulge my true self to Peggy, I *would* be an outcast, and quickly!"

They both laughed. "Tom, I've always loved your sarcastic humor. I'm through with my drink. We're short for time, so why don't you go get a room and I'll meet you in the lobby after I settle up here."

Tom charged the room to his company card and turned from the desk, motioning to the elevator with his eyes so that George would catch the signal from the wing-back chair thirty feet away. The desk clerk handed back the credit card with a, "Thank you, sir." Tom could sense that the clerk knew well what was going on, thinly disguising his disgust. "Another one for our Mr. Williams," the clerk muttered to his co-worker.

Tom opened the door to room 303 and motioned George inside. "Nice room. Nice view."

George said, "Yeah, nice." He pretended that he'd never been in the room before.

Tom turned suddenly and took George in his arms. "You drive me crazy with desire," he said. They fell to the bed, kissing passionately and pulling at each other's clothing.

• • •

George woke with a start and looked at his watch. "Oh, my God, my flight leaves in twenty-two minutes!" He hurriedly dressed while Tom watched.

"George, are you all right? You seem less of a wild man these days."

"You're right. I haven't been up to par lately. I think I'm working and partying too much for my own good. Probably I just need a little rest."

"You look like you've lost some weight, too. Maybe you're anemic or have mono or something."

"I did have mono a while ago, but it cleared up. I feel better than I did then. Still not quite back to normal, though."

"Maybe you should get checked again."

"Yeah, I'll do that. I hate to be a jerk, but did you bring me that stuff?" His timing was great, he thought, tying his shoes in order to avoid eye contact. He still had some morals, still felt embarrassed about sensitive topics.

"Get my pants over on the chair. The money and cocaine are in the right rear pocket."

Still purposely avoiding facial confrontation, George reached into the pocket and removed a wad of bills and a small white paper wrapper. He walked back to the bed and kissed Tom. "I'll see you again soon, I hope. I'd better zip outa here."

"O.K., call me again when you can."

"Sure will. Bye for now." He exited the room and sped down the hallway to the elevators. On the street, he flagged a taxi and got in with a "Airport, main terminal—fast!"

"Yes, sir." The cabby gunned the engine and sped away from the curb.

George pulled out the money and smiled. "West Hollywood, here I come!" He counted out ten fifty dollar bills. The paper wrapper was heavy, maybe two grams. Good haul. "Driver, got change for a fifty?"

"No sir, twenty dollars max."

"Damn! Well, I'm in a hurry, so give me a twenty for this fifty and we'll call it even. Easy come, easy go!"

"Right on! You can ride in *this* cab anytime!"

George was nervous about making his flight as the cab wove its way through the snarled traffic, the driver honking and swearing at every other car. His thoughts were laden with fleeting moments of the pleasures that awaited him in L.A. How he loved that town! All the bath houses and parties and bars. He intended to spend a full day at the exclusive Blue Moon, where the upper crust of gay men hung out, soaking in the baths and partying. All the men there were lovely, refined, and well-moneyed. The last time he was there he'd had three different lovers in one afternoon. This time he'd get there at mid-morning and stay as long as he wished—or until he involuntarily burned out. And then, to continue his four day furlough, he'd hop a flight up to the Bay Area for the gay parade and ball. He knew he'd have to pick up more money along the way to fully enjoy his time off, but that would be easy enough. He snapped forward in his seat as the cab lurched to a halt.

"Here you are, buddy. It's as close as I can get. It'll be quicker for you if you jump out here and cross the traffic on foot."

"Sure, O.K., thanks." He exchanged his fifty for a twenty and jumped from the cab. Inside, he ran down the long concourse, panting as he reached the check-in desk. "Are you George Williams?" the agent asked.

"Yes, I'm sorry. I'm running late," he panted.

"You'd better get on board. There was a flight delay posted until your alternate could get here. I'll cancel the delay and the on-call attendant."

"Thanks, I really appreciate it. I went to see a friend and his car stalled on the way back from lunch and so—"

"Uh-huh, sure." The agent was more than obvious when she rolled her eyeballs upward in a dramatic show of disbelief. "Hustle. You're assigned to first-class."

"So where have *you* been?" Brenda asked, as she checked the door. She'd been on the same flight with George since LaGuardia. "You look like the proverbial cat who ate the canary, if I may. Where do you disappear to on these short layovers, anyway? You come back, always with two minutes to spare, and a smirk on your little-boy face."

George blushed and glanced downward, a manipulative little gesture he'd found to be tremendously effective in throwing the focus back at the inquirer. Brenda blushed a little, too, realizing it was none of her business. She changed the topic to be more palatable. "I suppose you've been out buying a little gift for your mother, and it's none of my business." She smiled and exited through the small doorway from the galley to give the preflight instructions.

You've done it again, you master, you, he thought to himself. What control! George went about his business checking the beverage stock, and then slipped into his seat and fastened the belt just as the plane began thrusting down the runway. He smiled as he thought about L.A. again. So what if his co-workers questioned his behavior? Screw 'em, anyway!

• • •

Tom had dozed again. He awakened and glanced at his watch. "Seven-thirty, wow! I'd better get home!" Peggy had been in a foul mood lately, and now she'd be really red! He shook the cobwebs out of his head and went into the bathroom. A splash of water on his face revived his thinking. "Aha!" He picked up the phone and dialed, scheming while it rang.

"Hello, Brodesky residence."

"Marge, this is Tom Pillen. Is Ralph in, please?"

"Sure, Tom, he's out in the garage. Just a sec."

Tom could hear the television and the screaming kids in the background. How lucky he was to have his children fairly matured. He had a sense of guilt, though, because he'd missed so much of his children's early developmental years due to demands at work. On the other hand, he'd moved up quickly in the corporate structure and could justify this guilt by the fact that the kids lived a very comfortable life.

"Hi, Tom. What's up?"

"Ralph, I'm here at the Hilton. I'm in a jam. I need to call up the note for the time I covered for you, when you were with that cutie up at the cabin."

"Uh, yeah, yeah. And so you want an update on the accounts receivable, Tom?"

"Gotcha, she's there, huh? Okay, if anyone asks, we went out and had a drink to discuss the mortgage branch audit, right?"

"I believe that's right, and I'll get back with you in the morning." Click.

Tom put the phone down with mixed feelings of relief and guilt, the overall sum being a vacillation between guilt and depression. How long could this self-torture go on, anyway? Thoughts of the easy way out recurred. STOP IT, STOP IT! He fought the powerful, overwhelming images of a self-inflicted perpetual state of peace.

1977

NEW YORK CITY, MARCH

Green was everywhere. The street lamps, signs, and restaurant and bar interiors were all festively decorated with the color of the day. The fabled green beer poured from keg taps and iced mugs. *My Wild Irish Rose* blasted from the loudspeakers in front of Kelly's, while people sang and danced and sloshed their mugs to the rhythm of the music. Thousands of people filled the streets and bars, some celebrating their heritage, and the rest simply taking advantage of another reason to party.

In one area of the Village, strikingly beautiful men gathered and had a truly wild party every year, with each year gaining more notoriety among the gay population. Gays came from all over the world for this event. Most were dressed in their most flagrant finery—skin tight leather, silk tops splayed open to the waist, wildly mixed tuxedos, and a myriad of other unimaginable human coverings.

The day took on the atmosphere of Mardi Gras in the French Quarter of New Orleans, complete with impromptu parades, banners, and constant street dancing. It was a day tailored to the personality of the eccentric, and even the more subdued took advantage of the day to surface their deepest audacities. The transvestites were abundant, dressed full tilt in multi-colored sheer slinky adornment. High heels and seamed fish net stockings, garters and lace, camisoles and feather boas. All had beautifully done makeup, some with wigs, others with short, close-cropped hair. If, from a reasonable distance, one observed the crowd for any length of time, one could witness the lustful spontaneous coupling and disappearance of these raffish people, to reappear perhaps an hour later, only to repeat the self-indulgence again, moments later. The corners of the alleys nearby were occupied with couples and groups engaging in flagrant sodomy.

Police patrols, afoot and mounted, patrolled the area sporadically, closing their eyes in disgust to the debauchery. They were ordered not to interfere unless there were complaints involving property or victim crimes. Most of the retail shops, with the exception of the bars, closed their doors this day every year.

As usual, 'heteros' milled along the outskirts of the party, verbally insulting and taunting the partiers with shouts of, "Queers!" "Faggots!" "Fruitcakes!," and other equally hateful prodding. It was plain that those throwing the remarks travelled in the protection of gangs.

A street preacher stood on a pile of wooden pallets, Bible in one hand, flailing the other, shouting condemnation and quoting Genesis 19 1:11. "As God destroyed the cities of Sodom and Gomorrah, so shall He destroy you," he screamed at the passersby. Shouts of "Screw you!" and "Go to hell!" drifted upward toward him. Occasionally empty bottles and food scraps were hurled from the crowd. A can hit the preacher on the right side of his forehead, causing a trickle of blood down the side of his face. Unshaken, he persisted in disparagement, now comparing the sin to the orgy of the frustrated heathens awaiting the return of Moses at the base of Mt. Sinai.

"So where's *my* little piece of the golden calf?" a mocker yelled. The crowd laughed.

This particular year there must be four thousand gays here, the stoned young man-boy thought to himself as he watched the revelers.

I think I've died and gone to heaven! He took another gulp of beer, spilling it over his chin and neck and allowing it to run down the front of the green sequined leprechaun suit he'd rented. He'd lost the hat somewhere earlier in the evening, but that was okay, he'd just pay for it. Could be he'd left it on the floor of the cheap hotel down the street, where he took his first pick-up. Or maybe it was in the car in the alley with his second? That was just after he'd done a 'lude' and then a hit of cocaine to temper it, and he was spaced. He laughed out loud to himself, losing his balance from inebriation, and caught himself again before going down. His current prospect for number three was tipping his mug, just as George caught himself, and suddenly laughed so hard he spilled beer down his front as well. Laughing, they both fell drunkenly back into the bar booth, landing on the laps of the other men who had sat down there immediately after George and his friend had gotten up.

"Whaa's yer name, anyway?" asked George's latest.

"Georgey . . . Georgey Williams," he slurred. "Whaa's yers? No, no, I don' wanna know. I like your ear ring, but I really like the shape of your mouf. I wanna take you down an' get dirdy, kay?"

"I thought you'd ne'er aks! Le's go find my car."

They staggered out of the bar, laughing crazily, staying upright only because there was no room to fall in the tightly packed crowd of bodies. Once in the alley they encountered a three man orgy.

"Forgit the car. This looks *fun*!" George took his pants down to his knees and joined in.

"Hey, guy, you into S&M?" the transvestite asked.

"I'll try anything," George said. "Why, do you like it?"

"Yeah, but I thought you looked too cute for that sort of thing."

"No, not me. Anything, honey!"

They carried on in the alley for a long time. George was tired and high when he finally broke away.

He came to with his head lying on the table in some crummy bar, as the lights came on.

"O.K., everybody out! Closing time," someone yelled.

George crawled from the booth and staggered to the door, then felt the heave burning upward through his esophagus. He just cleared the threshold when he lost it, projectile vomiting onto the sidewalk.

It was three-thirty a.m. The street was quiet. "What street is this!" he exclaimed. He let his stomach settle for a few minutes, then laughed, "God, I don't know where I am or how I got here, so I must have had a good time! My butt hurts." He was still wearing what was left of the sequined leprechaun costume. "Oh, yeah, I need a place to stay." He had just flown in that afternoon and left all his belongings in his rental car so he could hurry to the Village several hours before the celebration. Sleeping arrangements were never a problem for him. He had friends that would take him on a moment's notice anywhere he went.

He staggered half a block down the street and found a pay phone, then dialed a number he had on a slip of paper in his money clip. The phone rang.

"Hello?" The responder sounded asleep.

"Joseph, this is George Williams. Got an extra rack for the night?"

"Hi, George, what time is it, anyhow?"

"Three forty-seven in the a.m. Didn't you go to the Village tonight? I tried to call you earlier, but you didn't answer, so figured you were down there. I didn't see you, but, shit, man, there were thousands of beauties! I think I got boned a dozen times!" His slurred speech had cleared while he was asleep, passed out in the bar.

"You're such a whore! Come on over, I'll leave a key under the mailbox. See you in the morning." Click.

George fumbled for another coin, then deposited it and dialed the cab number that someone had conveniently stuck on the phone. "Yeah, hello, Yellow Cab?" Pause. "Pick me up at the corner of 13th and Broadway."

The cab arrived in minutes. "Get in," shouted the cabby through the open window. "Kinda slow this morning." George slammed the door behind him and the cab pulled away. "You one of those fags from the Village?" the cabby prodded.

"Fuck you."

George woke up on the couch, his head throbbing, his stomach churning, the smell of frying bacon from the small apartment kitchen making him nauseated. He let out a long moan........ "Woe is me, my poor head, my poor gut!"

"You awake, buddy?" called Joseph.

"Awake, but barely alive.... What time is it?"

"Eleven-thirty or so. Bacon and eggs?"

"Oh, God, no. You want me to throw up on this expensive virgin white carpet?"

"You do and I'll throw you off the balcony. Speaking of physical abuse, what have you been doing to yourself lately? You look like hell, gaunt, bad color, you know?"

"Probably because of last night. You should have been there!"

"No, I think your color is bad anyway. Do you feel all right?"

"Well, actually, I've been feeling kind of puny for a while now. Just a phase."

"Maybe you've been letting yourself get too run down with all this partying. Maybe your liver is becoming affected with all the drugs and booze. Lots of maybes. At any rate, you don't look very good. Seems like you're losing weight, too."

"I've been going to doctors more often lately for different things like colds and stuff. They keep telling me that I have a virus infection and that it'll go away. I quit running 'cause it was too much and I get pooped out easily. I noticed my weight loss, too, even though I'm eating as much as I ever have."

"Sounds like you've got an Outer Mongolian sheep disease or something!" They both laughed. "Really, though, you should go to some kind of specialist and get a real good checkup."

"Yeah, I've been thinking about it. Now that you've made me out to look like shit, I feel like shit! I'm going back to Toronto in a couple of days, so I'll try to find a good doctor instead of these emergency guys who size you up and throw you out in ten minutes or less. Woe is me. I feel like doggy do-do! And I still have to find my rental car. Shit. Damn booze."

Part Two The Agony

1979

TORONTO, JUNE

George was tired of all the illnesses he'd had for the past two years. There was nothing major, really, except for having mononucleosis diagnosed for the second time in two years since his return from the St. Patrick's celebration in New York. Since then, his mono test had never gone back to negative, and he caught all the colds and flus he came into contact with. The lymph nodes on his neck had stayed swollen, too.

His doctor had blamed everything on the chronic mono infection, until this latest problem surfaced three months ago. The doctor decided to monitor the purplish, funny looking spot on his neck, but when it started to change and grow, he thought it odd enough that George should see a dermatologist. George was tiring of doctors, but he knew something was wrong.

He sat in the examining room at the dermatology clinic.

"How long ago did you notice it?" asked the specialist.

"Let's see . . . Probably three months ago. But it started out smaller."

"It's growing?" the doctor asked.

"It's getting bigger, and now it itches all the time. I just want it removed. It makes me look terrible."

"Hmm, I've never seen a lesion quite like this one. You say it's getting larger?"

"Yes, slowly," George responded. "Can you remove it here, now?"

"Sure, but I'm going to take a good skin border all the way around it because it looks suspicious. I've been a dermatologist for twelve years and haven't seen anything like this. It has a poorly defined border, and that's not a good sign." Dr. Reedy, the chief of the dermatology department at the hospital clinic, was baffled. "How long have the lymph nodes in your neck been swollen?"

"Two years. I have chronic mono, too, and my doctor told me that's what's causing the swelling. He told me not to worry, they would go down in time. But then when this spot showed up, he got concerned and sent me to you. I've never really felt bad, other than being chronically tired from the mono, but I've been sick a lot more recently, with colds and things like that. Do *you* know why?"

"Well, to be straight up with you, the worst scenario is cancer, but it may be simply a benign lesion of some kind. I'm going to send it to the pathologist for an evaluation. I'll inject a local anesthetic, before I remove it, and you won't feel a thing. Be all done in twenty minutes, and you can go home."

"I have two questions. Will I have a scar, and how long before it heals? You know, the cut from the surgery."

"Because it's on the visible area of your neck, I'll use a plastic technique to keep the scarring down. The incision won't even be noticeable, unless you get very close and stretch the skin. It'll be about an inch and a half long. It should be well healed in two weeks or so. You'll need to come back here in four days, and I'll take out the sutures. Probably by the tenth day you'll hardly notice it. When you come back for the suture removal, I should have the pathology report in hand to discuss with you."

"My biggest concern *was* looks... Now you think I might have cancer? It just *can't* be!" His lack of insight was mirrored by denial. "I'm planning on going to the parade in San Francisco. God, I hope it's not cancer. What would I do?"

"For right now, try not to get too worked up about it. Don't let this interfere with your vacation. It looks a little funny, but so do a lot of other lesions that come back as benign pigment changes. What parade are you going to, anyway?"

"The yearly Gay Freedom Day Parade. One of the most fun days of the year. It's kind of like the Halloween celebration in New York City. People come from all over the world! It's a great time."

"Uh, well," clearing his throat, "okay. Please follow me into the surgery room." The doctor cooled suddenly.

That was expected. George long ago learned of this typical reaction from straights. Without further conversation, he followed the doctor down the hall into a small, sterile looking room with an electric surgery table, stainless-steel instrument trays, glass cupboards, and large lights mounted in the ceiling.

"Lay down with your head at this end, please," the doctor requested. "Ann, could you come assist in this surgery?" he called.

"One second, be right there."

Ann, the nurse, came around the corner and entered the room. She laid out sterile gloves, syringes, and a package wrapped in blue cloth which she carefully opened on one of the stainless trays.

"Two percent xylocaine, a number 15 blade, 6-0 nylon and 5-0 chromic suture, and a small formalin specimen bottle," Doctor Reedy barked. "Mark the lab slip as follows: 3 cm. x 1 cm. purpuric lesion from left suprasternal notch. Send the specimen to the lab as soon as we're finished. Scrub the area and I'll be back in a minute." He left the room.

"What does all that mean, anyway? Is it bad? Will it hurt?" George was anxious.

The nurse turned and smiled. "It's just technical terminology for the kind of anesthetic, scalpel blade size, type of suture material, and so forth. Don't worry, it won't hurt a bit. When he first injects the skin to numb it, it will feel like getting novocaine at the dentist, then you won't feel a thing."

She opened some large cotton swabs soaked in antiseptic and started scrubbing the area. "Right now, I'm cleaning the area with a bactericidal agent to prevent infection. Try to relax." She finished up and focused the overhead light on the area. "I'll go get Dr. Reedy."

They returned together, then Dr. Reedy sat on a steel stool next to George. The nurse handed him a syringe and he inserted the needle several times around the area. George first felt a slight burning sensation, then nothing. The nurse placed a paper drape, with a precut center hole, over the surgical site.

George's thoughts drifted away, trying subconsciously to remove himself from this.

The next thing he was aware of, after overhearing mumbling and chatting during the procedure, was the doctor placing a glob of skin in a small jar the nurse was holding. Then he picked up an instrument, with a needle and thread protruding, and George felt some tugging as the knots were tied.

"There, that ought to do it." The doctor pulled off his gloves and threw them in the trash.

The nurse removed the drape and cleaned the incision area before covering it with a gauze dressing. She instructed George to watch it for infection and to come in, if needed, before the four-day follow-up when he was to have the sutures removed. Then she walked out.

George overheard mumbling from the hallway, some laughing, and a distinct, but quiet, "damn queers" in the doctor's voice.

"Screw 'em," he said just loudly enough to be heard.

Doctor Reedy returned and told him he could leave, but to come back as discussed for the follow-up.

George felt fine until two hours later, when he began to have pain as the anesthesia wore off. He took some pain pills and slept. Luckily, he'd been given the next four days off.

The next morning he felt better and decided to enjoy his free time. He called a handful of his most promiscuous friends over for a party.

"You just need a good lay!" one of them exclaimed, and the party was on.

• • •

At three p.m. on the fourth day, George found himself in the same surgery room for his suture removal. He'd been worried about the possibility of cancer, in spite of the reassurances he'd had from the medical people and his friends, and the mind-bending drugs and booze he'd consumed over the past three days. He was about to get the answer. He paced nervously in the small room.

Doctor Reedy entered the room. "So you made it back all right." His attitude had changed noticeably since George bared his homosexuality on the last visit. The doctor was overtly uncomfortable.

"Let me see the incision." He pulled the dressing off and studied the fine line traversed by black thread. "Looks good. I'll take the sutures out." He went to a tray on the counter and retrieved a small scissor and forceps, then began clipping and pulling the fine black threads.

"Well?" asked George.

"Well, what?" He continued clipping and pulling.

"How did the report on the specimen come back? I've been going absolutely crazy with worry. If it's cancer, I think I would just die."

"Oh, you types are so dramatic! No offense, but you *are*. Just a minute. Let me finish here. One more to go. Nurse, would you get me Mr. Williams's chart, please?"

George didn't like the evasiveness. Something was wrong.

The nurse brought the chart and Doctor Reedy flipped to the back page. "I am afraid I have some good news and some bad news, as the line goes."

"What?"

"The bad news is that your lesion was a very rare form of cancer, called Kaposi's Sarcoma, that affects the connective tissue in the body. The good news: it's fairly benign."

"Meaning?"

"Meaning, if you have to get a cancer, it's not a bad one to get. It's treatable, to a large extent, through the normal methods, radiation or chemotherapy being the best choices.

"It's seen mostly in blacks and elderly Mediterranean men. That's why I'm so puzzled by its appearance in you. The next step is to stage it by doing some biopsies of lymph nodes and a scan to determine the extent."

George was stunned. "*Any* cancer is bad, Doctor! What are these other tests?"

"We take some lymph node biopsies, from various areas, under local anesthesia, like you just had, and check them to see if the cancer has spread. We'll do a CAT scan, too. If it hasn't spread below the diaphragm, were in good shape, treatment wise.

"I want you to see Dr. Steinberg. Here's a referral form with pertinent information." He handed George a typed form. "He is an oncologist, a cancer specialist. His address and phone are at the top of the page. Call and get an appointment."

George didn't feel that bad. He had cancer, so *they* thought. Doctors had been wrong before. Even if it was cancer, so what? Lots of other people had cancer, too. I have the world by the balls, he thought to himself. I'm not going to let this thing get to me. The treatment will cure me, and I'll be fine. In the meantime, no sweat, I'll just try to have a good time.

He went home and called the oncologist to schedule an appointment for right after his return from San Francisco.

• • •

After packing a light bag, George drove to the airport and caught the first flight to San Francisco for the celebration. Upon his arrival he took a cab to see Frank, an old San Francisco lover, and arranged to stay with him. Then he took the trolley down to the highlight of the gala event, the Galleria.

Beautiful men were everywhere, dancing in the streets, in the corners of the atrium. Lesbians gathered in small clusters, prostitutes abounded. The clothing was extravagant, vibrant in form and color. There were the usual whips and feather boas, seamed fish net stockings, high heels, wild earrings, facial makeup, and long manicured nails. All could be found in both men and women. Distinguishing the sexes was difficult at best.

Music floated through the crowds from all directions. There were banners and placards proclaiming and demanding 'Gay Liberation' everywhere. Live impromptu bands and ghetto boxes boomed and clashed, and the odor of marijuana wafted through the air. Under a stairway a small group was doing amyl nitrate poppers, laughing, and smoking joints.

George ran into many old lovers, remembering only the names of his favorites. Some he met for the first time, and collected their names and numbers on napkins and matchbooks. He danced for hours.

How could anyone with cancer do that? He was alive, zestful, invulnerable! Maybe they were all wrong and he was fine, just a purple bruise from a violent sexual encounter or something.

Gay men knew of George Williams, he was one to conquer and boast about. He was continuously propositioned, a perennial favorite at popular gay spots around the world. He thrived on attention, languishing in the knowledge that he had his choice of any man there. Money, drugs, sex, and youth. Cancer? No way!

George was high, high on poppers, cocaine, pot, speed, booze, and whatever anyone passed his way. It was getting late, the crowds were thinning, and the dinning music was slowly dying away. He looked at his watch — 2:15 a.m. But he wasn't ready to go back to Frank's. The bath houses. *Yeah, there'd be some action there.*

He made the rounds at the Bulldog, the Hothouse, and then the Club Baths with two new 'friends': it seemed he just couldn't get enough of any of it. More orgies and drugs, more, more! Even those who knew him as a partier were surprised at his almost neurotic search for fun. His friend Barry from the Club Baths finally persuaded him to go back to his hotel and spend the remainder of the night.

"Wha nigh', it's seven a.m.", George slurred, as he got in the cab.

• • •

The afternoon sun struck George's face. He stirred and sat up, confused and dizzy. His head pounded as he read the note on theother unused bed. "Here's my number in Paris, dearie. You're a wonderful lover. Call me. Love, Barry."

George groped on his hands and knees to the bathroom, his belly knotted with cramps and heaves. He knelt by the porcelain rim and vomited, then fell to the floor.

It was dark when he came to again, lying by the toilet on the cold tile floor. Groggy and with his head still pounding, he wrapped a towel around his naked body and gargled the mouthwash left by the hotel, then looked in the mirror and combed his hair.

"You *really* look like shit this time, stupid. Look at those bloodshot eyes. Actually, I guess it means I had a good time!" He smiled to himself and giggled. "No cancer in this body." He rotated his upper torso around in the mirror, looking for any other spots on his shoulders and neck. "Oh, shit. Is that one?" There was a small discoloration just below his left ear, slightly posterior, so he couldn't see it without stretching the skin. "Shit, it looks just like the other one!"

He dressed and took a cab back to Frank's place, knocked three times on the door, and got no answer. No change of clothing, no way to clean up. Everything was in his bag inside the apartment. "Shit!" He walked back down the narrow hall and out onto Castro Street.

His money clip contained forty-eight dollars, enough to get back to Toronto, if he could hop a standby flight. He flagged a cab, "Airport," and hopped in the back seat. Twenty dollars.

He had to wait two hours at the airport before catching the midnight special back to LaGuardia with a connecting flight to Toronto. Nine dollars and his airline attendant I.D. bought his flight home. It cost more to get him the last five miles, via taxi, than to fly three thousand miles across the continent. His room mate was asleep, when he quietly opened the door and slipped into his room. Tomorrow was his day with the oncologist. Back to the real world again. He slept.

• • •

The door to the office suite read: Carl Steinberg, M.D., Oncology. George was still down from the partying in San Francisco the past couple of days. He'd had trouble getting out of bed, even though his appointment wasn't until 2:30 in the afternoon.

He pushed the heavy, solid oak door open and stepped inside to the smell of leather furniture. *What opulence! This guy makes a lot of dough! The decor is something else.*

It was a large room, expansive enough for a dozen over-stuffed leather recliner chairs, interpolated with chrome and brass accent tables and lamps. There were smaller leather chairs for the people who accompanied the patients. In one corner, a brass room divider shielded a small galley area, which provided freshly brewed coffee and snack foods for the waiting patients. It reminded him of an airliner galley.

The tables near each setting of chairs had a current *Wall Street Journal* and classy magazines like *Bon Appetit.* The walls were of black walnut panels, with vertical columns in a bas-relief effect rising to the high ceiling. Vertical windows, on the exposed south wall, rose from the floor to the ceiling, throwing natural light throughout the room to nourish the huge tropical plants. How deceptive this place was, based on the outmoded exterior of the office building, twelve stories below.

He approached the L-shaped desk in the corner. "Hello, I'm George Williams. I have a 2:30 appointment with Dr. Steinberg."

"Oh, yes, Mr. Williams," the receptionist said, handing him a clipboard. "Please fill out this patient information form, and return it to me when you're finished."

George took it to one of the leather chairs by the brass writing table and filled it in. The form required everything, particularly emphasizing insurance information, but obviously trying to downplay finances to secondary importance. It was well done, he noted. *Must have hired a professional, subliminal psychologist to design this one.* He carried it back to the desk and handed it to the receptionist with a slight smile.

"Please have a seat. The nurse will be with you in a little while."

George picked a chair where he could engage his favorite pastime of people watching. He sat in a corner with his back to the huge glass wall. From here he could observe the comings and goings of the employees and patients. He tried to be unobtrusive by holding the newspaper in front of him.

There were six other patients in the room, accompanied by their relatives and friends. There was a young man, maybe his own age, seated by the galley area. He was wearing a stocking cap, even though it was quite warm. He nervously fidgeted with his shirt tail. He must be some kind of blue-collar worker, wearing a work shirt with a company name tag over one pocket and his name, 'Jim', sewn on the other side. A young woman sat with him; his wife, George decided. Jim shifted his position, and George noticed that he had no hair under his cap, and now the different light cast on him revealed an ashen, pallid color to his face. He looked much older and frail in this different light. He coughed with a disturbing, barking quality. His wife took his hand to comfort him. He stopped coughing and looked over at George, a dull look in what should have been sparkling blue eyes. George shifted his gaze across the room to avoid eye contact.

There was an elderly man accompanied by a younger man, possibly his son. The old man had a walker next to his chair. He sat, sunken eyes fixed mindlessly at the far opposite wall. He couldn't have weighed more than eighty pounds. His hands continuously trembled, and he had large black and blue areas on his inner elbows, some with small bandages. A living, breathing skeleton. His son, for the most part, ignored him, reading a magazine to occupy himself. Frequently the old man would groan, and the son would look up for a moment. "It's okay," he would say. "We're at the doctor's office, and he'll make you feel better with the treatment."

"No-o-o-o, no-o-o-oh," the old man groaned.

He must have been ninety years old, George observed. If I'm that miserable, when I get that old, *take me out and shoot me.* George never considered any real disruption in his own mortality, but, at the same time, he had trouble accepting the value of prolonging this pathetic old man's life via medical miracles. Let the poor old sucker go. He hoped the son of the old man was telepathic and picked up his thoughts.

A vivacious, young, pretty nurse came into the room. She didn't fit in here, in this place of suffering and chronic pain and doom. If the idea was to boost the patients' morale by using superficial niceties, it was a dismal failure. *That woman should be selling flowers at the beach, not working here.* "Mr. Harley, please," she called out with a pleasant chirp.

The young man helped the skeleton up from the recliner and placed the walker in front of him. The old man moved the walker, with the aid of his son, and slowly shuffled his feet to it, moaning all the way. He didn't know, or apparently care, where he was. *That's disgusting. The old man should be home in bed or in the hospital, anywhere but here. He would be more comfortable stretched out in a coffin.* George's opinions on voluntary euthanasia rekindled, as he watched this poor wretched shell of a human being shuffle interminably the twenty feet to the doorway, moaning with each step.

God, he'll *never* make it. He couldn't watch anymore, and turned his attention back to the younger man, Jim.

The young woman picked up his look and nodded with a tired

smile. She didn't look much better than Jim did, her face exposing chronic worry. George was becoming melancholic; the impact of what he witnessed here was getting to him. He stood and walked over to the couple. "Mind if I sit?"

"No, not at all," the woman said. "It's depressing, sitting in here every week, with no one to talk to." The man looked up, nodding what seemed to be agreement, and cast his eyes toward the neighboring chair for George.

"We don't know anybody in this city. We're here for Jim's treatments, and living in an apartment for patients sponsored by the hospital. She tried to smile, "Betty Carlin," extending her hand, "and this is my husband, Jim." He nodded again.

"Where are you from?" George asked, attempting to rid his depression by indulging in light conversation.

"From Sudbury, up north. We were sent here by our old family doctor when he found that Jim had cancer. I'm sure glad we have the government insurance, because there's no way we could afford this. Dr. Steinberg was the only cancer specialist we could see on the government plan, so we had to come the three hundred miles and stay here. Jim's treatments are over next week, then we can go home. He's doing so much better." She turned to him. "Aren't you, honey?"

Jim looked up and said slowly, "I'm doing much better, honey." His voice was sluggish, almost retarded sounding. He had no personality, and spoke mechanically, struggling to repeat Betty's words.

George was bewildered. What was wrong with this guy, anyway? "If you don't mind, what kind of cancer do you have?"

"Cancer of the . . . of the . . . of the b-rrain. But I'm doing much better, honey," looking back at his wife.

He had that last sentence by rote, George noted. Damn, if he was truly much better now, what was he like before? He shuddered. These people are sick and dying from cancer. *I don't feel that bad. Maybe it will turn up that I really don't have such a big deal, after all. This is all too depressing.*

The woman cut in again, anxious to talk to someone. "Jim has been having radiation treatments to shrink the size of the tumor in his brain. The doctors said that the cancer is too widespread to operate, but with the radiation and shrinkage of the tumor, he could live longer, and he *is* doing much better."

Stop saying that, George thought. He was certain these people had either been sold a bill of goods or that they were denying the poor man's deathbed status!

"Yes, he looks like he's doing okay," George lied. He was sorry now that he'd started a conversation with these pathetic people. He actually felt genuine sorrow for them, and it made him deeply uncomfortable.

He hadn't felt this way since he was a small child and his grandfather had passed away, just after his father had abandoned him. He hadn't thought about this for years, apparently psychologically repressing it. He'd resolved to himself, subconsciously, that he would never allow those feelings to surface. They were too disturbing. Compensating, he made certain that he never subverted himself to other people's feelings again. He would do what he pleased, and if others were hurt in the process, so be it. He was not going to be the one to feel the hurt again.

"Mr. Williams?," the flaky nurse chirped, scanning the lobby.

"Gotta go," George said to the disconsolate couple as he stood. "I hope everything works out for you." He started for the door that the nurse stood near.

"Good bye, sir," Jim called out. And then, curiously, "D-d-don't let them do it t-to you."

What does that mean, he wondered. He followed the nurse back through the exam and treatment area. With his peripheral vision he saw patients in small rooms, either lying on tables, or seated in comfortable chairs, with intravenous tubes and bottles hanging next to them. A few of them looked like they were in good health. Then he heard moaning coming from the doorway just ahead. He looked inside as they passed, and saw Mr. Harley lying on a table with restraining straps on his wrists. A nurse was trying to put a needle in his forearm. She talked soothingly, trying to calm him. The old man glanced in George's direction, seeming to look directly at him for a second, but George sensed that he really didn't comprehend anything.

"Right in here and have a seat," the nurse waved into a doorway, "and Dr. Steinberg will be here in a minute."

George entered a beautiful, comfortable office, even more nicely furnished than the waiting area he had just left. There was a large walnut executive desk, with a comfortable high-backed chair, and behind it the same exterior full-length window from floor to ceiling. He sat in one of the chairs meant for visitors and fidgeted nervously.

A man in a white coat appeared out of nowhere into George's ongoing daydream.

"Hello, I'm Dr. Steinberg. You must be . . . George Williams," he said, looking at the name on the top of the chart through the half-glasses hanging on the end of his long nose. "Nice to meet you."

George reached up and shook his hand, the hand of a cold, dead fish. "Likewise, I'm sure." He hadn't had time to stand for the salutation, still trying to shake his daydream.

Perusing the chart, without looking up, the doctor said, "So you have that oddball cancer that's been showing up recently in queers."

Stunned, George replied, "The proper term is 'gay.' And yes, I'm homosexual. How did you know? Did Doctor Reedy tell you?"

"No he didn't. I've heard, through the grapevine, about this weird disease appearing in homosexuals, so I assume you're gay. Excuse me, but if you prefer the term 'gay,' I can live with that. It's just another linguistic stigma avoidance tactic, as far as I can see." He looked at George over the top of his glasses, then back at the chart. "So, it appears that we need to stage the extent of the malignant cells, and then determine the best course of treatment. I'm sure you've had ample explanation of the problem from Dr. Reedy, as that is *his* responsibility. My current task is simply to evaluate and treat . . . fine, fine . . . ," a brief pause. "Any questions?"

"No." What an arrogant asshole! "Yes." George lisped as effeminately as he could, throwing in a flick of his wrist. "What's next, Doc?"

The doctor caught his gesture and chose to ignore it, looking quickly back at the chart. "I'll have the nurse arrange a CAT scan to determine if there are any periaortic nodes, indicating a more serious involvement, and we'll go from there. Go to the front desk and get your instructions from the receptionist. It's been nice to meet you, I think, and I'll see you again in a few days to discuss the results of the test." He rose and extended his limp-fish hand over the desk. George shook it lightly and gave it a little affectionate squeeze.

"All right, then, Doctor," he lisped. He left the office and returned down the long hallway through the treatment area, still hearing Mr. Harley's moans until he exited into the lobby. He approached the desk. "Do you have the instructions ready for me yet? Williams, George."

"Yes, sir. Dr. Steinberg just buzzed me. You get the standard forms with an appointment for a staging CAT scan." She handed him three pages of pre-printed material with his name and a time and date on the final page. "If you have any questions, please call." She turned back to typing.

A well-oiled machine. A well-oiled *money* machine. George scanned the last page of the instructions. CAT Scan Wednesday morning at 8:30 at Toronto General, then return to this office Friday at 1:00 p.m.

• • •

"Hands at your sides, breathe slowly and deeply, and remain perfectly still until I tell you otherwise. This test will take about thirty minutes, so relax as much as you can." The technician was readying equipment while he spoke. "You won't feel a thing."

George lay supine on a long, concave surfaced table in the hospital's radiology department, awed by all of the ominous high-tech equipment. He was in a small room with a large donut-shaped machine, with the table he was lying on about to be sent into the hole of the donut. He humored himself with the thought that this might be the ultimate destruction of mankind, being eaten alive by their own machines. The tech left the room, and George was alone. His only contact with the tech at this point was via a large glass window and a two-way speaker system. The tech gave last minute instructions about a motor noise and some motion. Suddenly he heard a high-pitched, electric whirring noise, and the table he laid on started moving into the giant donut. The table stopped at about his gut level, the tech again reassured him and told him to remain still throughout the test, then turned on some relaxing music.

Forever passed, and again he heard the tech's voice telling him they were finished and the table would move outward. *It's about time they finished.* He'd been here for his appointment since 8:30, and it was now 11:45. How typical. "That wasn't too bad," George told the tech. "I thought it would burn or something. Especially when you said I wouldn't feel a thing. I know how you people lie to prevent fear in us poor victims you call patients!"

"Oh, now, now. You know I couldn't lie to a handsome man like you," the tech audibly lisped. "Are you the George Williams who works for the airline?" he queried. "If you are, I've heard about you through friends. You know, your travels and delightful escapades and everything."

"That must be me," he boasted. "I've traveled all over the world, and had more fun than most men could have in two lifetimes. I've been everywhere but the 'lectric chair, seen everything but the wind. I'm handsome and then some, I'm agile, I'm fragile, and some people even call me hostile!" He chanted, using his best lines. This kid was kind of cute, maybe he could go out for a drink.

"You're too much," the kid laughed. "Just like I've heard. My name is Jamie Murchison." He was beaming.

Maybe eighteen or nineteen years old, good looking, nice body. "Listen, Jamie, what time do you get off work? Maybe we could go have a drink, maybe dancing." By this time it was apparent they wanted the same thing.

"I'm out of here by eleven tonight. I work twelve-hour shifts, but I'm off tomorrow. Going out with you would be fun! That is, if you feel like going out. Are you sick or something? Why the scan?"

"I feel fine. The doctor just wants to check and see if I have anything wrong in my belly, I guess." George intentionally downplayed the questions. He wasn't going to lose a lover over having a little cancer, even if he really did have it, and people might shy away from him if they knew. Might think it was contagious or something. "Let's do go out tonight. I'll pick you up at the front door at 11:15."

• • •

Noon the following day came too quickly, and Jamie had to leave.

They got out of bed and had coffee and bagels in the sunroom. "George, I really enjoyed last night. It was only the second time that I've ever . . . oh, well, never mind. I've got to go to my mom's house to take her to the store now. Can I call you again, or will you call me?"

George smiled that wiry smirk. "Please do, anytime."

Jamie clumsily got up from the breakfast nook and headed for the back door. "S-see you later, huh, George?"

"You bet," the same smirk on his face, looking over the rim of his cup.

The door closed. George picked up the papers he'd been given at Doctor Steinberg's office and began reading them, more carefully, as he drank his coffee.

Cancer cells are mutated normal cells that multiply very rapidly, wherever they are in the body. Cancer itself does not actually kill, but the effects of erosion or pressure on other vital structures, over time, from the rapidly growing tumor, causes symptoms and, if not treated, can be fatal. Three choices of current cancer treatments are surgery, irradiation, and chemotherapy, depending on the type and location of the cancer. Surgical intervention is utilized to remove small ,localized tumors, if they are caught early before they grow too large or spread. Focused irradiation is utilized to shrink large tumors to facilitate surgery, or to reduce tumor size to alleviate pressure on vital structures. Chemotherapy involves the use of intravenous anti-cancer drugs to destroy cancer cells, useful in the treatment of diffuse cancers such as lymphatic types, leukemias, and skin cancers. Any of these three treatment modalities can be used in any combination on an individualized basis.

George looked out the window to watch the Bluejays in the giant silver maple tree in the backyard. Their squawking had disrupted his concentration, and given him a chance to digest what he'd read, after they momentarily departed across the cedar fence. *This cancer stuff is something else, but there are treatments for it.* He'd always associated a diagnosis of cancer with the kiss of death, and was horrified by the thought that he could ever have such a disease. Now that they *thought* he had it, it wasn't so bad. He felt no better or worse for it. *Probably still turn out to be a fluke.* He turned back to the information sheets and began reading again.

Surgery can result in the same complications as any surgery, number one being infection, then anesthesia after-effects, scarring, failure to heal properly, and all of the complications associated with other neighboring structures and organ systems affected by the surgery; a myriad of possibilities which would be discussed on a case-by-case basis prior to signing any operation consent. Irradiation can cause loss of hair, nausea and vomiting. There is a slight chance of radiation burns and skin discoloration. Many patients benefit psychologically by the use of wigs until hair growth recurs. Nausea and vomiting can be reduced through the use of medication, which is usually given to the patient as a preventive even before the treatment. Burns are extremely rare due to modern technology and specialized radiographic equipment , which uses a minimum of radiation. Chemotherapy can cause hair loss, also, and nausea and vomiting frequently occur. Both of these side effects are treated in the same fashion as discussed previously for irradiation.

That sounds like some pretty mean stuff. I'll bet it's a lot worse than a little nausea, too, the way these medical people are. Why don't they lay it on truthfully, and say you're going to barf your guts out? Maybe the drugs they give are good shit. I'll play it up like I'm *really* sick so they give me the best they have. I wonder if they still prescribe pot smoking to control the vomiting like I read somewhere? I could go for that pharmaceutical quality pot! Hopefully, when they find out I don't really have the cancer in the first place, I can still fake my way for the pot.

• • •

Friday lived up to its forecast of a dismal, rainy day. It was the kind of day when people would like to stay home and sit in front of the fireplace, maybe watching a good football game, with the wonderful smell of mama's roast in the oven. Wrong season, George realized in the middle of his conjecture. It was still early summer, not the preferred cool autumnal season that was required for his daydream. It was one of those hot, muggy rains that come on slowly and hang overhead for days, with thick gray cloud covers and occasional fog banks. George sat with his feet up on the sill of one of the full length windows, looking downward at the traffic below. It was a pleasant daydream, however, and he tried to get back into it.

"George Williams?" The cute little nurse was calling him from the doorway to the doom-and-gloom area. She watched him snap to and rise from the chair next to the window. "Dr. Steinberg will see you now." She held the door open for him.

George walked over and passed through the doorway. "Where is everybody today, you know, all those sick people that were here last Monday?"

"Oh, we don't do treatments on Fridays, just consultations. Go on in to Dr. Steinberg's office, he's waiting in there for you."

He walked down the hall, past the empty treatment area, and entered the office.

Dr. Steinberg was poring over a chart, looking down that long nose through his reading glasses. "Good afternoon, Mr. Williams. How are you today?"

"About the same, can't complain. Did you get the test results yet?"

"Yes, I've just been going over the radiology report." He took his glasses off and looked at George with the most condescending attitude he could muster. "The cancer has spread into the lymph system below the diaphragm, meaning that you not only have the Kaposi's lesions on your skin, but also a lymphoma. How long ago did you notice the purple spot on your neck?"

"About three months before I saw the dermatologist. I had them on my feet for a while before that."

"You didn't mention the lesions on your feet to Dr. Reedy?"

"No."

Dr. Steinberg shook his head, perturbed.

George couldn't help but feel stupid. "Guess I should have . . . my legs have been a little swollen."

"It's too bad that you didn't come in right away," the doctor scolded. "Possibly we could have caught it before the lymph system became involved. Localized radiation or electrocoagulation could have treated the spots then, but now we're forced to do chemotherapy. For prognostic reasons, I want to get a lymph node biopsy to differentiate the type of cancer cells involved. We'll do that today, and have the results back from the pathologist next Tuesday."

• • •

Tuesday afternoon found George back in Dr. Steinberg's office, with another surgical dressing on his left lower neck. His concern about his cosmetic appearance had dwindled, in direct opposition to his increase in anxiety and depression, over these new developments. "I'm back again. This is getting old, and fast. What's the latest?"

"You have Reed-Sternberg cells in the node we biopsied, meaning you have Hodgkin's disease along with the Kaposi's. We're finding that they seem to go hand-in-hand recently, so this is not unusual. At least now we have a treatment plan and a prognosis of sorts. Actually, you can consider yourself fortunate. Both these cancer forms are in the easier group to treat. I want you to read this information," handing George more sheets, "and we can get started on the chemotherapy tomorrow. You'll experience some nausea and vomiting, but I'll prescribe some powerful tranquilizers to counteract these unpleasant side effects of the drugs, vincristine and procarbazine."

"Start tomorrow? Do I come here?"

"No, be at the hospital at seven a.m., and we'll start the I.V. drugs at ten o'clock. You'll possibly be in the hospital overnight, depending on the side effects. The treatments will go on weekly thereafter, probably for five to eight weeks. I'll be getting lots of lab work, too, checking your immune system along the way. These drugs can adversely affect that system. Now, go back out to the front desk and get more information."

"But what about . . . ?"

"All of your questions will be answered in the information pamphlets at the front. I'll see you tomorrow."

BUDAPEST, JULY

He had arrived at his office one morning at the university and answered his ringing telephone. "Buenas dias, er, good morning, Doctor Jurado speaking," with his thick Cuban accent.

"Listen carefully. I will only say this once." A man, mature, with an Italian or possibly Spanish accent. "There are three, maybe four people involved in spreading a virus-caused disease into homosexual men in Europe and the United States. This disease may be a worthwhile tool for covert terrorist activity, better than your infiltration of the U.S. with drugs. I tell you this because I am a Cuban sympathizer. I know you are a Cuban agent, Colonel Jurado. Go to see Leonardo Mazzone at his bakery of the same name in Palermo, Sicily. Go now, by yourself, and see him personally. Offer him a large sum of money to tell more." Click.

Luis was startled, puzzled. He looked at the phone as if he expected it to divulge more, then slowly replaced it in its cradle. "Que paso?" he said aloud to himself, wondering what was going on.

He made his excuses to the university about the sudden death of his sister in Havana, then made flight plans to Cuba via Athens. He could then take a side trip to Palermo from Athens, and, if what he found out in Palermo warranted a trip to Cuba, he would continue on. If not, a few days on the beach never hurt anybody before returning to work. He had arranged for ten days off for his sister's supposed funeral, so he had to use the time to cover his excuse anyway. He actually hoped this anonymous tip would turn out to be a hoax. It wouldn't be the first time he had been played with.

Luis bought a round-trip ticket to Havana and boarded the night flight. He arrived in Athens at four-thirty a.m., then bought another ticket to Palermo, and arrived there at ten that morning. He went to the language interpreter and found the bakery in the phone book, then got a map to it's location downtown. He was there at eleven-thirty.

"Habla usted Español?" He queried the clerk in the bakery. The woman looked at him and motioned for him to stay, not understanding him.

A burly man came out in a white tee shirt and pants, wiping his hands on his apron. "Ella no habla Español, pero yo, si," stating that the woman did not speak Spanish, but he did.

Luis continued in Spanish. "I'm looking for Leonardo Mazzone. Is he here?"

"Why do you want him?"

"My name is Dr. Luis Jurado. I'm a scientist from the university in Budapest, and I received an anonymous phone call yesterday that I should contact Señor Mazzone personally. He is supposed to have some information that is valuable to me."

"Do you have your passport, Doctor? I must have some identification."

"Si, just a moment." He fumbled in his sport coat pocket and produced the blue covered document.

The man took it and examined it carefully for a few minutes. He handed Luis a blank piece of paper and a pen. "Please sign your name as you did on your passport."

Luis did so, then handed the paper back.

The baker turned the signature paper and the passport upside down to compare the signatures, then held the passport up to the light to examine the safety paper engraving. "It appears to be in order." He handed the passport back to Luis. "I am Senor Mazzone. What can I do for you?"

"Like I said, I want to find out more about this phone call I received. The caller said something about a virus developed by a handful of scientists that was being spread intentionally. Do you know of it?"

"Well, I don't know. I do know of it, but there are many issues to consider, and it could be a major biologic weapon and so . . . "

"I see. Ten thousand U.S. dollars . . . would that help you remember?"

"You see, Señor, I came into this through my trusted cousin who is an American-born Italian, and it is difficult to put a value on his life if the wrong people were to get this information."

"Is his life worth perhaps fifty thousand? I mean, it had better be very worthwhile information, with something to substantiate it."

"Es posible!" It's possible. "Do you have the money?"

"Not with me, but, obviously, whoever called me knows who I am and that I can get it easily enough."

"Un momento." Mazzone went to the back room momentarily and returned with another man. The man was tall, dark, very handsome, very smooth in his demeanor. And dressed classically in expensive continental attire.

The man came to the rear of the counter and extended his hand. "Nice to meet you, Colonel, my name is Phillip Ash, er, *Sal Danella*, to you. Apparently I have something you're interested in. Let's go in the back. Please follow me."

Luis followed him into the small office at the rear of the ovens. "So what is this all about? Who called me? How do you know of me?"

"That was Leonardo, whom you just met, who called at my request. How I know of you is not important. Now, I have come into a very interesting situation. I cannot give you specific information, but I also know I can fear for my life if I attempt to defraud you. You must settle for that." He placed his overnight bag on the desk, and retrieved a disposable enema bottle that had been relabeled. It had a number on it, and the name Enrique Sosa, Madrid. "Now, I know how your government has been trying to erode the moral and political fiber of the U.S. for many years, hoping to bring that country to chaos. I have here, in this small bottle, a biologic agent that has the potential to cause religious, social, and financial upheaval throughout the entire country. Slowly but surely, covertly, like a cancer, the disease this agent causes will spread nation wide."

"That is quite a claim, Señor. I need some kind of explanation."

"Please allow me. I am an independent contractor, in a way. I make a living doing things for people that they need done, but for whatever reason cannot do themselves. I am paid a premium price to complete assignments in a professional and timely fashion, and quietly. I was contracted by a small group of men, two of whom are world class biogeneticists, to seek out a handful of very active homosexuals and infect them with this biologic agent that they had engineered. The agent seeks out and slowly destroys the human immune system, wrecking health, with no known cure. It is spread through homosexual behavior, basically from the colon of one through the prostate and into the seminal duct, where it spreads to the next victim's colon through anal sex. Imagine the financial burden placed on a country's economy, trying to treat, as well as eradicate, an unknown, highly contagious disease."

"That all sounds like science fiction, but predicated on reality, I suppose. Who, in their right minds, would initiate such a disease?

And to what purpose? And why target homosexuals? I can understand their choice of a viral agent, being extremely difficult to even first diagnose. And then, to find a treatment? That could take forever, literally!"

"You pose several legitimate questions, Colonel. But I am under a personal oath not to divulge any more information, even if I knew more. I will be candid with you. These people are paying me over one hundred thousand U.S. dollars for each of the seven homosexuals that I successfully infect by injecting this agent in the enema bottle into them. Therefore, fifty thousand does not interest me."

"So, what would pique your interest, you know, enough for me to buy that bottle?"

"I don't believe I could sell you the bottle, I need it for evidence that I completed my mission. Perhaps, I was thinking, that you could take an amount of it to study and maybe duplicate."

"No, no, I want the entire bottle. I'll give you *two hundred thousand* for it. You could replace the contents with water; who would know?" Luis picked up the bottle and studied it as he spoke, then looked directly at Sal. "And, as you stated, if this turns out to be a fraud, your life is worth nothing."

"Well," Sal paused, "make it two hundred and fifty, and you have a deal."

"You're a wise man, Sal." Luis smiled. "I would have ended up with that bottle *somehow*, you realize. We might as well be gentlemen about it. Do you have another clean container to pour the contents into?"

Sal looked at him coldly. "Certainly, let me get one." He left for a few moments, then returned holding a small glass jar with a plastic lid. After donning rubber gloves, he opened the enema container very carefully, afraid of the contents, and poured the solution into the glass jar. Then he screwed the lid on tightly. Damned Spaniard, anyway, Sal thought to himself. He would still find Sosa and inject him with water to collect the other money. Wentworth was becoming angry at the long delay in Sal's finding Sosa. Sal needed to hustle.

"Thank you, sir, I will look into this." Luis reached for the jar, as Sal caught his arm.

"Money . . . " Sal said.

"Come on now, Sal... Nobody carries that kind of cash around. You know you'll get it."

"Money . . . " Sal repeated, still holding Luis's arm and smiling.

Luis looked at him, not smiling back. He'd come prepared for buying this information, but had only brought a hundred thousand. Luis had assumed he wouldn't need anywhere near this amount. "Oh,all right."

Sal released Luis's arm as he reached for his briefcase. He opened the lid and retrieved two thick envelopes. "Here is a hundred thousand, that's all I have with me."

Sal opened the envelopes and fanned through the sheafs of large bills. "O.K., this'll do for a down payment. But I want to call my bank and find that the rest has been deposited within forty-eight hours." He handed Luis a slip with a bank name and account number on it.

"It shall be done." The two men smiled at each other, not a trusting smile, but cold and tolerant. They shook hands and Luis departed through the front door with the jar in his briefcase.

He was pleased with himself for taking advantage of this opportunity, and the good will he would generate, on his own behalf with General Castro. He flagged a cab and was on his way back to the airport. The return flight to Athens went quickly, and he barely caught another evening flight, his ultimate destination being Havana.

• • •

HAVANA, JULY

"Hace mucho calor, no, Generalissimo?" Colonel Luis Jurado fanned himself with his hat as he spoke of the heat.

The entire city was bathed in the mid-summer's broiling sun. The normally busy market areas were quiet, merchants relaxing under their canvas shades, while awaiting the cooler hours for business to pick up. The palm trees stood perfectly motionless in the sultry, still air. They drooped as though even they could not tolerate the seventy-four percent humidity and one hundred and three degree temperature. The only noise evident throughout the city was the sporadic laughter of children playing in the streets, and the din of barking dogs. The residential areas were devoid of people, all of them staying inside out of the sun. Ceiling fans turned quietly in every building, trying to create human cooling, as minimal as it was, by convection. Wealthier sections of the city were vacant to the eye, the residents inside, staying in the few rooms with air conditioning. Automobile traffic was diminished, as only the ultra rich could afford air conditioners in their cars, if they were fortunate enough to own a car at all.

The capitol building's air conditioning had been over burdened, functioning more poorly than usual in the intense heat. Workers in the less important levels of government had their areas turned off altogether. They were told that the government needed to conserve energy, and therefore they must bear the heat as a patriotic gesture. All of them knew that the upper echelons had their air conditioning at least running, even though the best hoped for in this extreme heat was eighty degrees. Out of patriotism, however, one did not discuss this inequitability, even with one's trusted co-workers. There were many less desirable jobs that needed filling. At least the lucky workers on the second floor could imagine an ever so slight breeze through the open windows.

"Si, hace *mucho* calor," General Fidel Castro replied. "Como esta su familia, Colonel? Que bueno tenerlo aqui." Fidel made the usual niceties about Luis's family, and it was good to see him.

Luis acknowledged the general's obligatory interest and thanked him. It was rare indeed to have an audience with Castro personally. Luis was a high ranking official in intelligence. He was educated, having obtained a doctoral degree in zoology in Hungary, through the auspices of the Cuban military, in order to fulfill his dual role. By virtue of his acceptance in the eastern bloc countries' scientific community, he was appointed Minister of Sciences at the university in Budapest. That was his official sanction, but he also acted as an unofficial agent for the Cuban government. His role in this capacity was to monitor clandestine activity in the scientific arena, with a particular interest in biological weapons research.

"Tell me about this important news you have, Colonel." Fidel said. "It must be very intriguing to bring you here on such short notice, to see me and me alone."

"Yes, General, it is very exciting. I was in my office two days ago in Budapest when the phone rang . . . " He recounted the entire story.

Fidel listened all the while, fully absorbed. When Luis had finished, Fidel asked "De veras?" For real? "This is an amazing story. You have done well to buy the biologic agent. Do not worry, the money will be deposited in Sal Danella's account." They both realized with whom they were dealing, definitely not to be cheated. Those people could ruin anyone, including a small country and its heads of government, if they were maddened. "So what do we do now? We have but one bottle."

"I think it would be wise to call a meeting of our most trusted scientists, no more than three or four, who are well experienced in viral and genetic research. I only have eight days remaining before I must return to Budapest, so we must act urgently. If the original geneticists could duplicate this virus, I should think we can as well. If all else fails, we can infect one of our undesirable citizens and let the agent replicate in his body, then study it further."

"Muy bueno, Colonel." Very good! "You are brilliant! Why have we not become better friends in the past?" Castro put his arm around Luis's shoulder and gave him a congratulatory squeeze, inadvertently blowing thick blue cigar exhaust in his face.

Luis fought to refrain from coughing violently, almost becoming ill from the General's foul breath. He pulled away subtly but quickly. "Thank you, sir, thank you. I am tired from all this drama and would like to relax for a day. Can you arrange a meeting for the necessary scientists on, say, the day after tomorrow?"

"Certainly, Colonel. You be here again at one o'clock p.m. the day after tomorrow and speak. I would like for you to stay and head up this project. Is it possible for you to obtain an extended leave from your post in Budapest without any suspicions being raised? We could feign a car wreck, in which you suffer injuries where you must recuperate for a period of time, no?"

"With pleasure, General. I am honored." They shook hands, and Luis departed.

Luis went to the beach to seek relief from the heat after he checked in at his sister's home. She was shocked, but pleased to see him, and it was arranged that he would stay at her house while he was in Havana. She dared not be too inquisitive about his presence. She knew that he could tell her nothing.

The cool ocean breeze blowing across the white beach felt good after his long trip. It was good to be home, even for a short stay.

Forty-eight hours later Luis was back at the capitol in Castro's office, where he met three scientists from the university. Castro assured him that all three had been through a stringent security clearance. After they had been introduced and settled in, Luis again recounted the entire story, much to their confoundment.

"To what end do we research this agent?" asked one of the men.

Castro smiled and said, "That question has baffled me since Luis first presented me with this surprise. You gentlemen all know that I would like to see the great United States of America come to its proverbial knees, especially since their laughable attempt in the Bay of Pigs. And even more so, I am filled with hatred since it has become common knowledge that their CIA was responsible for failed attempts on my very life. Such self-righteousness in the face of such flagrant hypocrisy cannot and will not be tolerated. Our friends in the Kremlin would be duly impressed were we to somehow cause the government of the U.S. to fail, especially since they themselves have harbored this desire for decades. We, a tiny country of three million people, will show the Russians!" He looked at the men, then continued.

"As you know, my compassion for the well being of our citizenry is great. That is why I have allowed the week long visits to our country from our extended family of Cuban-Americans living in the U.S. over the past year. However," he smiled, "I would be remiss if I failed to mention the approximated figure of well over one hundred million U.S. dollars we have netted, from our visitors' local spending, by this arrangement!" He smiled again, and the others laughed on cue.

"What I did not predict, however, was the backlash that this program would create amongst some of our less patriotic. The Cuban-Americans, on their visits here, demonstrated their superior standards of living in the U.S., contradicting our last twenty years of anti-American propagandizing about the hard life there. From this, I have discovered that we have a small percentage of unpatriotic citizenry within our country, starting anti-government undercurrents. For this reason, I have decided to allow emigration of those undesirables, free choice, to Peru and Costa Rica next year. Using that gesture of good will as a cover, I was considering opening the port of Mariel, for a limited time, to allow direct emigration to the U.S. as well."

The group listened intently, hardly breathing, not believing what they heard.

"You may calm your reactions, gentlemen," Castro continued, "you have not heard the remainder of my intent! Concealed in this emigration from Mariel, I plan to cleanse our prisons of criminals and *them* to deal with!"

The group laughed and applauded, praising their general's ingenuity.

"Gracias, gracias! And now, for the coup de gras. I want you very talented and trusted men to work quickly and earnestly to duplicate this biologic agent, so that we may infect these prisoners before they are released next spring."

There was stammering and side chatter, the men repositioning themselves in their chairs, all expressing favor with this plan.

"Quiet, please, gentlemen," Castro continued. "Our continual infiltration of the U.S. with drugs, and our incitement of subversive behavior, has indeed caused disenchantment with the U.S. government, at least in part, in the affected groups. However, with the planned introduction of this ever-so-malignant disease, we can force economic upheaval because of the tremendous burden on the health care needs of those infected. The spread of the disease will increase in a pyramidal fashion to huge numbers over the years to come. From what I have learned, this agent was developed to wipe out the practice of homosexualism by limiting its mode of transmission to the disgusting act of anal sex. Possibly, I hope, scientists of your caliber can alter the virus and make it transmissible through other human body fluids as well. That is why Dr. Jurado and I have called you here today, to attain these goals I have underscored. I have appointed him chief of this endeavor, and his orders are to be followed explicitly. Does this explanation satisfy your questions about the value of this project?"

More rumbling and shifting. "This project may indeed bring the

U.S. down, but you have not granted us much time, General," one of the scientists spoke out.

"This I know, but I have every faith in each and every one of you. A word of caution, gentlemen. This mission is absolutely top secret; you must carry it with you to your death. If this ever leaked to the world press, our country would be persecuted for eternity, even, I daresay, by our allies. Therefore, if it is ever discovered, or even strongly suspected, that someone leaked any of this information to any others aside from those in this room, the traitor will be sought out and executed immediately. Do you all understand?"

All indicated their commitment to the conspiracy.

"Bueno, bueno. Now, go about your business as usual and await instructions from Dr. Jurado. He will begin this work within the next few days."

They arose and talked excitedly amongst themselves, shaking hands and chatting about the project, then left, one by one, as their personal comments diminished.

TORONTO, AUGUST

"Oh, God, Wednesday again," George moaned. He rolled over and turned off the blaring clock radio alarm, then strained to get out of bed. He was so weakened, tired. Wednesdays mentally drained him. He had lost thirty pounds since the onset of the chemotherapy six weeks ago. His appetite was non-existent, and the mere aroma of food nauseated him. It was a physical accomplishment to get out of bed and get going in the morning; all he wanted was to lie there and sleep. Had he known then what he knew now, he would have refused the treatment. "I never felt that bad in the first place."

He forced himself into the bathroom and turned on the shower, allowing the water time to warm while he brushed his teeth. He tried to smile, looking in the mirror at his Yul Brynner hairstyle. Most of his hair had fallen, just like he was warned, so he shaved the rest. It actually didn't look too bad . . . he even got compliments from his friends that he might be more attractive! No doubt he stood out in a crowd, at any rate. He turned sideways to check his physique. Much too skinny. I'm going to have to start that damn high calorie pudding again. The bathroom was steaming up when he got in the shower. "My shampoo bill has dropped one hundred percent!" With that remark he burst into laughter.

"What's going on in there, anyway?" It was Corey, his roommate. "I haven't heard you laugh like that in weeks! You got a hot one in there or something, fool?"

"No such luck," George hollered. "I can barely hear you with this shower running. I was just laughing about my shampoo bill!"

"I gotcha!" Corey began to laugh. "I'll wait 'til you're finished and then we can hear each other!"

"What?"

"Nothing!" Corey went back to the kitchen and mixed some pancake batter. It was refreshing to hear George laugh, he thought. He was careful of aromas in the house, and pancakes were one of the few George could tolerate lately. He put two slices of bread in the toaster, hoping George would eat them.

George came out into the kitchen with a towel wrapped around his waist and a second towel over his head. "Good morning, my friend. What are you doing?"

"Slaving over a hot toaster, so to speak. You look silly with that extra towel over your head, like a nun or something. What do you need to dirty an extra towel on your head for, anyway?"

They laughed. "Sheer force of habit of twenty-some years, I guess. Here, you use it." He threw it at Corey. "See, it's not even wet!" They laughed again.

"Even when the chips are down, old George hangs on to the humor! It amazes me that you don't mope around more, knowing what you're going through."

"The first roll out of bed in the morning is the absolute worst, but once I get going, look out! Oh, yeah, it's Wednesday again."

"I know, I know. You needn't remind me. Same treatment time?"

George's mood briskly sobered. "Yeah, damn it. Hopefully only two more after this one."

"Great. I suppose I can bear your barfing for a day just three more times. Did they give you any more of that good dope?"

"I told you I wasn't going to give it to you anymore. I need that shit! Would you rather have me barfing my guts out twice as bad?"

"I don't think you could get any worse, and my being loaded on *your* drugs sure makes it easier on me!"

"You're a real pal, fruitcake. Hey, can you give me a ride down and back?"

"If you promise not to throw up in my car again, sure. It took five days for my car interior to dry out after I had to run it through the car wash the last time. Bring a barf bag with you. Want to try some breakfast?"

"Ugh, thanks, but no. Even when I'm hungry, all I can eat is bread and crackers and that calorie pudding. Hurry up, we've got to leave in an hour."

They walked into Dr. Steinberg's office at ten-thirty and checked in at the desk. The sickeningly sweet little nurse came out and took them back to the treatment area. The usual nurses came in and started the I.V. George winced as they poked the needle into his forearm, all the while telling him it didn't hurt and to lie still. "Tell me, honestly, have either of you ever had one of these steel pipes rammed into your body?"

They looked at each other, caught off guard. Alice, the younger one, said, "No, but we learned in nursing school that it's not that painful." Just as she finished George felt the burn of the fluid flowing into his vein.

"Ouch, that burns! Why don't you two have somebody do this to *you* sometime, then you can teach the *truth* to other students! You better have the barf tray ready, I feel like it'll be a bad one today."

"Oh, you mean the emesis basin?" Alice asked.

"Whatever you call it, it's just a nice word that you people dreamed up for barf. Oh, get me the medicine that's supposed to keep me from throwing up that doesn't work worth a shit, OKAY?"

"Knock it off, George, you're being an ass," Corey said. "I know this isn't a picnic, but don't take it out on the staff, OKAY? They're doing their jobs."

"Yeah, I'm sorry, guys, but this is getting to me. It seems endless. I come in here, get beaten up, then go home and vomit for two days. I can't eat, I feel like hell, my hair has fallen out, I'm skinny as a rail, and—"

"All right, already! At the least this ordeal may have preserved an otherwise very short life. Anybody would feel the way you're feeling if they went through this," said Corey.

The older nurse said, "You're friend is right. This is not easy for anyone, and you are holding up as well as can be expected. It's all right to emote your feelings; it's healthy. Much better than closing up like some do. They *really* have a tough time. Some people just give up, and their attitudes alone decrease the treatment's effectiveness."

"Speaking of that, what ever happened to that old man named Harley that was in here a couple months ago? You know, when I first came in?" George asked.

The nurses looked at each other, then the older one said, "We can't discuss other patient's conditions."

"Croaked, huh?"

They looked at each other again, then went back to taping the I.V. in place. "I'll be back to check on you in a little while," the young one said. They finished and left.

Four hours later George was home, crouched over the rim of the toilet, vomiting. "Damn!" Dr. Steinberg had checked him this morning and told him that they would stop the treatments for awhile. It seemed his lymph nodes were shrinking faster than expected. George was thrilled.

"What are you doing in there? You all right?" called Corey.

"What d'ya think I'm doing? I'm riding the porcelain rim, like every Wednesday." He finished his dry heaving and went back into the living room. "This is killing me— There must be a better way. But no more! At least for a while. Maybe I can grow some hair and gain some weight."

"Yeah, that's great. When you quit barfing I'll take you out for a steak dinner." Corey smiled.

George slapped his hand over his mouth and ran, dry heaving, for the bathroom once again.

He's right, that anti-nausea drug doesn't work worth a damn," Corey said to himself. His *last* treatment! Two more trips to the clinic just for checkups, and all done. George is back!

NEW YORK CITY, NOVEMBER

The first significant snow of the year was falling as Dr. Gregg scraped her windshield free of the heavy ice from the condensation the night before. It had been fairly warm only yesterday, with the high temperature hitting sixty-five degrees, but the heavy cloud formation to the east had been the usual precursor to today's weather. "Damn, it's cold!" she trilled as she leaned over to get the center area. "Where are my gloves, anyway?" She hadn't been able to find her gloves from the year before, and she was running late for work at the medical center. She didn't want to miss her first patient. He was coming in today to discuss his strange skin disorder and get the results of the dermatology consult.

Her fingers froze to the chrome door handle for a moment. In her hurry, she had forgotten the standard childhood experiential lesson regarding skin and frozen metal objects. "Damn!" She waited until the metal warmed sufficiently and released her fingers.

She entered her small office in the family practice department and slipped off her heavy coat and scarf, hanging them behind the door. Then she lifted the phone and buzzed her receptionist. "Loretta?"

"Good morning, Helen, beautiful day, no?" in her heavy Puerto Rican accent.

"Sure is, I can't believe it," she returned the sarcasm. "Say, has my first patient arrived yet? Umm, Mr. Larsen, the school teacher?"

"Not yet, Doctor, but you know how the traffic is snarled. He's only ten minutes late. I'll buzz you as soon as he arrives."

"Thank you."

Helen dug through the pile of incoming interoffice memos, looking for the dermatology report. Loretta left all the previous day's memos on her desk every morning. "Aha, got it. Let's see . . . ", she read the conclusion, " . . . consistent with Kaposi's sarcoma. What's that, I've never heard of it. It must be a zebra disease!" she chuckled. A zebra disease, to any medical student, is one that is quite exotic. But, being a student, one tends to 'look between the stripes,' and come up with exotic etiologic explanations, while overlooking the simple but usual diagnosis.

She left her office and passed Loretta. "I'm going to run down to the library for a few minutes. If Mr. Larsen shows, have the nurse get his vitals and put him in a room."

"Si, Doctor."

Helen took the stairs to the third floor and entered the library's oncology research area. She took several general research volumes from the shelf and proceeded to a table. Twenty minutes later she was back in her office with her newly gained knowledge.

"Mr. Larsen is waiting in room five." Loretta said over the intercom.

"Good morning, Mr. Larsen," Helen said as she entered.

"Good morning, Doctor Gregg," he robotically responded.

"Well, to get right down to business, Mr. Larsen, I've received the report from the dermatologist, and it seems you have a rare form of skin cancer called Kaposi's sarcoma."

"Cancer!" His color faded. "Am I going to die?"

"Wait a minute, let me finish explaining, then you'll be much more at ease."

"Sorry, but— cancer, God!"

"That's quite all right, a very normal reaction, I assure you. Now, I will admit very openly that I had never heard of this cancer type, so I was just in the library doing some research, and now I can speak somewhat intelligently about it. Tell me, have you ever done any travelling in Africa, or possibly the Mediterranean area, or is there any African or Mediterranean heritage in your family bloodline?"

"No, I've never ventured overseas, and my family lineage is pretty much Scandinavian, to my knowledge, why?"

"According to my reading, the only endemic areas in the entire world for this disease are those two places, and even in those areas the occurrence is rare at best. I thought maybe there might be a hereditary factor, or, for some unknown reason, that you may have been exposed to an endemic virus while travelling at some point in your life. Extremely odd, indeed. At any rate, you have it, and there is no evidence at this time that it has involved anything other than the localized lesions on your legs. So the treatment is irradiation of the lesions. It is a fairly benign cancer form, given there are no complications, and yours seems to be a simple case. I'm going to give you a referral to the oncology department for treatment, and I'll follow your case very closely out of personal interest. Keep in touch, OKAY?"

"Sure thing, Doctor Gregg. I want to get rid of this as soon as possible. I'll do whatever you say." He ascended from the chair.

"Good luck to you," Helen said as she looked up from her notating.

Helen picked up the phone and dialed an in-house number. "Hi, Kris. This is Helen Gregg in family practice. Can you meet me later for lunch? I've got a really interesting case I want to go over with you."

"Oh, hello. I'd like to, but I'm tied up here. What've you got?"

"Well, Dr. Bean, you are the tropical med specialist with the greatest knowledge of the 'zebra disorders', no?"

"Well, I've never had it put to me quite that way, but, sure, I guess!" She laughed. Kristine Bean had finished an internal medicine residency three years earlier, and then developed an interest in exotic diseases, mostly of tropical origin. There was an increasing interest in this area of medicine, a necessity created by the advent of high-speed global travel. There were many cases in the medical journals of diseases endemic to an isolated area of the globe turning up, out of place and elsewhere, and the suffering patient was either misdiagnosed or, worse yet, never diagnosed. Some of these illnesses had even resulted in fatalities. If properly identified, they could have possibly been appropriately treated in a timely manner, thus possibly restoring the hapless patient's health. There were a handful of doctors, knowledgeable in this field of medicine, spread across the country. Most were centered in epidemiologic centers, such as the National Institutes of Health in Washington, D.C., and the Centers for Disease Control in Atlanta. Dr. Gregg was fortunate that she had Dr. Bean at hand. "Why, what have you got for me?"

"Two weeks ago I saw a thirty year old male school teacher who presented with a chief complaint of purpuric lesions on both ankles. He had noticed them one month prior. His medical history, review of systems, and exam were all unremarkable. I was unable to identify the lesions, so I sent him to dermatology for a consult. This morning I saw him again, and the derm report stated he has Kaposi's sarcoma, which I'd never heard of."

"Kaposi's . . . Kaposi's . . . Not Kaposi's varicelliform?"

"No, Kaposi's sarcoma. I recalled the varicelliform eruption skin disorder, but not a sarcoma."

"I haven't seen that one before. Did you check it out?"

"Yes, uh-huh. The oncology section in the library had a small amount of information on it. Apparently it's a very rare, and quite benign, sarcoma that is endemic to elderly men in the Mediterranean area and certain areas of Africa. There is no knowledge of its occurrence anywhere in this country, and here we have a Scandinavian man who has never done any foreign travelling. What do you think?"

"Strange, I must say," Doctor Bean commented. "I'm not sure what to say, actually. Say, listen . . . how would you like to present it at the epidemiology luncheon the day after tomorrow? I'll help you do the preparation. Maybe somebody else has some knowledge to share."

"Yes, that's a good idea. See if you can get me on the agenda and I'll call you tomorrow evening at home. We can get together before the presentation." Dr. Gregg was excited; it would be her first case presentation since she was a student. Family practice didn't really offer much in the way of exotic illness. "Maybe I'll really get into this one!"

There were eleven doctors present at the luncheon, all of them apparently bewildered by the case presentation of Kaposi's in the U.S. Two of them had vague recall of the disease, and none had ever encountered it personally.

"A splendid presentation, Dr. Gregg," said Kristine as they walked out of the cafeteria together. "You should consider epidemiological medicine. You were quite thorough and precise in your approach."

"Thank you. I couldn't have done it without your guidance. It's been such a long time since I had to present a case!"

Two weeks went by, with Mr. Larsen being treated by the oncology department with irradiation. His case had initially created great interest throughout the medical staff. Dr. Gregg kept herself informed of his progress. His lesions were, in fact, clearing with the treatment. The fervor over the bizarre disease had waned in the past several days, and the staff was returning its attention to the mundane medical problems of a multifaceted university hospital. The thinking was that possibly Mr. Larsen did, in fact, have some unknown Mediterranean lineage.

Dr. Gregg went into her office one morning the following week, and found an urgent message to call a Doctor Foller at the nearby Veterans Administration hospital. "897-3654," she read aloud as she dialed the number. "Yes, good morning, this is Dr. Gregg at the university returning Dr. Foller's call."

"One moment, please."

"This is Dr. Foller. Dr. Gregg?"

"Yes, I found an urgent note to call you. What's up?"

"My colleague over here told me you presented a case on Kaposi's a little while back. Is that correct?"

"Well, yes, why?"

"Are you seated?"

"Why, what's going on?"

"I've turned up another one over here!"

"Excuse me?"

"I say I've picked up another Kaposi's sarcoma over here. A twenty-two year old male with a presentation and findings identical to yours, according to my colleague that attended your luncheon. Same history, too. That is, no known Mediterranean blood and no foreign travel, and Anglo. My patient is gay by admission during his sexual history. I have yet stranger news. He personally knows your patient, Mr. Larsen. By the way, is Mr. Larsen homosexual, to your knowledge?"

"Wait, *wait!*" She was stunned. "This is too much! Ok, just a minute, let's see. I would have to say maybe he is, based on his effeminate behavior only, but don't quote me."

"I think we'd better get these two men together for a little chat, don't you? I mean, they know each other and all, so it shouldn't be embarrassing for them."

"Yes, I agree. Maybe we can get some common ground out of

this. I need to call my patient and clear it with him first, then I'll call you back and set up the time. We could meet here in the private dining room."

"OKAY, then, you call me soon. My patient has already agreed to a meeting. Oh, see if you can get a sexual partner history from your man before we meet."

Helen hung up the phone in disbelief. No way! They must have found a patient with spots on his ankles, then jumped on the bandwagon for lack of an appropriate diagnosis. It happened all the time in the medical world. Poor diagnosticians, that had to be. What about his patient's personal knowledge of my patient? What an amazing coincidence! Are they lovers, perhaps? Too much!

She called Wolleson Elementary School, the work number listed on Larsen's chart, and left a note for him to call her. He returned the call during his class break, agreeing to a meeting the next afternoon after school.

The meeting room was stuffy. The patients were unnerved over discussing their sexual habits, but were overall very cooperative. They answered questions for over an hour. "More coffee, gentlemen? I'm going to get some for myself," Kristine said as she got up from the table. Negative responses.

"Are we finished here, then?" Dr. Foller asked.

"I believe I have all I need to know," replied Helen. "We still have no obvious etiologic factors, and the only commonality is that you men have had sex with one another. And there is that airline attendant you both have had sex with, uh—"

"George Williams." Mr. Larsen interrupted.

"And you don't know whether he has anything like this?" Dr. Foller asked.

Both nodded negatively. "He lives in Toronto, and from what we've learned just now, we each see him at about the same time, maybe every three months or so, when he stays in the city on furlough. I haven't seen him for four months now." Mr. Larsen replied.

"Do either of you know where he lives or how to contact him?"

"No, I don't," responded Larsen. The other man, eyes cast downward, nodded no.

"If it's not too personal, do all gay men engage in such flagrant sexual behavior? I find it amazing." Doctor Gregg paused at the door.

"Many do, especially at gatherings like parades and such. Once it's known you're gay, by being at these events, you become active sexually. Let's face it, we are persecuted by the public, and have only each other for companionship and sexual gratification. We're forced to make the best of our situation," Larsen said.

"Well, I guess I'll forget the coffee, I don't need it anyway. I'd better get back to the clinic. Thank you, gentlemen, for your candor," she said to the men.

She returned to her office, back to the cold and flu jungle, all the while contemplating the unusual recent events. Maybe she would do some research and submit an article to the New England Journal. This was a great opportunity for both personal and career stimulation. "Yes, I believe I will!"

HAVANA, DECEMBER

Fidel sat behind his large desk, feet propped on an opened drawer. He sucked his fat cigar, with its incessant thick blue-black smoke malodorously fouling the air. His office stunk with the permanent sour aroma of old cigar smoke, in spite of his having it painted and the carpet cleaned every six months. Like male cat urine in a house, Luis thought; once its there it smells forever. Frankly, the odor sickened him, but nobody tells that to 'El Presidente' without some kind of imagined horrid repercussions, at least that was rumored. I wonder if anyone has ever actually said anything to challenge his ego? It's not up to me to disprove rumors.

Fidel took a long draw on his cigar, pondering Luis' progress briefing on the replication of the covert biologic agent. "So you've been successful without having to resort to actual human experimentation? It's very impressive, what science is capable of doing these days, no? I am but a simple man, without knowledge of such things, and so I am that much more amazed at you scientists' capabilities. The reason I sit in this office before you is because of the respect and love from my people, not because I was highly educated in the sciences. I want you to know that, my friend, because then you will know to present your case to me in understandable terms, rather than scientific hyperbole."

"Si, Senor Presidente. You must realize that the single slight difference between your ability to comprehend highly technological science and ours is simply that we scientists spent many years in our specific scientific education process. It has nothing to do with levels of intelligence."

Castro turned and smiled a big smile. "Then you understand exactly my meaning. Your insight pleases me." He gloated over his newfound intelligence.

Luis knew he had a well calculated winner with that one. The oaf, stupid as a mature cucumber, actually. He was a big man physically, at least by Cuban genetic standards, and quite possibly that fact made him just *appear* less intelligent. He did possess an uncanny manner of exercising influence, however, and Luis knew he was not a man to be regarded lightly. He had held his position of power for twenty years, in spite of multiple attempts, both foreign and domestic, to overthrow him. He sat where he did, not by the "love of his people," but because he controlled all the guns in Cuba and maintained the people's respect via strong arm tactics. Nonetheless, he controlled the power, at this point in time, anyway. The smart man manipulates the current system to his benefit; the dumb man bucks it like all the martyred 'heroes' lying in graveyards throughout the world.

"So tell me, you know, in common language, what you have done and what happens next." He took another draw on his cigar.

"We have replicated the virus in eggs, much like vaccinations are manufactured for use in medicine to prevent childhood diseases. The virus did mutate to some degree. It is a very unstable one to begin with. I am curious to know where the European scientists first got this agent. It is unlike any previously known as human pathogens, or, excuse me, as producers of disease in humans. But it is not an artificial creation, either. It does mimic very closely the behavior of other human viruses. Very puzzling to all of us, indeed. Not that any of that matters in our plan, just a curiosity."

"In other words, you don't know where it came from, but we can still use it and mass produce it."

"Exactly." He smiled while thinking, *what a dumb shit!*

"Well, have you discovered what it does in the human, and how long it takes?"

"The original virus we bought in Sicily slowly breaks down the body's natural ability to fight off infections, finally leading to chronic sickness, from repeatedly contracting minor contagious illnesses. For example, colds, strep throats, fungal infections, everything and anything. Eventually, when the body's fighting system is sufficiently weakened, antibiotics don't work anymore because the body can't assist the fight against infection like it should."

"But I thought that antibiotics were what killed infections, so why don't they work in this case?"

"That is the common thinking, General, that antibiotics kill infection. And, yes they do, to the extent where the infection is diminished enough for the body's own system to finish the job. You can look at them as helpers of the body, not curative agents by themselves. That's why, when this virus ruins the body's own system over time, nothing can be done except to try and have the patient stay well by avoiding possible infections. A self-imposed personal isolation, if you will. It would be a miserable existence. There is nothing else that would help anymore. Because we inadvertently altered the virus during our reproduction, we are unsure as to how it will transmit from one person to the next. The original inventors engineered it so it would pass through proteins in the colon and genital organs of males, but our new version has not been tested."

"And why not?"

"Frankly, General, we didn't have the time. Much of these studies are based on preliminary results. It would be helpful to study their effects on primates, such as monkeys, before we begin human implantation, but that could take another year or more. And now, the question I came to ask of you. Is it possible that you could delay your planned mass exodus of undesirables to the States? If so, we could attempt better studies, and be much more accurate in our planning."

"You said possibly a year?"

"Well, yes . . . but it could be longer than that since this is such a slow disease process. I couldn't promise you a hard deadline with specific results."

Fidel looked at his calendar. "Hmmm . . . But the virus right now will do the job, no? You're just not exactly sure of the final results, or how it may spread?"

"That's correct, General. But I must make you aware that lacking adequate knowledge of the virus, something catastrophic may occur. Do you remember from your childhood the myth of *Pandora's Box?* There is a chance that we may be toying with nature to an extreme. I use as an analogy the import of the African bee into South America to increase honey production. Now the hybrid is called the killer bee because of it's aggressive nature. And that has been in very recent history, not a mythological pretense. There are many other examples where man has intervened in nature and caused catastrophe."

"What kind of problem could occur here, with our plan?"

"For example, what if it took another transmission route into people and really spread wildly. What if, perchance, it were to mutate itself further and spread through simple sweat? That would mean it could be passed by a handshake, or using someone's pencil!"

"What is the reality of that happening? It sounds rather exaggerated, no? I prefer to work within the bounds of reality, Colonel." Fidel was becoming irritated.

"At this time, yes, it is exaggerated," Luis relented.

"Colonel Jurado, I was planning on this emigration for possibly next April or May. You may be brilliant in your work, but you don't understand the intricacies of political prowess. I have deliberately leaked my intentions to intelligence officers and newspapers, both here and abroad, of this upcoming hiatus to the U.S. Families of our citizens in the States are delighted about the reunion with their loved ones. It makes me appear to be a benevolent person in the eyes of the political world. I cannot now renege on those plans, for fear of political defamation."

"So you won't allow any more time for research?"

"No, Colonel, I'm afraid we must work within these time constraints."

"Very well, then. There is nothing further we can do with our research in such a short time. Upon your order, we'll commence injecting the prisoners." He looked downward, slightly shaking his head in disappointment. "I think we should tell them that we're injecting an anti-helminthic agent into their rectums because there has been an outbreak of pinworms in the prison."

"What did you say we would call the injection? Anti..?"

"Anti-helminthic. That simply means anti-worm medicine, and worms are common in the bowel tract. They are contagious in closed, unclean living quarters, such as prisons."

"Ah, si, bueno. A good plan."

"And I think it would be wise to go ahead and do the injections now, because over the next several months the prisoners will have forgotten about this and won't bring it to the attention of the U.S. health agencies. Their authorities would raise questions about this oddity, because de-worming medicine would appropriately be administered in pill form. These prisoners, I'm sure, are poorly educated, and won't know the difference. Anyone with a higher level of education should not have it administered, as they may suspect something foul."

"I agree fully, Colonel. How soon can you get started? I'll arrange it with the prison warden to 'de-worm' them." He grinned. "Even if he knows this is an odd technique, he will say nothing to anyone, I guarantee it."

"I'll speak with my co-workers, and I should think we can begin as early as tomorrow. I was told there are approximately forty-five hundred hard criminals and mental patients who will be released. The rest are political prisoners, and they probably comprise the more intelligent group, so we will avoid them. Is that accurate in your estimation?"

"I'm not sure, but I believe I have heard those figures somewhere."

"We have enough injections for possibly one thousand. I think it would behoove us to have the prison warden first bring all of the men that are known homosexuals. If memory serves, I believe I read somewhere in an American study that as many as twenty percent of all men are homosexual or bisexual, so one thousand injections should be enough. We could manufacture more if needed. Most of these men will settle in Florida, but others will migrate to other cities in search of opportunity, spreading the disease. Florida, I predict, will be the major epicenter, or focal point, for the disease."

"Colonel, again I congratulate you on your ability and intelligence. None of this could ever have transpired without your loyal dedication to myself and your country. Continuation in your dedication could earn you many wonderful opportunities."

"Thank you, General. I regard this as nothing more than fulfillment of my patriotic duty, but I thank you for your flattery. I'll call the prison warden and arrange to do possibly three hundred tomorrow."

"Bueno, Colonel. I want you to come and see me personally whenever you wish. My door is open to a man of your stature. Oh, incidentally, when this project is finished, I will see to it that you are returned to Budapest without suspicion."

"Thank you. I look forward to personally working with you again, General." Possibly with *me* on *your* side of the desk, mi Presidente, he thought as he left the office.

1980

NEW YORK CITY, MARCH

Dr. Gregg held the envelope that had arrived with the morning mail. *Who do I know in Paris?* The envelope was heavily stamped with express mail instructions and marked 'URGENT'. It's probably another foreign medical seminar flyer. More junk mail. These private vacation-type seminar promoters were worse than magazine sweepstakes brokers in their brazen manner. She picked up the letter opener and slit the top, retrieving the sheets from inside. The letter fell open and she was attracted by its personal nature, hand signed by a Dr. C. DuBois. The letterhead read L' Institut De Medecine A Paris, Rue Victor Hugo 10988, Paris.

Maybe he was fluent in English, or at least had provided the courtesy of exact translation to English for her benefit. Very nice. She read aloud as she always did. Her retention was better that way.

> Dear Dr. Gregg. I read with great interest your submission in the February, 1980, issue of *The New England Journal*."

Wow, she thought, a response! Somebody reads journals, after all. She read on with renewed excitement.

I am a board certified family practitioner at the above institute. I did my residency at the University of California in San Francisco prior to returning to France, thus my language fluency.

I am writing to inform you that we have been seeing multiple cases of Kaposi's sarcoma, much to our chagrin, over the past twenty-four months. We have seen fourteen cases, to be exact, all homosexual. Three of the patients are also intravenous drug abusers. We have noted two other curious developments. All of the patients are autoimmune depressed and pick up minor illnesses readily. The other curiosity is the incidence of a normally nonpathogenic unicellular organism, pneumocystis carinii, causing severe pneumonias in three of our Kaposi's patients. We have isolated the same organism as the cause of pneumonias in two other homosexual patients, neither of which have the cancer form.

Our medical staff discussion group speculated that Kaposi's cancer had simply broken out of the previously known demographic factors of geographic area and older age groups, as only three of the afflicted are in the age fifty-plus range. We are now faced with the question of the immune system failure and the resultant pneumonias from pneumocystis carinii.

Most of the cancers are being treated successfully at this time with radiotherapy, but four cases have proven refractory to both radiation and chemotherapy, and the patients are doing very poorly, indeed. Certainly the expected leukopenia state from the cancer therapy is not helping, but we have no other alternative.

Two of these patients have died from the pneumonia, with antibiotics only helping for a short while against the organism. But, obviously, when the immune system is in complete failure, no known treatment is of benefit.

I am very interested in exchanging complete case histories with you. All of us at the institute are extremely concerned about the gravity of this mysterious syndrome which seems only to afflict homosexual men. Please call me as soon as possible at my office number on this letterhead to make arrangements. Keep in mind the five hour time difference.

Helen was in a state of emotional shock. She let her hand fall to the arm of her chair, the letter fluttering to the floor. "This can't be real! Some joker is jerking me around." She thought hard for a moment; who would have reason to pull such a monstrosity, for what? Her mind was blank. *No one.* Searching through the waste can, she retrieved the envelope. It was real, all the proper French postmarks and everything. Maybe this doctor, or whomever, was having fun in his off-time or something. Still shocked, she read the letter a second time, a third time, then a fourth, hanging on every word. Whoever had written it certainly had some inside information and had done his homework.

She picked up the phone and dialed. "Dr. Bean, please. This is Dr. Gregg." She waited a few minutes.

"Hi, Helen, how are you?"

"I am in a state of absolute shambles," she replied.

Kristine was taken aback, paused, then, "What's the matter?"

"I have in hand a letter from a Dr. Claude DuBois, from the Paris Institute of Medicine in France, in response to the journal article I submitted."

"So, big deal, you should expect some letters of interest. You know you've reached someone. That's great!"

"No, no, no. You don't understand. Pay close attention, I'll read it to you." She read the letter slowly, clearly, concisely, in its entirety.

"Wow, no shit! Is that for real? No, you're screwing around . . . Aren't you?"

"No, Kristine, I am *not* screwing around."

"I'll be right there." Click.

Minutes later Dr. Bean burst through the door. "Let me see that." She snatched the letter from Helen's closed hand and began poring over it, wild-eyed.

Helen sat silently, staring blankly at her diplomas on the opposite wall of her small office, her fingernails tapping rhythmically on the hard desk top, shattering Kristine's concentration.

"Stop that, please," Kristine said angrily, still wild-eyed. She read the letter again. "O.K., level with me, is this some kind of prank? Are you bored or something?"

"No, Kristine, I'm not bored or anything," Helen said softly, still blankly staring. "What do you think? Here's the envelope, check it yourself."

"I think we should call this guy, and *now!* What time is it there, anyway?"

"Let me see, it's eight forty-seven here, that's one forty-seven p.m. there, still office hours." She picked up the phone and punched the long stream of numbers.

Several minutes passed while the call went through, then a French speaking woman answered that Dr. Gregg couldn't understand. Helen soured; she had forgotten in her frenzy that they would speak French! "Uh, uh, uh . . . " Her high school French came back enough to get, "Parlez vous English?"

"No." Then some other gibberish, and another woman was on the line speaking English in a heavy French dialect.

"This is Dr. Helen Gregg from New York City calling for Dr. Claude DuBois. Is he there, please?"

"Oui, please stay," was the reply.

"Hello, this is Dr. DuBois. You've received my letter so soon, Dr. Gregg?"

"You are for real, then?"

"I beg your pardon?"

"Oh, I'm sorry." Helen returned to reality. "I honestly had trouble accepting your letter as genuine, it is so shocking! We—my colleague and I, that is, thought maybe it was a joke."

"No, Doctor, we do not joke about such serious matters here."

He was French, known for their stoicity, she remembered. "I apologize, Doctor, but you must realize that the receipt of a letter of this nature is quite overwhelming."

"Oui, certainly I understand. We have been grappling with this problem for quite some time, not realizing there were other cases elsewhere. I'm afraid my sense of humor has failed me recently."

Aha, he is human, after all. An older, mature voice. "So you have had these cases appearing for two years? I was not aware. In all honesty, I had never heard of Kaposi's sarcoma until these cases spontaneously manifested themselves. In the time since I submitted that article, we have diagnosed three more cases in this area, again, all gay men. I have not seen any of the pneumocystis cases; however, all of our cases are also compromised in their autoimmune responses. But no fatalities as of yet."

"That is fortunate. It is a terrible feeling, watching helplessly as these people slowly become emaciated and weakened, then die from an illness which remains a mystery. Have you done sexual partner tracking?"

"To a certain extent. I was amazed to learn of the promiscuity of these men. They can remember some of their more special encounters, but most have had multiple partners in gay hangouts that they barely recall having had."

"Oui, oui, we have encountered the same behavioral quirks here. The reason I asked that question is because several of the names we have raised are Americans."

Helen sensed an affront, as though he was implying that Americans were responsible for this disease. Foreigners always seemed to blame their problems on the U.S. She knew he was aware that Kaposi's was not endemic to the United States, but instead to his own geographic backyard! She chose to overlook the implication. "That is interesting to hear. All our names so far are limited to the U.S. and Canada."

"Would you please send me all of your completed case histories and work ups, and I will do the same for you. Of great interest to me is a complete sexual partner list on each of your cases. I, of course, will send you the same information on our cases to date."

"I certainly will. This is a very bewildering situation. I thank you for your information and help, and we must remain in contact with new developments."

"Oui, we shall indeed. Au revoir, Doctor."

"Yes, goodby." She hung up the phone and looked at Kristine, who had been listening on the extension in the room next door. "What do we do now, Doctor? *You're* the exotic disease specialist."

"Absolutely astonishing. A new disease! There hasn't been anything like this since the Legionnaire's disease of what, ten years ago? My first inclination is to involve the CDC in Atlanta, but their initial bureaucratic response will be to have us watch it. Especially since it is so localized. I know, by past history, that they won't seriously consider the French element we have just discovered. They're concerned only with numbers of disease cases in the U.S. I do, however, feel obligated to inform them. At least we can *try* to hang the albatross on *their* necks. What the hell is going on, here, anyway?"

"I suppose the first order of logic is to compile all of our case histories and exchange them with the French to cross-check for other links in occurrence. I'll have medical records get the charts up here this afternoon to make copies, and send them to DuBois stat." Helen dialed the records department as she spoke.

Kristine scanned the letter once again as Helen read off the names of the charts she needed in the background.

Kris was uneasy. This disease had the potential and propensity to become a major outbreak, and soon. "See you later, I've got to run," Kristine whispered to Helen while she rattled names.

"Just a second, please," Helen said into the phone. "Kris, I'll call you as soon as I get the French records. Any help you can give me would be appreciated. Maybe you might pick something up from them that I miss."

"Sure, see you later."

Helen continued speaking with the records department, finishing the data on the last patient, then took an early lunch to descramble her thoughts.

She arrived back at one-thirty and found all the charts on her desk. She scanned through them to cull unnecessary information before the copies were made. The university had come out a month ago with a memo about overuse of copying machines, and how expensive it was on a per sheet basis. *I guess anything to save a buck. The pennies add up!* She was on Mr. Whinney's chart, the last one, when the phone rang. "Yes, Loretta?"

"Doctor Gregg, there is a long distance call for you on line two from a Doctor George Nesto in Chicago."

"Thank you, I'll pick it up in here." She punched line two. "Hello, this is Dr. Gregg speaking."

"I'm glad I could reach you. I'm Dr. George Nesto, with the county health department in Chicago. Listen, I saw your article in the journal recently, and I've got some interesting information for you."

"Yes, Dr. Nesto, what do you have?"

"We, too, have turned up a case of Kaposi's here. It was seven months ago. The man is gay, but we didn't give much thought to the case because he is, in fact, of Greek origin, and elderly. Then, yesterday, I personally encountered a patient with what I believe will be diagnosed as Kaposi's lesions. The patient is at the dermatology clinic now. Again, the patient is homosexual, but not of Mediterranean or African origin. I, like you, had never heard of this ailment until these two suddenly appeared. Have you any further developments?"

She had trouble focusing on the second half of his speech. *I can't take this.* "I'm sorry, but I'm in a state! You say you also have two cases there?"

"Yes, I believe so. Strange, huh?"

"Extremely! I've just been contacted by a doctor in Paris, France. They have turned up fourteen cases to date."

"*Really?* Any explanation for all of this?"

"No, none at all. The only common thread is the homosexuality. Would you please send me the records on these men? And if you should uncover anymore, send those, too. Oh, yes, and send the sexual partner history."

"By all means, I will." He gave her his address and phone number. "Keep me abreast of anything new, all right?"

"Definitely. And thank you for calling, good bye."

Again Helen called Kristine. "This time the call was from the county health department in Chicago. They have one confirmed and one suspect case, both gay."

"Phenomenal! Did you arrange for the records?" asked Kristine.

"Yes, this Dr. Nesto agreed to send them, and I'll send ours to him."

"I guess, at this time anyway, we're remaining on a holding pattern, then. Let me know when the records arrive."

"O.K., talk with you later." Helen put the phone back in its cradle quietly. She pulled back her lab coat and put her feet up on the desk, then picked up the phone and hit the intercom button. "Loretta, cancel the remaining patients, O.K.?"

"Sure, there are only two, and they're both late."

Helen put on her winter coat and decided that a nice crisp walk in the park down the street would be refreshing. To help her sort all this out, in a way. She left her office and told Loretta to go home at five.

Another week went by, and Helen and Kristine found themselves cross-checking lists of names of sex partners of the afflicted patients through the computer. They had all the names from Chicago, Paris, and New York to date. A half dozen names surfaced frequently, three of them being common between New York and Paris. Francois Le Monde, George Williams and Clancy Pfizer came up on the international compilation, and George Williams surfaced on all three lists.

"This George Williams guy must be one virile son of a buck," Kristine said. "I think we need to find him, but he's a real question mark. All we know about him is that he lives in Toronto and works as an airline attendant. The way he flies around the globe, though! I wonder which airline he works for?"

• • •

The next morning Dr. Nesto called Helen again. "Hello, Dr. Gregg, how are you?"

"I'm well, thank you. What's up?"

"I'm calling to report that we now have a total of three cases of Kaposi's, the most recent man also having the Pneumocystis carinii pneumonia, and failing fast. He, too, is gay. All three are immunodepressed as well, per usual."

"I guess it's time to call the CDC again and get them motivated. Dr. Bean, my colleague on this investigation, called them once already and got the standard wait and watch order. This is obviously beyond the realm of coincidental occurrence, even according to their conservative epidemiology guidelines."

"I whole-heartedly agree. I will call them also to ask assistance."

"Very good, thank you. I'll speak with you later."

She called Dr. Bean again and told her of the newest case. "Kris, this is getting scary. People are becoming gravely ill, even dying, and no concerted effort is underway to determine the cause. I'm calling the CDC again and insist that they initiate a work up. If necessary, I'll go over their heads politically and get someone of importance involved."

"That sounds like the proper track. Keep me posted all the way."

"Sure." Helen hung up the phone. "Loretta, get me the number for the CDC in Atlanta, please," she called out.

"Here, Doctor," Loretta handed her a note paper with the CDC's number written on it.

"Thanks." She dialed the 800 number, then waited. "Yes, this is Doctor Gregg calling from New York City. May I speak with someone in the epidemiology department, please?"

"Hold, please."

Six minutes passed, by the clock, when finally some one answered. "This is Dr. Rounds. Can I help you?"

"Yes, Dr. Rounds, my name is Dr. Helen Gregg. I'm calling from New York City."

"Helen Gregg . . . Helen Gregg . . . Oh, the one who wrote the article about Kaposi's recently in *The New England Journal.*"

"Yes, that's me. Are you aware that there are over a dozen cases of this disease diagnosed in Paris, France, at this time? I also received a call from the county health department in Chicago. They have three cases there, too. I am calling to see if you people will become involved, as the incidence of this disease is well beyond reasonable coincidence. And there is the common thread of homosexuality."

"We've been aware, yes, of the disease in Paris, but we don't concern ourselves with foreign health problems. That's the responsibility of the World Health Organization. Now, the occurrence in this country is still quite limited, to my knowledge. No one but yourself and another female doctor from up there has notified us of anything. As I'm sure you know, our funding resources are limited, and we can't jump every time a seemingly new plague of some kind crosses our threshold. Many such reports are made to us every month. Some, indeed, are weird increases in rare illnesses, but they tend to fade back to their known parameters of occurrence. Therefore, at this time, I recommend that you still be patient and keep accurate records."

"So you will do nothing?"

"Not at this time, as I said. We will watch for further

developments, however."

"I, quite frankly, find that response disgusting! Let me speak to the department chief, please."

"I'm sorry you feel that way, Dr. Gregg, and I am the chief of the department. We, like you, must work within established guidelines. Please feel free to contact me personally if you have further information. Good bye, for now."

Helen slammed down the phone. *"What kind of shit is this, anyway?"* she yelled.

"Dr. Gregg, please!" Loretta said. She came in the room and whispered. "There are patients out there."

"I don't give a goddamn! Tell them I went home!" She put on her coat and stomped out the door.

It was freezing outside as she walked the three blocks to her car, but she hardly noticed. Her mind was locked in frustration the entire way. I can understand them not exploring an increase in the amount of bladder infections, or perhaps back strains, but this . . . Damn! This is a life-threatening illness, and it is definitely a threat to the public domain, even though they are gay men. Aha! Perhaps that's it! Dr. Rounds hates queers, and therefore doesn't give a damn. He's probably glad they're dying of an unknown!

HAVANA, APRIL

> "Good evening, and welcome to the early evening news. I'm Tom Danlau, reporting live from New York City.
>
> "In the top of the news tonight on this, the twentieth day of April, Fidel Castro opened the small Cuban port of Mariel as a quote 'good will gesture' to allow free passage to Cubans who wished to emigrate to the U.S. and Central America. More on this story after a word from our sponsors."

The blaring volume of the commercial messages pounded from the television. Fidel hit the mute button on the remote control transmitter and turned to Colonel Jurado. "Very interesting. I made the national news in America for the first time in possibly ten years." He was beaming with pride, his cigar-yellowed teeth flashing. He sat, eyes fixed on the muted television, watching new car promotions. He rapped his finger nails absent mindedly on the desk. "I wonder if Americanos hate these silly, boring car commercials as much as I do. Half of their television programming is insulting to the intelligence. Do you know of that country music show with all of those ridiculous comedy skits?" He belly laughed. "That was the number one popular show in America for several years! I couldn't believe it." They both laughed.

The ads terminated and Fidel resumed the volume.

> "The small quiet port of Mariel, Cuba, today became the site for the first emigration since Fidel Castro established himself as dictator twenty years ago. General Castro states that he presented this opportunity for Cubans to emigrate to the U.S. and join their families as a 'gesture of goodwill' to his people.
>
> "Throughout the past two years, Castro has allowed visitation of Cuban-Americans to Cuba for periods of one week to visit family members who remained in Cuba after the closed door policy of Castro's first eighteen years in power. Our sources tell us that, based on these visits, unrest amongst the Cuban citizenry developed after witnessing the higher quality of life in the U.S. that was apparent in their American counterparts. The situation apparently became an embarrassment for the Cuban government.

Contrary to Castro's statement of goodwill, reputable sources have reported that dissension amongst the Cuban middle class is responsible for this exodus. There are reports from captains of small vessels hired to sail to Mariel and transport emigrants that the Cuban military is forcing them to transport Cuban prisoners and mental patients to the U.S. Official confirmation of this development is pending, and will be detailed in a later broadcast. It is estimated that as many as one hundred thousand Cubans are taking part in this mass exodus.

"In other news, there have been three new cases of the bizarre cancer, Kaposi's sarcoma, reported in the San Francisco homosexual population . . . "

Castro clicked the off button on the remote control hard in frustration. "Damn! They play down my benevolent gesture and instead condemn me as a liar! And such a short news item. Some cancer in San Francisco takes billing over me!" He threw the transmitter at the sofa. "I remember twenty years ago. You were just a boy, mi amigo. I was the headliner in the nightly news for many months. It was glorious!"

"I'm sure, General," Luis said, *you egotistical jerk.* "Possibly there will be much more news coverage for you when their government verifies the transport of prisoners and mental patients!"

"That kind of news coverage I don't want. It didn't take them long to get that out, did it? I wonder when I will receive a call from the White House, begging me to take them back?" he jeered.

"I would hope not for a while. Our disease transmitters need time to function and disseminate the virus. Knowing how sexually active homosexuals can be, I should think we will have a good base of infection in a reasonably short time. That initial foundation of prisoners will do well to propagate the infection in the Miami slums. It would be wise to delay any acceptance of returnees for as long as possible."

"Yes, sound advice. By the way, how did the implanting of the virus go here, at the prisons? It must have been quite funny, sticking enemas into the squirming prisoner's butts. I'll bet it was not pleasant for your men, however, doing one thousand enemas on murderers and rapists!" Castro belly laughed.

"Please, General, we're not that stupid! We made the prison guards do it!" They both roared with laughter, Fidel nearly falling from his chair.

"Mi amigo, I should have known!" continuing his laughter. "How about a whiskey?"

"Sure, as a 'self congratulations' for completion of this mission."

Castro went to the bar and pulled two shot glasses from the shelf, filling them with Jack Daniels black label. "Only the finest from America, in spite of their trade embargo! And at this very moment, I am quite certain, that somewhere across the Straights of Florida someone is enjoying a fine Cuban handmade cigar. I toast you, you capitalist bastard, wherever you may be!" He raised his shot glass in unison with Luis, then both gulped their whiskey. "Have another!"

It was commonly rumored that you did not refuse an offer of drink from El Presidente. He supposedly became belligerent if you didn't accept, but in the end, with a load on, he was belligerent anyway.

"Si, Presidente. Why not?" Luis smiled an empty smile. He had hoped he could get away, but once the whiskey bottle appeared that thought was gone. *Might as well get drunk!* "How do you come by the Jack Daniels? It's my favorite whiskey."

"There are ways, my friend, of getting whatever you need for pleasure from this life. Speaking of that, want a woman, perhaps? I can arrange for you to have the most beautiful woman in all of Havana. Her name is Lolita. Ooo-lala!" He formed the shape of an hourglass with his index fingers and laughed.

"I don't know."

"Carmela!" he hollered to his front office girl. "Call Lolita and tell her to come right away. I have someone for her to meet, a brilliant scientist, no less!"

"Thank you, General, but I really don't think . . . " Luis interceded.

"What do you mean? You bring me the answer to my dreams, a way to get back at the Americanos for all they have done to me, and I want to repay you handsomely, like a prince. Have another whiskey!" He poured the shot glasses full again. "Salud!" They downed their shots, and Fidel belched and wiped his mouth on his sleeve. "You know, mi amigo, the Americanos have been responsible for the two most humiliating episodes of my life. Did you know, when I was younger, I went to Los Angeles to become a movie star with my brother?" He laughed and hiccuped. "Well, as you can see, I'm not one!" They both laughed, then Fidel stopped abruptly. "It's only funny to me. I dislike being laughed at by my citizens."

"Uh, I'm sorry, sir."

"Sure, sure." He became somber. "The other time was when Khrushchev backed down, like a coward, in 1962. He fell for Kennedy's bluff! I have never been so angry and humiliated in my life as I was that day, learning that the Russian ships had turned back. I could be a very powerful man if I had those nuclear missiles here now. Don't you think the almighty United States of America would respect me if I had nuclear warheads aimed at them? Of course they would. It's all they understand. Have more whiskey!" He poured more.

They drank again, Luis sipping this time. "Drink, drink!" Fidel bellowed. Luis picked up the glass and downed it without hesitation. Maybe the rumors were right.

"On the other hand, the stupid Americanos gave me my most enjoyable day, too. It was the Bay of Pigs invasion. What buffoonery! There they were, unloading their weapons and troops at the water's edge for their assault on my government. A bunch of untrained, lazy fools. First they move to America to escape the rule of my iron fist," he smacked the desk with his fist, "then the U.S. supplies these clowns with shrapnel helmets and weapons and little else and dumps them on my shore to retake their country! And the U.S. thinks it is a covert operation, and it would appear that the people rebelled and returned their country to a sniveling puppet democracy! Aha-ha-ha-ha . . . I don't remember that I lost so much as one man! Sent them scurrying back to the ocean like rats from a burning pile of refuse! Aha-ha-ha-ha-ha-ha . . . " He laughed until he could laugh no more, then sighed and poured the glasses full again. "Salud!" This time Luis didn't hesitate to drink his whiskey.

Luis was tiring of the stench in Castro's office, the blue cigar haze burning his eyes and throat. "Yes, General. That is a funny story. That woman you spoke of . . . she sounds delightful. Why don't I arrange to go and pick her up?"

"Suit yourself, Colonel. I will have Carmela call her and tell her to stay at home. My driver will take you there." The mood settled. "So, tell me, Colonel, how long before you expect that we will see the results of our ploy?"

"Honestly, sir, no one can be certain. It is a slow virus. But, depending on the overall health of the person infected, it could show effects in as little as a few months. Don't expect that the entire country will fall overnight. That was never intended. Too suspicious."

"I guess we just wait and watch. How many of those queers that we shipped over there today are spreading it right now, as we speak, I wonder?" He laughed again.

"It would be difficult to offer a guess. But it is known that men of that sexual leaning can be uninhibited, and take on sexual encounters with great spontaneity. In all fairness, though, let's give them a couple of days to settle in!" They laughed.

"I like you, Colonel. So you will be returning to Hungary shortly, no? You have become a good friend, and I will miss your presence. But you have your work to do there. You are much more valuable to this country there than you would be here. Perhaps more information will come to you at a later time, while you are in Budapest. Your bits of intelligence information from over the years certainly have been worthwhile to us and our allies."

"Thank you. I will continue to try to live up to your expectations, General. I must leave by week's end. I, too, have enjoyed this opportunity to get to know each other." He stood and put on his jacket. "I'd better go now. Lolita is waiting!"

"Si, si." Fidel laughed. "Enjoy yourself, my friend. Adios y hasta luego!"

TORONTO, MAY

"So, how do you feel these days?" asked Dr. Steinberg. He had finished reviewing the chart, and was palpating the lymph nodes on George's neck. "The last time you were here was June fifth, correct?"

"Yes, it was early June, I remember. I don't know, I still think that the chemotherapy wiped me out. I haven't felt up to my usual self since then. I tire easily, and—"

"I think that you're laying too much blame on the treatment. My feeling is that you would be much worse than you are right now if not for the therapy. Your lymph nodes still seem to be of fairly normal size, that's a good sign. And I see you've regained twenty pounds."

"Yes, but the fatigue . . . "

"And looking at your scalp, I see that you will probably regrow a full head of hair. Why do you still keep it shaved?"

"I don't know, I guess because it would look too dumb while it was growing, and what if it didn't grow evenly?"

"I think you're depressed more than anything. Are you sleeping all right, eating all right, sex drive normal . . . That is, for *you*, anyway?" He looked down when he asked that question, not comfortable dealing with homosexuality.

"I'm sleeping too much, I'm eating better than I was during that six weeks of hell in therapy, and, yes, Doctor, my sex drive is strong as hell, but I can't get it up like I used to. My party life has quieted down because of that."

"Well, I think it's all in your head. I want you to keep coming in here for checks on a monthly basis for a while. If we can get you through five years without a recurrence, we consider you cured. Here is a prescription for some antidepressants." He tore the prescription from the pad and handed it to George. "Now, good day to you."

"So you can't do anything for the tiredness and the sex problem?"

"That's up to you, son. Try some vitamins."

George walked out of the office feeling like he'd been had. That bastard just screwed his insurance company out of twenty-two thousand dollars, and created more problems than he cured. And then there was that poor old Mr. Harley. "Hell, he killed that guy. I wonder how much he got for the murder?" He said it just loud enough to where he hoped he'd be heard by other patients and their families in the lobby. A few looked up, then receded to their own little troubled worlds.

• • •

The following Saturday night Corey came home from his flight to Florida. "Aren't you working yet?" he asked.

"No, I'm still on disability leave. I wish I could go back, but I don't think I could hold up."

"Oh, yeah, poor baby! All you have energy for is flying around the fun towns and screwing lately. You must be worn to a frazzle, poor man. How could you work?" he chided.

"Eat shit!" George threw a pillow at him.

"Oh, yeah, I forgot to tell you. There was a message on the recorder from a woman named Helen something a couple weeks ago. She left a number to call her back. It probably fell behind the dresser 'cause I haven't seen it for a while."

"I don't know anyone named Helen. Must be one of those charity seeking idiots, invading the sanctity of people's private homes via the telephone, then intimidating them by use of guilt to squeeze money out of them. There ought to be a law against those bastards. That one outfit, that athletic league outfit, calls every month trying to sponge more. I tell them 'How dare you invade my privacy to beg! Take me off your list immediately!' and then I hang up. To hell with this 'Helen' woman, and all the rest of them!" He raised his coffee cup in salute, as if expecting massive crowds to yell "Hear, hear!"

"You're a good soap box man! Hey, you'll be interested in this. I was reading one of those weekly news magazines on the plane, and there was an article in it about the same kind of cancer you had, Kokos, or whatever it's called. There's a woman doctor at the university in New York City who's been seeing a lot of patients with it. She was whistle blowing on the CDC, which is the government agency in the States that is supposed to investigate diseases. She said that three or four doctors have asked them for help in figuring out where this disease is coming from, but they are refusing because they claim they don't have the funds. She's really pissed off because some patients have even died! It said, too, that pretty much all of the patients who have it are gay."

"What? Run that by me again! People are dying from it?"

Corey looked at him, then highlighted the article again.

"Damn, that's scary. Did it say anything else?"

"That's about it. It was in one of those news column pages. I'm sorry, I should have brought it home for you." Corey had a sheepish look on his face. He could tell when his older and seemingly wiser roommate thought he screwed up.

"What magazine was it? I'll go buy it."

"I'm sorry, I don't know. The cover was torn away."

"Damn! I'm going down to the store and look through the news racks to try and find it."

"Ummm, Are you coming home tonight?" Corey asked awkwardly.

"Sure, I don't have anything else to do, why?" George was startled.

"Well, in case you had any wild plans, maybe we shouldn't sleep together anymore. I mean, until this disease stuff is cleared up."

"Oh, bullshit! I mean, if the scientists at the CDC in the States aren't all that worried about it, why should you be? They are the quickest country on this earth to make a mountain of a molehill. It's all journalistic sensationalism, just to sell magazines. Another cheap shot! That woman doctor probably has a hard-on to make a big name for herself."

"Well, it did say that they're finding it in France and the Netherlands, and several cities in the States. Don't get so wired. I only told you about it thinking you might want to check her out. Who knows, maybe she has a treatment that works. This quack doctor you have here doesn't seem to be doing much for you."

"Thanks for your concern, but no. I'll stay here with my quack. That chemotherapy crap is what made me this way. I'm getting better all the time. It just takes awhile to get the chemicals out of your system."

"It's up to you, but if I were you, I'd think about some opinions from other doctors."

George stretched and yawned. "Well, I'm kinda beat. Those magazines will still be at the store in the morning. All this crap makes me depressed. I'm going to bed. You can sleep in the guest room if you want to," he whined. He had become juvenile, the way he always did under stress. He stood up and threw the newspaper he'd been reading on the sofa and huffed into the bedroom.

He tossed and turned for a long time, unable to sleep, thoughts of disease and despair floating through his mind. He would seem to fall asleep for a few minutes, then have a nightmare about himself looking into a full length mirror and seeing a groaning, emaciated black and blue rotted skeleton. There were I.V.'s in each of its arms, and it would vomit constantly between groans. He jumped up in bed, startled, and found himself screaming. Corey was sitting at the bedside shaking him.

"George, George . . . it's just a nightmare, like you've been having, but worse this time."

"O.K., O.K., I'm O.K. What's wrong with me? I hate it." He looked at Corey. "You know, maybe I should go and talk to that woman doctor in New York. Who knows, maybe she can do something.

In the morning I'll call Gary to see if I can fly down to the city and stay at his house, then I'll track this woman down on Monday."

"A wise man. Here, take this sleeping pill and try to sleep again." He handed George a glass of water and a small capsule, then left the room.

"Hey, Corey?"

"Yeah?"

"I love you, man."

"I know. That's because I'm so good to you!"

• • •

Sunday afternoon George was on the plane bound for New York. I hope I make it in time for the ball game, and an ice cold beer would be great. He napped for awhile.

When the plane arrived at two-thirty, Gary was waiting at the gate. "George, my man, how the hell are you? It's been a year or so since I've seen you! Decided to go the Yul Brynner look, huh? Looks good." He took one of George's heavier bags. "Hey, what's going on with you, anyway? I had some woman from the university call me a couple of months ago, asking if I knew how to get hold of you. Out of the clear blue sky. Are you in trouble with the cops or something?"

"What?"

"Yeah, she said it was very important that she contact you. I told her I didn't know where you lived. I mean, she could have been a weirdo or a bill collector or something."

"Yeah, uh, thanks. Could have been anybody." George was confused.

• • •

They watched the Mets lose their fifth game in a row, and the beer was all gone when George announced that he was tired and was going to bed. "I'll see you in the morning."

"Just like that? You're not going to sleep with me? Thanks a lot, pal. I've been looking forward to this since you called yesterday, horny as hell! See you later, prick!"

"Hey, Gary, I'm sorry. I should've explained. I've been sick lately, and I just went through the most god-awful time of my life. I'm still not feeling all that great. I had a real rare skin cancer."

"It's not that Kaposi's stuff that everybody's talking about, is it?"

"How did you know about it?" George was shocked.

"Everybody knows about it, all through the Village. There are, I don't know, maybe ten guys with it at the last count."

"O.K., yes. That's why I'm here. I want to go to the university medical center to see if they have a better treatment than what they had in Toronto."

"Oh, shit! I'm sorry I jumped at you like that. I didn't know."

"No sweat. It's O.K. Maybe in the morning or something, when I'm not so tired, we could have some fun, if you know what I mean." George smiled.

"Well, maybe it's better for you if you just rest while you're here. We don't have to do it." Gary was hardly interested anymore.

"O.K., maybe that would be better." He knew that Gary was turned off because of the cancer. If he didn't need a place to stay, he would have told him off and walked out. He was just too tired.

Monday morning George was on the phone with the university switchboard. "Hello, I'm trying to reach the woman doctor who's handling the Kaposi's patients. Do you know who she is?"

"Oh, that would be Doctor Helen Gregg in family practice. May I say who's calling, please?"

"Uh, sure, my name is George Williams, but she doesn't know me."

"Please hold."

"Er, excuse me, Dr. Gregg," Loretta said, tapping on the door to the patient exam room, "but there is a Mr. George Williams on the phone!" She heard some hurried, muffled excuses being made to the patient, then Dr. Gregg came out and closed the door.

"What line, Loretta?"

"Three."

She ran into her office and picked up the phone. "This is Dr. Gregg speaking," she panted.

"Um, hello. My name is George Williams, and I'm calling because my roommate read about you in a magazine, and said that you were working with patients with Kaposi's cancer. Are you the one?"

"Yes, I'm the one. You are Mr. Williams, the airline steward from Canada?"

"H-how did you know?" He was thrown.

"Mr. Williams, I have been actively looking for you for months! I've called people up there, and finally tracked down your employer who said you were out on disability leave. I even called your number and left a message on the machine. I was going to try you again this week."

"Oh, that was you!" George hadn't put it together until just now. "My roommate told me that a woman named Helen had called."

"Where are you? Where are you calling from?"

"I'm at a friend's house, here in the city. I came to find you to see what's going on, to see if you could help me. But why were you trying to find me?"

Helen was emphatic. "Listen, I want you to come over here right now. It's extremely important that I see you." She gave him the address and her direct phone line number. "When you get to the lobby, take the second bank of elevators on the right to the seventh floor. Get off the elevator and turn to the right and go to the end of the hall to the door marked Family Practice Department, it's suite 722. Got it?"

George was writing notes as he listened. "Yeah, suite 722. I'll call a cab now."

"Please don't fail!" Helen pleaded.

"I won't. I'll be there shortly." He put the phone down, bewildered. Why was she looking for me?

He called a cab, then looked at his watch. "Put a rush on it, O.K.?

• • •

George walked through the door marked 722 just after noon. "Hello, I'm . . . "

"George Williams," said Loretta. "Come right this way, please." She showed him into Dr. Gregg's office.

Helen stood up, somewhat awed by his presence. He surely must be one of the most sexually active men in the country, possibly the world. "George, I assume." She held out her hand to greet him.

George shook her hand. "That's me. So you're Dr. Gregg. Pleased to meet you. Now, tell me, why were you looking for me?"

"Please, have a seat." She motioned him to a chair. "If you don't mind, I'll call you on a first-name basis. I feel as if I already know you. George, your name has come up repeatedly in the investigation of this disease pattern. From gay men in Los Angeles, Miami, Chicago, Dallas, Omaha, San Francisco, here in New York, and even Paris, France!"

"What are you talking about?"

"Part of the task of an epidemic investigation is to identify common factors. In this case, over ninety-eight percent of those with the disease are gay. The other two percent or so deny homosexual behavior, but we have to think that they are lying to us, for whatever personal reasons they may have. Anyway, the common thread is homosexualism. The next step is to track anyone involved with the diseased persons, so we obtained as many names of their past lovers as possible. Your name came up on a phenomenal amount of lists as having had sex with them. For this reason, I was trying to track you down and see if you have the disease also."

"No shit! Oh, excuse my tongue." He turned on the charm, "I am an airline attendant, and I do enjoy myself and try to hit all the good times, including Paris, yes. But I didn't know I was that popular." He gloated. "And yes, I do, er, that is, I did, have the Kaposi's cancer. Well, he said I did, anyway, but I always felt great until he started jamming those chemicals into my bloodstream. I'm talking about the chemotherapy that my doctor, er, Doctor Steinberg in Toronto, treated me with."

"Your condition must have been fairly serious if it required chemo. Was it in the lymph nodes?"

"Yes, uh-huh. Now for the reason I came to see you. Do you have any cures, or vaccines, or anything at all that will kill the disease? I mean, I hear people are dying from it! The doctor who first diagnosed it said that it was a mild cancer from Africa, and I've never been there. He didn't tell me it could kill people!"

"Well, I know it's frustrating, but there have been new and even worse developments since we started on this. But no cures or treatments, because right now we don't even know the cause. There is also a pneumonia turning up in gay men, with or without the Kaposi's, that normally doesn't cause illness in humans. That is what is killing most of the dying patients. We think now that there is maybe an environmental factor, or possibly a biological agent, such as a bacteria or virus, that is causing these diseases. Quite possibly the cancer and pneumonias are just manifestations of the agent. The agent seems to attack the person's immune system and render it useless, thereby letting these usually nonpathogenic organisms manifest themselves. A few of the patients have died of various other types of infections, too, because their immune system is wrecked and can't fight them off. So, right now we are still trying to identify the actual cause, then maybe we can develop a treatment."

"So there isn't a cure?"

"No, I'm afraid not." She glanced away.

"What the hell is wrong with the science world, anyway? I mean, this is 1980, not the damned Dark Ages. I didn't know there were any diseases that couldn't be cured with modern medicine."

"I know it's frustrating, believe me! Actually, there are hundreds of diseases that medicine cannot cure, beginning with the common cold. All we do is treat the symptoms, so the patient isn't so uncomfortable, until his own immune system kills the virus. There is the standing joke about a cold taking seven days to go away with an antibiotic, or a full week without it."

"Ha, ha, that's very funny," he sneered. "Well, so you found me, and yes, I have it. So what? You can't cure it."

"Like I said, we need to study it, and the only method we have to attempt a cure is to study patients that have it, meaning you. Especially since you seem to be involved so deeply, based on our investigation. Are you willing to get a complete work up? That means a hell of a lot of testing, every inch of your body, inside and out. One never knows, we might find something."

"Oh, in other words, become a test case? Let me think about it for a few days. I grew real tired of that other medical crap, and I'm more than a little reluctant to be one of your lab rats."

Helen sighed with disappointment. "Yes, I guess I can understand. Listen to me, though. The only thing I can theorize right now is that this is an unknown disease, quite possibly venereal in nature, meaning transmitted sexually. Why it's appearing only in gay men is unknown. Maybe male hormones interplay somehow. At any rate, be advised that you may be spreading it through sex, so please avoid sexual behavior."

"What? Are you kidding? No way, I might as well be dead. This is my body and nobody, including you, tells me what I can and cannot do!" With that, he stood and stormed out of the office, slamming the door behind him.

Helen jumped up and pulled open the door, yelling down the hallway after him. "At least think about the work up, George! Please call me later!"

1981

NEW YORK CITY, JANUARY

"I decided that I want to go through the tests, but on one condition." George said, seated in Dr. Gregg's office.

"I'm very glad you're here," Helen said. "It took you a long time to come back. That was seven months ago you walked out of here mad. Tell me, what made you change your mind?"

"It's quite simple. I'm still sick. I seem to catch everything; colds, stomach flus, *everything.* And I had pneumonia and was in the hospital until only a week ago. While I was in the hospital I decided to come back. In Canada, they haven't had enough cases of this to know what to do."

"George, you have to understand that they probably are treating this problem the same way we are, medically speaking. There still isn't much we can do until we isolate the actual cause of the disease, and even then it may take some time to develop agents to combat it. Right now all we can do is just as they did in Canada, treat the various infections with antibiotics. In other words, don't expect too much. At least you can take comfort in the knowledge that you are doing something to help. Now, what's the condition you mentioned?"

"The only condition is that if any cures or treatments develop, from me or anyone else, I get first crack at trying them. I don't want to die like the others. How many are dead now, anyway?"

"The last I knew, there have been one hundred and seven deaths that are GRID related—"

"Excuse me, what's 'GRID?'"

"Oh, I thought you would know that term. That's the acronym the CDC has given this syndrome. It stands for Gay Related Immune Deficiency, and it encompasses the two diseases, both Kaposi's and Pneumocystis carinii pneumonia. There are, I think, about three hundred seventy-five confirmed cases throughout the U.S. right now. The numbers are growing daily. Back to your terms for study. . .I don't have the authority to absolutely guarantee your wish, but I'll do everything in my power to see to it. And, you must understand, that even if treatments are discovered, they will probably be experimental for *years* before the FDA gives the O.K. for any widespread use. Prior to that, the treatments, if any, may be actually worse than the disease itself, perhaps even fatal."

George looked her straight in the eye. "Dr. Gregg, you know as well as I that by doing nothing, I'm a dead man *anyway.* I mean, look at these spots!" He pulled his shirt open and exposed his chest. There were multiple discolorations of various sizes up to his neck. "They're all over the rest of my body, too. That's the deal, I get first crack at treatments. Right now I have to wear makeup all over my body to cover the spots."

"Yes, I see. So it's all over your face, too?"

"It's *everywhere*, and it's ugly! Do we have a deal?"

"Like I said, George, I'll try my best. That's all I can do. Did you give any thought to my request last time we met? You know, about curbing the sexual activity?"

"Well, sort of. I've been doing a lot more travelling on my free flying, living on my disability insurance as best I can. And I've had a few more lovers, but not as many." He lied. He'd been flying to different cities almost constantly, going to the celebrations; Halloween, St. Patrick's Day, Gay Rights parades, New Orleans, the Hooker's Ball in San Francisco, and so on. And in between he'd hit bathhouses all over the country, meeting new and beautiful men. He found recently that he had to go to dark bathhouses so his spots were not noticeable.

He still maintained his old established lovers, but he had to be careful in bedrooms and hotel rooms to insure that they were dark. He actually was living much better than usual financially, too, being able to talk his older, financially well-heeled lovers out of money at the least suggestion that he needed it.

"At least you've cut down," Dr. Gregg said "That's still my own pet theory, that the disease is sexually transmitted. But there are a myriad of other theories, too. Some feel that it is a genetic failure, somehow, and propose that gay men have a genetic defect that predisposes them to homosexuality, and possibly the defective gene is mutating to this disease. Others are still considering environmental possibilities, possibly something chemical in Vietnam vets."

"So no one is any closer at all, huh, to finding the cause?"

"No George, still working at it."

"Oh, Dr. Gregg, you said that the CDC has named it GRID. I read in the newspaper that they had finally gotten involved. What made them come around, your article in that news magazine?"

"No. Actually, I'm not sure. One day two investigators just showed up and took copies of all of my records. I guess it was because they finally had so many reports that they had to act. At any rate, I'm glad they're in it. They have the best resources and experience for this sort of thing. They'll be talking to you, you can bet on it. They come here about once a month to get the latest crop of reports and developments. That reminds me, they're due here very soon. I'd better get to work on my updates."

"Well, what do you want me to do? I do have insurance, you know. But if you're using me for a guinea pig, maybe you wouldn't have to stick it to me too bad, right? My insurance only pays eighty percent."

"I'll talk to the proper people, and maybe we can waive the twenty percent you would normally pay, I don't know. For now, go home and get everything you need to live here for three weeks or so, comfortable clothing, toiletries, books, and so forth. We'll house you across the street in the dormitory for families of extended treatment patients. There are two other men over there with GRID, too, that we're testing.

When you get back here with your things, check in at the inpatient desk downstairs, and they will take care of you from there on. I won't be directly involved in the testing, but I'll keep tabs on you. I'm kind of out of the picture except for finishing up what I started before the CDC came in. Now it's the hot item to be involved. Frankly, I'm tired of all of the responsibility! Now, get moving, your first day of testing is tomorrow."

"O.K.," he sighed. "They do every test possible on a human, huh? Is any of it painful?"

"Some things are a little discomforting, but for those you'll be semi-anesthetized. Don't worry about it."

Sure, right! Famous last words, lady. Whenever medical people say it won't hurt, it's excruciating! "If it gets too bad, I quit," he said as he walked out the door. Dr. Gregg hadn't heard him. That's good.

Over the next two weeks George was tested to the brink of physical exhaustion. Everyone kept telling him it was due to his disease, and that actually he was maintaining quite well. He had blood tests daily, sometimes twice daily. He kept hearing words like SMAC, CBC, gases, profiles for this and that, genetic testing, cultures, hormone levels, and on and on. They took urine every other day for drug screens, cultures, chemistry, microscopy, and so forth. And then there were the *big* ones. Tubes were stuck in his rear end for colonoscopy and washings, and in his penis for checking the urinary tract, and down his throat for scoping in the lungs and the gut for *more* washings and biopsies. He had to masturbate a half dozen times for semen studies. He had huge I.V. needles stuck into arteries for radiographic dye studies of different organs, including his brain. He had CAT scans on every inch of his body, and then more blood draws. He had been drugged many times for studies, especially the tube insertions and the biopsies of his liver and kidneys. Dr. Gregg *hadn't* lied about the pain question, though. He had been so drugged during those procedures that he hardly remembered them. According to the doctors, that was as should be with good anesthesia.

And there was psychological testing between the druggings for the physical tests. There was a three hour long personality factor test;

would he rather go hunting for antiques or plant flowers, did he ever hear voices, did he ever think people were talking about him. He answered every question conceivable, he thought, about his upbringing, sex life, religious opinions, life ambitions and so on. His entire being, both physical and mental, was thoroughly exposed, as though he'd been placed on a microscopic glass slide.

He laid in bed for two days recuperating from severe fatigue; him feeling that it was due to the testing, them feeling that it was secondary to the disease. Only two more days to go!

He was angry, moody, snapping at people who came in to poke and prod. But, they all 'understood,' that is, until they got outside of his room. Then he would hear comments like "what a jerk, you know he's a *queer,*" and others. That made him angrier. Why didn't other people get this crap, people that were lesser than he? There were a lot of sleazy people out there, people with no class. If it was truly sexually transmitted, he must have picked it up from one of those sleaze balls. Why didn't they get it? *I'll show 'em!*

Friday morning came. It was check out day! George was packing his things when there was a rap at the half-open door. He turned around, and there stood Dr. Gregg with two men. "Good morning," she said.

He grunted, and turned back to his packing. "So where the hell have you been? You said you would be checking on me, and this is the first time I've seen you." He turned and looked at her, upset. He threw a shirt in the bag. "This has been the worst two-and-a-half weeks I've ever lived through. At least what I can remember of it. Look!" He pointed at the dressings over the sites of the puncture biopsies. "And you said no pain? Bullshit!" His childish side resurfaced.

"I told you this study would be *very* involved, and I would follow the case, not care for your personal needs!" Helen blew up. "I wanted you to come in long ago, when you were stronger, and quite possibly could have tolerated this a hell of a lot better. Now, you show up in complete desperation, and want to make deals to save *yourself,* and to hell with everybody else. Don't lay that crap on me, I've had it!" She turned and abruptly left the room.

"So what do *you* want?" George asked the remaining men. "More bullshit?"

"Settle down, son. I'm Dr. Fellows," said the thin one, "and this is Dr. Schuster. We'd like to ask you just a few more questions. We know what you've been through, so we'll try to be brief."

"Oh, yeah, the disease hounds from the CDC, right? If you don't mind, I'm in the middle of leaving right now."

"Mr. Williams, please . . . This could be the most important phase of this testing. We need the names of as many sexual contacts as you can possibly remember." Dr. Fellows said.

"I've already done all that, it's in the record you have in your hand. Oh, what the hell! But then this is it, I'm getting out."

Dr. Fellows opened the chart to the history section. "Let me read them to you, and if there are any others that you had forgotten, you can give them now. He began reading the names, "Fred Hammond, Robert Jaramillo, George Vetrovec, Clancy Pfizer . . . " When that name came up, Dr. Schuster perked. "How do you know Clancy Pfizer?"

"Oh, he's a diamond broker for the jet set. He travels the world. He and I met in Jamaica once, then spent a few weekends together here and there. He's a great guy, lots of friends." George had become strangely compliant, seeming to be enjoying this recognition of conquests.

Fellows continued through the list. "That's all you put on the list. Are there any more you can remember?"

"No, those are the ones I know. But, you know, there are a lot more than that, maybe two hundred and fifty a year, on the average. I can't help it if I'm well liked." He smiled. "Say, what made you boys get in on this investigation, anyway? I thought you were refusing. At least that's what I read in a magazine a while back."

"Actually, my friend, we've been watching the increase in these diseases, which we now refer to as 'GRID', since about 1978. Until recently, the cases were so sporadic and seemingly disconnected that we couldn't do anything. But now, however, with the explosiveness of the situation, we stepped in. There are several cases, too, of victims who swear they are not homosexual, but abuse I.V. drugs like heroin and cocaine. More water thrown in the mud for us. Most researchers and physicians think that these people are gay, too, but won't admit it, and that's all we have to go on."

"That's what Dr. Gregg said. I guess everybody thinks queers are *liars*, too. So you've been aware of this crap going on for quite some time."

"Yes, but we can't indiscretionately take every disease report that comes across the desk without first watching. We don't have the money, nor is it usually necessary. Most of these unusual disease outbreaks are self limited. Oh, George, please refrain from sexual activity until we get a handle on this. To be candid with you, your name has been cross-referenced more than any other in the entire U.S., including way over on the West Coast, and right now we feel that you may be spreading it sexually."

"Uh, oh, sure. I sure wouldn't want anyone *else* to get it." George continued packing. "Is that all, then?"

"I believe so." Dr. Fellows closed George's chart. "We have your address in the event we need you later." They exited the room as George closed his bag. He went into the bathroom and smothered his face with makeup, making the purplish lesions barely visible for his grand entrance into the outside world.

Dr. Schuster fumbled in his coat pocket. "Have you got the keys? Never mind, here they are." He fished them out of his pocket and opened the car door. "Interesting development, I would say. Both Williams and Pfizer are multiple repeaters on our lists, and they have had sex together. I see now where there is an elitist group among homosexuals, and on an international level. I still wonder why the same names appear so often, and others we only encounter possibly once or twice."

Fellows got into the car. "It does appear to be a close-knit group. That Williams character is crazy. After observing his self serving behaviors, I wonder if maybe he's a little sociopathic? He could be *trouble*."

"Apparently you didn't get to the psychologist's reports on his personality inventory testing. He's *definitely* sociopathic, and he'll do whatever he damn well pleases, in spite of all of us."

"Lord, help us! So he *is* trouble. If indeed this is sexually transmitted, he wouldn't stop screwing around even if he *knew* he was contagious. Pleasures of the flesh, a penchant for vengeance, and no real conscience to validate his behavior."

"Yeah, that's the textbook example of a sociopathic personality, right there! Well, let's check the county hospital next and see how many more times his name turns up." He backed the car out and drove away.

George stopped at the desk and checked out. He had to sign seven documents for insurance claims and release of information forms. The medical center had agreed to waive the twenty percent in exchange for his permission to openly use the test results. "Thanks a bunch, see ya!" he said flippantly as he headed for freedom. Now he could do what *he* wanted, not what others told him to do every hour of the day and night, even planning what he could eat and when.

God, I'm *horny!* Three weeks without getting laid! He decided to go eat a greasy burger and shake, then head for some action in a sleazy bathhouse. If indeed he *was* spreading it, he was going to give it back to the dirtballs in the street, probably where he got it to begin with. Some carefree back alley fun at one of the celebrations somewhere along the way. Maybe it was that really weird guy with the bull ring in his nose and the mohawk haircut. "I'll teach those scumbags for giving me this!" he mumbled.

He walked into the Hot Room two hours later. He *never* would have set foot in this scummy place in the past. The sweaty fat man at the desk took his three dollars and pointed to the bath area door. George entered the filthy changing room and went into a bathroom stall to take off his clothes so that no one would see the rash. He wrapped himself in a big towel and put his clothes in a locker, then headed for the hot tubs marked 'Candle Lights.' It would be dark in there, perfect. There was some giggling coming from beyond the second door, and the sweet smell of pot, so he went in. "Hi guys, mind if I soak for a little while?"

"Oh, not at all, please do!"

That one was a wimp, skinny and hairy, dirty looking. He had a ring in his right nare, and several in his left ear. There were tattoos of devils and spiders on his chest and arms, and George could make out a large lettered one that read 'OIL HERE,' with an arrow pointed at his navel.

The tub room was grimy, and reeked of body odor intermingled with the pot. The other guy was facing him, between his legs, with one arm out of the water holding a joint to his lips and giggling. "Want to get high?" he lisped effeminately, then giggled again. He handed the joint to George, who bent over and took it as he dropped the towel away and slipped into the water.

"Oh, thank you. I haven't smoked in weeks." He took a big hit and held it momentarily, then burst into a forceful, barking cough, his face wrenched. He coughed so hard his lungs hurt.

The others laughed in ridicule. "Not big on smoking pot, huh? Just learning?" said the wimp. They continued their roar.

It was the harshest, cheapest pot George had smoked since high school. He held his chest with one hand and covered his mouth with the other, face bluing, continuing to cough. I'll teach you bastards, he thought, still coughing. "Shit!"

"Maybe you just need someone to hold you and rub you softly," the tattooed one said. He reached under the water and took George in his hand. "Is that better, darling?" They both laughed again.

George held his temper... He'd get 'em. "That is some *mean* shit!" His cough finally subsided, and his voice returned to normal.

"Yes, I *do* say. I've never seen you here before. Is this your first time at this palace of pleasure, this den of inequity?" the effeminate one asked.

"Uh, yeah. I was walking by and thought I'd stop in for a good time, if you know what I mean." George stroked his buttocks.

"Ooooh, I like you *already*." He turned and kissed George hard on the lips.

The three of them engaged each other for an hour, each taking turns. George serviced both of them, something he had been incapable of recently due to his compromised strength. Twice in an hour! He was in a subdued rage, and he meant to *get* them.

There was a hard knock on the door. "Hey, you, sweetie pie . . .the one who only paid three bucks . . . time's up!"

It sounded like the pig from the desk. "All right, I'll be right out." He made a big show and stood up in the water. "See these spots, 'dearies?'" He pointed to his chest. "I have the gay cancer! I'm sure you've heard about it! I may have just given it to *you!*" He jumped out of the tub, laughing. The two dirtballs just sat in the tub, dumfounded, staring at him, then one another, eyes wide in fear. George left the tub room and hurried for the lockers, retrieving his things and throwing his clothes on as quickly as he could. He was just about to don his shoes when he heard them coming after him, cursing and yelling that they would sexually mutilate him. He ducked out the fire exit and ran barefooted down the alley, laughing, the fire alarm blaring behind him. "Two down," he squealed with delight.

George tired and slowed down when he reached the next alley, then entered it. He listened and heard nothing, so he came out of the shelter and sat down on the curb to put his shoes on. "That was kind of exciting!" he said loudly to himself. Maybe after a little rest he'd go check the action at the Underground, another good sleazy joint down the street. He could surely get a couple more!

1982

CHICAGO, FEBRUARY

"Mrs. Pillen?" Dolores called into the waiting room. She had been the office nurse throughout the twelve years that Peggy had been coming to this clinic.

"Yes, right here," she raised her hand as she stood. Peggy had never grown any more informal with her, in spite of the fact that the nurse knew much of her personal social and medical history. Peggy was unsure as to whether she was being professional, bored, or just indifferently cold and calloused after so many years of listening to people complain about their aches and pains.

Monday morning, and the office was crawling with patients. Children from various mothers were coughing and hacking, crying, screaming, laughing, and climbing all over the furniture. It was the same furniture that had been there for twelve years, Peggy thought. Solid dark wood, with thick green imitation leather upholstery on the seats and backs. Not comfortable, but not uncomfortable either. It actually complemented the lobby's aged appearance, done in green paneling and carpeting, and set off with artificial plants. She wondered if you could buy this kind of an indestructible room.

Being ill, then having to come in on a Monday, the busiest day of the week, was almost intolerable. Medical offices all over town were busy on Monday, mopping up the illnesses and injuries from the preceding weekend. Many patients, like Peggy, suffered through the weekend to avoid the high cost of emergency rooms and urgent care centers, commonly known as "band-aid clinics" anyway. The "doc-in-the-box" usually came up with a diagnosis of "just a virus" and then charged eighty dollars! Most people improved by Monday, in spite of themselves, thus saving their time and money. Those still ill, like Peggy, probably *should* come in. Maybe their cold had converted to pneumonia, or their simple cut had become infected. It was comforting to know that you were in the hands of your own medical provider, who kept a running record of your problems and could tie them together.

"You can come back, now." Dolores held the door to the patient exam area open. "Follow me, please." She waddled down the hall, barely enough room for others to pass. The approaching lab tech stepped sideways into an exam room to let them through. "Room four. I'll be in shortly to get your blood pressure."

Peggy stepped from the hall into the standard eight by twelve exam room, equipped with a sink, stool, and exam table. Everything in this place was dated, from the light green tiled floor, cracking in the corners, to the ugly patterned acoustic ceiling panels. At least the walls had been painted within the past couple of years. The exam table was of real, genuine wood! It had been years since she had seen white metal cabinets anywhere but here, the kind that were popular during the fifties. The center one, under the sink, still had the "WARDS" insignia plate, proudly bearing the manufacturer's name. Everything smelled slightly musty, with the pervasive heavy vitamin smell common to all medical clinics. She sat on the stool and waited the expected twenty minutes before hearing the nurse coming down the hall.

"So you're back again? You're certainly coming in a lot recently." Dolores put the stethoscope in her ears and wrapped the cuff around Peggy's arm.

"Well, I can't seem to shake . . ."

"Shhh, I can't hear your blood pressure." She watched the little dial intently for a few seconds, then released the pressure from the cuff. "There. Now, what were you saying?"

"Good morning!" Reed interrupted. "How are you this morning?" Peggy always found it amusing that people in clinics asked that obligatory question, knowing there is only one possible response from patients in a medical office.

She wanted to answer, *"I feel like shit!"* just to elicit some kind of reaction. Then she thought no, maybe she would say, *"Oh, everything's delightful! I just came in because I had some extra money to pay an office visit and say hello!"* Oh, well. Be quiet and do the routine.

She had felt rotten for the past few months, picking up colds, intestinal flus, bacterial infections, and anything else that may be contagious, every time she went out in public. Reed Robinson, the family nurse practitioner she had come to trust over the years, was just being himself with his canned question. She liked him, actually. He was very up front in his approach to illness and patients. She had never encountered a nurse practitioner until him. He had a degree in nursing, and then pursued specialized education at a university somewhere in Kansas, she remembered, to gain his specialty title. He did everything that a doctor did.

He was divorced and had two young kids whom she'd seen around the office once before, nice kids. He spent more time with her than any doctor she had ever seen, and elicited unusual insight into the patient's situation just by speaking on a person-to-person level. She had grown tired of the pompous "holier than thou" attitude of physicians, and now preferred the more humanistic approach of this man. This clinic was based on the osteopathic medical philosophy. It was the personal attitude that attracted the patients, many of whom had been coming here for years. A young doctor and his wife, also an osteopath, had recently taken over the practice. Peggy didn't know these new physicians, and preferred Reed for that reason. He had properly picked up on things others had missed, and dealt effectively and honestly with her. But this time she was dubious of his belief that she was just having a bad time in her life, and she was under emotional stress which prevented her immune system from fighting these common problems.

"I'm sick again, same old stuff," she finally answered. "Slight fever off and on, I have big lumps under my jaw and behind my neck, and I can barely get out of bed, I'm so tired. And I'm still having burning when I urinate and have to run to the bathroom all the time, even though I'm taking that antibiotic you gave me. And I've noticed a vaginal discharge, and I hurt in my lower belly now. Two years ago, when I had a bladder infection, the medicine cleared it up in just two days. It seems I get just slightly better for a few days, then I get something else. How long can this go on, anyway?"

"You really *have* been getting ill a lot recently. Are you eating properly, and getting sufficient sleep?"

"I'm one of those awful health nuts! I'm very conscientious of good dietary habits. I've always gotten eight hours of sleep nightly, but lately I can't get up at all. I want to sleep all the time."

"Peggy, be square with me. Are you on pills or booze or anything? Over time, a problem like that could cause this sort of thing."

"No, sir, I didn't even have my usual brandy eggnog this year at Christmas!" she chuckled.

"How about your personal life? How are you and Tom getting along lately?"

"There *has* been a little more rift between us than usual. But as you know, we never have been the ideal happily married couple; more like a comfortable old pair of shoes that you hate to throw away," she smiled. "We are those old-fashioned types who stay together for the kids' sake."

"Well, then that hasn't changed. You've talked that way since I've known you!" They laughed. He flipped back through her chart. "Let's see . . . ten days ago you had a bladder infection. Three days before that you had cervical lymphadenopathy, a week before that you had a febrile episode, etiology unknown. Bronchitis before that, cellulitis prior to that. This has been an odd string of illnesses, yes . . . This pattern looks like it started a little over a year ago with that mononucleosis bout. Now, for the past four months, you've been increasing, both in frequency and severity, of complaints and illnesses. Have you had any unexplained weight loss, blood in the stools, or anything else unusual?"

"Well, I'm losing some weight, I've noticed, but I *like* that!" she grinned. "It's a hell of a way to do it, though."

"That's for certain! I think we'd better do a thorough exam today. It isn't right for you to be ill *this* long. We'll draw some labs too. Dolores, come in here, please," he called out.

"Yes, sir."

"Set up Mrs. Pillen for a pelvic exam and get slides for a Pap smear. Get a CBC, UA, SMAC, thyroid profile, and PA chest also."

"What's all that stuff, anyway? Sounds like you think I'm dying!" The kind, middle aged man laughed. She liked his smile and usually pleasant disposition. She'd always thought Reed was in his early thirties by his demeanor, but had recently learned he was actually thirty-eight.

"No, no, no. Just running some general tests to see if we can pick up anything that's not obvious by your recent history. I'm probably doing these things for your mental well-being as much as anything! Maybe we'll pick up a little anemia or something." Half the job of a medical practitioner was instilling assurance in his patients, but he knew she was not completely settled. Neither was he. "I'll leave for a few minutes while you undress".

"God, I hate these damn Pap tests," she muttered as he closed the door. She took off her clothes, covered herself with the paper drape the nurse had left, and sat on the end of the table.

The door opened again after a few moments, and Dolores and Reed entered. "O.K., Peggy, you know the position." She laid back on the table and put her feet in the stirrups with a displeased groan, then slid her buttocks to the end of the table.

"How's that? See, it's just like riding a bike, as they say. One never forgets!" She laughed.

The nurse handed him the lubricated speculum, and he placed it in her vagina. "Hmm . . . How long did you say you've had this discharge?"

"I don't know, maybe a week or so, why?"

"It's kind of an unusual type. Nurse, would you go get a Thayer-Martin plate? We won't be able to do the Pap today because of the discharge, Peggy. The pathology lab will send it back as unreadable, and charge you for it anyway. I'll get some other tests to determine the cause of the discharge, then, when the infection is cleared, you can get the Pap done." He removed the speculum just as the nurse entered with the culture plate. He took a swab and streaked some of the discharge onto the plate, then replaced the lid. He swabbed some glass slides. "Gram stain, KOH, and a wet," and handed it to the nurse. He held out his gloved fingers, and the nurse squeezed some lubricant on them from a tube. "O.K., relax these muscles again," he said as he inserted his fingers. He pressed downward with his left fingertips on her outside belly while pushing upward from within.

Peggy suddenly tensed and jumped in pain. "Damn! That *hurts!*" She pushed his hand away.

He removed his fingers and sat down as the nurse left the room with the lab specimens. "Now, scoot back a little so you don't fall off the table, then sit up," he sighed. "Are you faithful to Tom, Peggy? Be honest."

"For nineteen years, now. Why? Are you interested?" She laughed as she scuffled back and sat up.

"Come on, now," he blushed. "Is he faithful to you, too?" He was looking in her ears with the otoscope as he spoke, routinely carrying out the time-honed physical exam. "Open your mouth wide, say ahhh."

"AAHHH. Why are you asking me this?" she queried. "Do you know something I don't know?" She knew he was serious. "Well, I know he had one affair, several years ago, when we weren't getting along. But it was short-lived and he promised me he'd never do it again. I actually kind of mentally blocked it; it's too painful to think about. We went to counselling together and decided the incident was stress induced."

He was listening to her lungs with his stethoscope after finishing the head and neck exam. "So you don't have any suspicions recently that he's seeing someone? Breathe deeply with your mouth open several times."

She did as he commanded. He listened to her heart for a few minutes, then removed his stethoscope and left it hanging on his neck, seemingly a permanent fixture. She was stunned, aching. "Well, not really. He's had to stay late at work a few times, not often, but he comes home fairly early, not like when he'd stay out all night when he was having the affair. Tell me why . . . Why these questions?" She began to cry.

"I won't know until the lab work is done, but you have a purulent discharge and a very tender abdomen, consistent with a possible sexually transmitted disease. But let's not jump to conclusions, other things can cause these symptoms as well. Now lie back for a minute so I can examine your abdomen and breasts." She eased back down, oblivious to his poking and then the cold stethoscope on her belly. "You can get dressed when I leave the room, then go to the lab down the hall and get the other tests done. We should have several of the results in a few minutes, so come back in here and wait. Please, for your own good, try not to be too upset until we get the results back. Like I said, it could be something else, too, like a persistent bladder infection."

Reed exited the room, overhearing her whimpering. He was distraught, trying not to openly display his concern. "Days like this I wish I did something else for a living," he mumbled.

"Excuse me?"

"Oh, nothing, Dolores, just mumbling."

Peggy was numb as she dressed, then trod down the hallway to the door marked 'LAB.' The tech handed her a small cup and some antiseptic towelettes. "Take this to the restroom and use the towellettes to clean up before you take the specimen."

"I know, I know," Peggy snapped. She took the cup and went into the bathroom. She cried hard for a few seconds, then tried to regain her composure as she took the specimen back to the lab. "I'm sorry for being so short with you."

"That's O.K.," the tech interrupted empathetically. "Please sit here so I can draw the blood."

She sat in the chair with the padded arm rest and looked away while the tech said, "A little poke, now." A quick pricking sensation which she barely felt. Now she was becoming angry. He finished and directed her to the x-ray room. She had her chest x-rayed and returned to the exam room.

"No way," she said to herself. Tom actually did love her deeply, there's no way he would have screwed anyone, much less some woman who was dirty enough to have given him V.D.! It must be a mistake. She waited. She realized she was biting her nails. She hadn't done that in years.

Twenty minutes later Reed walked in with some slips of paper. "Well, you *do* have a resistant bladder infection, and by the tenderness in your back and your fever, I think it has involved your left kidney. You also have a lot of yeast in your urine. These findings could explain your tender belly and discharge. The gram stain isn't done yet, that'll be another few minutes. Something odd, here. Your white blood cell count is extremely low, and I would expect it to be elevated with what you have going on."

"So what does that mean?"

"It appears that your natural infection fighting system isn't working properly, and—" He was interrupted by a knock at the door. The tech handed in another slip and the x-ray film. He tried not to show his disappointment upon glancing at the paper. He hung the film on the lighted view box on the wall and pronounced, "Appears normal." He wheeled around. "Peggy, there's no easy way to tell you this. The preliminary gonorrhea test, the gram stain, is positive," holding the small slip. "There is a chance, though, that it's either another organism or just misread. It's happened before. But with the character of your vaginal discharge, I think we should treat you. I'll tell the lab to run a syphilis test, too, just to be safe."

She burst into tears, intermixed with feelings of rage, and didn't really hear the tail end of his sentence.

"I'll leave you for a few moments, then we'll talk about the therapy." He left the room and quietly closed the door. She was approaching an anxiety-induced panic state before she rationalized herself into straight thinking.

He came back in the room. "A little better, now?"

"I . . . I think so." She blotted her eyes with a tissue.

"O.K., some serious stuff to deal with here. Let's get a plan. First, here's a prescription for three and a half grams of ampicillin and a gram of probenecid. Take it all at once. And here is another prescription for a vaginal yeast medicine. Use it as directed on the instructions. Then I suggest that you talk with Tom candidly, and get *yourself* some counselling, regardless of whether he goes with you." He handed her a business card with the name of a clinical psychologist. "This guy's good, tell him I sent you. Item number three, I want you to call this immunology specialist, Dr. Fitzgerald, for a consultation dealing with your immune system. The women in the front office will give you a copy of your recent records for him to review." He handed her another card. "And finally, call back here in two days to find out the result of your gonorrhea culture, and the culture and sensitivity on your urine specimen. We may need to change some medicines. Do you have any questions?"

"No," she whimpered.

"I know you're very upset right now, so you may have a question later. Call me at any time."

"Th-Thank you for being honest."

"No problem. You call anytime." He reached out and laid a hand on her shoulder. "You're strong. You'll do all right."

• • •

"My name is Tom Pillen, and I had an appointment to see the nurse practitioner at 10:00."

"Yes, Mr. Pillen. Have you been seen here before?" the receptionist asked.

"No, first time. My wife told me I was supposed to come in."

"Oh, you must be Peggy's husband. She's such a dear." She handed him a clipboard with a form on it. "Please fill out the information and return it to me."

"Thank you." He took the form and sat down in one of the chairs in the lobby. *Thanks a bunch, lady. I already feel like shit, and then you have to tell me how wonderful Peggy is. The receptionist must know, yeah, that's it, and she's really rubbing it in. Try to keep cool, just keep cool.* He filled in the information, address, insurance, etcetera, and took it back to the receptionist with a scowl.

"Please be seated. The nurse will be with you shortly."

He sat down again and picked up an outdated magazine. Well, I guess it fits this place just fine. He replaced it on the table and sighed. What a jerk, what a *disgusting* jerk am I!

The nurse came through the door. "Mr. Pillen?"

"Yes, ma'am." He stood and followed her down the hallway and into the exam room.

"Please sit on the table while I get your blood pressure."

He sat as he watched her go through her routine, thinking that hers must be a boring job. She left the room, mumbling something about somebody coming in shortly or something. He glanced around and thought how old everything was in this place, and that god-awful odor. They should replace the musty furniture and carpeting, possibly the entire building.

The door opened, and in walked a man in a white lab coat. He was reviewing the chart, then looked up. "Mr. Pillen, I assume." He extended his hand. "I'm Doctor Bloom. Reed isn't in today, and anyway, I was interested in this case after he explained what's been going on. By the way, some bad news," he sighed. "Your wife's gonorrhea culture *was* positive, so she'll be getting a call from the health department to track possible contacts. That's a legal requirement."

"I'm her *only* contact," he replied adamantly. "So you know the story. My wife said I was to come in and get checked out. Sure raised hell in my little world. She hasn't talked to me since she was here two days ago. I think she might take the kids and leave, the way she's talking. I guess I can't blame her, doing what I've done."

"Want to talk about it?"

"What the hell, it's all out now! Keep this confidential?"

"Yes, it's legally privileged information, anything you tell me. It's also *unethical* to release information without your authorization."

"Well, O.K. Here goes. I'm bisexual. I don't think I knew it before I got married, but then over time curiosity got to me and I started staying out and picking up guys in bars and stuff. Then I liked it, and I started picking up guys on the street and away on business meetings and conventions. I just happened to be away for a weekend meeting about two weeks ago, and I picked up a teenaged boy, a hooker. We had sex, then I dumped him back downtown. Then I noticed a little burning with urination about five days ago, and then, this morning, I started having a discharge from my penis, just like when I had the clap when I was in the service. Too late, though, obviously. Peggy got it from me, I guess."

"Does she know you're sexual preference?"

"Are you kidding? No way! I'm Mr. Macho around my social circle."

"O.K. Well, all we can do now is treat the problem. Maybe you should get some counselling, too. Now, being a new patient, I need a little history. Any chronic medical problems, blood pressure, heart disease, diabetes, lung problems?"

"No. Healthy as a horse."

"Any medications you take daily, or any allergies to anything, particularly medicines?"

"No."

"Have you ever been hospitalized for anything, surgery, illness, or accidents?"

"No."

The doctor took notes as he spoke. "Fine. Are you possibly anemic or something? You look a little pallid."

"Not that I know of, but I haven't had much energy for a few months. Would that have anything to do with it?"

"Maybe, maybe not. Slip your shirt off and let me look you over." The doctor went through the routine exam, checking eyes, ears, heart and lungs, all the way to Tom's feet. "You've got a little supraclavicular lymphadenopathy."

"What's that?"

"Those swollen lymph nodes above your collar bones. How long have they been like that?"

"I don't know, a little sore for maybe a month."

"How about those purple spots on your legs and chest, how long have they been there?"

"About the same. I just thought they were bruises."

"I want you to see a dermatologist about them. I'm not sure what they are. Now, let's test you for gonorrhea." He took from his pocket a petri dish filled with a brownish culture medium. "Drop your drawers." He put on a rubber glove and grasped Tom's penis, then took a cotton swab with the other hand and inserted it into the meatus. "A little discomfort."

"*Yow*, that smarts!" Tom jerked away.

"Finished with that part." He rubbed the applicator swab on the culture plate. Now, take this slip and go to the lab down the hall, then come back here."

The doctor left and Tom adjusted his clothing. He went to the lab and had blood drawn and a urine specimen, then returned to his room. *I wonder if I'm really sick or something?*

Ten minutes passed, and the doctor returned. "Very curious. You have a lot of yeast in your urine, and that's uncommon for a man. Also those spots on your skin. Your white cell count is way down, too, which means you can't fight anything off properly. Your immune system is down."

"So what does all that mean?"

"I'm not sure right now. I'm going to treat your gonorrhea, and then I want you to see this dermatologist as quickly as possible about those spots." He handed Tom a business card with the name of the specialist. "When you call for the appointment, tell his receptionist I want you to be seen quickly, then to send me the consultation report. See me again a few days after you've seen him so we can go over this. I should have his report by then."

• • •

Tom was scared. The small exam room closed in on him. He couldn't catch his breath, and his heart was pounding. "Got to get out of here!" He opened the door and hurried down the hallway to the door marked EXIT, pushing it hard as he went through. The alarm horn blasted. Patients and employees appeared from everywhere to see what had happened. Tom stood, loosening his tie and shaking, trying to breathe. He had been a basket case since he'd seen the dermatologist and had the biopsy.

Dolores came outside. "Are you all right, Mr. Pillen?"

"I can't breathe, and I'm light headed, and my hands are numb," he panted. "I think I'm having a heart attack or something."

"I think you're hyperventilating. Come on back inside and I'll get the doctor to see you right away."

"O.K., thanks." He went inside and she closed the door behind them. The blasting alarm ceased abruptly, and the crisis atmosphere quickly subsided as everyone went about their business. She walked him back to his room, then brought in a paper bag.

"Lie on the table and rebreathe your old air in and out of this bag for awhile. That will correct your blood gas levels, and you should start feeling better. What you are having seems to be a panic attack. I'll leave the door open, you try to relax." She left him.

Dr. Bloom entered in a few seconds. "Feeling a little better?"

"Not much."

"Nurse, give Mr. Pillen fifty milligrams of hydroxyzine I.M., please," he called out the door. "Tom, I want the medicine to calm you a little before we talk. I'll be back in a little while." He turned and walked out, humming to himself. He caught himself and stopped. He always hummed when he was stressed.

How could anyone be so nonchalant when things were so serious, Tom wondered. He was breathing in and out of the paper bag, slowly feeling better, slowly regaining his composure.

Dolores came in with a syringe. "Just relax. I'll give you this in the arm." She helped him bare his shoulder, then darted the needle into his arm and injected the medicine. "There, you should start doing much better in a few minutes." She rubbed the site again with an alcohol wipe and pulled his shirt sleeve back down, then left.

It seemed like an eternity before the doctor returned. "Sorry, I had several patients, but I'm glad the medicine had time to work. Are you better now?"

Tom pulled the bag away from his face. "Yeah, I'm O.K. This surgery incision is awfully sore, though."

"Let me look at that." Dr. Bloom removed the sterile white gauze from Tom's left upper chest. "It looks like it's doing as expected, no infection. The stitches make things itch a little more. He took quite a chunk, huh?"

"Sure seemed like it to me. It was really gross, all that globby crap hanging on the skin he cut out. I wanted him to gas me, but he wouldn't. Said it wasn't necessary, so instead he injected novocaine or something."

"He was right. General anesthesia should be avoided unless it's needed. Too dangerous, actually. How's Peggy, are you patching things back together?"

"She's gone. Took the kids and went to her sister's house in Iowa. She said she could never forgive me again, and she didn't want the kids exposed to a homosexual father. You know, all the problems at school and everything if the other kids found out. Now all I do is sit around the house and drink scotch. I haven't been able to work . . ." He broke down and sobbed. "I just don't know what to do anymore. I wish I could end it all right now," he cried.

Doctor Bloom put a hand on his shoulder. "Tom, you need some psychological help, and right *now.* I want you to go straight to Heights Hospital and check in. I'll call ahead and make arrangements for you to see Dr. Ryker. He's a very fine psychiatrist. They may keep you for a few days, so take a toothbrush and some extra clothes and what have you."

"Yeah, I'm falling apart. D-D-Doc, what did the dermatologist say? Have you talked to him yet?

"Uh, no, er, it usually takes a few days," he lied.

• • •

Tom checked into the hospital and sat around for two hours before Doctor Ryker came by.

"Hello, I'm Dr. Ryker," he shook Tom's hand. "I talked at some length with Dr. Bloom about you. It seems you've had some real personal life crises the past few days." He sat in the visitor's chair and took out a note book. "I don't like to play games with people, so no bull, O.K.? I find a direct method gets direct results. Now, Dr. Bloom tells me you've holed up at home, and you're drinking heavily since this crisis started. Taking any pills, too?"

"Uh, yeah, I've been taking a few valiums and percodans that were lying around the house. They kind of take the edge off, you know?"

"Are you having any thoughts of suicide?"

"Well, kind of, once in a while. I mean, shit, what's left? I'm a goddamned faggot who screws young boys or anybody else. I've been hiding it for years, feeling like hell all the time. My therapist just tells me, 'feel it, come to terms with it, and accept it as the way you are.' He's a damned queer, too! Then I give my wife the goddamn clap, and my life *really* falls apart. Now I've got nothing, so why live this rotten existence, anyway?"

"Have you thought about how you might commit suicide . . .if you did it, that is?"

"Um, I thought about pills, but after reading about it, I decided a gun would be more certain . . . so nobody could find me unconscious and revive me. That would be even greater hell, to live through it and then have to face everything."

"Do you have any guns around?" Dr. Ryker had stopped writing and looked straight at Tom, observing for any body language that might suggest lying. Suicidal patients would lie and not think twice. After all, they would be gone soon, and so who cared about what others thought of their personal characters.

"Yes, a small pistol, I think it's a .32 caliber, that's been in the desk drawer for years. You know, for burglars or whatever. I've never even fired it before, and I don't know if the bullets in it are any good. Do you know if they go bad over time?"

"I'm picking up on the sense that you are asking me to indirectly condone your intent with that question. If I say no, they don't go bad, then you might think that I approve of your decision and chosen method. If I say yes, then you might feel that I am against you by showing indirect disapproval for your plan. That would interfere with our working relationship. I think it's best if you don't place me in a position to answer questions at this time."

"Whoa! Pretty heavy stuff, there, Doc. To me, that was a very simple question about bullets, and you turned it into all of *that.* Now I know why you guys make the big money. It's compound thinking. In college we called it psychobabble. It never led anywhere, except for maybe a few fights, and a state of profound confusion."

A slight laugh, "Well, call it what you will. I think that the only two fields of human study where we can bend the rules like this are psychology and philosophy, and, obviously, I'm in one of them. After interviewing people for fifteen years, one gets a feel for ulterior thinking. Professionally developed intuition, I suppose. Back to the focus of our meeting here. Point blank, I feel that you are a threat to yourself, and I'm recommending that you stay here for several days. I'll put you on some medication, and we'll do some therapy to get you over the hump with this depressive state. What you are experiencing is not abnormal; the sense of loss of your family and way of life. Very much like a grief reaction for a deceased loved one. On the other hand, what makes this an unusual problem are the circumstances. You've finally admitted your homosexuality to others, and most importantly, a complete confession to yourself. There is probably some good in that, somewhere. At least you can stop the chronic self-punishment through the guilt you've carried all these years. Now we must deal with the depressive impact of how this occurred, meaning giving your wife the gonorrhea that you picked up through homosexual behavior. We'll start on that tomorrow."

"How long will I be here? You keep saying, quote, 'a few days.' I have things to do. If I don't stop drinking and get back to work, I'm out. Mortgage V.P.'s aren't that hard to come by, you know."

"Honestly, it depends on how well you come around. I'm pleased to hear that you are thinking about your future needs, however. A good sign. I need to tell you, by reason of the 'patients' bill of rights' that this hospital adheres to, that you may sign yourself out at any time. I would prefer to put you on a three day legal hold, but you don't fit all of the strict criterion."

"After this little session, I think I would *like* to stay. I feel safe here, at least for now. Kind of isolated from the world."

"Good, you're being rational. I'll see you in the morning." Dr. Ryker started to leave.

"Oh, Doc, by the way—"

He turned from the doorway. "Yes?"

"You're being honest with me, and I need that to validate my judgments. I felt Dr. Bloom wasn't levelling with me. Tell me, honestly, do you know the result of the biopsy from my shoulder?"

The doctor looked uncertainly at him for a moment, then returned to the chair he had been seated in. He sighed. "It's not good news. I had hoped you wouldn't ask until you were more settled, but in order to maintain your confidence in me, I think we'd better discuss it." He sighed again. "You have what is known as Kaposi's sarcoma, a rare and serious cancer of the body's connective tissue."

Tom was stunned, his face paled. "Am I going to die?"

"If you agree to chemotherapy treatment, no one knows. Your life can be prolonged, at any rate, for an undetermined amount of time, possibly years."

"Wh-what causes it, how did I get it, where?" He sat motionless, a blank rigid stare at the window. Not through it, but at it, as if reality ended at the invisible barrier of glass.

"Well, Tom, like I said, it's a very rare form of cancer, and for some reason, it's being seen more and more in homosexuals. You are only the fifth person diagnosed in this city with the disease. I was going to wait until our talk in the morning, but I guess now is appropriate. There are some doctors from the National Institutes of Health and the CDC that are tracking it, trying to get a fix on it. They'll be here late tomorrow morning. For now I'll order some tranquilizers, and a sleeping pill for later tonight. Perhaps you'll feel a little better in the morning. Is there anything else I can do right now?"

"No, absolutely nothing," Tom said flatly, still blankly staring at the pane of glass. He had not altered his position during the entire session, legs drawn, and squatting on the bed.

"I'll see you tomorrow, then." Doctor Ryker stood and walked out.

"Nurse, would you give Mr. Pillen two milligrams of haloperidol I.M., please?" Doctor Ryker asked as he stood at the nurse's station, writing admitting notes. "Make it every six hours as needed for agitation. I don't think he'll act out physically, but he impresses me as one bearing watching, and I'd like to settle him down a little. I also want him to get flurazepam, thirty milligrams by mouth, at bedtime so he'll sleep. I hope he doesn't go catatonic on us. Oh, he's on suicide precautions with fifteen minute checks. See you in the morning." He closed the chart and laid it on the counter, then walked down the hall.

"Good afternoon, Doctor," the nurse called out as he left.

"God, that burns!" Tom exclaimed as the nurse injected the tranquilizer into his buttock.

"Yes, I'm afraid that's expected with this medicine, but it will fade in a minute or so," the nurse said, wiping the injection area after withdrawing the needle. "I'm glad to see you are responding, anyway. A while ago you were so withdrawn."

Tom avoided eye contact. "I've been having a few problems here the past couple of days. Nothing I can't take care of."

"Want to talk?"

"No, not really, no big deal, and it's none of your business. Thanks for the shot, I guess," he snapped. He had had enough psychology to know when he was being manipulated into involuntary soul searching. "Forget the dinner part, O.K.? I can smell the food from the hallway. Just leave me alone. I want to be alone."

"If that's what you want, but I must tell you we'll be watching you closely, on physician's orders, over the next day or two."

"No sweat. Now, if you don't mind, please leave." He returned to his upright squatting position, staring at the window.

• • •

The day nurse was wrapping the blood pressure cuff around his arm when he awoke the next morning.

"Good morning, Mr. Pillen," she chirped pleasantly. "I'm Shirley, and I'm going to see to your therapeutic plan as your primary nurse. You'll need to get up soon so you can clean up and eat breakfast. The doctors from the CDC will be here soon to interview you."

"Knock off all that happy shit, O.K.? Get real! I'm lying here rotting because I'm a goddamn faggot, and you act cute!" He grabbed the water pitcher off the table and threw it at the door. "Screw you and everybody else in this place, too. I don't need this shit!" He broke down and sobbed again.

Shirley retreated from the room quickly, then returned long enough to give him an injection. He quieted down after twenty minutes, staring at the window again. He caught his reflection in the mirror in his peripheral vision, then looked at himself straight on.

"You garbage," he mumbled. He looked like hell, like one of those schizophrenic street bums he had seen hanging around the bus station downtown. He hadn't shaved in several days, and his hair was matted and dirty. He had black circles under his eyes. "You even *look* like garbage!"

The nurse returned a while later, accompanied by two men in casual clothing. One was opening his brief case on the bedside table as she spoke. "Mr. Pillen, these are the doctors from the CDC. They need to talk to you, as you already know." She then turned and left.

"Hello, I'm Dr. Fellows, and this is Dr. Schuster," the taller lanky one said. "You know why we're here. You have contracted a rare cancer which has been spontaneously appearing in homosexuals for about four years, and the situation is worsening. We are trying to establish any common denominators that may give us clues to its origin, and your help is crucial to our investigation. You have the disease, and there's not much to do but treat you with the standard forms of cancer therapy. Perhaps, though, through this investigation, we can stop the trend and hopefully discover a treatment before it gets too widespread. For these reasons, your candor would be appreciated."

Tom gawked at them. *These guys are heavy!*

They sat in the visitor's chairs, and Schuster pulled some forms from his briefcase. He took the cap off his pen and began. "Hrumph," clearing his throat very officiously. "First we need demographics. Please answer all questions, as mundane as they seem, thoroughly." He started down the list with name, age, address, occupation, marital status, and so forth. Then he pursued the avenues of genealogy and family medical history, personal medical history, foreign travel, health care preferences, an extensive social and mental health history, dietary habits, and physical activities, including hobbies and other interests.

During the ensuing hour and a half long battery, Tom became increasingly fatigued, but responded appropriately. Then the weighty questions began.

"Now, I want you to think back to your earliest sexual experiences and run through your history on a chronologic basis, as accurately as possible."

"Jesus, leave me alone! Can't a guy die in peace? This is bullshit." He glared from one to the other.

They glanced at each other and nodded. "We think it's best if we give you a little break. It seems you are tired. We'll come back this afternoon. In the meantime, eat a little something and get some sleep, then try to reconstruct your sexual history mentally, so you're prepared."

"You never stop! Get the hell out of here!" He picked up the water pitcher again and threw it at them. It ricocheted off the wall and splashed on Dr. Fellows.

Schuster slammed his briefcase lid, with the files still protruding, and they quickly retreated to the hallway.

Shirley returned with another injection. Tom knew he needed it and took it passively. Besides, it took the rough edges of the torment away.

Lunch trays came and went, with Tom declining again. He continued in his drawn position, staring at the window, now rocking on his buttocks and mumbling nonsensically.

"Mr. Pillen, we're back," said Dr. Fellows. "I hope you have rested over the past few hours. We'll try to make this session as short as possible, but we must have thorough information. Let's get started. About your sexual history. Have you reconstructed it mentally?"

"Yes . . . yes, *yes!*" he paused. "Get it over with! O.K.! When I was seven, er, how far back do you want?"

"At what you consider your first sexual encounter, not necessarily intercourse."

A long sigh, "O.K., at age seven I played around with a neighborhood girl who was about my age. No big deal, just experimenting. We would go into an old empty house and touch each other and look. My friends all asked me what it was like; the ten or twelve year olds, that is. It was no big deal. I wasn't interested.

"As I got older, maybe thirteen or so, I noticed all the guys were crazy about pictures of naked girls. They were driven to necking and petting and talking about it in school. I wondered what the big excitement was, but to be part of the crowd, I pretended the same. I wondered if they were pretending, too. I actually liked it much better when we boys got together and looked at each other and played with each other. There was a group of about, I dunno, six or so. We hung around together.

"Getting into high school, all the guys in the class were dating and necking, parking at lover's lane to see how far they could get with the girls. Some actually got laid in the tenth grade, at least they claimed. My group still hung around together, not interested in girls. When we were seniors in high school, my gang knew what intercourse was, but we liked each other more than chasing after girls.

"One night we got drunk at a lake, I remember, in the spring. We thought that if everybody else could screw, why couldn't we? The drinking and talk became heavier, and pretty soon we were necking and feeling each other, then we had an out-and-out orgy. Boy, did I feel like shit the next day. I wanted to tell someone, but I couldn't. It was one of the most emotionally draining times in my life, purporting that I liked girls when I really liked boys . . . men. Since then I've had many encounters with male lovers, and women too, but I preferred the men. I think I became bisexual, instead of straight homosexual, as a smoke screen. That is, if I could be straight queer and fully accepted and guilt free, I would be straight queer. But for the sake of maintaining a guise of normalcy, I needed women too . . .to secrete my preference for male lovers.

"I got married on that pretense, attempting a facade of normalcy. Don't get me wrong. Peggy's a wonderful woman and a good mother, but she doesn't satisfy me sexually. So I have sought out that satisfaction outside my known social world by hiring street hookers, and going to gay bars and bath houses, and that sort of thing. I've had, I don't know, maybe two hundred men over the years. Once I confessed to Peggy that I was having an affair with a woman, but it was really a man. Then, recently, I picked up a street hooker and he gave me the clap. Peggy got it too, from me, and when I went to see the nurse practitioner they picked up this cancer. Any more questions?"

"It must be hell, living a dual existence like that, always guilt ridden," Schuster sympathized. "Well, now then, we need names of all the homosexual contacts you have had, and in what city, at least those that can be recollected. Then we'll leave you alone. Try to affix a time frame too, please."

"This will be it, then, huh? You'll *really* leave me alone?"

"Yes," said Schuster sincerely.

"O.K. The last four or five, I don't know, local street queers for twenty bucks. Before that, I can't give you names, man! Jesus, I'd be ruined if anyone found out! Several are very respectable men, with families!"

"Confidentiality and discretion are absolutely the best tools we have in this investigation, so we're not dumb enough to blow it and cause mistrust wherever we go. Rest assured, *no one* will ever know we spoke with you."

Tom stared hard at Fellows, then Schuster, who was nodding in agreement. "No one, huh?"

"I give you my solemn word."

"What the shit, I'm a dead man anyway. Before the street queers there was Charles Blake, the east side city councilman. His wife doesn't know he's bisexual either. Also in the past couple of years there has been, on repeated occasions, flings with Dave Allison from Hartford, Connecticut, Steve DeBoer from New York, Nathan Murphy from here, Brandon Waller, the president of First International in Miami, and two of his friends that were with us at a convention last year, George Faye from Dallas..."

"George Faye, the CEO of Dallas Aeronautics?" Fellows asked.

"Yeah, he and I met in Kansas City for a real estate development proposal several months ago. Oh, yeah, and we picked up some young guys around the Plaza and took them back to our hotel."

"Go on." The doctor's amazement showed.

"Fred Ringold from L.A., George Williams from Toronto, Canada, Marvin Morris—"

"Wait a minute. George Williams, an airline attendant?"

"Yes, he's probably my favorite of all. I used to see him fairly often when he flew through, and sometimes we would spend the weekend together when my wife was away".

The doctors looked at each other, then looked again at Tom. That name caught something, Tom noted.

"Still see him?"

"No, he called a while ago and said he was ill so he wasn't going to be flying as much. Why?"

"Oh, just asking," Schuster said. "Tell me, out of curiosity, do you think that all gays lead such active sex lives as you?" He hoped to throw the focus from Mr. Williams.

Tom wasn't thrown. "Sure, I guess, a lot of them do. It's kind of exciting, actually, to go different places and meet different people. Now, it's my turn to ask a question. What about George Williams?"

"Well, we've interviewed him in the past. Let's leave it at that."

"Really . . . Does he have this crap, too, being sick and everything? I don't even really understand what it is I have."

"What you have is one of two diseases that are rare in humans. Yours being Kaposi's sarcoma, the other being a pneumonia called pneumocystis carinii, caused by a one-celled organism that a healthy body fights off quite readily. Both diseases are appearing in the gay community at an alarming rate, with no explanation. They both seem to be resulting from the body's immune system dysfunctioning. We have tentatively called the complex of both illnesses Gay Related Immune Deficiency, or GRID, for short."

"So you think I might have caught this from George, that's what you're thinking?"

"We can't legally or ethically divulge his medical condition. We must offer him the same confidentiality that we are giving you."

"Oh, uh-huh, I see. I'm really tired again, and I'm getting pissed off at your condescending crap. I want to sleep. Come back later."

"That would be impossible. We have to catch a plane in two hours."

"Tough." Tom looked toward the window again and ignored their further grilling.

The men walked out, tired and frustrated. They stood in front of the elevator. "Boy, those boys *really* get around!"

"Now, now . . . But yes, it seems so. I hope we get a handle on this one, and soon. Mr. George Williams is frightening me. I mean, that *one* guy has spread himself all over the world. His name came up in three out of seven interviews in Paris. The other one, uh . . . Pfizer, the international jeweler, that has come up. It's interesting that the same handful of names tend to recur."

The elevator bell dinged and the door opened. They boarded and pressed the first floor button, still talking as the doors closed.

• • •

Tom was enraged at first, then started to sob. The nurse and an orderly came in and told him they were instructed to give him four milligrams of Haldol this time. "Stay away from me!" Tom threatened.

The nurse immediately left, and came back with yet another orderly, a big man. They told Tom they were going to give him the injection and to settle down.

"Bullshit! I know my rights; the goddamned shrink told me I could check out, and that's what I'm doing, *now!*" He flung the closet door open and grabbed his things, throwing them into the small flight bag he had brought. The nurse and orderlies watched helplessly as he stomped down the hall and exited through the fire escape doorway.

"Call the police and Dr. Ryker. He's dangerous. See if we can get a hold order," the nurse instructed. The orderly ran for the desk.

Moments later Tom stood in front of the hospital watching for a cab. "Damn, don't they ever drive by here?" He paced nervously back and forth, wringing his hands, watching. A cab appeared down the block headed his direction. He stood in its pathway with his arms extended, forcing the cabby to screech to a halt.

"Hey, you, get out of the way! You crazy or somethin'?" The cabby bent his head out the window, snarling viciously.

"Yeah, and I need a *cab.*" He walked around the side and jerked the door open. "Excuse me, but I need this cab worse than you do," he said as he took the startled woman's hand and pulled her from the back seat. He slid in and shut the door. "Now, you will take me to 12122 Grange Avenue, got it?"

"Sh-sure, buddy, sure. Now you just relax a little, O.K.?" He tromped it, noticing the police car pulling up to the curb in the rear view mirror where he had just lost his fare.

The cabby pulled into the driveway, and Tom threw a twenty at him. "Here, this should do it." He got out and slammed the door behind him without looking back. "Keys, keys," fumbling in his pocket. "Shit, gone." He rounded the house and broke the glass pane in the patio door, then reached in and released the lock.

Once inside, he headed straight for the liquor cabinet. He retrieved a bottle of scotch and poured a large glassful, then tipped his head back and downed it. "There, to hell with everything!" He went into his wife's bathroom at the top of the stairs and frantically searched for the valium bottle. "Where is it, come on, where is it!" He pulled the drawers from the vanity, dumping the contents on the counter top. He dug through the pill bottles until he found the one labeled 'Valium 10 mgs.' He took two, thinking about what he had to do.

It was five-thirty by the clock radio next to the bed. He opened the dresser drawer and pulled out the locked box, then turned the rotating combination lock to 0-0-0-1 and opened the lid, dumping the stock certificates and insurance papers on the bed. He found the small address book at the bottom of the pile. Running his finger down the list of names, he found what he needed. He went to the bedside table and picked up the phone, dialed the long distance number, and waited while it rang several times.

"Hello, Maxwell and Williams residence," the man answered.

"Yeah, yeah, is Georgey-boy there? This is his old pal, Tom Pillen, calling from Chicago."

"Oh, yes, Tom, George has spoken of you. This is Corey Maxwell, his room mate. George isn't in right now, but he should be home in a couple of hours. Can I take a message?"

"Yeah, tell him to call me as soon as he gets there. It's urgent. He has my number."

"Will do, sir, and, by the way, if you're ever in Toronto, please call. Maybe we could get together for a drink or something."

"Uhhh, I don't think that will be possible, but maybe I'll see you in hell, faggot." Click. Tom fell to the bed and passed out.

The ringing phone startled him and he slowly crawled over to the table. The clock said 7:43 p.m. "Hello."

"Tom, this is George returning your call. What's up?"

"Are you sick, George, I mean *really* sick?"

"Well, uh, yes, they tell me I am, why?

"Do you have spots?"

"What do you mean? Why are you so upset?"

"Spots! Do you have spots?"

"Some kind of rash, yes."

"And you knew you were sick when we met in the airport hotel in Chicago that time you flew through in the afternoon, when I said you didn't look good? And then all the times since?"

"Something was wrong, yeah. Why all the intensity?"

Tom was digging through the bedside table as he spoke, and found what he needed. "So then you gave me the gay cancer and you probably knew it?"

"No, no, I didn't know it at the time, no. I'd never—"

"Bullshit, you bastard! Listen closely and live with it." He put the revolver to his temple.

George heard a sharp report, a moan, and the phone fell against something hard. "Shit— *TOM, TOM, TOM, COME ON TOM, ANSWER ME!"*

1983

NEW YORK CITY, JULY

"I-it's s-o-o c-cold!" He shivered, his teeth chattered. His skin was blue, ashen. Frost covered the windows, icicles hung just outside. "T-turn up the heat and bring more blankets!" He hadn't been this cold since he had been stranded on a stalled chairlift when he was fifteen. The wind chill factor was minus thirty-seven degrees that blustery mid-January day. It took four hours for the ski patrolmen to get everyone off the malfunctioning lift by using ice covered ropes. He suffered severe hypothermia, and was hospitalized for three days for re-warming by warmed I.V. fluids and a special thermal blanket. Another twenty minutes of that temperature and he would have been dead, like the man two chairs behind him had died.

Now he was on the chairlift all over again. He could see the snow falling, feel his hands and feet numbing, the tips of his nose and ears burning sharply in the freezing temperature. His frozen breath hung in the air in front of his face. Sitting, waiting. He could hear the muffled sounds of the snowmobiles below and behind and the hollering of the rescue crew, helping people into sleds for the ride down to the waiting ambulances. "Take me next, *please!*" he hollered.

"George, George!" He heard from somewhere in the distance. "It's O.K. You're all right." It was Corey's voice.

"H-how did you get here, Corey?"

He felt a warm hand stroke his face, a *burning* hand in contrast with the frigid, cold winds. He drifted in and out of the freezing temperatures, finally realizing that he was inside, smothered in blankets. Was he really inside or still in the chairlift, only *dreaming* that he was inside, out of hopeful desperation for warmth? Frost and icicles on the window again. He must be inside! He had been saved! Again he felt the burning, soothing stroke across his face.

He opened his eyes and looked up. "Mom, where did you come from? Where are we? Is it you?"

"Yes, George, it's me." She tried to smile, but couldn't. It was not a happy time, but a time of dread, of sorrow. It wasn't unexpected, but that made it a time no less difficult to bear. "You're in the hospital, sonny, and Corey and I are here." Mary Williams had known about her son's homosexuality since he was twenty years old. She'd known that there was something different about him well before that. He was a loner; only an occasional friend came and went from his closed little world. Girls, nice girls, beautiful girls, would call frequently, but he showed no interest. Then at age nineteen he suddenly became very sociable, he blossomed. He had many friends with whom he spent time away from home. But there were never any women, only handsome young men in his circle. Her suspicions were confirmed when she took him aside one evening and confronted him with it

"Yes, Mom, I'm gay.""

It had broken her heart to hear it, but she'd known that there would be no other answer. She cried now as she thought that, again, she was in the same position. There was no other answer.

The hospital had called early that morning and told her that her son, the son she loved without question, probably would not make it through the day. He had been in and out of hospitals for the past year. Pneumonias, skin infections from minor cuts and abrasions, urinary infections, strep throats. Every slight little infection, which in a normally healthy person would have been treated with a few days of antibiotic pills at home, knocked George to the ground. She had been called on two previous occasions, when he was hospitalized, just to be prepared in the event she would need to come quickly. This call was for real; she was here.

It was a terrible, shattering disease. Maybe it would have been better if it were a *quick* killer; not this long roller coaster ride of ups and downs, emotional drains, constant worry. Maybe . . . maybe it was good that it would finally end, releasing her from this never ending strife. No, no! Don't think that! It's repulsive to even *dare* to harbor that thought! She broke down and cried, hoping God would forgive her selfishness and self-pity, and then she prayed for George.

Whatever he's done, God, he's a good boy, he was just lost in this warped, unstable world. Please take him to you.

She wept. Corey stepped forward and put his arm around her, and she cried on his shoulder. She could not bear to let thoughts of what she'd read in the newspapers enter her mind. Some twisted religious fundamentalists had been publicly preaching that this disease, this terrible disease, was the work of God, His way of condemning and ridding the earth of the satanical manifestation of homosexualism. God, all merciful God, would not allow such suffering!

"What are you doing here?" George's eyes had regained some of their sparkle, losing the dull look that accompanied his intermittent bouts of delirium.

"I'm here to be with you, George," Corey said. "And your mother is here, too. She flew down from Toronto."

"Oh, so . . . maybe it's time . . . I think it is. Maybe it will be peaceful . . . I hope so." His eyes dulled again.

"How is he doing?" Dr. Gregg asked the nurse in the hallway.

"Not well. His pressure is down to seventy over twenty-eight and his pulse is in the hundred and twenty range. His respiratory rate is down to six per minute when he's quiet, and he's doing some Cheyne-Stoking. His mother and friend are in there with him."

"Good, he won't have to go alone. Oh, just so you know m feelings, as much as is humanly possible, I try to see that my dying patients are not alone. I have this thing about people dying alone, even if they're comatose. Please, if nothing else, if you can ever sense that one of my patients is going soon, stay with him and at least hold his hand; especially now that I have all these GRID patients coming here. Their families and friends have abandoned them."

"Yes Doctor. I'll get the word to the rest of the staff, too. We'll make do, even if we're one short on staffing for a little while."

"I'm especially involved with George, here. You know he has the dubious honor of being dubbed 'patient zero' by the CDC? As far as they can tell, he fairly single handedly started this whole nation wide epidemic. His name was at the bottom of every tracking list they did. He either slept with the other victims, or slept with one of *their* other lovers, indirectly transmitting the disease to all of them. An interesting legacy for a dying man. Anyway, I'm not going to interrupt them. Keep me posted and I'll sign the death certificate." She walked on down the hall.

"Oh, look at all the beautiful flowers!" George cast his now sharpened eyes around the room again. There was only one floral arrangement this time, and the flowers had wilted during the past week that George had been here. The rooms full of flowers had begun dissipating with earlier hospitalizations. His friends and lovers had become weary of sending flowers every time he, or another friend of theirs with the same illness, was hospitalized with different infections. Only one small arrangement of blue carnations, from ever faithful Corey, sat on the bedside table, slowly dying along with George. It had struck everyone odd that the potted flowers had wilted, despite the best of care, along with George's deteriorating condition.

He started hallucinating again, blubbering incoherently about the freezing cold. He shivered and his teeth chattered. It was, in fact, mid July, with an early afternoon temperature of ninety-two degrees. "C-C-Cold!"

George's eyes again went dull, blankly staring through the window. "Look, a white dove!" A pigeon sat just outside on the window sill preening itself. "God, if you are there, please don't leave me." And then an intense, ever warming pleasant glow started in his legs, then consumed his body in a strong, rippling wave. His body lay still, eyes openly fixed on the 'dove'.

"I think he's gone, Mrs. Williams," Corey said.

Mary sobbed and laid over his body. "My boy . . . my boy . . . my boy . . . "

Corey stroked George's cool hand. "Good by, my good friend . . . "

Part Three
The
Avarice

1984

VATICAN, SEPTEMBER

Dining al fresco in the crisp autumn air was always enjoyable for Monsignor O'Casey, so he chose D'Alesandro's, on Via Angelo Emo, two blocks north of the Vatican City. The patio, with its customary red-and-white checked table cloths and Cinzano umbrellas, was typically Italian, and one could order to his taste from a widely diverse menu.

"A most enjoyable lunch," Dr. Thomas said, his hands emphatically patting his belly. "Monsignor, I must applaud your choice of restaurants. Not often can a group of four, with such diverse tastes in dining, no less, each have his personal craving satisfied as we've just done in this single establishment."

Brian, in fact, hadn't eaten anything but a light dinner salad. His appetite had been nonexistent for several months. "I'm glad you enjoyed it," he said, feigning a smile. He was concerned that he was losing too much weight. He had once prided himself on his robust good looks, physical conditioning, and healthy mental state.

Dr. Bjorgstad nodded in agreement, while Cardinal Wentworth maintained his non-involvement in such a trivial matter as lauding a silly lunch. The world was fraught with much more significant issues that needed attention. He finished before the rest, and his only concern was to get on with the purpose of the gathering. "Are we finished, then, gentlemen?" He looked at the check and cast a wad of bills on the table. "Shall we take a walk down near the river?"

It had been a year since the conspirators had last met. This luncheon meeting had been arranged to discuss the progress of the mission. Brian had suggested that they not discuss business until they had finished their meal, then they could walk down by the river to insure privacy. For him personally, this arrangement would assist his already troubled digestion before the anticipated heated disagreement commenced.

Brian had been taking increasing amounts of antacids since this project began. He noticed an even more significant increase when he'd recently learned that health researchers had discovered that the virus was spreading via blood transmissions, and now threatened the general population. And, worse yet, it was a confirmed *killer.* Of the known count of afflicted, about half were dead.

Careful to wait until they were out of earshot of other diners, Dr. Bjorgstad opened the conversation. "So, how many are dead now . . . of the seven we implanted?"

"Uh, let's see," Dr. Thomas answered as he packed his bulldog pipe with cheap, foul-smelling tobacco. It reminded Brian of burning wet leaves. "I think four of them . . . Stefan Cristobal, the film maker; Artie Verheyen, the Dutch socialite, Clancy Pfizer, the jet setter, and George Williams, the flight attendant."

They were so *cavalier* in their attitudes, Brian thought. How had he become involved with these weird men? As he glanced around, they were *all,* with the exception of Dr. Thomas, physically and mentally ugly. Hans was a skinny little man with crooked teeth and a high-pitched, scratchy voice. And his *clothes!* He always wore mismatched plaid pants and shirts in wild colors and rumpled, patterned coats. He had a way of twitching his long, skinny nose, reminding Brian of the rats in his high school biology lab. It was a surprise to Brian when he'd seen a picture of Hans's wife and kids. All of them appeared normal. His wife was even somewhat attractive.

The cardinal still had his tic, his goiter had become more

prominent over the years, and he'd developed red, ruddy splotches on his cheeks from the booze. In strange contrast to this odd group, Dr. Thomas was always confident, assured, and seemingly normal in his mentation. He was conscientious in his dress, always classy, and a noticeably handsome man for his age. The awful tobacco he had chosen was his only downfall.

Brian listened inattentively to the men's conversation, thinking to himself while they walked. *What would be the final death toll from this horrible disease he had been accessory to, one hundred percent?*

It made him physically and mentally ill, and his health continued to deteriorate in a downward spiral. He'd been hospitalized twice with bleeding ulcers and chest pain, each diagnosed as stress related. The doctors had told him he needed some rest. They treated the ulcers with acid blockers, and put him on tranquilizers. He was told to seek stress reduction psychotherapy to stop this downward spiral. He must identify his personal life stressors and deal with them, soon, he was repeatedly told, or his health could be in serious jeopardy.

He'd been relieved of his duties as pronuncio, a blessing, he later conceded.

The other men made light chatter about the autumn weather, and when the foliage color changes would occur this year, as they walked down the street toward the bank of the Tiber.

"This looks like a good place to talk." Noah pointed off the walk into a small clearing. They entered, away from the street noise, and sat on fallen trees.

Brian was nervous, occasionally leaning against a standing tree, then pacing in circles. He heaved a sigh, "Well, so what's new? Do you men know anything other than what's been in the news recently?"

"I believe the premise of that question, if I may, is that you feel we've created a new plague upon mankind that has escaped our projections," Dr. Bjorgstad responded.

"Don't put words in my mouth, and don't be so defensive, Doctor," Brian snapped. He would have preferred someone other than this meek little wimp to answer his question.

Bjorgstad turned to him. "You have been *extremely* agitated over the new developments, Monsignor. We're all aware of that." He twitched his nose again, forcing Brian to look away.

Cardinal Wentworth added, "Brian, we . . . that is, the three of us, have had two conference calls since we last met a year ago. We intentionally didn't include you because we didn't feel that you were thinking clearly about these developments, and therefore you couldn't make valid, objective decisions as to how to proceed. You have been, self-admittedly, confused and depressed. You have become much too emotionally distraught over these unpredicted circumstances. Knowing this, we felt it would be better if we kept the decision making amongst the three of us."

"So, I've not been consulted for my opinion on any of this for the entire past year, and when I've been refused my repeated requests for meetings, it was because you'd already talked among yourselves and determined the course of action? Like when I wanted to discuss the discovery of the blood transmission route and its ramifications?" Brian was livid.

"Monsignor, please try to get hold of yourself," Doctor Thomas retorted. "It couldn't be helped. In *none* of our computer analyses and animal testing did we encounter the virus's mutation like this. We have two theories. The first is that there is a certain protein combination in the human that isn't present in the monkeys we studied and tested, and this protein has led to the mutation of the virus, allowing the blood transmission route—"

"And what's the *other* theory?" Brian asked.

"The other theory is that someone has discovered the virus, and has *intentionally* mutated it. Far be it from me to know who, or why, but it's extremely unlikely that the virus could mutate so drastically in this short a time period without assistance. Anyway, we didn't consult you because we must regard you with some skepticism, if you want the straight truth. You fail to see the scientific reasoning we all endorse, and must be treated like a child."

Brian turned to him. "Doctor, your condescension has no place here. And please, don't hand me any more of that 'theory' crap. I've had it with *'theories.'* Your scientific method has been eighty percent dead wrong thus far. The only theory that has become a reality is the virus's passage through the lining of the colon. Yes, that worked well, infecting the homosexuals as planned. But now—here and now—how do we so easily explain away the transmission into the non-homosexual drug abuser? How do *we* rationalize that issue to our consciences in order to carry on this 'mission of God?' Don't you think that God wouldn't have let this project go so far awry? If, indeed, *He* were responsible for it, through us as the chosen ones, to carry it forth? Or, are we, as a group, or perhaps *singly,*" he added, looking straight at Wentworth, "the lost ones, pursuing our own misguided desires to rid mankind of homosexualism, based on our own bigotry?" Brian's face was bluish from the rapid speech.

The cardinal, who had been watching a squirrel dart around the underbrush, spoke. "Monsignor, this conversation is very tiring. We, in our phone calls, that is, already considered these questions, and came to the realization that possibly God had *indeed* intervened, deciding to remove yet another scourge from this planet, that of drug abuse. It's apparent to the three of us, and I think you'll have to concur, that drug abuse yields the entire spectrum of crimes against mankind. The drug abuser, like the homosexual, is foreign to God's plan. The whole issue of drug use yields further spiritual regression. Drug abuse involves the user directly, and the victims of his crimes indirectly, in its ugly degeneration of the soul. God's greatest creation, *man,* created in the likeness of Himself, must be returned to its original holy state."

"My, how Utopian! That ideology certainly has a pleasant aroma, when compared to its *opposing* viewpoint," Brian said sharply.

The doctors gawked in dismay. "Monsignor, I think that remark is emotionally vulgar and has no place in this discussion!" Dr. Bjorgstad responded.

Brian relented. "Er, yes . . . I'm sorry," he paused. "I'm obviously very frustrated. But there is *another* untoward effect of our toying with nature. How do you, I mean *we,* accept the introduction of the virus into hemophiliac children and God fearing people ,via life-saving blood transfusions? Supposedly, people who have had transfusions as long as *four years ago* may have been infected!"

"May I?" As the cardinal spoke, the doctors remained silent, both uneasy with this further prodding. "Monsignor, that's another issue we've already discussed. We needed to consider an historical perspective to yield this resulting philosophy. From Biblical prophecy we have accepted that God has punished humans with floods, famines, and disease. In most cases, the mere scope of the particular catastrophic event inadvertently involved and afflicted innocent people. Analogous to this, in our present world, are the children born to drug addicts. Innocent children are born, unwanted, and addicted to heroine and cocaine. After discussing the unintended involvement of innocents, we each tried to justify the occurrence of the virus in the innocents. We concluded, based on these historical precedents, that we have to accept this phenomena as God's will."

"*What?* I'm sorry, gentlemen, but I can't accept this trash. If I were to accept your rationalizing, I would no doubt lose my faith in God. If I were to lose my faith in God I would be nothing . . . *Nothing!* I want to stop this warped self righteousness immediately, then confess our involvement in this horrid scourge to both God and humanity." Brian wrung his hands and paced as he talked. "Then we'll have to deal with the consequences, no matter how severe, as best we can. Is the vaccine still available, to at least spare those who haven't yet contracted the disease? Or has *that* been misrepresented to me as well? Does a vaccine really even exist?"

"Yes, there is a vaccine!" Bjorgstad answered, shuffling his foot in the dirt. "But it's effective against the virus we *originally* engineered. You are aware that the virus is not behaving in the manner we theorized."

"Meaning?"

"Meaning that the virus has mutated several times, and the vaccine may not have the preventive effects it had against the original form."

"But that's all we can offer, right?" Brian looked at Hans squarely, as if to prevent any more possible double talk.

"Uh, yes, right now. But we could do further research, and test its efficacy, by using blood samples from people recently infected. I think that if we are going to consider admitting what we have done, we'd better have the appropriate vaccine available."

"I think you're suggesting a ploy to buy time, hoping to spare yourself," Brian snapped.

The cardinal stepped in. "Brian! How dare you insult this man's moral integrity! I think, Monsignor, that we're obliged to test the vaccine. Now *you*, in essence, are proposing your *own* theory, and hoping prematurely that the vaccine will be effective. What, for example, would happen if the vaccine had an opposite effect, and caused the virus to further mutate? We need further study on the vaccine's effects on the current mutated virus."

"Yes, yes, all right. But we must put a time limit on the research. If the agreed upon time limit is surpassed, without satisfactory results, we'll have to act immediately to expose ourselves. Possibly we could turn it over to the world science community and let them deal with it. Is six months sufficient?"

The doctors looked at each other. "Six months is unreasonable to evaluate long-term effects," Thomas said. "And besides, the disease has actually been slowing in numbers of new cases this past month. Possibly we've reached the peak of the natural occurrence curve, as *all* diseases do in time. Maybe this discussion is all for naught, and we've been blinded to our own success in the original goal. As a side note, have any of you seen in the news where prominent television evangelists are continuing to call this a plague upon homosexuals and drug abusers from God? At least *that* aspect of the plan has been realized. And I, Monsignor, still share the belief with the cardinal and Dr. Bjorgstad," motioning their direction, "that we *were* chosen by God for this mission. It all fell together too smoothly for there to be any other explanation."

Brian realized he was hopeless in this argument. "O.K., O.K... Let's put all of this philosophizing to rest. I think, then, that if in one year's time we're still groveling for answers, we should meet again, with the intent of exposing ourselves, and deal with the consequences. I need to leave now . . . I must go to prayer to seek consolation from God. This experience has been much too trying, and I fear it's not over yet. I'm going back to Chicago to visit my family for a month or so, to think." Brian left the clearing and walked briskly back toward the Vatican.

"Perhaps he is misguided," the cardinal sighed. "I sometimes wonder if he's our weak link, sent by God to test our strength in this task. Let's hope that through his prayer and meditation, God will help him see the truth." He left the doctors and proceeded toward the street.

"What do we do now? What if Brian loses control of himself and exposes us?" Bjorgstad looked at Thomas, brows drawn in worry.

"I think we have plenty of time to see what happens over the next year. But, we may have to deal with him in an unfortunate manner. For now, however, I think he bears watching very closely. He seems to be on the verge of a breakdown."

"D-Doctor, do you mean what I think you mean?" The timid Dr. Bjorgstad was aghast.

"My good friend, we are old. We are respected throughout the world for our distinguished careers in the biological sciences. We have each published many significant scientific papers. We have legacies of pride to pass on to further generations. With this in mind, do you want to die as a criminal, perceived by the ignorant world lay community as the greatest mass murderers in world history? Shamed for eternity? Is that the kind of heritage you want for your children's children?"

"Obviously not, but—"

"Then we have to consider the monsignor as a very real threat, and deal with him as best we can. However that may be, unfortunately."

CHICAGO, NOVEMBER

Bonna and Douglas O'Casey sat in the sunroom off the kitchen in their modest, older home, chatting over a leisurely breakfast. "More scrambled eggs, dear?" Bonna asked. "They're going to get all dried out."

"Oh, thanks, no. Why don't you call Brian down?"

"He said he was going to sleep in this morning. He needs the rest. I'll fix him something later." She began clearing the dishes.

"You know, I'm sure glad I enclosed this old porch way back when. Sunday mornings are so pleasant out here." He watched some sparrows pecking at the bird seed trough outside the enclosure. Douglas was still proud of the job he'd done on the room, soon after they bought the house in the forties. The sunroom was cozy, and the favorite gathering spot for parties and leisure activities, to say nothing of their traditional Sunday breakfast.

Douglas was a lawyer by vocation, and a self taught carpenter by avocation, incessantly sawing and banging his way through unoccupied weekends. The neighbors had complained often, more about his loud cursing when he'd hit himself with the hammer, than the construction noise itself. He often laughed about how he needed to continue practicing law beyond his retirement in order to financially sustain his mistakes around the house. In reality he'd become fairly expert.

Bonna, a retired high school teacher, was forever reminding him not to build outbuildings too near the easement on their over-sized lot. The tall, graying woman kidded him often about an earlier "problem." He had spent six months constructing a beautiful redwood gazebo, only to have an anonymous neighbor call the city to have it removed. He was *one* foot too near the property line!

"Well, should we reschedule our Canada trip for next month and do a little *ice* fishing?" he laughed.

"You're not *serious!*"

"No, no. I'm a fair weather fisherman. Let's plan on sometime in the spring." He watched as two male sparrows fought over the only available perch on the outside trough.

The couple had recently celebrated their golden anniversary, and Douglas was actually going to retire. They'd been planning their fishing trip when the call came from Brian, their only son. He wanted to come home for an extended visit, "to get away from it all." He'd told them he was suffering from "burn-out" and needed a break.

"So, dear, what do you think about Brian? There's *definitely* something wrong," Bonna said as she stirred the sugar into her coffee. "He's been home two weeks now, and does nothing but mope around. He told me how sick he's been, with ulcers and headaches and everything. *He was always so healthy*—no appetite now, either, and have you noticed how frail he looks? I'll bet he's lost thirty pounds. And I don't think he's shaved in three days. He hasn't even been going to mass!"

Douglas knew it was coming. They'd walked on eggshells long enough, and both of them were becoming a little unnerved. "I don't have a clue. But, hell, Bonna, the man's over forty years old, and a priest, yet. He's probably seen it *all!* He's probably just tired of listening to people whine." He knew there was more to it, but didn't want to cause undue worry for her.

"Remember, Doug, when Brian was just a kid?" she smiled, looking out through the window while wiping the dishes. "How happy-go-lucky he was, always the perennial joker? He started off wanting to become a train engineer. Remember the engineer's cap he got from Santa Claus? He wore the silly thing to bed for nearly a year!" she laughed with delight. "And then, when he came home after his sophomore year at State, and said he wanted to go to the seminary. Remember how upset we were at first, our only boy wanting to become a *priest?* No grand kids, we cried?"

"Yes, I remember speaking to Father Carroll down at the church, trying to get him to make Brian change his mind. And he told us, in so many words, how selfish we were! The *nerve*, we thought. Brian stood right up to us, proud and tall as he could be. He was ecstatic when he was admitted to the seminary. And *we* turned so proud, then, of our boy, wanting to help humankind. We decided we would indirectly have *throngs* of grand kids, wherever Brian was!"

Bonna began to cry, not from sadness, but sentiment. She wiped her tears with the dish towel. "Remember how thrilled he was at his ordination ceremony? I thought I would burst with joy!" she sobbed. "What's wrong, Doug . . . what's gone wrong?

Douglas went to her, taking her in his arms. "Sh-h-h, it's all right, dear." He wanted to cry, too. He took her by the shoulders and forced her back at arm's length, smiling, trying to hide his own welling tears. "Remember, honey," he smiled, "how thrilling it was when he was made monsignor? And slam, bam, next thing you know, he'd been appointed *pronuncio to the United States of America!* It was the most spectacular thing I'd ever seen!"

"Yes, yes. I remember it as though it were yesterday! The happiest day of my life!" Her tears abated, and she wiped the few remaining with the towel, then reached up and wiped Douglas's face. "You old softy, you!" she laughed, looking into his strong, blue eyes. They'd defied aging, unlike his thinning, gray, once jet-black hair. "I believe *you're* crying, too." Deep inside, she knew that Brian wouldn't, and possibly *couldn't,* talk about what was eating at him.

Douglas released her. "Please try not to worry, dear, things will work out. Brian is a strong man, and when he's ready, he'll talk. Let's not pressure him." He kissed her forehead.

"Yes, you're right. He'll do fine," she smiled half-heartedly. She laid the towel on the counter, then walked back to the sunroom.

Douglas stretched his arms and yawned, "Well, I believe I'll go out to the garage and get started on the bread box for Mrs. Foltz. I promised her last night at mass that I'd make one for her." He left through the back way.

"Are you up yet, Mom?" Brian called as he entered the kitchen. "I can smell your perfectly cooked bacon, of *course* you're up!" He wished he could eat, but he had no appetite per usual.

"Yes, Brian, I'm in the sunroom reading the paper. Do you want me to fix you some breakfast?"

"No, I'm not very hungry. I'll just have a little bowl of cereal. I'll get it." Bonna heard him rummaging through the cupboards, then the refrigerator door slammed. Brian joined her at the table. "So, how did you sleep?"

"Wait 'til you're as old as I am, then you won't bother to ask that question of *anybody,*" she smiled. "The answer isn't pleasant. It's called arthritis. Brian, it's *so* good to have you home. What's it been, two weeks now?"

"Two weeks exactly. And two weeks left. Then, back to the real world."

"It seems that you only arrived yesterday. Time goes so quickly!" She paused. "Brian, are you feeling all right? I know something's wrong. Is there anything I can do?"

He looked at her, then at the spoonful of cereal he was about to put in his mouth. "Uh, no, Mom . . . but thank you. I just have a few things I need to work through on my own." He could tell *no* one that he knew the cause of his torment. He had no solution to allay the wretchedness. There wasn't one. He had tried, doing his confessions with Cardinal Wentworth, begging God's forgiveness.

The cardinal had granted him absolution, but at the same time tried to impress upon him that no sin had been committed. He was one of the *chosen,* and was involved in God's plan to stop man's self destruction by spiritual disintegration.

"Remember, Brian, the homosexuals were chosen because they are disordered in God's plan, and are unfortunate to be the most recent outcropping of demoralization. It's time to rid mankind of its worst pestilence, immorality, by example. Hopefully, and only then, will the rest of humanity see the light and return to a holy spiritualism in the love of God."

The cardinal had been so persuasive when he had given Brian this pep talk. Brian, from sheer fatigue, wanted desperately to believe him. He'd tried repeatedly to accept that reasoning, and had repeatedly failed, questioning his own motives, his faith in God, his very being.

He thought back, possibly three years, to when he'd realized that the cardinal was becoming more extreme, more obsessed with the war on immorality. The cardinal continued to blame it all on the Vatican Council II. *Was he insane?*

There was nothing overt that one could readily identify, but small, seemingly meaningless occurrences, things he said, the way he said them, implications.

What, indeed, *was* he, anyway? A man, as the cardinal himself stated, chosen by God to direct this house cleaning of humanity? Or an old, disgruntled and self-deluded, sole-surviving dinosaur from ages past? Did he really know what he was he doing? Was he still in control of his mental faculties?

The *tic,* the unbearable *tic.* Brian could clearly picture it in his mind. It reminded him of old horror movies—the crazed, maniacal antagonist *always* had some kind of identifying peculiarity. All the uncertainties continually streamed through Brian's consciousness, furthering his own emotional fragmentation.

"Mom, I can't let you sit here like this, day in, day out." He needed to tell her *something.* "I've been having some problems with Cardinal Wentworth—some philosophical differences. You probably remember him from when you and Dad were in Rome a couple of years ago."

"Yes, I remember." Her boy was opening up! She felt warm, needed, internally reminiscing on how she felt when Brian used to seek her advice when he was an adolescent.

"We've had this ongoing disagreement over something I can't divulge, *yet,* anyway. It has affected my work, and they've relieved me of my duties as pronuncio."

"What?"

"Yes, yes . . . I'm sorry I didn't tell you sooner, but I didn't want you to be upset. *I'm* O.K. with it, so don't worry. I was burned out anyway, and I'd been thinking about relinquishing the position to someone with more enthusiasm."

"Well . . . All right, Brian, I'm not upset then." She wasn't sure if she'd hidden her disappointment.

Brian noticed her neck veins distending, the way they did when she was concerned. "You see, the cardinal's getting on in years, and does some things that I consider questionable. Not *bad* things, but just—I guess he just has odd ways, rather eccentric. Some of the younger priests think he's too conservative, dogmatic. Old fashioned, I guess. They think of him as once powerful, but they feel he's outlived his usefulness in this new, more tolerant era." He played with another spoonful of cereal. "Some of the young priests make jokes about him behind his back. Some even believe he's *crazy!*"

"What do *you* think?"

"Oh, I don't know. I *do* think he's somewhat of an oddball." He laughed. "Pass me the funny papers, please."

She slid them across the table. "Well, dear, take your time, and stay here as long as you'd like. I *do* so like having you. Like your father says, 'It will work out.'" She raised the newspaper again, gratified that he had finally confided in her. She felt like a mother renewed! Replacing her reading glasses, she folded back the metro section to the last page and began to read. "Brian?"

"Huh?" He threw down the funnies. He hadn't had much of a mind for humor lately, not much of a mind for anything. He wished he could seem more enthusiastic.

"It's such a shame! Yes, he was your age, Brian, it says right here. It *must* be him." Bonna's face paled.

"Who's that?"

"Remember Arlin Fischer?"

"How could I forget? He was *only* my best friend from the third grade on up to our sophomore year in high school. I remember when his family moved across town—my first episode of depression in life."

"He *died!* It's in the obituaries . . . from that terrible AIDS disease. I didn't know he was *gay!*"

Brian choked on a spoonful of cereal, then became quiet for a few moments. His blood seemed to fall to his feet, he went pallid, he became light headed. Bonna continued to speak, blocked from view by the paper.

"That disease, oh my, so-o-o terrible. You know, the TV evangelists are calling it a disease from God to wipe out the homosexuals."

Brian dropped his spoon into the bowl. "He *wasn't* gay, Mom. He was a *hemophiliac!*" he snapped. His mind began to rage uncontrollably. *My God, my God, will it stop? My innocent childhood friend, killed by my own hand!*

Bonna pulled the paper to one side as she heard the spoon bounce from the bowl and hit the oak parquet floor. "Oh, dear. All those years, living right down the block, and I didn't even know!" She studied Brian carefully. "Are you all right, son?"

"Yes, yes, I'm just fine." He hoped his deceit wasn't obvious. "Don't mind me, I'll find the spoon." He bent beneath the table to hide his color. Suddenly a burning surge coursed violently through his esophagus; he tasted the vomitus in his mouth. He quickly held his breath.

He was successful. He controlled the vomit, choking the bitter, acidic bile back into his stomach. "I've got it," he said in a raspy, guttural voice.

Bonna placed the obituaries back in front of her, assured that he was all right. "That illness, it's so mysterious," she went on. "I don't understand how modern medicine can be so lost. I was under the false impression that just about *anything* could be treated these days." She laid the paper on the table in front of her, then wiped her fingers on the napkin, leaving black smudges from the news ink. "After all these years, you'd think they could come up with a more stable ink. Do you remember Peggy, son, the Moore's daughter? She married a very successful banker. It was such an extravagant wedding. *Pillen*, yes, that was his name. It's so tragic. He apparently had AIDS and killed himself, and then his *wife* came down with this AIDS disease, too, and *she* died recently! The poor kids—boys—are living with the Moores now."

Brian stood dizzily from the table, his face long and sweating. He wildly bolted to the sink, bawling, vomiting, his gut twisting and wrenching the entire distance. "Oh, *please*, my God, *please*, NO!" he wailed and sobbed, interspersed with violent heaves, totally insensible to his surroundings, and his mother, who hysterically had run to his aid.

"BRIAN! BRIAN! DOUG. DOUG!" she screamed, hoping her husband could hear her. "Oh, *Brian*, what's the *matter* with you?" she sobbed. She stood, barely, hanging onto Brian's middle as he retched over the sink. His limp body suddenly slumped to the floor, a final act of exhaustion.

Bonna raced out the back way, glass shattering as she bounded through the French double doors. *"DOUGLAS*, oh, please, *DOUGLAS!"* The scream of the electric saw stopped suddenly, and she fell into Doug's arms as he appeared at the garage door frame.

"WHAT IS IT?" he yelled. Bonna pointed at the house, unable to speak. Douglas slid her to the grass, then sped into the kitchen and immediately saw Brian sprawled on the floor by the sink. Yes . . . Brian had a pulse! His breathing was raspy, but he was breathing. Doug raced to the phone. "Hello, 911? *Please, please come quickly!"*

1985

ROME, DECEMBER

Dr. Thomas's cold, drab gray office seemed a fitting place for the meeting. The semi-cool greetings had been hurriedly completed.

"So, where is Cardinal Wentworth?" Brian asked. "His displeasure is conspicuous by his absence, I suppose."

"You're quite right, Brian," Dr. Thomas said. "He doesn't want to be associated with us unless it's *necessary.*"

Thomas loaded his pipe.

"Well, that's to be expected," Brian went on. "Now, I'm sure you doctors know why I wanted to meet with you."

"Yes, we *know,*" the rat-faced Bjorgstad responded with a sigh. "You don't look good, Monsignor. You've lost a lot of weight." He stalled.

"We're not here to discuss my *weight!*" Brian barked. He settled down with some deep breaths. "O.K., then . . . Your year to develop a vaccine was up three months ago, and I, stupidly, gave you this extension." Brian looked back and forth at the two men. "Have you been successful?"

"Allow me, Dr. Bjorgstad," Thomas said. Bjorgstad nodded his approval. "There's no way we could come up with an adequate vaccine against the mutated virus in such short order, Monsignor. We suggest that maybe in another year's time—"

"Absolutely *not!*" Brian shrieked. "Your time is up! For the sake of mankind, I am giving you gentlemen until the end of the month to prepare a public statement on this entire, sick undertaking. If you don't contact me within this time, I will go to the press! *End of meeting!*" He turned abruptly and stomped out of the office.

Thomas sucked on his pipe and exhaled the thick gray smoke. "Well, Hans, my friend, our options are *exhausted.*" The two remaining men looked at each other sadly. "No choice now. We need to proceed quickly."

"I agree," Dr. Bjorgstad said. "We have no other choice. Let's make the call in the next couple of days." They shook hands firmly and parted.

• • •

"Yes, hello. I can barely understand you. Must be a bad connection. Can you hear me?" Noah asked into the phone.

"I hear you fine. Who's calling?" Mr. Mazzone asked.

"I can't understand you. It's fuzzy and distant. I'll call you right back." Dr. Thomas recradled the phone slowly, pensively. He disliked paying the high rate for his phone service to begin with, and then to have it cost money for bad connections *really* annoyed him. He turned to his friend. "Do you know anything about phone tapping, Hans? I've noticed for the past month how this phone gets fuzzy like that, especially on long distance calls. The phone company says there's nothing wrong with it."

"No, I'm not familiar with that kind of thing. Do you think it *might* be tapped? Have you ever looked around the office, here, to see if anything looks out of place?" Hans began darting his beady little eyes suspiciously around the room.

The office was medium sized, large enough for Noah's desk, two tall file cabinets, and several visitor's chairs. Noah used it to conduct scientific meetings, and therefore kept the decor plain to avoid inattention to business with clients. The walls were gray block, and all were bare except for the one bearing Noah's certificates of accomplishment.

"No, I've never looked. Maybe I'm just a little edgy recently." He picked up the phone and looked at the number written on his note pad again. "Damn! Another long distance call," he said as he redialed. "Hello again, can you hear me?"

"Yes, I hear you fine."

"Good, that's much better now. Is this Mazzone's Bakery?"

"Yes it is. How can I help you?"

"This is Dr. Noah Thomas, calling from the Thomas Independent Research Laboratory in Rome. I need to speak with Leonardo, the proprietor."

"This is Leonardo, what do you need? If you're trying to sell something, I'm not buying."

"No, no, you don't understand. I'm trying to contact Sal Danella. Do you know how I can reach him?"

"Uh . . . " Leonardo paused apprehensively, "How do you know him, and what does this concern?"

"He's done work for me in the past, and I have another job for him."

"Oh, yes, I remember, Dr. Thomas. He's spoken of you. He's not here now. I think he's in Paris, but he calls every two days for messages. Give me your number, and I'll have him return the call if he wishes to talk to you."

"Sure. I'm calling from Rome. My phone number is 396-555-3254. Have him call me Saturday morning at this number, please. I'll make it a point to be here until noon."

"I've got it, Dr. Thomas. I'll give him the message. Good bye."

"Danella sure wanders a lot," Dr. Thomas said as he put the phone down. "Right now Mazzone thinks he's in Paris. He's supposed to call Saturday morning. Do you think he might do this sort of thing, *really?* I know there are people who do, but he seems so charming. One just expects that someone who would do what we have in mind would be rough and mean looking, plain nasty."

Hans replied, "Well, he *did* stick us with an exorbitant fee on the work we gave him last time. It takes me five years of legitimate hard work to *gross* what he *netted*, while flitting around the world and having fun to boot. I'm rather ambivalent in my opinion of him. I suspect, for the right money, he'd do just about *anything*."

"I suppose you're right," Noah said, "and he's the only one I know who we could even *talk* to about it. He did that other distasteful job for us, and he seems reliable and discreet. He knows he can't tell anyone else about what we're going to ask him. We could still implicate him in the AIDS plot."

"If *he* won't do it, he may know somebody who will. We've got to do something, and soon, or we're all in deep trouble. You still don't think we should tell the cardinal?"

"Absolutely not!" Noah emphatically banged his pipe on the overflowing ashtray. "He could *never* condone anything like this. But I think that if we *do* take care of O'Casey, he'll figure out what happened. It would be too coincidental. We should never mention anything about this to him, *never*. Let him suspect. I just hope Mr. Danella will be expedient in handling this. He sure took his time to finish the implantations, you know. That last one, anyway. When did he finally send the last envelope on that Spaniard, uh, Sosa? Wasn't it 1979, 1980?" Noah rolled his eyes upward.

"Yes it was, but he really had a time of it finding the guy," Hans said, rubbing his chin. "But Sal did ask, several times, if we wanted to use one of the alternates. If you'll remember, we told him no. We *wanted* Sosa for the same reason he was hard to find. All he ever does is tramp around the world and practice his perverted sex with other homosexual maniacs. A beautiful spreading agent. By the way, did you ever analyze the remnants of that last bottle he returned, like you did the others?"

"No, I didn't bother. All the others checked out fine, still had plenty of residual virus, so I figured that one was O.K., too. He had no reason to pull any tricks."

"Yes, I suppose you're right," Bjorgstad paused contemplatively. "About our current situation. Are you sure this is the only possible way? Couldn't we just scare the monsignor or something? Maybe threaten him with harm to his family? I don't even like *that* prospect, but it's highly preferable to getting *rid* of him."

Noah turned to him. "Hans, we've explored every possibility we could brainstorm. We've brought most of our ideas up many times, and ruled them out as unwise as many times..."

"It seems we, *ourselves*, have deteriorated to immorality, just what we thought we were ridding from the world when we took this damn project on in the first place." Hans squirmed. "Now the whole thing makes me sick. And poor Monsignor O'Casey! God help him. I, too, must admit that I'm using more anti-depressants than I used to."

"I don't see a problem with that, as long as—"

"The count now," Hans interrupted, "is seventy some thousand confirmed cases in the U.S. alone, and one third of them dead. And in Paris, and London, God only knows. And the misery in Africa. How do you explain how hard *they've* been hit?"

"I don't know. Possibly their bodies don't possess enough immunity, or maybe they have an affinity for the virus, how the hell do I know?" Noah drummed his fingers on the desk.

"Maybe we should reconsider somehow letting the vaccine out. There must be a way to do it without exposing ourselves. There *must* be. Then we wouldn't have to do this, you know?"

"Hans, please! Don't make this harder than it is. We've been through the possibility of releasing the vaccine, too. We've been damned lucky so far that no one has talked, and exposed us for the monster we've created. We have no other course of action."

"Does the cardinal still feel that this plague is the will of God? I mean, does he *really* feel that way, truly?" Dr. Bjorgstad's faith in the mission had been faltering since the virus had turned up in hemophiliac children and blood transfusion patients, then heterosexual women, and finally babies born to women infected with the disease. "How does he explain the women and babies?"

"He still thinks that some innocents will be inadvertently afflicted, like in *past* pestilences God has put on humans, and God has His reasons. I last talked to him a week ago, to discuss the possibility of releasing the vaccine. He seemed more opposed to the suggestion than ever, and refused to even *consider* it. He told me he thinks God took advantage of this opportunity to wipe out immorality by allowing the spread through the heterosexual population, scaring those who are guilty into stopping drugs and extramarital sex. He seems to get more rigid as time passes, I must admit, rationalizing everything as God's will."

"Noah, *what* do we do? How do we live with this? How do *you* live with it? You're always so damned self assured." The chair squeaked as Hans leaned forward inquisitively.

"I don't like this any better than you do, actually. But at the same time, I'm a pragmatic, functional man. I don't let my emotions eat away at me like Monsignor O'Casey did. My primary concern, as should be yours, is self-preservation. With that in mind, I accept the fact that there are things that I must do that I find personally disgusting, but still they must be done. Remember, we have legacies to protect. Consider what would happen in the world scientific community if two of its most respected researchers were exposed as the perpetrators of the AIDS plague? That thought alone keeps my thinking clear, my goals in focus."

"Yes, you're right. I guess I must continually reassess the ramifications of exposure. Maybe *that* will help. I'm *so* very tired. I suppose it's the anti-depressant. Well," he stood to leave, "thank you for the tea and the advisement. I want to get back to Stockholm soon. I think I'd be more comfortable in my own home. This hotel life in Rome isn't for me. Oh, have you committed the vaccine formula to memory, like we agreed?"

"Yes, I *have,*" Noah adamantly replied. "And you?"

"Yes. We must *never* divulge it to anyone. I think we should deny its existence. Creating the disease was bad enough, but then not coming forward with the vaccine sooner than this. To the grave, right, my old friend?"

"To the grave! Good night, Hans."

"Good night. Call me and let me know when Mr. Danella will be here." Hans put on his maroon striped coat and wrapped his scarf in preparation for the cold winter wind. "Possibly it's the cold, and the gray overcast sky, that has us all down. And then it's Christmas time, too, which *should* be a happy time." He gave a quick nod and left the room.

• • •

Saturday morning found Dr. Thomas pacing the floor in his dismal office. He'd been trying to catch up on his research journal reading, but he was unable to concentrate, always returning to the pacing. The phone rang abruptly, startling him. "Hello, Dr. Thomas speaking."

"Yeah, Dr. Thomas? This is Salvadore Danella. Leonardo told me you wanted to speak to me. What can I do for you?"

"Yes, Mr. Danella. Hans Bjorgstad and I need to talk to you in person, right away. He's here from Stockholm, and he must return soon. Can you come here?"

"What's the problem? You sound scared or something."

"I am. We all are. When can you get here?"

"I'm on a job right now, but I think I can finish up and be there Tuesday. Here's the deal, though. You tell anyone who might happen to ask that I was with you all day Monday, got it?"

"Uh, well, I guess so, Sal. Why?" Noah queried. He shivered from the chill of his office. He rarely turned the heat on anymore.

"You don't ask *me* questions, I won't ask *you* questions, O.K.?" Sal snapped.

"Uh, O.K. Be here Tuesday then, all right?"

"See you then." Click.

Dr. Thomas replaced the phone and put his coat on. Hans was right. The cold gray of winter had a negative effect on everyone's attitudes. It made them more jumpy, irritable. And Christmas . . . it wasn't going to be a pleasant Christmas for him, either. All this turmoil and no way out. He closed the drapes over the frosted windows and shut the office door behind him, then walked through the empty lab area where he had once done such magnificent and honorable research. Work he was tremendously proud of.

There used to be a bustle of activity, with students asking his help in straightening out their bumbling, and accidents that sometimes produced positive changes and new insights. Some he had even patented! Things were different now. All had been quiet for the past two years. His heart wasn't in it anymore, so he'd stopped bidding for research work. Thomas Laboratory, once proud of it's fame in the science world, was now just another red brick building in a dying neighborhood. The sign over the front of the building was peeled, and the old building was showing its age from the lack of maintenance. He had sold off much of the equipment to newer, upscale labs that had aced him out of the bidding in the private research market.

He locked the heavy front door behind him and walked to his car at the front curb side, intentionally not looking back. Maybe he *should* just sell the building and be done with it.

• • •

Hans and Noah sat in the office in the old laboratory building Tuesday morning. They were nervous, chatting about how they might approach Sal when he arrived.

"Do we *dare* come right out and ask him? What if he doesn't do this sort of thing, and turns us in?" Hans asked.

Noah turned. "Let *me* approach him with it. First, I'll remind him of how deeply he is involved with us already. That might scare him a little, at least enough to protect the confidentiality of this meeting." Noah's eyes suddenly turned cold. He could feel the change as he realized he could no longer think of himself as a kindly old man, but an ogre, driven to self survival through animal behavior.

"Yes, I think that's best," Hans said. "*You* do it, then. Does he know about the *vaccine?*" He asked in his timid voice.

There was a rap at the door. "Uh, no . . . Keep that quiet. Come in," Dr. Thomas cried.

The door swung open, and in strode Sal Danella, as smooth and composed as ever. "Good morning, good morning, gentlemen," he bellowed, "Great to be alive!"

The two doctors looked at him, not sharing his sentiments. "Sal

Danella, I want you to meet my colleague, Dr. Hans Bjorgstad."

"H-how are you?" Hans held out an unsure hand, "I've known of you for quite some time. It's good to finally meet you."

"Yes, of course. You are the other partner in this little enema bit." Sal smiled accusingly.

"Er, I helped with the project. I hope we didn't pull you away from anything important, you know . . . in your work."

"No, not at all! Your call couldn't have come at a better time, if I do say." He turned to Noah. "Remember the agreement we made during our phone conversation, about Monday?" he sneered.

"I haven't forgotten, but let's not get into all of that. I don't want to know anything about it. I want you to know before we begin, Mr. Danella, that I still don't like you."

Hans' jaw dropped as he gawked at Noah. "Noah, please! You must excuse him, Mr. Danella. Sometimes he speaks without thinking."

"Oh, no problem. He let me know the first time we met that he didn't like me. Why should he start now?" Sal chuckled. "So, with that out of the way, what do you gentlemen need me for, more gory enemas?" He laughed.

Dr. Thomas stared at him coldly, trying to figure his approach. He cleared his throat. "Sit down, please. Now, it seems you remember the enemas very clearly."

"Sure. I was hoping you had more for me to do. The wages were fair enough." Sal smiled, drilling it in, then took a seat in the wooden chair by the door.

"Did you ever figure out just exactly what was in those bottles?" Dr. Thomas raised an eyebrow.

"Not for a while. I didn't care. But yes, I know now. I should call you 'Typhoid Noah,' huh?" Again he chuckled. No one else laughed. "Lighten up, guys, that was funny!"

"Frankly, I don't see the humor," Noah said. "But you know you're just as open to any possible repercussions as we are, right? You realize that?"

"What did you bring me here for, to threaten me or something?

What is it you want?" Sal started to get up.

"Please . . . stay seated. I'm sorry, I've gone about this improperly." Noah leaned back, then stared at the ceiling as he spoke. "I simply wanted to point out that we are all as guilty individually as we are collectively for this plague. And then one can add conspiracy charges as well. My purpose in rekindling this topic was to imply a loose threat, so you wouldn't expose the request we have for you."

"All right, I'm listening. What request?" Sal sat back down.

Noah heaved a deep sigh, and then, "Have you ever *killed* anyone?"

Sal squirmed a little in his chair. "Uh, no, never. Why?"

Noah played with some paper clips on his desk. "Then . . . *Would* you kill someone?" He looked up, straight into Sal's eyes. He was puzzled by Sal's coolness, having expected something of a more startled response.

"I don't know. I've never thought about it before. Why, what did you have in mind?" Sal remained unshaken.

Noah was still negatively impressed by Sal's aloof nature. *Had he killed someone?* "You know Monsignor O'Casey."

"A priest? You want me to kill a *priest? Are* you out of your *minds?* Why in hell—"

"Because he cracked up. He wanted us to develop a preventive vaccine for the disease within a year's time, or he would blow the whistle. The first deadline passed last September. We pleaded with him and he gave us a three month extension. We've been unsuccessful." Noah intentionally didn't tell him of the existing vaccine. "Now, just two weeks ago, he gave us an ultimatum. He's going to expose us if we don't make a group statement by the end of this month. We have exactly thirteen days left. And, oh, if it might influence your decision, he's no longer in the priesthood. He quit when he cracked. Now he works in a slum neighborhood, in a youth center." He maintained his eye contact, watching for any sign of hesitation.

"He's no longer a priest, huh? What happened?" Sal asked.

"He had become guilt ridden, and had a break down. He was

hospitalized for a month in a psychiatric facility when he went home to visit his parents in Chicago. He told us that a close friend, a hemophiliac, had died from AIDS. And it took the life of another family friend, too. We thought he'd probably told someone then, but he didn't. We've had our share of sleepless nights along with him, believe me."

Sal was concerned. "So what'd he say?"

"A while ago when I talked to him, he told me he couldn't bear the hypocrisy of living the role of a priest and condoning what he'd done at the same time. The cardinal tried to snap him out of it, but to no avail. We're *convinced* he'll tell. We have no other option but to get him out of the picture. Will you do it?" Noah pleaded.

Sal leaned back in his chair. "I don't know. *Kill* a man of God. Shit. What's the money like?"

"Money? Are you serious? You're in this too, remember. Up to your greedy little neck," Noah responded.

"Look, I don't have to do *anything* I don't want to do, understand? If you won't do it yourselves, you'll have to pay somebody, and I don't think I could do it because I know he's still a priest at heart. I'd have to contract somebody else for the job." He looked at each man with the calculated coolness of a stalking lion. "If you want it real quiet, to look like a burglary or an accident or something, it'll cost you plenty. I'd say two hundred thousand for a professional job."

"That's *ridiculous!"* Hans exclaimed.

"Have it *your* way. Good day, gentlemen. At the least, I'll expect payment for my time and expenses for this little meeting." He stood once again.

"Wait, wait. All right," Noah said. "But I'll need to speak to the cardinal, first, to get the money. I'll have to lie to him, because he'd *never* condone this. I'll think of something. Call me later this afternoon." Noah flushed with anger.

Sal smiled. "Always a pleasure doing business with you gentlemen. Something new every minute. Kind of exciting, isn't it?" He nodded smugly and exited the room.

"Wh-what do you think, Noah? Can he be *trusted?* I think he's some kind of a weirdo, and would probably double-cross his best friend for money."

"We have no other choice. You leave now. I have to go see Cardinal Wentworth, and I don't think there's any reason for you to stay. Why don't you go on back to Stockholm?"

"Yes, I believe I will, as soon as this is set up. I'm not very good at this kind of thing." Hans visibly trembled as he stood, put on his coat, then walked out.

Next morning Noah phoned the cardinal's office to verify that he was in, then drove to the Vatican.

"Good morning, Eminence. I'm glad you're here."

"Good morning, Dr. Thomas. Why so sullen, and to what do I owe this spontaneous visit? I thought we'd agreed never to be seen together again unless we could cover it with some kind of officious sounding story."

"Yes, Eminence, but something very urgent has suddenly come up. I'm afraid I'm in a bind and need your help quickly."

"And what kind of help do you need?" The cardinal straightened his collar.

"Please, sir, suffice it to say only that I need a large sum of money. It concerns our project . . . some loose ends. I thought you could maybe pull it from your discretionary fund."

"The obvious questions, Doctor, are how much money, and what for? The well is only *so* deep, you know!"

"You know you can trust my judgement, Cardinal. You know that I would *never* approach you with a request like this, unless the situation was dire. Please don't ask me *specifically* why I need the money, because all I can tell you is that it involves the protection of our project. You wouldn't want to know the remainder. Now, the amount." He sighed. "Two hundred thousand dollars, U.S."

The cardinal looked silently at him for a few moments, then folded his hands on the desk in front of him and leaned forward. "Two hundred thousand dollars? That's a tremendous amount of money to have readily available. And no *explanation*. I'm to work on blind trust?"

Noah swallowed. "I beseech you, Eminence, for the sake of all of us. I wish I could tell you more, but I can't. I need the money quickly."

"Just a moment." He pulled a key ring from his pocket and sorted through it, locating a small brass key. He unlocked the file drawer in his desk and retrieved a hanging file, from which he produced a ledger sheet. "Hmmm . . . Doctor Thomas, this fund only has a hundred and eighty-three thousand dollars remaining in it. It hasn't been this depleted since we made the last payment to Sal Danella several years ago. It was near a zero balance when we finally paid him off, and I've been trying over the past four years to replenish it. I've managed to transfer small amounts at a time back into the account to cover our huge expenditures. If I give you the money, I'll have to start from zero again!"

"Eminence, I *swear* to you that this is *absolutely* necessary," Noah pleaded.

"Dr. Thomas, it was difficult to get the first amounts of money out of this account years ago. *This* ledger," he tapped on the sheet, "is the actual balance. There in the corner, in the large file, the *official* ledger sheet indicates a balance of well over a million dollars!"

"Oh, my." Noah put his hand to his chin. "What if you get audited?"

"Some may call it embezzlement. I don't. The money was appropriated to me to spend as I might see fit to further the teaching of the church. I could use it for a new roof on a mission in South America, for example, or possibly school books. I chose to give the purpose of the account a little broader horizon, in that the teaching of the church *does* include the issue of morality. We, *you and I,* are increasing morality through the spread of AIDS. Now, my successor might come into this office and realize the discrepancies of the dollar figures through an audit. Without proof of worthwhile spending, I would be branded an embezzler. My only other choice would be to expose what we have done, which I refuse to do. To avoid long explanations at an audit, I *must* get the account back to a million. Do you understand my precarious position?"

"Yes, Eminence, but I see no other way to resolve this problem. If I can't raise the money, and *quickly*, all is lost anyway, and soon. We'd be exposed for certain."

Wentworth placed both index fingers on his chin and leaned back in the chair. "You're as sincere as I've ever seen you, Doctor. Well . . . yes, the money is yours."

"Thank you, *thank you*. You've just saved us all." Noah stood and bid goodbye, then made his exit. The cardinal peered out the window, watching Noah enter his car and drive away. "O'Casey . . . " he mumbled to himself.

Noah returned to his office to await Sal Danella's call. He felt certain the scumbag would settle for the hundred and eighty thousand. He wondered how a man could exist with the few values of this unscrupulous carrion eater!

He sat at his desk, reviewing old files and discarding outdated material, passing time leisurely while waiting for the call. He pulled out the old ISV-1 research files and scanned them. What a noble plan this *had* been. The idea of cleansing humanity of its immorality and perversion through biogenetic engineering had been so intriguing, so challenging a prospect. *Everyone* was so sure of themselves, so convinced of their heavenly calling, so dedicated. There had been such an overwhelming sense of camaraderie amongst them. The research students, too, were so very dedicated, though unwittingly and under false pretenses. It had been a happy time in the old brick building.

"And now, there's *nothing,*" he muttered to himself, shifting his vision aimlessly out the bay window into the dull gray cloud cover. He closed the thick file, wondering whether to save or destroy it. "Ah, what the hell do I need it for?" He tossed it in the large trash can in frustration. *"Gone forever!"*

He continued staring out the window, day dreaming of his earlier life. He could picture past, happy Christmas seasons, with his now deceased wife and now adult children. They were so proud of him when he'd received his doctoral degrees, and various fellowships from scientific fraternities.

He glanced at the wall where the certificates hung, gathering dust, four rows of frames attesting to his distinguished past. But that was the *past.* The pride he used to feel when he would sit in this very chair and admire them had faded, now they had lost their meaning. "Just a bunch of paper," he muttered.

He pulled an old novel from the desk drawer entitled *Excellent Memory.* He'd started reading it what, twenty years ago? It had grabbed his interest, but he was pulled away on a research project and never finished it. "Plenty of free time now." He opened the cover and found the book mark on page one hundred sixty-six, but he couldn't recall much about it, so he started again at page one. The pages were yellowed and brittle. "My, how ironic!" The plot slowly crept back into his memory. "My God!"

There was a handful of men involved in a conspiracy to cause doom in the world by creating a drug that diminished human moral inhibitions. They were members of a cult, obsessed with doing Satan's will, of purposefully opening Pandora's box to bring evil into the world. The drug proved to be unstable, and instead had a reverse effect of creating *goodness* instead of evil. Ironically, publicly esteemed *good* men, the world leaders, the men of power in the religious community, and so forth, wanted the personal integrity that the unstable drug had inadvertently created to *stop!* The balance of good versus evil had been thrown in favor of the good, generating chaos in the delicate balance of world politics and economics. There *needed* to be a gray zone for proper equilibrium! The conspirators were about to be exposed when he'd had to stop reading it several years ago. "Fascinating!" he exclaimed. He briefly scanned to where he had left the book marker years before, then sat, perusing every word, oblivious to everything. The phone rang abruptly and snared his attention.

"Yes, hello."

"Dr. Thomas?"

"Yes. Sal, I presume?"

"Yeah, it's me. What did you find out?"

"Why don't you come here to talk? I don't know about this phone." Noah traced the burlwood grain on his desk with a finger as he spoke.

"Sure, gotcha. I'll be there in thirty minutes." Sal hung up.

Noah returned to his book, even more fascinated by its content, as the time passed quickly.

The exterior doorbell rang. Noah marked his place, then put the book on his desk and went out through the lab area to greet Sal. "Hello, come on in. Follow me back to the office. It's the only room I keep up any more."

Sal wiped his feet on the inside rug, then followed the old man. "Yes, it's considerably nicer in here," he said as they entered the partitioned office area. He removed his overcoat and threw it on the chair next to him. "So what did the cardinal say? Did he give you the money?"

Noah sat and leaned back in his chair. "I was able to get *most* of it, but it will wipe out his entire account. Can't you get somebody for less money? I mean, you've expressed your *shared concern* with our motives in the past. And it's your own church you are taking the funds from, I'm sure you know. Not us personally. And then the fact remains that you are protecting *yourself*, too, in this whole mess. Don't you think somebody would do it for less?"

"Why? How much does he have available? Let's face it, the Catholic Church ain't *broke!* And, my friend *isn't* Catholic, he's not even religiously inclined, so *he* doesn't give a damn about religious sentimental reasoning."

Noah leaned forward. "It has taken the cardinal *four years* to accumulate this hundred and eighty thousand dollars. The four years that have passed since your greed depleted the account to *nothing*. And that's all there is. If you can't find someone to do the job for that kind of money, then we're all ruined. You, too, if I may remind you."

"All right, all right. I'll make a deal with my 'friend' to cancel another debt he owes me, if he'll accept the discounted price. It'd be a *super* deal for him! Then I've completed my contribution to your cause, right? Then you'll stop riding me?"

Noah smiled. He had come out on top. He felt venerated in his perception of being taken by Mr. Danella years ago. "Yes, if you can work it out at this price, I'll think better of you. And the fact that you're cancelling out a debt to assist this project, which, knowing you, is *probably* quite a significant debt. That makes me feel better."

"Fine, then. Send the money to the same account number as in the past, and once it's in my hands I'll proceed to hire my man. The job will be done within the thirteen day remaining time limit, I assure you."

"We have a deal, then." He extended his hand.

"Noah, Noah, the handshake went out years ago. It's now a money world. *Trust* me. Now, where's O'Casey living? What's he doing with his time? What are his personal habits? I need to know all you can tell me about him, to cut down on planning time."

Thomas gave him all the information he could about Brian's current situation. "He's involved with a youth program. He's working in a young people's runaway house where they deal with drug addiction, prostitution, and so on. He's living in a crappy little apartment in a slum area. His standard of living went *way* down."

"All right, leave it to me. I'll call my bank in three days to verify the deposit, then I'll take care of the problem. Again, if anyone at all asks you about me, you need to alibi me. If I end up in jail, I'm calling *you* to get me out, got it?" Sal stared at him coldly.

Noah disliked what he found himself faced with more than any other aspect of this entire ordeal, but he was obligated to an agreement. "You have my word. The money will be there."

"The job should be done within a week, then. Now, I must be going. Dr. Thomas, I want you to know that I feel as remorseful about what we must do as you do. I wish we all had better control over these unfortunate turns in our lives, and there could be other, more pleasant resolutions. It's too bad we don't live in a perfect world. I'll let myself out." He donned his coat and left the office, closing the door quietly behind him.

"Yes, it's too bad," the doctor repeated.

• • •

Sal buttoned his coat against the wind as he exited the building. He *really* didn't like what he had to do. It was the first time in his life he must kill a man of integrity, a man of *God*, yet, whom he personally felt to be the *only* one of the conspirators righteous in his convictions. Nevertheless, the job must be done. If his own involvement in this maniacal scheme came to light, he would *surely* be convicted with the other men. He thought about how many times he had literally gotten away with murder, then to be faced with the possibility of a criminal conviction in a mad scheme like this! "It has to be done," he said, convincing himself, "and I can't do those cowardly men's work for nothing. None of *them* would ever have the guts to do it, in spite of themselves." He rationalized his motive. He had become *expert* at rationalizing, somewhere during the course of his life.

• • •

Several days later Sal shivered as he sat in his rented Porsche across the street from the shabby, plain apartment building. It was seven thirty a.m. Brian should have left twenty minutes earlier, if he was to make it to the youth center on time. It was frigid outside, the temperature hovering at minus twenty-two degrees Centigrade. He had been running his car intermittently to avoid being noticed by the engine noise, while parked on the quiet street. He would wait until he could no longer tolerate the cold, then start the engine to heat the cabin and clear the windshield of frost. Then he'd let it run until he was overheated, and turn it off again. "I've had *worse* jobs for *less* money," he said to himself.

People had come and gone from the building during the busy morning rush hour. Fortunately, he would know Brian by sight from their previous meetings. Brian's phone was unlisted, so he couldn't call to check his being there. He could have used the 'sorry, I must have misdialed' excuse, if only he knew the number. Instead, he had to resort to *this* stalking method. "Shit, it's cold!" He started the car once again, wincing when the starter malfunctioned with a whine. *Good, no one's looking.* Then he perked up, noticing Brian exit the front door and head toward the parking lot provided for tenants. He watched while he got in his car, then heard the starter grind until the small engine in the old compact finally rattled to life with a burst of black smoke. The car backed out and left through the alley exit.

Sal left his car and entered the building. He ran his finger down the building directory by the mailboxes. He found Brian's name, number 207. He climbed the stairs and walked down the dark hallway, finding it on the left side, half way to the rear of the building. He took a quick glance up and down the hall to check for residents. It was empty. A stroke of luck, actually, that Brian had been late getting started this morning, after the other residents had left. He wouldn't be observed by any of the neighbors. He produced a lock pick and rolled the tumblers until the door knob released, allowing entry into the apartment.

He stealthily entered the living room. *Maybe* the man who left had just *looked* like O'Casey. All was quiet, so he crept down the narrow hallway, looking and listening for untoward sounds. A toilet flushed and he froze. He decided it was a distant sound, probably from an apartment on the floor above. He continued the five feet to the next open door. It was the bathroom. The two bedrooms he had passed were empty. That *had* been Brian he'd seen leaving, he was sure now. He breathed a sigh of relief and made himself at home, warming himself near the wall heater in the living room.

"So far, so good, at least that's what they say," he muttered to himself. "Brrrrrr-r-r," he shook and hugged himself, flapping his hands on his upper arms. He took off his scarf and coat and threw them on the sofa. Maybe the heat from the wall heater would absorb into his chilled body faster without all the insulation covering him. His teeth chattered a little, and he shivered. "I didn't know how *cold* I was until I got in here!"

After a few minutes of warming he started. He put on gloves and shuffled through the drawers in the kitchen, loosely remembering where everything was. Then he proceeded to the bedrooms and went through the drawers, careful not to disturb anything, and then the bathroom. "Good, no guns to worry about." There was nothing unusual here, he noticed.

Most people have their little hidden "embarrassments" that he delighted in finding. Maybe a pile of dirty magazines under some towels in the linen closet, some porn flicks hidden behind the VCR, or possibly a notice from a collection agency stuck underneath other papers on the bulletin board by the phone. A common finding was an adulterer's little black book hidden in a shoe, maybe, on a top closet shelf. He'd discovered that he personally was no different than anybody else with his own secret idiosyncracies. But *this* man, Brian, was *clean.* All he had were worn missals, an old rosary in one of his drawers, and papers and letters from his family in the U.S.

He opened a letter and read it aloud. "Son, We know you haven't been doing well, even since you left the hospital. We know you are carrying something terrible on your shoulders and that you can't tell us because of your faith. I thought that maybe it's something someone told you in confession that you're struggling with. I want you to know we're all thinking of you, and praying that this ordeal will somehow end soon. The flowers you got were cabled by your Uncle Ted. I hope that you're doing better, and you'll get well soon. Please write soon. All my love, Mom."

Sal was taken by the letter. He sat and read it several times over. This man was *honorable*, truly worthy of respect. Sal had killed others that were 'respected' persons, but not truly *worthy.* Civic leaders, lawyers, and politicians; all of them were underlying crooks. He was engrossed in a personal dilemma of whether he could take this man's life when there was a sharp knock at the door. He froze. Somebody outside the door was turning the handle; he watched it turn. Had he remembered to lock it after he came in? He quietly slipped into a small closet and closed the door; his heart pounded, he breathed hard. He tried to control both.

He heard muffled voices and the door creaked open. "Brian, are you home?" Two voices, sounded like boys. "I guess he went to the center already, let's go over there. Weird that he left his door unlocked." The door closed again.

Whew! That was too close. *I hope they don't tell him about the door.*

He replaced the letter in the drawer, being careful to place it exactly how he'd found it. People had a way of placing things in a certain fashion, and subconsciously sensed anything out of place. No need to alarm the target. The drawer on the old dresser stuck as he closed it. He couldn't close it completely without pounding on it, possibly drawing attention. "Damn!" He left it ajar.

The furniture was sparse, extremely worn, and mismatched. Two homely pictures hung above the couch, the only attempt at decorating. A crucifix hung near the door. Brian lived an apparent life of poverty. Social service professions usually didn't pay worth a damn, he knew. People were expected to work out of benevolence, a love of mankind, dedication. Brian truly *did* work for these reasons, he thought. The kind of crap that led to a boring life and an early death. How come? He was educated. He could get a nice, fat job somewhere and live a more than comfortable life. Instead he chose this. Sal pondered that philosophy for awhile. This was a *good* man.

The longer Sal considered this job, the less interested he became. He sat on the couch for a minute, bent forward and wringing his hands, elbows resting on his knees. He stared at the floor. Great money, but hard on the slight remainder of his emotions that secretly harbored his conscience. "Damn!" He stood up, having decided that he couldn't do it. He *would* have to subcontract it after all. He paced.

Gino, an old acquaintance, would be good for this one. He set a mental image of the apartment's layout to pass on to Gino, took the number from the label on the phone, then opened the entry door. He glanced up and down the hall while stuffing the gloves in his pocket, then sneaked out quickly while no one was about.

He crossed the street and climbed into his car, noting the physical layout of the immediate area. Then he drove around the building, checking for fire escapes, bushes, parking areas, and other pertinent information to pull off a job. He was sure that Gino would repeat the same, just to assure himself of the setup, before he actually did it. Everything looked good.

The building planners had conveniently located a heavy steel pipe up the wall within a few feet of Brian's living room window, probably a gas pipe. Gino could climb up to the ledge on the second floor and make his way into Brian's living room window, or maybe use it to get out in a hurry if he needed to. There was a fire exit at the back end of the second floor, and plenty of bushes at the base of the escape stairs.

There was parking readily available near the foot of the escape.

The only drawback was the parking lot light near the back of the building, but a pellet gun would quietly take care of that. The automobile traffic was light in the front street; only one car had passed in the few minutes it took to case the building. That was good. A quiet street, with little traffic after the rush hour. Timing could be used in planning the escape. It was dark by five-thirty p.m., and darkness was *always* the best cover possible. Probably wouldn't need to use the fire escape. The careless amateur might boldly exit through the front door, but the back way would be the prudent professional's way out.

Sal turned his car out of the parking lot and drove quietly down the street, headed for Carlo's Meat and Poultry. He was still contemplating his emotional involvement in this hit, even if he wasn't actually to be the trigger man. He would tell Gino to make it clean, and as painless as possible. Yes, that helped some.

An hour later he walked into the small butcher shop. Gino stood behind the counter, wearing a blood-spattered apron over a dirty tee shirt, and dirty white pants. He had finished wrapping a woman's freshly-butchered chickens and was making small talk as Sal entered. He looked at Sal, then quickly looked away, smiling back at the woman.

"Thank you, Mrs. Quaglia." He smiled and handed her change over the counter. "Have a nice day, now." She thanked him, smiled back, and left.

Gino wiped his hands on his apron while he spoke. "So what do *you* want, Salvadore? I haven't seen you for what, a couple of years? And so I repeat, what do you *want?* Maybe a nice dead chicken, no?" He laughed, holding a chicken by the neck.

Sal chuckled. "Hey, look, my old friend, I've been busy and couldn't come to see you like I used to. I travel a lot, you know. Tell me, do you really like killing and chopping up all those poor little animals?" He picked up the butchered chicken, looked at it, and threw it back on the counter.

"It's not so bad. I feel as though I'm doing everybody a favor, doing their dirty work for them. With that in mind, what brings you in?" Gino chopped the head from a chicken.

Sal laughed. "You are truly a funny man, Gino. Always a wit. Is anyone else around?"

"No, I'm here alone."

"Good." Sal sombered. "You looking for any work? You know, other than carving animal carcasses?"

"Well, I'm quite happy here, Sal. But it doesn't pay much, so I *do* take on some moonlighting, you might say, once in a while. What did you have in mind?"

"In a minute, my friend. What have you been up to?""

"I'm but a simple butcher, in a small shop, where I've worked daily and dependably since I've been paroled. But," he smiled, "it's truly amazing what a man can do in his off hours, if he's careful."

Daredevils and dummies were the ones filling the prisons, and Gino fit neither group. Not since he had been paroled six years earlier from a twenty year prison term on a racketeering conviction. He, rather than society, had been the one to benefit by his prison experience, in essence going to school on the stupidity of the daredevils and dummies. He vowed not to be so stupid as *they* had been. He hadn't been suspected of anything foul since his release, thanks to his excellent prison education, in spite of being three times as active, and on a much grander scale, than his pre-prison days. The police approached him only once, four years ago, to question his knowledge of a Sicilian ring operating in Europe. Gino was the *perfect* choice for the subcontractor. Sal leaned forward on his elbows on the high glass cooler. "You want to do a contract job?"

Gino paused in his ongoing chopping and stared at the wooden block below his cleaver. "A *hit*, huh? Damn, I don't know. I haven't done *that* in a long, long time. Never did like it. I only did it when I was in a bind for cash." He gave Sal a side glance. "Know what I mean?"

"Yeah, yeah, of course. Forty thousand U.S. dollars. Easy hit. Preliminary casing's all done."

Gino picked up his cleaver and continued. "I don't know. That *used* to be big money, once."

"Fifty thousand, and no more." Sal raised an eyebrow.

"Make it *eighty*, and I won't have to think anymore." He looked up.

"Sixty-five, that's tops. If you can't do it for that, I'll get someone else." Sal looked toward the door.

"Don't be in such a hurry, old friend," Gino laughed warily. "I was just about to take it. No need to threaten. Why don't you do it yourself? I thought that was your big thrill, playing the hunter."

"Er, I'm sort of personally connected to the guy, so I can't pull the trigger."

"*What?* Do I hear the distant conscience of Salvadore Danella?" Gino roared with laughter. "Getting soft, eh?"

"I guess so, maybe. You'll do it?"

"What are the terms?"

"Say, ten down, the rest on completion." Sal would have to front the first ten thousand out of his own pocket to circumvent questions from the employers.

"Who's behind it, and for what?"

"That, my friend, is privileged information. However, I can assure you that it's a clean job, no strings attached. The employers are quite upstanding men and sworn to secrecy because if one goes, everybody goes. They've proven themselves many times before in past dealings with me. And you know that you are dealing with *me*, Sal Danella, not some amateur flake. *That* should be more than good enough for your decision. With the price you're charging me, I'm not going to make any money other than a minimal agent fee."

Gino disjointed the thigh from another chicken, thinking while he worked. "Well, sure, I could use the money. O.K., no questions. Deposit it in my Lucerne account?"

"Done." Sal extended his hand, then retrieved it when Gino laughingly attempted to grasp it with his bloodied hand.

"Yeah, done." Gino wiped the blood on his apron, then they clasped hands.

"All right. Here's the guy's address and phone number, in case you want to call and see if he's at home before you go in." He handed

Gino a matchbook with the information written inside the cover.

"I cased it this morning. He lives alone. He leaves for work early in the morning, and gets off at four-thirty in the afternoon, so I suppose he's home by four-fifty p.m. After you do it, hang around until about five-thirty, then use the darkness to cover your exit."

Sal pulled out a penciled sketch of the building. "There's a fire escape at the back end of the building, and there's a lot of shrubbery, here," he indicated with his finger, "for cover if you need it. It's a real quiet apartment building, so there's probably not much activity after all the neighbors are in for the night. There is a light in the parking lot, here, near the back door, so if I were you, I'd knock that out before I did the job. There's a heavy pipe up the side of the building, near his living room window, that you can use to get in or out if you get into a tight spot. The apartment itself is on the second floor, about midway down the hall on the left. Pretty simple, small living room, small kitchen, short hallway, with two bedrooms and a bath."

"Any weapons around?"

"Some kitchen knives, but no guns."

"How soon? A rush job?"

"Take care of it within the next week, or we're all in deep trouble, and no pay for you."

"O.K. Let me go check the place out for myself in the next couple of days, then I'll take a day and follow the guy. I'll have to get my good pal, Lanzo, to alibi me. I've got something on him, too, so he takes good care of me. I'll get the job done within the week. What does this guy look like?"

Sal described Brian in full detail, including his physical characteristics, and abstracts of Sal's own impressions.

• • •

Gino called in sick to work the next day so he could go look at the set up. He was careful to go during mid-morning, after the neighborhood would be cleared of traffic. He went through the front door of the building and up the stairs to number 207, then turned the tumblers in the door lock, opening it quickly but cautiously. He had called first to insure the victim's absence. He found the apartment just as Sal had told him. *Simple.* This guy didn't have any money, that was apparent, a poor working man. Deeply religious by his assortment of artifacts. Why did anyone want *him* dead?

The pipe on the outside wall was convenient, but hopefully he wouldn't need to use it, only if he was surprised. Much wiser to use a regular exit. Anyone seeing him hanging on the pipe *wouldn't* forget him, yet they probably *would* if he simply bypassed them in the hall. He could even say hello! He left the building via the rear entrance and descended the stairs to the ground, noting the bushes and parking lot light, then left the area.

The next morning he called in ill again, then went to the apartment to observe the victim's routine. He sat across the street, awaiting the man Sal had described. He watched several people come and go, all working-class types. Suddenly he was roused by the man who fit the description perfectly. Mid thirties, tall, handsome, reddish-blond hair, light complexion, like nobody else from *that* building. Clean-cut, American look. The other inhabitants were all definitely Italian, judging by their dress and physical attributes.

Gino watched him saunter into the parking lot and get into an older model compact car. It chortled for a moment, then chugged with a plume of black smoke. That was the car Sal had described.

Gino started his own car and pulled into the parking lot, being careful not to follow too closely. He followed the victim out through the back of the lot, into the alley, and then onto the street, still trailing at a safe distance.

They wandered through the neighborhood and turned onto a major street, then drove for ten minutes and turned back into a quiet area.

It was one of the barrios. The victim pulled up in front of a one story building that appeared to be a medical clinic of some type. Gino pulled to the curb, safely back, then watched his man get out of the car and enter the building. He drove his car slowly past in order to read the faded sign over the front door. "A *youth center?*" he puzzled aloud.

Why did anyone want a philanthropical working man killed? Maybe this was a *cover* of some sort, and in reality the guy was a crook, maybe running a racket of some kind. He parked his car across the street and watched.

Teenagers and young adults came and went, staying from a few minutes to a couple of hours. Maybe a drug dealer with a good front? He continued to wait and watch. The man didn't come out at lunchtime. "How boring!" He would've liked to read the book he'd brought, but the last time he'd done that, his mark walked out the door, right under his nose, without his notice. No, he had to endure the boredom, and keep an eye on the door at all times.

It was late afternoon when the victim finally came out and entered his car. It was four thirty, just as Sal had predicted. Gino followed him home again, then went to his own place to plan.

Gino was 'sick' a third day. This was the day. He'd told his friend Lanzo, if truly one had friends in this business, to cover him. Actually, as he was aware, these 'friendships' were really just symbiotic relationships. If one of the co-survivors was burned by the other, *both* were dead. "It's a dog eat dog world," he lamented. The alibi story would be that they were at Antonelli's Bar, from noon until ten that night, when both went home drunk.

Gino drove to the rear of the apartment building at four in the afternoon, stopped briefly to get out his pellet gun, then scanned the area for witnesses before pulling the trigger. He heard the 'poof' as the vapor escaped from the parking lot light. He then pulled his car into a space marked 'visitor' and turned off the motor.

He walked to the front of the building, still lucky to have no one about, and climbed the stairs to the second floor. His heart pounded a little from an escalating anxiety level; he felt a fullness in his chest, and breathing became a little more difficult. He tried to act as though he had reason to be there; not to look suspicious to anyone who may come into the hall and not recognize him as a tenant. He approached the door marked 207 with pick in hand and nervously turned the tumblers, fumbling this time.

"Come on, come on," he mumbled to himself. Click. The door

swung open and he slithered in sideways. His first hit in four years. Had he lost his nerve for this, the ultimate in underworld work? He quickly closed the door behind him and scanned the apartment.

After donning gloves, he went into the bedrooms and riffled the drawers to set up a 'burglary-motivated crime scene.' "Good, no guns." He went to the kitchen and repeated the process, then returned to the living room to wait.

Fumbling through the pockets of his heavy coat, he retrieved a 9mm Beretta, and attached a home made silencer from the other pocket. Then he waited. Turn on the radio? No, someone might hear, even turned down low. He could hear the muffled sounds of a television next door, indicating the poor insulation within the walls.

Would someone hear the shot, even the slight 'zip' sound of the silencer? Maybe use a pillow over the gun? No, the investigators would find the powder burns and then suspect premeditated murder, instead of the planned scene of a startled burglar.

His mind roiled with anxious thoughts; his breathing and heart rate accelerated again. "Hey, you, slow down, take it easy. You've done this before. No big deal." He consciously tried to reconcile his anxiety, to regain control. He took a few deep breaths and sat on the sofa, head back, eyes closed. He wished he could take off the damned gloves. His hands were sweating inside, making his whole body feel clammy. He toyed with the gun, aiming at small targets like light switches, just like a boy with a wooden gun.

It was four-thirty. Just another fifteen minutes. *What's best? Do it in here, or in the bedroom?* If he hid in the bedroom, the victim might go to the kitchen first and find everything amiss, blowing his element of surprise. *No, no, in here.* But he'll see me when he opens the door. "Aha!" He went into the kitchen.

Now, when he comes in, I can wait until he closes the front door, then step out and do it. He trembled, his breathing became erratic again. How the hell does Danella do this so *easily?* He found a glass and drew some water from the tap to wet his parched mouth and lips, then carefully wiped it with the towel and put it next to the sink. "Damn! Hurry up, guy."

Footsteps approached the door. He heard a muffled, "Oh, hello, boys, how are you?" The grating sound of the key sliding into the lock came into focus.

Shit, there are people outside! Now his heart raced uncontrollably, his breathing developed a short staccato pattern. The door opened and the man entered, humming to himself. The footsteps went down the hall way, then a pause.

"Is there someone in here?" the man asked in a wavering voice. The footsteps returned toward the living room. Gino stepped into the hall, in front of the frightened man, with the gun pointed at his chest. The bewildered man froze and looked at Gino, then down at the gun.

"The *animals* . . . They're all *mad!*" He began to pray and mumble, then asked God's forgiveness for 'the plague.' Then he held out his hands, curiously, as if *inviting* death. The man harbored no fear, Gino sensed, but peace, acceptance. Gino's hand shook as he squeezed the trigger. *ZIP! ZIP!* The victim slid down the wall to the floor. Gino rolled him over. The man mumbled something, then he went limp.

"A what, a priest? Oh God, forgive me!" Gino pleaded. He stood, stunned, quizzically looking down at the dead man. His gun hung at his side, he was shaking. "I killed a *priest?"*

After several moments he regained his senses. He stuffed the gun in his pocket, then hurried to the living room and threw open the window. He didn't even think to check the hall for neighbors; he just wanted *out.* It was just turning dark outside, and there was no one in the parking lot. He crawled out onto the ledge and inched his way to the pipe. Grasping the pipe, he slid down, his hands burning from the friction. He fell the last five feet, then crawled behind a bush. After insuring his gun was still in his pocket, he calmly stood and stepped onto the sidewalk. He brushed himself off, then tried to act casual as he walked toward his car. The expected sound of sirens never came. He started his car and backed out without incident, then pulled down the alley and onto the street. At the third intersection he finally heard the distinct wailing of sirens, but he was safe now.

Should he get Sal Danella, the unconscionable bastard, and

make him *pay* for conning him into killing a priest? He had thoughts of shooting the creep. No, it was too late, it was done. He'd have to live with it. He vowed that somehow, someday, he'd get the son of a bitch.

The next morning Gino returned to work as usual, trying not to display any residual anxiety over what he'd done. Maybe it was good, because Carlo thought his peaked appearance was due to getting over the flu, and he just wasn't up to his usual jovial self yet.

"Glad to see you're feeling good enough to come back," Carlo said.

"Yeah, thanks," he replied.

Gino spent the remainder of the work day much to himself, avoiding conversation with Carlo by always being certain to distance himself physically in the butcher shop.

Gino watched the news that evening to see what had developed over the murder. There was a longer than usual news clip on the former priest, stating that he'd left the priesthood for personal reasons. The reporter continued with a long story about his career, what a respected man he was, and how he'd taken work at the youth center to "help those that could still be helped." No one knew, the reporter commented, what the priest had meant by that statement.

The murder was reported as "appearing to be burglary motivated," but the Italian state police were investigating. "Oh, shit!" Gino exclaimed. The priest had called the state police a few days earlier and told them that he needed to discuss something of great importance, and that his life might be endangered. The police hadn't put real emphasis on his personal protection because he'd mysteriously said that he couldn't divulge any more details for another two weeks.

"What the hell's going on here?" Gino asked himself. "Do I contact that slime, Sal? No, better I leave it alone, wait until things cool for a while. Then I'll figure a way to get him." He didn't want any more ties to *that* source of trouble. He'd keep the money and try to live with his conscience—until the timing was right, anyway.

1989

HAVANA, APRIL

The wheels of the Ilyushin-62 jetliner screeched as they bounced down onto the runway. The huge plane screamed past the cheering onlookers, then taxied back to the terminal and quickly rolled to a stop on the tarmac.

The ground crew placed the stairway as the military band commenced playing *Gimn Sovetskogo Soyuza*, the national anthem of the U.S.S.R. The door on the jet opened and several security men deplaned, followed by the guest of honor, Mikhail Gorbachev. The pre-planned crowds roared their appreciation as he descended the steps to join their own national fixture, Fidel Castro, garbed in his perennial revolutionary military fatigues.

The men greeted each other warmly, playing up to the international news cameramen waiting to record this historic event on videotape. They clasped their hands together and thrust them upward together in a victory motion, then immediately began an animated and seemingly warm verbal interchange as the cheering died down.

Castro approached the microphone, smoothing his beard. "Comrades! You stand witness to a truly historic occasion! This is the *first* time in our revolutionary state that we have had the distinction of a visit by a prime minister from our friend and ally, the Union of Soviet Socialist Republics. I give you Prime Minister Gorbachev!" He clapped as he backed away from the mike. The crowd cheered.

Mr. Gorbachev's port-wine stained pate stood out in the morning sun. He quieted the crowd with out-stretched arms. "My fellow comrades! It is with great pleasure that I find myself a guest in your humble country! Your president and I will meet today to further bolster our countries' relationship, by a renewed commitment to common purpose, to strengthen our lasting ties through truth! My presence here is a mission of *friendship!*" He smiled broadly, waving to the crowd. The cameras rolled as the limousine pulled up behind the two leaders. The men climbed into the car and sped away from the giant plane, surrounded by police cars and motorcycles.

Newsmen from the communist bloc reported the scene as a truly warm greeting, while newsmen from the western nations reported it as a prearranged sham for the cameras. Cuban-Russian relations had been faltering again, according to the western nations' political analyses.

Unknown to the Cuban people, Gorbachev had also come on a mission of accountability, making known his dissatisfaction over Cuba's handling of financial aid. Russia had poured millions of rubles into the Cuban economy for extravagant community projects, but had seen nothing come to fruition.

Also unknown to the Cuban people, Castro wanted to discuss his displeasure with Gorbachev's reform programs. Castro felt Gorbachev had become too soft in his dealings with the U.S., and leaned too far toward personal freedoms within the Russian citizenry.

Havana's streets were lined with over a half million people to cheer on the motorcade. Western analysts viewed this as an awkward publicity stunt. The entire population of Cuba totaled just two million, and this huge turnout was regarded as a feat of no uncertain terms.

The motorcade arrived at the capitol, and the dignitaries and security men entered the building. The dignitaries sat down to a gala luncheon, still smiling and appearing as if there was no strife between them. When the luncheon ended, the leaders retreated to Castro's office to discuss international issues and their unique symbiotic relationship.

"Mi amigo, at the very least I am happy to meet you personally, and I know that in spite of your determination to try your reforms, we can still rely on each other as fast allies and friends." Fidel made his opening remark, fishing for Gorbachev's deeper rationale.

"Yes, our commitment to one another shall remain strong. We

may disagree in our opinions, but perhaps that will allow us to become stronger in our alliance." Gorbachev motioned the cameramen away so they could talk privately.

The ambience dissipated. "You must understand that my country has wallowed in the doldrums for too many years, and I must seek out innovative methods to further stimulate economic growth. We must plan for the future, not rely on the past. I must take limited action to enhance the standard of living for the Russian citizens. Possibly allowing limited entrepreneurialism will give them a new ambition, a new drive, a new zeal. That is why I have opted...no, been *forced*, to make change. We shall see. The winds can always shift again, Presidente."

"And so they can! But, Mr. Gorbachev, *Perestroika... Glasnost, public debates, and elections!* All of these issues are in direct conflict with the philosophy of purist Marxism, and that upsets me tremendously. I'll be most anxious to witness the outcome of so flippantly altering our founding fathers' political philosophy."

Gorbachev smiled, "My new programs have increased the trust of our people in their government already. They're very happy to see that we are responsive to their needs."

"We shall see. By the way, I wanted to ask you what, if any, effect this AIDS disease is having in your country? We have a handful of cases here, but we immediately put them in a quarantine colony, similar to the leper colonies of years past." He laughed. "The Americanos think this is barbarism! Muy estupido! We only have maybe forty cases, and *they* have hundreds of thousands, possibly millions! Fools!"

"Don't be too quick, my friend. The Americans aren't *that* stupid! You *really* hate them, don't you?" Gorbachev asked.

Castro was stunned. "But, of *course!* And *you* don't?"

"They are a power to be reckoned with, not to be quickly judged. Certainly they have their reasons—"

Castro cut in. "It's those idiotic human rights advocates. They maintain that quarantine colonies are a scarred remnant from the Dark Ages. According to them, society miraculously became enlightened, and let these poor sufferers of *contagious* diseases disseminate into the population at large. If the fools would only think back and learn from history, the colonies for lepers and tuberculosis disbanded, actually, when cures became available, not due to enlightened humanity! I understand that recently, though, the health department in the U.S. has talked about instigating such colonies again."

"This baffling disease is such a tragic situation. In Russia there are many thousands, but I can't quote an accurate figure. But, we too have had quarantine colonies for several years. No one knows how the disease originated, or how to cure it, but until we have answers we must prevent its further expansion by keeping these people confined. To hell with human rights in the face of a lethal epidemic!"

Castro smiled. "Unfortunate for the Americanos, their stupidity. I'm glad you have taken intelligent steps to prevent its spreading in your country. Some day the truth will be known, and I will have my vindication." He said the last sentence in Spanish.

"What does that mean, what you just said? I didn't understand."

"Oh, nothing, really, just an old Spanish saying," Fidel sneered.

They returned to the topics of politics and economy. They couldn't, as expected, agree on Marxist philosophical interpretations, with Gorbachev remaining firm on his decisions regarding reform.

Gorbachev tactfully threatened the dictator of the Marxist island that he'd better show some progress in public works with the appropriations of Soviet money. If visible progress wasn't quickly forthcoming, Cuba would suffer major cutbacks.

The next morning the black stretch limo sped to the airport with the men saying their farewells. Nothing had been resolved, with the exception of Castro's agreeing to making frequent reports on Cuban progress.

Gorbachev stood up to the microphone to make his departure speech. "Well, Comrades, in spite of our differences during yesterday's prolonged session, I feel we have a bilateral understanding that we *will*, at all costs and without regard for these differences, maintain our alliance into the future. I bid you farewell." He waved to the cheering crowd, turned, and climbed the stairs to the waiting plane.

The free world news media had a field day reporting on this historic meeting, labeling it the meeting of the 'International Odd Couple.'

1990

ATLANTA, MARCH

"So, what did you do over the weekend?" Dr. Arthur Fellows asked. He sat with his long legs extended at the knee, feet upon the desk, aimlessly chatting with Charlie Schuster.

"Nothing much. I took the kids out to the North Fork Stables and we rented some horses. It's tough, being a divorced dad."

Arthur didn't say anything, thinking back to when he was divorced from his first wife, and the adjustment problems he'd had trying to be a weekend father. He sat and looked at Charlie with an understanding smile.

Schuster continued "My rear end is paying for it now! I haven't been on a horse for fifteen years." He patted the side of his buttock and smiled. "The kids loved it, and it was good to spend some time with them." Charlie sat in Fellow's visitor's chair, sharing some infrequent idle time. "Did you *really* read all those books?" he asked, pointing to the floor-to-ceiling shelves lining the entire south wall of the office.

"Most of them, and of course the medical books are there for reference. I plan to get them *all* read sometime, but that'll take a while." Arthur looked at the overwhelming mass of books, sitting neatly organized on the rows of shelves. "Books are my true weakness in this existence. I wish I could retire and stay locked away in a little idyllic mountain valley, with nothing to do but an endless stream of reading." He sighed. "When I was in school, the kids used to tease me because I'd rather stay home and read nonfiction books than play football, or anything else!"

"A real, genuine nerd, huh?" Charlie laughed. "No wonder you're akin to a walking encyclopedia! I always wondered why you chose the boring field of epidemiology. Now, I know. You're a *nerd!*"

Arthur was tall, lanky, and had a pasty appearance, with thick black eyebrows and thin lips that he could contort into many different expressions. He didn't have to speak to make his feelings known. His brows pulled together and his lips puckered. "I *beg* your pardon!" He tried without success to act unaffected. "Hey, I like *books*. And if I *am* a 'walking encyclopedia,' I don't have a problem with that. I'll state with *pride* that I read all fifty-plus volumes of the *Great Books of the Western World* by the time I graduated from high school."

"Oh, crap, Art! Pretty sensitive about it, huh?" Charlie grinned.

"Just because I chose stimulation of the mind over the gonads . . What a cross to bear!" His brows raised, and he tipped his head back so Charlie couldn't see the widening smile. "On the other hand, many of my *athletic* classmates chose football, being tough and machismo, chasing women. I took to books. I needed to make a place for myself in this world, to prove my self worth."

"Aha! So you're out to prove that the brain is mightier than the back, or some paraphrase like that." Charlie *had* seen the smile.

"I guess so. And look at the mighty football warriors, who now suffer from chronic injury problems and headaches. But, I'll admit, they're happily working as crew chiefs over the teeny-bopper hamburger flippers at McDonald's. And *I* have to work fourteen-hour days, trying to save the world from the ravages of unknown disease!" His chair squealed as he smugly sat back.

"Bravo! Bravo! I *love* it! By damn, you come up with some arrogant *crap!*" Charlie clapped and stood in adulation.

Fellows stood and nodded, as if taking applause from a full auditorium, then sat down again. He waited until he was settled. "What about *you?* Why did *you* get into this scientific calling?"

Charlie had seated himself again. "Oh, I dunno. *I* was the

football jock-type, until I realized that I probably would never outgrow my five-foot-six skeleton, so I decided to get smart and pay attention in academia. Things change, people change, times change, styles change. It kind of fell into place from there." He was a short but powerfully built man for the age of fifty-two. His hair was thinning and lifeless, and he'd stopped using Grecian Formula long enough for the gray to be showing.

"Yes, things *do* change, all right. Ain't no guarantees in this life," Arthur mused. "By the way, have you seen the morning paper yet?"

"No, not yet, I ran out of time this morning. It was *so* beautiful that I sat outside on the deck, drinking coffee, and watching the sun come up, reflecting off the back pond. The reflection warped the rays into glowing beams, fingers of light cast over the still, barren trees above. It was *sensational*, I'd never seen that happen before."

Arthur Fellows was fascinated, watching Schuster's graceful gestures as he swirled through the poetic oration. Fellows felt as if he could picture *exactly* what Schuster had experienced. "My, what a silver-tongued hummer. Your gift of communicative speech is surpassed only by your ability to communicate sensorially. You're obviously still writing poetry."

"Oh, yes, that. I couldn't stop it if I wanted to. It's just kinda *there*." Charlie smiled sheepishly, as though he was embarrassed.

Arthur realized his friend's uneasiness. "Do you get *embarrased* to talk about your gifted talent? My word, if only *I* had what you have. It's not something you're born with, but something that's developed over a lifetime of keen observation and wit." He watched Charlie blush. "*You* create, but I am left to *read* people's creations. Maybe I *read* so much because I'm a frustrated *creator* at heart! My, how I envy you."

Schuster glanced downward, not out of modesty, but sincerity. He cleared his throat. "Well, uh, thank you, kind sir. If I could make a living at writing, I'd give up this humanity saving garbage tomorrow. But, one must eat and feed his family, and this *is* better than assembling electronic parts in some microchip factory." He folded his arms across his chest. "Anyway, you were talking about the morning newspaper."

Fellows played with his ball pen, rolling it between his fingers. "The news media got hold of the Salk plan already."

Charlie shook his head. "Christ, they're fast! Who got it first? Let me guess. The *Enquirer?*" They laughed. "Or *another* legitimate rag?" Schuster kept the momentum up with his shrill, hoarse, ha-ha-ha-ha cadence. It made Fellows laugh all the more, then both were in tears, laughing at themselves laughing.

Charlie quieted down first, wiping the hysterical tear from his eye, and blowing his nose. "Really, though, they broke the news *already?* We just made the decision three days ago to pursue the vaccine testing. Old Jonas Salk's been negotiating the deal for two years, and in all that time the news *rarely* had any stories about it."

Fellows had regained his composure, but still snorted once before speaking. "If it wasn't for the fact that we're working on the virus with the Salk Institute, *I* wouldn't be aware that there's one in progress. The AIDS hotline doesn't have anything about it, either. The whole damned country thinks we've been sitting on our butts, doing nothing, for the past ten years."

"Maybe we should've thrown Jonas's name around a little more, for PR reasons, if nothing else. *His* name seems to have been the attention-getter."

Art threw his pen end-over-end and caught it between his fingers. "Do I detect a slight case of 'green-eye syndrome?'"

"Maybe just a *little,*" Charlie laughed. "It's too damned bad that *I* wasn't the one to come up with the polio vaccine in the fifties. Salk was just a *baby!* He was only thirty-five or so. I'm in the gray zone of my career, and still don't know if I'll make the eternal *Brittanica* listings! Then here comes Salk once again, using basically the same approach as he did with the polio research, and makes the big play."

"*Definitely* green-eyed," Art laughed as he obnoxiously peered into Charlie's eyes.

"Now the news people are going crazy, fighting like a bunch of dogs over a quarter of beef, since he made the announcement."

"And the *other* big topic in the AIDS game. Have you been keeping up on the controversy in the money game?" Charlie tossed a written report at Fellows. "Read this."

Fellows quickly scanned the news piece. "So, the *experts* are saying we're spending too much on AIDS research, to the detriment of cancer and heart disease research. Now I've seen it all!" He handed the paper back. "Don't they realize how many other scientific developments have come out of AIDS research?"

"You didn't read far enough. They *do* concede that, but it's conveniently hidden, later in the article. The argument, from the other side of the fence, is that many more people die of heart problems and cancer than from AIDS. They want prioritizing."

"Oh, hell, we all know it's a game of pocketbook politics, like everything else in this world." Fellows hesitated. "Of *course* they don't want their funds cut in favor of AIDS, but who, in their right mind, *ever* wants their funding cut? Get real! Salaries and jobs are the big part, we all know that. *I* don't want my job threatened, either!"

Schuster glanced up at the clock above Arthur's desk. "Ten o'clock, coffee time *officially.* Want to go downstairs and get a *fresh* cup?"

"Sure, let's go. Be prepared to get congratulated, or accosted by, *everyone* on the way down. It seems that no one else in our own *building* knew about the vaccine testing until they watched the news last night, so how could we have been so dumb as to have expected any recognition from the *John Q. Public?"* Fellows wheeled his executive chair out from the desk as he stood up, straightening his lab coat.

"Live and learn, huh? Damn that Salk," Charlie rambled on, "That old saw about it being *who* you know, not *what* you know, proves itself again." The men left the office and walked down the hallway, then took the steel-cased fire exit stairway down to the basement coffee shop.

"Yep, *bad* case of *green-eye."* Fellows turned to look at the still mumbling little man.

"Hey, Dr. Fellows. Great to hear about the vaccine testing," said a passing lab technician. "How many subjects do you have lined up so far?"

Fellows stopped and faced the female tech. *"None."* He waited impishly for a response, his eyes twinkling.

The tech blinked and looked straight at him. *"None?"*

"That's right, Nancy, *none!* But we're *looking* for test subjects, you know," he smiled menacingly. "Would *you* possibly be interested?"

She tried to read him, half smiling, half serious. "I . . . I'm afraid I wouldn't be a good candidate. You see, I had a hysterectomy several years ago, and I'm not sure if I had a blood transfusion, so—"

"Oh, that's too bad, Nancy. A nice, clean-liver like you would have been a tremendous subject. Why don't you let us run an HIV on you to see if if you've been exposed to the virus, and we'll base our decision on that?" He had a villainous leer, his teeth bared.

Nancy looked at him warily, making a few slight sidesteps to bypass him. "Well, Dr. Fellows, let me think about it for a few days. Er, I've got to run. I think I left a centrifuge running in the lab, and the timer isn't working. It's a very critical test, so—"

"Bye Bye, Nancy," Fellows bellowed with laughter as she darted off down the hall. "See how easy it's going to be to find volunteers, Dr. Schuster?" he said cynically.

"Yeah, terrific," Charlie languished. "What about you, Art? Why don't *you* volunteer?"

"I, uh, never told you this, but I had a problem with I.V. heroine abuse, and I used to frequent the whore district nightly, and before I *outgrew* my hemophilia..." They both laughed sarcastically. Fellows became reflective as they continued down the dark hall. "Not on your life, my friend! I'm as healthy as a horse, and I plan to stay that way. I feel sorry for the poor bastards that have the disease, and of course I hope that Salk's vacine *works*, but I don't think I'm man enough to voluntarily subject myself to the possibility of the vaccine's actually causing the disease. It'll be *years* before anything is made public on the outcome of the vaccine's efficacy, and I might end up on the bad end of the stick."

"I don't think I'm dedicated enough to sacrifice my life, *literally*, to my work, either," Charlie added. "Even though the testing over there on, what, ninety subjects, at the University of Southern California's cancer center, has been promising. Getting injected with components of inactivated pieces of the virus is a bit chilling."

"But, you know, the legendary Salk is volunteering his own bod, just like he did with his polio vaccine. A true American hero, and we don't have many. I don't think the man has been appreciated enough. He ought to get the Congressional Medal of Honor." They entered the cafeteria line. "Two black coffees, please," Arthur said to the portly woman behind the counter. He laid a dollar on the counter, and the men went to a table.

Charlie slid into the booth. "Does the name 'Jonathan Edwards' ring any bells for you?"

Fellows's brows furrowed, then an enlightened calm slid over his face. "Ah, yes, of course. From our early epidemiology classes, if I'm not mistaken . . . a clergyman. Let me think . . . the year 1758, smallpox. He volunteered himself for the experimental vaccination program, and it *got* him!"

"That's right . . . fairly young man, well, *old*, in those days, at age fifty-four. He'd just been appointed president at Princeton when he died from the smallpox." Charlie looked at his friend. "Come on, Art, *you* could go down in the *Britannica*, after all!"

"Thanks, but not for me. Let other, more humanity-oriented people put *their* toes in the water first!" He sipped his coffee. "How many priests and nuns are lined up so far? I *doubt* that they could get the ten they requested."

"You're way behind, Dr. Fellows. USC went to Archbishop Mahony in L.A. with their request and so far have over *sixty*, half of whom are priests and nuns."

"Wow! No kidding!" Fellows paused with his cup to his lips.

"That's right! Even Cardinal O'Connor in New York volunteered, but he was turned down because they already had enough. I thought you *knew* all this stuff." Charlie shook his head. "You'd better get with the program, Dr. Fellows!"

"I guess you're right. The last I knew, they were preparing to ask the old religious celibates, because they'd have the least likely exposure to the virus when compared to the population at large. And, it was thought, the older ones would be more likely to follow the old doctrine of Christian humanitarianism. But they *got* them, huh? Incredible!" Fellow's eyebrows almost touched his hairline, raised in a new expression that Charlie had never seen before.

"Uh, you'd better pull your eyebrows back down before they get caught in your toupe," Charlie laughed. Fellows blushed. Charlie started again, "And the old ones' lives have been fulfilled, so if they *do* contract the disease, it won't be as socially traumatic, using humans for test subjects."

"Are they still getting flack from the gay activists, who already hate the Catholics, for not condoning the use of condoms because of their birth control standpoint?" Fellows asked.

"Oh, sure, they claim that it's all a public relations scam on the part of the church." Charlie tipped his styrofoam cup all the way back, getting the last few drops of now cold coffee. "Done." He looked at his watch. "Let's go back upstairs, we've got some PR work to do ourselves." They stood and walked out of the coffee shop, back into the dark basement hallway.

Part Four
The
Transcendence

1992

PALERMO, OCTOBER

The bell tingled as the glass door closed behind the short, squatty woman who had just come in. She unbuttoned her long dark woolen coat, exposing the cotton print dress of a European commoner. She wore her hair in a tucked up bun, covered by a large scarf.

"Hello. Are you Mr. Leonardo Mazzone?" she queried.

"Yes, I am. How can I help you, ma'am?" he asked sweetly, then, "Oh, another damned charity solicitor?"

"No, no. Do you know a man named Sal Danella? I was told he is your relative. I have some urgent news for him."

"Who are *you*, if I may?" Leonardo decided that he needed to speak with Sal about having people locate him through Leonardo's shop. He didn't like it. He'd spent too many years building the business to have it destroyed by Sal's dealings.

"My name is Ruth Lommori. I'm the daughter of Dr. Noah Thomas, and he asked me to find Mr. Danella as quickly as I could. He told me I might be able to find him through you, and gave me the name of this bakery."

"I don't know of a Noah Thomas," Leonardo lied. "Is Sal supposed to know him?"

"That's what my father said. He wouldn't give me any other information about this matter other than what I've already told you.

All I know is that my father is dying of brain cancer, and during his moments of lucidity he pleads to talk to Sal Danella, and gives your name as the way to find him. *Please*, can you help me? It seems to be my father's last request. He is failing quickly. He's in Saint Joseph's Hospital, in Rome."

"I'm sorry to hear about your father," Leonardo was truly sympathetic, "but Sal isn't available. I think he's in London."

"Is there a way to contact him?" Ruth broke down and cried.

"No, I'm sorry. When he's traveling it's impossible. What day is this... Wednesday, yes?" He threw his hands up and smiled. "Aha! In two more days he'll be calling me for messages! I'll tell you what. You write down your name and phone number, and I'll give him the message when he calls." He wiped his hands on his apron, then handed her a pen and paper from near the cash register. "Here, use this."

The woman pulled her scarf back so she could see better, then scribbled the information on the paper and handed it back. "My father . . . I don't know how long he has." Tears welled in her eyes. "Please have him call me, *please!*"

Leonardo took the woman's hand. "I promise you, I will get the message to Sal. You can expect a call on Friday or Saturday. Now, go to your father. He needs you."

The woman walked out with her head down, wiping her eyes. *"TAXI, TAXI,"* she called out. A cab pulled to the curb and she jumped in. "Airport, please."

• • •

"Did you find him?" The old man's irregular breathing and raspy voice made him difficult to understand, and he stuttered frequently.

"I went to the bakery in Palermo, yes, and I talked to Leonardo Mazzone. He said Mr. Danella is in London."

"Oh, no-o-o," the old man groaned. "I *must* talk to him, I must!" Thomas's head lolled from side to side, and Ruth didn't know whether he was lucid or not.

"Father, he said that he'd give Sal the message when he calls tomorrow, and then Sal will call me... He *promised* me that."

"I must talk to him, I *must!* No one . . . else . . . can . . . know." He fell unconscious again.

Ruth got up from the bedside. *What can this be that is so important to a dying old man?* She spoke loudly, hoping he would stir. "Father, would you like to talk to a priest again? Perhaps Father Benedetto could help you. The one who heard your confession last week."

Thomas didn't respond, he just made unintelligible garbling noises and continued to slowly toss and turn.

Ruth remembered how shaken the priest had been when he exited the room. She'd asked him if there was anything wrong, but he just shook his head no and continued walking. He'd looked deeply troubled, she remembered, and left hurriedly without a word to anyone. And he was such a *pleasant* man when he first entered her Father's room. *What's going on here?* She tied her scarf, preparing to go home to await Sal Danella's call.

Ruth arrived at her apartment and made dinner for her husband, the one who rarely showed up at home for dinner. "Probably *drunk* again," she moaned.

She read a book, frequently stopping to worry about her father, then fell asleep in the chair. She was sleeping, dreaming a pleasant dream about the time, as a child, when she and her family vacationed at a resort in Austria. The cold ring of the telephone startled her awake. "Hello?" The bedside clock said four twenty-two a.m. It was Saturday.

"I'm sorry to awaken you at this hour. I'm calling for a Ruth Lommori. Is she there, please?" It was a smooth voice, very masculine.

"Sal . . . Sal Danella, is that you?"

"Yes, it's me. I got your message. What's going on with Dr. Thomas?"

"I don't know if you're aware, but he was told he had a brain tumor a year ago. Well, now he's dying, in the hospital. The doctors only expect him to live for a couple more days. For some reason, he's been pleading to see you whenever he wakes up a little. He keeps calling your name. Can you tell me what this is about? He's *so* troubled. The doctors think he would do better if he wasn't so tormented by this thing that he refuses to speak of." She cried.

"Why would he want *me?* The last time I saw him was four or five years ago, when I handled some personal business for him. Honestly, I hardly remember him." Sal lied. He would *never* forget that distrusting face.

"Oh, I don't know . . . I don't know," she wailed. "But *please* go to him!"

Sal had been anxious about making this call; his muscles tensed as he thought that maybe this was a trap of some kind. *Had the old man told the authorities what they'd done? Had he finally discovered, after all these years, that the bottle meant for Enrique Sosa had been tampered with? That it contained only water when he finally caught up to Enrique, and that he hadn't really injected him?* A lump formed in his throat as the paranoid thoughts streamed through his mind. His head ached. He'd been worried, putting off this call until now, even though Leonardo had given him the message the day before. He hadn't been able to sleep, the same thoughts churning over and over throughout the night. Was he finally *caught*, after all these years? Had Thomas told the authorities, from his deathbed, if truly he *was* dying, how they had arranged Monsignor O'Casey's murder? "Uh, how do you know of me again? I think this is a very strange call."

The woman recounted her story and continued pleading for him to come at once, to end the poor old man's suffering.

She sounded sincere. "Tell me again . . . " His thinking was muddled. "What does he want of *me?* I have nothing that could interest him anymore." It could be a trap.

"Please . . . " she begged.

He gave in. "O.K., Mrs. Lommori, I'll come and see him. What hospital is it?"

"St. Joseph's, downtown Rome. *Please* come quickly."

"Sure, uh, yeah. I can probably get there late this afternoon."

"Oh, thank you, *thank you,*" she sobbed. Then he heard the dial tone, and put the phone down. *If she is setting me up . . .*

He picked up the phone again. "Yes, this is room 208." He'd

called the hotel operator. "Could you arrange a call to St. Joseph's Hospital in downtown Rome, and call me when they're on the line? Thank you." He recradled the phone and waited, watching an old black-and-white movie on television. It was four thirty a.m.

The phone rang. "Hello," he said as he snatched it.

"Yes, Mr. Danella, this is the hotel operator. I have St. Joseph's on the line for you. One second, please." There was a series of clicking noises.

"St. Joseph's Hospital, good morning."

"Yes, I'm calling about a relative of mine in your hospital, Dr. Noah Thomas. Could I speak to the nurse who is taking care of him, please?"

"One moment." Sal heard a distant ringing sound while the call transferred.

"Fourth floor, Anna speaking."

"Er, yes, this is a *cousin* of Dr. Noah Thomas. I'm calling to check on his condition. I've heard he has taken a turn for the worse, you know, with the brain cancer."

"Dr. Thomas's condition is critical, yes, but he's being medicated and seems comfortable. Would you like me to get a family member on the phone?"

"Er, no, no, that won't be necessary. I'll come in and see him later today."

"Very well, then, good by."

Sal hung up the phone and heaved a tremendous sigh of relief. He turned off the television and climbed into bed, reflecting on his life of chronic fear. When he thought about it, this was actually just a repeat of many, many past nights, but each recurrence seemed to make the *last* one seem less stressful. Maybe he really *should* abandon this life and retire. He had plenty of money, more than he could ever spend.

But as many times as he'd tried, something exciting would arise once again. For whatever reason, he was drawn back into the thrill of stalking prey, then expertly planning the kill to cover any signs of foul play. The actual kill was not that thrilling, but he felt no remorse, either.

The victims were blood-sucking *parasites* anyway, and the world was a better place without them. Maybe *that* was why the police never seriously investigated their deaths. As long as they could be *half* convinced that these deaths were suicides or accidents, it was sufficient enough.

He enjoyed the evasion tremendously; the cat-and-mouse game of cleanly breaking himself from the realm of suspicion. He would be across the country, or even around the world, within hours after the kill. The hunt, the kill, the evasion.

It was an addiction, perhaps, that he may never be able to break. He drifted to sleep.

He arrived in Rome at noon and had lunch at the airport before taking a cab to the hospital. St. Joseph's was a large old brick building, probably a hundred years old. By European standards, however, it was a fairly new structure. A fire escape had been added to the steep walls of the building sometime in the past. He could see the large bore holes that anchored the rusting black stairway to the building. The landings were situated underneath the windows. He shook his head, "What a place to die."

In modern buildings the fire escapes were enclosed, located just outside doorways on each floor, specifically for fire purposes. "I hope I'm never hospitalized *here* in the event of a fire!" He wondered how, in reality, they were going to get bedridden patients out those windows and down the steep, narrow escape.

He entered the dimly lit, depressing old structure and inquired at the front desk as to Dr. Thomas's room number, then proceeded to the fourth floor. He was still a little unnerved after his wretched, sleepless night, and kept watch for any unusual activity in his peripheral vision.

Throughout the building he'd continued to be keenly aware of his surroundings, but nothing seemed amiss so he proceeded. Room 410 was on the right, past the nurses' desk. There was a small waiting area just before the room, and as he passed, a woman who had been seated in one of the chairs stood and approached him.

"Are you Mr. Danella?"

"Yes, I am. You must be Mrs. Lommori, pleased to meet you." He took her hand gently. "How's your father doing?"

"Oh, no change. He continues to call out for you. What's the meaning of all this? I must know." She looked at him sternly.

"I honestly don't know, Mrs. Lommori. Like I told you, I haven't seen your father in years."

"I want to know what's going on. That priest, the one who heard his confession, he was so deeply troubled when he came out of Father's room."

"Priest? *What* priest? *When?*" Sal was suddenly scared.

"Uh, a week ago. Father Benedetto, from the chaplain's office downstairs, why?"

"Oh, just curious, I guess," trying not to show his alarm. He knew the woman saw through his feeble attempt at staying cool. "Let me go in and talk with your father. Before I do, however, I want you to know that whatever he tells me may have to be kept between the two of us. There are certain things in every man's life that are not to be divulged. Maybe to protect property, loved ones, like yourself, or self esteem. Do you understand?"

"I . . . I guess so. As long as he can rid himself of whatever is tormenting him . . . so he's at peace."

"Good, then." He went into the room.

"Dr. Thomas? It's me, Sal Danella. Your daughter found me and told me about your condition, and that you needed to see me."

"Dan . . . Danella . . . Thank . . . you for coming." His eyes opened slowly. "I am dying . . . soon." He licked his parched lips. "The vaccine . . . The AIDS vaccine . . . is in the basement of . . . of the science academy . . . at the Vatican. You must get it out of there and let the . . . Let the world know of it . . . that there *is* one. The suffering . . . It has gone on enough."

Sal's was bewildered. "Did you say *vaccine? What vaccine?* You mean the one that that old scientist, uh, Salk, is working on in the U.S.?"

Noah licked his lips again. "Water . . . " Sal glanced around the room for the water pitcher, then poured a half glass and held it to the old man's lips. He took several small sips. "Not the same. His is . . . different . . . new attempt. *Our* vaccine. The hope . . . in Pandora's box. We had a . . . vaccine before . . . before we spread the virus. It was planned for in case . . . this happened. That it got out of . . . control."

"Why me? Why are you telling *me* this?" Sal stood staring at the old man, dazed by the revelation of the existing vaccine.

"I tried . . . I tried to get the cardinal to tell the world. He refused to stop it. The death . . . He is *mad!* He still thinks it is . . . God's will. Thinks it's stopping fornication . . . sex . . . drugs . . . sin. He thinks God wanted it to . . . spread to heterosexuals. He's *mad!* It isn't . . . supposed to end . . . this way."

"But why *me?*" Sal interrupted. "What am *I* supposed to do?"

"You . . . You get it out of the Vatican. You can do it. Save the church! If the world found it . . . at the Vat . . . " he paused to catch his breath, "Vatican . . . They'd think the church was responsible . . . for the plague. The church would crumble . . . Die . . . " His eyes rolled back, then he refocussed on Sal.

"*Where* is the vaccine again? I'm sorry, I'm not thinking."

"Water . . . " Noah's lips were swollen. His breath smelled foul, like he was dehydrated. His saliva clung to his dry teeth. Sal helped him sip again, then lowered his head back onto the pillow.

"Basement of . . . of the Academy of Science. Vatican . . . Two crates. Marked lab supplies. Enough for maybe five . . . five hundred thousand."

"Who *else* knows?" Thomas was starting to drift away. Sal shook him. "Hey, Noah, who *else* knows?"

"Uhhh, no one." He licked his lips with his dry tongue again. Sal helped him with more water. "No . . . no, Hans Bjorgstad knows. He has the molecular formula . . . memorized." He fell back into unconsciousness.

Sal stared at him through glazed eyes. What can *I* do? I can't get it out by *myself.* He shook his head, wondering if this was for real, then walked out into the hall.

"What did he say? What's the matter?" Ruth asked as she neared. "Is everything all right now?"

"Uh, yes, he told me what he needed to tell me. He should be O.K. now. Like I told you before I went in, I *cannot* break his confidence in the matter. But he should be at peace now."

"I guess that's all that matters," she answered. *"Thank you* so very much for seeing him. It is his last wish."

"I'm glad I could help." He looked deeply into her eyes. He knew that she could accept her father's death now. "Good by."

Sal trod down the stairs. His mind veered to the priest, Benedetto, who had heard Thomas's confession. What had the old man told him that'd made him appear so anguished? Priests have heard it *all* in the confessional; *nothing* should be *that* troubling to him. He entered the first floor lobby.

"Excuse me, Sister," he asked a passing nun. "Could you direct me to the chaplain's office?"

"Certainly. Straight down that hallway, third door on your left." She pointed the way.

"Thank you."

Sal's hard-surfaced heels made a clacking noise in the dead silence of the lobby. He reached the office and threw open the door. A priest sat against the back wall, facing him from behind a desk.

"May I help you, sir?" The priest looked up.

"Yes, I was hoping to speak to a Father Benedetto about something that's been concerning me."

"Well, you're lucky then. I was just about to leave. *I'm* Father Benedetto. Please, sit down." He motioned Sal to a chair. "Now, what seems to be troubling you?"

Sal looked at the floor, then raised his eyes to meet the priest's. He brandished a perilous expression, meant to be menacing. "I understand you heard the confession of Dr. Noah Thomas last week."

The priest was startled, his eyes questioned. "I'm afraid that is a personal matter__"

"You appeared *very* anguished when you left his room," Sal cut in.

"I beg your pardon, sir, but the sanctity of confession is not to be discussed with *anyone* for *any* reason. Now, please leave." He started to stand.

Sal stepped forward and grabbed him by the shirt, pinning him against the wall. *"What did he say,* Padre?" he growled, tightening his grip.

The priest looked down at the hands on his shirt. His own hands hung limply at his sides. But he was not afraid. "Confession is an act between God and sinner, and I am only the intermediary. I would choose death before divulging a confession I have been entrusted with." The priest's look was strange. He took on a certain placid expression with those words, not the fearful tremble that Sal had hoped to elicit.

Sal released him abruptly. "Well, if you can't tell *me*, you can't tell *anyone*." He abruptly released the priest, then turned and huffed toward the door.

"May God forgive you and save you from damnation, Mr. Salvadore Danella."

Sal stopped dead, turned, and glared. He *knew*. Thomas *had* told him everything. The priest maintained his serene expression, no fear. Sal wanted to go back and threaten him further, but he *couldn't*. He experienced a bizarre, cold feeling, as though he was being repelled from there. He left.

MINNEAPOLIS, OCTOBER

"If you really think it's possible, I think you *should* call them, honey." Sue was talking to her husband, Dr. Peter Toscano. He was keeping her awake, and she had to be to work at the university in the morning. She was a striking, statuesque, auburn haired woman of thirty-two.

"Yes, but call who? The WHO, the CDC, the NIH, *who?*" He rubbed his chin as he spoke. He was sat at the bedside. "It's three o'clock in the morning, Sue," he responded. "I've got to be to work at *seven.*"

"Me too, you know. *You* haven't been able to sleep in three nights, so what's another?" Sue had grown tired of Peter's insomnia.

"I *really* think I'm right! I think it's the *exact* virus! And it's been right under my nose for the past *decade!*" He lit a cigarette. "I suppose the most *logical* agency to contact would be the CDC." He spoke in a light Italian dialect, in spite of his having lived in the U.S. for the past fourteen years.

Professor Toscano had immigrated to the U.S. in 1978, on a student visa, to do biological research at the University of Minnesota. He was pursuing a master's degree then, and liked living in the U.S. He applied for, and received, permanent resident status.

The only drawback with *that* status was competing against the favored U.S. students for graduate programs, so he became naturalized. He completed his doctoral requirements two years later, then stayed on at the university to teach. Recently he had been promoted to full professor.

He had met Sue several years earlier, but after he'd been naturalized. He looked at her. "I love you, honey. I wish I could just forget this whole damned thing." Then he lightened up. "You *must* know I *love* you, dear. I didn't *have* to marry you for citizenship . . . I already *have* it!" he teased. He was olive complected, with a strong, square jaw and black wavy hair.

"Your *only* flaw, dear, is the *belly,*" Sue would tease back, saying *belly* in a deep bass voice, and poking him in the paunch at the same time. "Stereotypical Italian," she laughed.

Peter became serious again. "I always thought it was strange that the AIDS virus was connected to primates. Now they say it's a variety called the green monkey, but *we* were working with others. Maybe that's why I didn't tie things together. And we were working in a small independent research lab that contracted with big companies, like pharmaceuticals and cosmetics outfits. We handled specific, isolated units of whatever project the employing company happened to have going on at the time. It was called the Thomas Research Lab, in Rome."

Sue lifted herself up on an elbow. "Do you *really* think there's a connection, or could it be pure coincidence? Small research companies like that do live biological testing all the time. Maybe it was totally unrelated. What did they tell you, while you were working on it?"

"It was weird. Every time one of us assistants asked questions, Dr. Thomas became offish, then told us how lucky we were to be able to help on a project of such great magnitude. We were told it was a cancer research project for a pharmaceutical company in Switzerland.

It was *strange*, the whole thing. Nowhere did I *ever* see any signs of a large company's involvement, you know, like company letterheads or requisitions or anything."

"So it was a cancer drug project, so what? Those go on all the time. Let's go back to sleep." She laid down and snuggled under the comforter.

Peter continued, oblivious to Sue's interjection. "Thomas was so secretive about everything. We figured he was safeguarding against industrial espionage or something. You know, he happens to be in the running for a Nobel award this year, come to think of it."

"In what area?" Sue yawned.

"Cancer research."

"Come on, honey, leave it alone then! He's obviously a legitimate cancer researcher. You don't get a Nobel nomination without a pretty intense background, right? And *certainly* not for engineering the white plague!" She laughed. "He sounds like a respected scientist to me. I'm going to sleep." She turned and clicked off the bedside lamp.

Peter remained sitting, mentally analyzing the reading he'd been doing over over the past month that made him realize that possibly he *had* helped create the so-called AIDS virus. "At the Thomas Laboratory, years ago, we referred to it as ISV-1. It doesn't matter, it's just semantics. You can call it anything you want, if *you're* the researcher. The true identification comes in its mode of biologic action and structure, not by merit of its name."

"Would you *hang it up*, please, and go to sleep? You're driving me *crazy!*" Sue was getting a little irritated.

He carried on, talking to himself as much as anything. "I read a medical journal article that piqued my interest in the AIDS virus's similarities to the virus we worked with in Rome. They're *both* retroviruses. They carry their genetic material in RNA rather than DNA. They both encode their genomes into DNA through a specialized enzyme called transcriptinase," he mumbled. "After infecting a host cell, the transcribed viral DNA permanently integrates into the host cell DNA. At that point, it's designated a *provirus*, making use of the host cell to reproduce itself."

"Would you *please* . . . " she begged.

"Damn it, there are too many *identical* virology traits to have the AIDS virus be *anything* else! Ignore me, honey, I'm talking to *myself.*" He did this commonly when he was working through a problem. "The immune deficiency can be traced, in both cases, to a subset of T lymphocytes called T4 helper/inducers. Now, healthy T4 lymphocytes are responsible for fighting off infection in the body, and when they're compromised, as in the case of this virus, the T4's are rendered useless. A malfunction in the immune system results!"

"O.K., I give up!" She hid her head under the feather pillow.

Doctor Thomas had implied that the pharmaceutical company was working on a cancer drug that damaged T4 lymphocytes inadvertently, and that altering the genetic composition of host cells would allow genetic manipulation to overcome the untoward T4 damage. In actuality, the inadvertent lymphocyte damage could cause transformation of the lymphocytes into leukemic cells. The research goal, supposedly, was to overcome the obstacles of immunosuppression and cancer. *What a crock of shit!"* he yelled.

Sue jumped. "Wh-what? When will this end? I've *got* to get some *sleep!"*

"What a *fool* I was! I think I helped create the AIDS virus! But *why?* Why would a sane, rational, likable human being like Dr. Thomas intentionally create and use such a virus? Especially a world renowned geneticist?" He walked to the dresser and pulled a cigarette from the package, then absent-mindedly lit it.

"You're *certain* now, aren't you," Sue stated.

"Yes, I *am.* I was in a state of denial for a while, I guess, in order to protect my self integrity." He took a long drag. "But that's past now. I just mentally reexamined the similarities of the viruses, and there's no residual doubt. But what . . . What was the motive? I have to think that the doctor wasn't an *intentional* perpetrator. Possibly it was accidentally introduced into humans, or maybe the result of some sinister foul play. Maybe a terrorist act. *That's* probably it. How else would it have spread so quickly?"

Sue became involved. "If you're right in your conjecture—"

"It's *not* conjecture." He cut her short.

"Don't get so angry! Will you settle for *theory?"*

"I'm sorry." He looked at her. "Yes, I'll settle for *theory.*" He smiled weakly. "I'm going to call the CDC first thing tomorrow morning and at least explore the possibility. If nothing else, the similarity in the viruses is so strong that the vaccine we developed might be of help in dealing with AIDS."

"A *vaccine?*" She repeated, fully alert.

"Yes, a *vaccine.* We developed a vaccine, in case anyone would become infected with the virus. At least, that was the story we stupid research assistants were fed at the time."

Peter couldn't sleep now, no matter how hard he tried. He was too worked up, grinding his teeth between drags on the cigarette. "And to think, the famous Dr. Salk's been working on the same thing for a few years now. How ironic! If only I'd tied all this together a long time ago. Honey, would you call my office in the morning, in case I fall asleep, and make an excuse for my absence?"

"Sure, dear. Now *I* can't sleep." She rubbed his thigh. "Rubbing you like this makes me *horny.* Would a little 'nooky' help you go to sleep, hmm-m-m-m?" She smiled seductively, then bared a breast for him.

He grinned widely, and then said authoritatively, in his best scientist voice, "Now that my resolutions are made, I think *yes,* maybe that would help a *lot!*" He laughed, she giggled. He crushed out his cigarette, then laid next to her and began passionately kissing her on the neck . . .

The sun was shining through the mini-blinds, into the mirror on the dresser, and reflecting brightly into his face. He rubbed his eyes and yawned, then stretched and yawned again. The bedside clock said ten-thirty a.m. Sue was gone. He got out of bed and went to the bathroom to clean up. "Ten-thirty, hmmm... Must be an hour later in Georgia, I think."

He showered quickly, then went to the phone in the kitchen and dialed long distance information. "Hello, Atlanta information? Could you give me the number for the CDC?" He wrote the number as the operator spoke. "Thank you." Then he paused, holding the phone. They're going to think I'm a *nut* case! Maybe I *am,* I don't know! No, no, it *was* the same virus, absolutely. He dialed the number and waited.

"Hello, Centers for Disease Control," the woman answered.

"Ummm, yes, could you connect me to the AIDS research department, please? I would actually like to speak to whoever is in the highest position in that department."

"That would be either Dr. Fellows or Dr. Schuster. One moment, please."

"Fellows here. How can I help you?" the man grumbled.

Peter hesitated. "Uh, excuse me . . . I'm not sure how to begin. You're going to think I'm crazy."

There was a pause. "Well, please continue, let's *see!*"

"My name is Dr. Peter Toscano, from the University of Minnesota. Well . . . Well, I'm calling because I think I helped develop the AIDS virus."

Silence. *"Come again?"*

"I *know* it sounds ridiculous, but I'm a full professor here at the university. My credentials are impeccable," he stammered.

"I'm sure your credentials are in order, but you're right, buddy, it sounds *ridiculous.* I'm a very busy man. Why don't you call . . . call your local police department." He chuckled.

"I know . . . I knew it. Listen. I'm talking about a retrovirus that affects T4 helper cells and—"

"So you've studied the AIDS virus. That's *good.* I *do* want to hear you out, though, this is great stuff! I needed a break!" Dr. Fellows was amused.

Peter rambled on for ten minutes, with the doctor becoming quiet, increasingly impressed. " . . . so we finished the project and stored the viral antibody, to be used as a vaccine—"

"Did you say a *vaccine?*"

"Yes, damn it, a *vaccine!* But no, not the same one as Jonas Salk is trying to develop. This one's been around all along, and I just put it all together—"

"Where? How?" Fellow's voice was edged, suddenly cracking.

"It was stored in some crates in the basement of the Academy of Sciences at the Vatican. I remember thinking at the time that it was an odd place to store an agent produced for a pharmaceutical company."

"So . . . *You're for real?* You're serious? Can you give me the name of the dean at your college so that I can verify you?" Fellows was astonished.

"Certainly. His name is Dr. William Morton, and he's been the dean for thirteen years. My employee number at the university is 000-324-65. He and I, and the personnel department, are the only parties privy to that knowledge. His direct phone line is area code 612-555-6217. Please, *do* call him."

"And what's your number, Mister, er, Doctor Toscano?"

"My number is area code 612-555-1264." *He believes me!*

"O.K., got it. Tell me, does anyone *else* have this knowledge? Have you spoken with *anyone* else about it?"

"Only my wife. She's had to put up with me while I spent some sleepless nights mulling it over."

"O.K., good. *Tell no one else,* all right? I'm going to call the dean right now, then I'll get back with you at this number in a few minutes." He hung up.

Peter sat staring, befuddled. He was glued to his chair. After ten minutes the phone rang. "Hello, Dr. Toscano speaking."

"Yes, Doctor Toscano. This is Fellows. Tell me, what's your social security number?"

"504-62-1252."

"O.K., good. How soon can you get here? Or, better yet, can you get to D.C. today, this *afternoon?* I'll call Continental and take care of the flight. Your ticket will be waiting at the desk."

"Uh . . . yes, I guess so."

"Good. As soon as you arrive, go straight to Langley, the CIA headquarters, and ask for me. I'll wait there until you arrive at whatever time. We'll speak with the *CIA director only,* got it? *No* one else. In the meantime, try to recreate as much as you possibly can about this whole project, and write notes to yourself so you won't forget anything. Now, pack a light bag and head for the airport. Here's how to get to Langley . . . "

Peter took down the instructions. His head was swimming when he hung up this time. "Damn!" He scribbled a hurried note for Sue, telling her where he was going and that he'd call as soon as he could, and to keep this absolutely quiet. He dressed, packed a bag, and drove to the airport.

• • •

The D.C. area was just as he'd remembered, grimy with the dirt of two hundred years, but proud. He checked his watch as he paid the cab driver and stepped onto the curb, looking up at the massive building. It was seven p.m. He walked through the glass doors, encountering two men by the security officer's desk in the lobby. It was apparent that the employees had gone home for the evening; except for the two men and the guard, the building was void of people.

"Hello, Dr. Peter Toscano, I presume?" asked one of the men. Peter was impressed by the man's awkward, lanky stature.

"Er, yes, I am. And you must be Dr. Fellows." He extended his hand and smiled. "It's nice to meet you." He was uneasy.

"Follow me, please," ordered Fellows. He led the way to the bank of elevators and pushed the button, then remained silent as they boarded the car and rode to the third floor. The other man had stayed behind.

"This way, sir." Fellows walked down the hall. He was not one for small talk. The only sound was that of their footsteps echoing down the wide hallway.

Peter followed him through some wooden double doors and into a large, plush office, with a U.S. flag behind a giant mahogany desk. The man seated behind the desk rose to greet them.

"Dr. Peter Toscano," said Fellows, "I'd like to introduce you to Stanton Douglas, the Director of the Central Intelligence Agency."

Peter nodded. "A pleasure, sir." The desk was too large to shake hands across. Peter felt out of place, vulnerable. He was overwhelmed by the magnitude of the past few hour's events.

"Yes, Dr. Toscano, likewise," said Douglas. "Please, sit down. It's late, so let's begin. Dr. Fellows arrived a couple of hours ago. We've had a long chat, so I'm knowledgeable, and admittedly shaken, by what I've heard. Suppose you start at the very beginning, what, twenty years ago? Then bring us to the present. Did you make the notes as Dr. Fellows suggested?"

"Yes, quite extensive notes. On the plane." He pulled them from his coat pocket.

"Excellent. And I trust you have told *no* one, except for what you've told your wife already?" Stan asked.

"No one. I certainly understand the importance of keeping this quiet." Peter darted his eyes between his notes and the director.

"Excellent. Then please begin. Rely on your notes as much as possible. It seems the memory is less erratic with a guideline to follow," he admonished.

"Yes, I know. I *lecture* for a *living,* and notes are an integral part of that."

"Oh, yes, I'm sorry if I insulted your intelligence," Stan replied.

"Quite all right." Peter was beginning to relax. After all, these were just people, like himself, behind their high powered facades. "O.K . . . " He put on his reading glasses. "I was studying at the university in Rome in the early seventies, I think it was 1972. I needed some part time work while I was in school, so I hired on with the Thomas Research Laboratory as a research assistant. I'd been there for a short while when Dr. Thomas took me into his office and told me he was impressed with my knowledge and work, and that he had a special, confidential project his lab was working on. Supposedly it was a Swiss pharmaceutical company that was doing research on cancer drugs, and we were going to work on a primate virus, engineering it to act in humans to affect the autoimmune system. I remember thinking it odd that I'd never seen any correspondence from the supposed pharmaceutical company. Whenever I'd ask questions about some of the strange research Dr. Thomas asked for, he'd balk and change the subject. He was good at that . . . "

Peter told the entire story, reinforcing it with a smattering of indepth research terms and facts about the virus's behavior and structure. The men in the room hung on every word. The large office was stifled with intensity.

" . . . and, after wrestling for the past week or so with what *was* just a suspicion, I had to conclude that the AIDS virus, which we now call HIV, actually started in our lab with the acronym ISV-1 twenty years ago. When I was *absolutely* certain, I called and spoke with Dr.

Fellows, this morning." He removed his glasses and looked up at Douglas. There was dead silence.

"Uh . . . So you admit that you assisted in the development of this deadly disease? Unknowingly, of course," Douglas responded, breaking the stillness.

"Yes, apparently I did. But I have absolutely no idea how it was introduced into the human population, or who in a sane mind would do such a thing. I don't know. Do you suppose *terrorists* could be involved? Possibly a form of biologic warfare?" He looked at Douglas.

"I guess *anything's* possible," Stan responded. "Dr. Toscano, would you please indicate on your notes that you are the author, then date and sign them?"

"I guess so. What for?"

"Just for our records."

"I guess that would be all right," he puzzled. He did so, then handed the notes to Douglas.

"Thank you. How many others do you know of who were involved in this project? Please try to think carefully. *Anyone* at all, even with loose knowledge of it." He laid the notes on his desk.

"Only myself and another research assistant, but for the life of me, I can't remember his name. I've *tried.* And, of course, Dr. Thomas."

"*No* other scientists? Seems like a big project for one man. And, no less, to have a vaccine developed and all."

"Thomas kept very tight control over the paper work and results, stating that it was the wish of the pharmaceutical company. If there *were* any others, it was kept secret. Incidentally, I read that he'd died just recently. Too bad . . . a brilliant man . . . a great loss to the world scientific community."

"Yes, I believe he was a Nobel winner, or at least nominated." Douglas then turned in his chair and picked up the phone. "Did you get all of it?" he asked into the phone. "Good. I think that's all we need. Come on in."

Peter turned to see the large double doors to the rear open. A man in a gray suit walked briskly in, followed by two other suited men. They approached Peter directly, with the lead man facing him. The others flanked him to the rear.

"Dr. Toscano," Douglas said quietly, "this is Lloyd Barber, with the United States' Attorney General's office."

Barber looked at Peter straight on as he reached into his breast pocket and retrieved a folded sheet. "Dr. Toscano, I have here a warrant for your arrest." Peter's eyes glazed. "You are charged with open counts of murder and conspiracy in the deaths of John Guthals, Stephen Homann, Andrew Leal, Foster Cash . . . " he read on, " . . . George Williams, Timothy Cavanagh . . . " The list contained dozens of names. "And I'm sure there will be several thousand more charges, as soon as the paperwork is completed. You have the right to remain silent . . . " he continued with the Miranda rights. The men behind Peter restrained him by the elbows while they placed him in handcuffs.

Peter's eyes then dulled with shock, horror. He sputtered, his mouth hung wide open. He was dumfounded, he couldn't speak. He choked on his words. They wouldn't come out of his dry, open mouth. Finally he was able to squeeze some air across his paralyzed vocal cords. "What? Wha?" He fought for breath. "But . . . But I came here to help *you!* This is the United States of America! I am a citizen of this country. I have my citizenship papers! This can't happen here!"

"Please, Dr. Toscano," Douglas said. "Try to get a hold on yourself. You must realize that this is the largest alleged mass murder, second only to the Holocaust, as of yet anyway, in the history of the modern world. We *must* pursue legal action."

"Come with me, please, Doctor," Barber said. He led Peter, flanked and supported by the other men, from the room. Peter cursed loudly in Italian as they left.

"So what do you think of this, Stan?" Dr. Fellows asked. "Quite a dramatic turn of events, huh?"

"Absolutely and totally *incredible!* Beyond my hitherto wildest imagination! I don't know that I can believe this has happened. I think it'll take some time before I can say I comprehend, yet actually *believe,* what I have just witnessed with my own ears and eyes!"

"Yeah. I'm still a bit dizzy myself, even after having most of the day to digest it all. It seems my brain just doesn't want to reason it through with any intelligence. Well, I believe I'll go back over to the hotel. I'll come by in the morning to plan our next move." He blew a frustrated puf of air from his cheeks and rapped on the desk with his knuckles, then turned and left. "Good night."

• • •

"So, how did you sleep?" Stan asked of Dr. Fellows. They were in the director's office the next morning.

"Not worth a damn, I'm afraid," Fellows answered.

"Me neither. I think I finally might have dozed a little at around four a.m., but I'm not sure whether I really did. I came into the office at about five-thirty to go through all of this in my mind again. Coffee?"

"Sure, black." Stan picked up his thermos and poured the hot liquid into a paper cup from his desk drawer, then handed it to Fellows.

"Thanks. I think I have some perspective now. By the way, what's going to happen to Dr. Toscano?"

"That's up to the Justice Department. Poor fellow. It makes me kind of ill to think what we'll have to put him through. He *did* come here to help, and, frankly, I believe he's innocent of everything other than being in the wrong place at the wrong time. I think he's been had. My intent, in having him taken into custody, was really to keep this whole thing hushed up until we can get that vaccine."

"Why?"

"Can you imagine the *explosivity* of this thing? What would happen if the news media got wind of the fact that there's a *vaccine?* And that AIDS may be a sick, man made plot, by unknown perpetrators? Jesus! There might be rioting. Fighting over the small amount of vaccine available. I think the Catholic Church would be placed in a real jam, innocent as it probably is. Remember a couple of years ago when the Salk Institute went to them for volunteers for it's vaccine testing, and how up in arms the gay activists were over it?"

"Yes, vaguely. This situation could be treacherous."

"We'd likely have a global witch hunt, with everyone looking for unknown conspirators. Everybody would blame everybody else that they already love to hate. Man against man, race against race, country against country. Possibility of a resultant war? I think pretty damn strong."

"Yes, I see. We must be *extremely* careful. I've had some major questions of mine answered, finally, with this revelation about the disease. We've never been able to figure it out. We knew the virus is present in a species of monkeys, but no one's ever been able to figure exactly how it transmitted into man. And the other mystery we've been unable to figure. Why did it start at a narrow focal point in time, with just a handful of individuals, but on a world basis? I see now where the conspirators, be they terrorists or whatever, first must have infected a handful of gay men, *intentionally*, to spread the disease." He took a sip of the coffee. Stan remained pensive, silent.

Fellows put his cup down. "Remember the one victim on the warrant that Lloyd Barber named, George Williams, from Canada? He was deemed 'Patient Zero' by the CDC several years ago. He was at the base of *all* our contact tracking. Hell, a friend of his wrote a book about him, and his involvement in the transmission of the disease was the topic of television shows, like *60 Minutes*, a few years back. A famous man. I wonder if maybe *he* was one of the original men infected. We told him early on to abstain from sexual behavior, because we felt that he was sexually transmitting the disease. Did that stop him? Hell no, it made him *more* active. There are tales that he had, I don't remember, maybe a thousand lovers, and that's *after* he learned of his illness, and before he died. Like he was *trying* to spread it." He shook his head in dismay.

"Yes, I recall all the hoopla about him. I'd read he was quite a colorful character, his lifestyle and all."

"That he was. He died, I think, in about '83. Anyway, let's move to the future. So, what's next?" Fellows queried.

Stan looked at his desk and sighed. "Well, we'd better plan, *clandestinely*, to get that vaccine before somebody *else* does, if it's still there. I suppose we must verify its existence, then arrange to have the Air Force pick it up. That could take some time to get the logistics arranged. Especially in light of the fact that we can't tell anyone what's going on. I'll do some figuring, then get some agents in the Rome area to monitor activity at the Vatican for a while. It'll probably take me six or eight weeks to scrutinize a handful of men to involve here. Men that I can trust with my *life*, basically. Then we'll arrange a flight, somehow, into the civilian airport in Rome to pick up the vaccine as quietly as possible. We can't even tell the Air Force, truthfully, what we're doing." He sighed again.

"It's too bad, you know. If the world was a trusting place, and there weren't so damn many crazies and profiteers, we could just fly over there and pick it up in the morning!"

"Yeah, dream on!" Stan rubbed his cheek.

"About the vaccine. *I* want it," Fellows remarked suddenly.

"See? *You too, huh?*" Stan laughed uneasily.

"Purely *scientifical*, my friend," Dr. Fellows retorted. He sensed the air of mistrust in Stan's remark, even though he'd tried to disguise it with a slight laugh. Based on this innocent, insignificant interchange, he could *see* how this situation could escalate to a war! "I'd like to have the vaccine flown to Miami, the site of the major epicenter of the disease. It could be stored there at Homestead Air Force Base while we checked its efficacy. If truly there's any merit to it, we could immediately begin vaccinations, and hopefully produce more, once we got the molecular formula. As an after thought, we could *desperately* use Dr. Peter Toscano's knowledge. I hope you see to it that nothing happens to him!"

Stan brightened. "Absolutely right. We never even *considered* him, did we? How stupid of us to *overlook*, yet criminally *prosecute*, what may be the very key to our salvation from this plague! All the frenzy, and no time to think clearly, I guess. But, of course, don't admit our oversight to anyone. We might be sharply criticized in our positions if we appeared so damned stupid."

Fellows nodded. "I'd better go catch a plane. Get the charges against Toscano reduced, or, preferably, dropped altogether so I can consult him, and immediately. Tell him to contact me again as soon as possible, and I'll work things out. And set up the pickup of the vaccine as soon as you can, then call me. I'll look for things to happen within a couple of months." He crumpled his empty cup, then threw it in the waste basket. "So long." He walked away from the desk.

"Have a safe trip. I'm sure we'll talk soon," Stan called out.

BUDAPEST, NOVEMBER

The phone rang as Luis entered his office. He hurriedly threw his coat over the chair and grabbed the receiver. "Good morning, Professor Jurado speaking."

"Yes, is this Colonel Jurado?" asked the creamy smooth male voice.

Luis hesitated. *No* one at the university knew him as a colonel. He kept his military affairs secret to protect his credibility with the university. Only the KGB knew he was an agent for the Cuban government. He had *never* been seen in his uniform in Hungary, being careful not to expose his dual role.

"Er, who's calling, please?" His voice was peppered with anxiety.

"*Colonel*, don't you remember my voice? This is Salvadore Danella. Long time no see!"

"Oh, yes, now I remember. It's been many years. What can I do for you?" He breathed easier.

"Sell me some shares in your newly found capitalism!" he laughed. "I hear your going great guns there in Hungary with your economy since you threw the damn ruskie commies out a couple of years back. Don't you feel a little shaky there, like a fish out of water, to use an old cliche?"

"All right, Sal, what do you want? And keep the politics out of it. I still have reason to be here."

"Yeah, sure Luis, sure. If that's the way you want it! To the point. I have some news that I know your government would be *very* interested in, but it will cost you plenty. It's about the AIDS thing."

"So, give me a clue. That covers a lot of territory, and we're not in the habit of paying for worthless information. Let's see what it's worth."

"Here goes! Did you know there's a *vaccine?*"

There was a pause. "So what, Sal, *everybody* in the entire world knows there's a vaccine. I heard about it three years ago, when Dr. Salk in the U.S. called for volunteers in the Catholic Church to test it. He succeeded, huh?"

Sal had to think for a moment. "I don't think it's the same thing you're talking about. *This* one was developed by the original doctor, way back before they released the virus in the seventies."

"What? An original vaccine? Why did he have a vaccine?"

Sal cleared his throat, "Uh, in case the disease got away from him, he had a way to abort the project."

"Hmmm . . . so there's an effective, tested vaccine already in existence?" Luis's mind churned with the possibility, then concluded with sarcasm. "Did you mix it in your kitchen? You must be bad off, calling me with an opener like this."

"I'm *serious.* I learned about it just recently, and until now didn't know exactly what to do with the information. The original scientists had one all along! The only person still alive with knowledge of it told me about it from his death bed, just a month ago," Sal lied. Bjorgstad was his hole ace.

"That would have to be Noah Thomas. I heard he'd just died recently. If you're trying to pull a fast one, you'd better think twice," Luis warned.

"Look, *friend,* don't threaten me. Have I given you any misinformation yet?" Sal countered, lowering his voice.

"Well, no. All right, let's talk. What do you want?"

"I want a meeting with you and Castro, in Havana, sometime next week. My price is a half million in U.S. currency, and for this, I'll tell you *exactly* where the vaccine is. You can pick it up at your leisure, then maybe destroy it, or possibly sell it to the Americans for some astronomical figure."

"Why would we want to sell it to *them?* We bought the virus and implanted it there to destroy their health care system, remember?"

"You've already established the disease in the U.S. so deeply that they may crumble financially in their fight to keep up with the cost of medical care for the victims *anyway.* So sell them the vaccine for billions of dollars and finish the job on their economy!"

"Very interesting, *if* you're on the level. Let me think it over and get back with you in the next few days. I'll call Havana to see if there's any interest. Are you still at that bakery, uh . . . "

"Leonardo Mazzone's, that's right. I'll wait for your call. And hurry. There are others who may be interested, you know."

"Don't be so hasty. I'll let you know if Castro wants to see you. Good by." Luis put the phone down. *A vaccine? There's been a vaccine all this time?*

• • •

Luis's call came three days later, and Sal spent the next night in a roaring, flying metal behemoth over the Atlantic. The jet dove from the wispy ocean clouds into the Havana airport in the morning of the next day.

The decrepit fifties model Ford with 'Taxi' hand painted on its side doors rattled through the streets, leaving a trail of blue smoke. Sal had flagged it at the airport to take him to the capitol building, and sat next to the cabbie in the front seat. "God, it's muggy here. How do you people stand it?" he asked the driver. A barely perceptible aura of humidity circumscribed the bright sun.

"No entiendo." The driver didn't understand. He stared straight ahead, lurching frequently to unexpected stops when the old brakes screamed of metal fatigue.

Luis was already in Castro's office when Sal was shown in. Sal had had second thoughts just before traveling to Havana. He would be out of his element and safety net. He could be made to 'disappear' in this little country, and no one would be the wiser. His friends would certainly look for him, but all the Cubans had to do was say he was killed in some kind of accident, and that would be it. His corporal safety took on a new frailty he'd never experienced. "Good morning, gents," he said as he strode into the ceiling fan cooled room.

Fidel Castro was unmistakable, garbed in his customary military fatigues and bearded. He looked, to Sal, just like he had always seen him in the news media, but his physical stature was impressive. Maybe his *size* alone, when compared to other short Latino men, helped influence the decision in putting him into the power seat of this dictatorship.

"Good morning," said Luis. "Salvadore Danella, please meet Generalisimo Fidel Castro." He waved his arm from Sal to Fidel.

"A pleasure to meet you, General." Sal extended his hand.

Fidel failed to take his hand, instead glancing at it indifferently, then at Sal's face. He remained seated behind the large desk. "Sit down, Danella."

Sal tried not to show his ire with this unexpected, rude treatment. *Who the hell does this clown think he is, anyway?* He sat grudgingly as commanded.

"Now, *mi amigo,"* Fidel sneered sarcastically, "I want to begin by telling you that I have *no* respect for you. You are a man with no sense of duty, no country, no loyalty, no personal integrity. I daresay you would do *anything* for money, given you didn't have to *endanger* yourself, of course! That also makes you a *coward* . . . a *gusano*, in my language...a *worm*. I've heard that you call yourself a *mercenary* of sorts. You are *mistaken*. A mercenary has the courage to place his life in danger, for a *cause*, regardless of the money he may command. You *run* from danger. Now, I am a busy man. Tell me what you want." Fidel looked back at the papers on his desk.

Sal trembled with rage, his face burned. He wanted desperately to spring from his chair and smack the pompous son of a bitch with the heavy gold ring he wore, just for moments like this. Had he a gun, he may well have used it! *Settle down, settle down, settle down.* He took some deep breaths to calm himself. "O.K., O.K. I know what you think of me, but I'm not upset by your scathing *opinion*, as it is *simply* that. One must *respect the source* of an opinion before he is affected by it."

Fidel's eyes froze, then slowly raised from the papers. "What *is* it you *want?* I want you out of my sight as quickly as possible."

Luis sat in the corner chair, watching in horror. "Gentlemen, may I act as intermediary here? It seems you have polarized opinions and need someone to intervene to accomplish anything. Try to place your emotions secondary to your business goals." It worked, he thought. There was a noticeable decrease in the tension. *Whew!*

Fidel spoke. "You have the floor, Danella. Luis has already told me the gist of your proposal."

"Good, we can keep it *short*. Noah Thomas, one of the engineers of the AIDS virus, told me from his deathbed that there is a vaccine, and there *has* been one all along. Apparently he wanted to die with his conscience cleared. The originators prepared it before they introduced the virus into humans in case the disease got out of hand, like it *has*.

But they wouldn't come forward with the information, after they'd lost control, for fear of recrimination. Thomas said that *no* one, except himself, knew the molecular structure of the vaccine." He lied. Of course there was Dr. Bjorgstad, but that would remain Sal's secret until he'd made this deal. "Only *I* know where the vaccine is right now. I'd told Luis, here, that I wanted a half million for the information, but I've decided that it's worth *more.* I now want a *million* U.S. dollars." He was still steamed from Castro's scathing oration.

Castro scowled. "My opinion of you couldn't have been more accurate." Their eyes locked in a spiteful glare. "I'll give you the *half* million only. You can either choose to accept it, or watch over your shoulder for the rest of your life. I, like you, am not without connections in this world."

"That's an *ugly* threat, and my people don't take kindly to threats. But to avoid the further deterioration of our *working* relationship, I'll accept your offer." He scribbled some information on a slip of paper, then laid it on the desk. "Deposit the money in that account, within forty-eight hours. I'll give the information to Colonel Jurado after I've confirmed the deposit."

"Bueno, done then." Castro turned to Luis. "Please, Colonel, remove this slime from my presence."

"Please wait in the hallway for a moment, Sal. I'll be right there." Luis still tried to maintain the peace.

Sal stood, still glaring at the general, then turned and strode proudly from the office.

"General, you are going to give him the *entire* amount?" Luis queried.

"Si, Colonel. A *deal.* I *would* have given him the entire *million,* and possibly *more,* for this information. But he's such a coward, he backed down right away!" He smiled.

Luis bade goodbye and joined Sal in the hallway. "My, Mr. Danella, you are a *surprising* man! I have *never* seen anyone speak to the general in that manner, and then be allowed to walk away! And with a *half million dollars,* no less. You did, though, take a fall in the amount you wanted."

"My friend, my friend... I got *exactly* what I wanted! Had I started my price at a half million, I may have had to settle out for half of that! I am not a *stupid* man, Colonel." He gloated.

Luis mused to himself about how each man thought he'd had the other. "Si, es verdad! Now, I think it best that you go straight to the airport and catch the next flight out to *anywhere*, for your own safety. You are not well-liked here."

"Ain't that the truth! I'll do *just* that. Thank you, Colonel, for your assistance. I'll call you in Budapest in a few days."

They shook hands and parted. Sal exited the building and caught another junked cab to the airport.

• • •

Luis was becoming alarmed by the third day without hearing from Sal. *Had Sal cheated them?* He sat in his office, wondering how Castor would reprimand him, when the call came. "Yes, hello, Sal. You received the money?" Luis was careful not to divulge his mistrust.

"Yes I did, and I wish to thank you. However, there was one more item of interest that I had forgotten. We'll call it a deal sweetener, *gratis*, for your past business." Sal had been scared for not revealing this information. It was best if he told, for his own future safety. Castro was, in reality, a powerful man, and Sal respected his ability to take care of little details on a global scale. "There *is* one other person who does, in fact, know the molecular formula for the vaccine. It's Dr. Hans Bjorgstad in Stockholm, Sweden. He's very old now, and will probably die soon. He has the formula committed to memory, and upon his word of honor, he'll take it to his death. For this reason I don't think his knowledge should be of great concern to you."

"All right, I see. Castro will be interested in that information, I'm sure. I won't ask you how long you've been aware of it, but I suspect that you reserved that information in order to make your deal with him. You're playing with fire, you know," Luis warned.

"That's why I thought it was a good idea to tell you. Like I've told you in the past, I'm *not* a stupid man. Now, let's get on with it. I called to give you the information about the vaccine. It's in some crates, I think two or three, in the basement of the Academy of Sciences at the Vatican. The crates are marked 'lab supplies.' You should retrieve them, however you can, before anyone else might learn of them."

"How much is available?" Luis asked.

"Enough to vaccinate a half million people, from what I understand. But by doing a little research, I should think you'd be able to replicate it. You boys did a hell of a job on replicating the virus, if I remember right."

"Yes, we did. But it wasn't easy, and it took a long time. I have another job for you. Would you stand watch at the Vatican and make sure there is no attempt at removing the crates by anyone other than myself? I'll see you are well paid for your time, but don't do any more *gouging*, got it? You're at the end of your rope now."

"Yeah, I guess I could arrange to babysit the stuff until you can move it. If anything unusual occurs I'll call you. Why are you asking me to do this? It's perfectly safe. Hell it's been lying in there for twenty years."

"I'm just being careful to protect our half million dollar investment. And, who knows, we may not be the *only* people on this phone line."

"Yeah, well, O.K. I'll take good care of it and let you know if anything weird happens. This'll be a boring job," Sal teased.

"Just *keep* it a boring job, then. We'll make arrangements to get it out of there as soon as possible, maybe a couple of months."

BUDAPEST, DECEMBER

"I've about had it with these lesson plans," Luis quipped to himself as he reviewed the upcoming month. He'd been teaching at the university for over twenty years, and since he'd revamped the biology department's program five years ago, nothing had been changed except for updating information in the texts. He felt as if his career was becoming a little stagnant. The phone rang. "Hello, Professor Jurado speaking."

"Yeah, Luis?"

This time he recognized the voice. "Yes, Salvadore Danella, how are you?"

"I'm fine, but maybe your purchase isn't." Luis heard auto traffic in the background. "I'm in a phone booth, so I gotta make this fast. I've got a friend on the inside at the Vatican who tells me there are some CIA agents quietly watching the merchandise. I can't get any closer than that without being discovered."

"CIA? How did *they* find about it? Have you been pulling any *shit* on me, Danella? You know, selling it to *me* and then to *them?* That's what's known as a double cross, and double crossers pay dearly for their mistakes. Got it?" Luis's voice was threatening.

"Sure, Luis, I go to the movies too. You've paid me well enough for my information and guarding this crap. I wouldn't screw you. Remember, I'm not *stupid.* If you even *suspected* that I was double crossing you, I'd be dead in a minute, I know that. Gimme a break!"

"Then we understand each other. So tell me about it."

"My friend, whose name I can't mention, but who's always been straight with me in the past, tells me that some Italian operatives for the CIA showed up here about three weeks ago. They're watching the Academy of Sciences very closely, but haven't even let on to the Vatican government as to what they're doing. From what my friend knows, the Vatican authorities may not even be aware of the agents. No one knows. But this friend, who has other friends at the academy, told me that the CIA's planning to send a long-range air force bomber in to land at the civilian airport in Rome, soon, to airlift some crates out of here. They supposedly paid off one of the mid level people at the Vatican to keep it quiet. Shit, the Vatican higher-ups have *never* known what's been going on here, under their very noses, for twenty years!"

"Are you *certain* of this?" Luis demanded.

"I wouldn't waste the dough for the call if I wasn't. Maybe, as your friend Fidel put it, I don't have any loyalties, but when I'm paid for a job I *do* it. That's what keeps me alive and insures future business."

"O.K., yeah. All right, then. So they're planning on moving this stuff out soon?"

"That's what I'm told."

"Then keep in touch with your friend, and we'll have to plan, somehow, to destroy the merchandise. If they fly it out on an air force jet, they'll need to go on to Aviano, to the U.S. Air Force Base, to refuel. Do you have any connections on the base? Is there anybody we could get to sabotage the plane?"

"*Anything* can be arranged, you know, if you're willing to pay the right people. I happen to have friends, yes, that I think could interfere with a flight out of Aviano." A bus honked in the background.

"In that case, I need to make an urgent decision. I'll *personally* guarantee that you'll receive *another* half million if you can arrange to handle the plane somehow, so the vaccine never reaches United States soil. I want it destroyed completely, irretrievably *gone*, got it? If you fail, no payment."

There was a pause. "Yeah, I got it. I'll take care of it. Fair price, too? Half a mil's a nice, round figure. That'll give me my retirement fund! I've always wanted to retire, you know, but the dice and the horses seem to get to me. Now I can *quit* all this crap!"

"Then we have a deal. If you fail me, though—"

"No way!"

"What about the other guy in Sweden who knows the formula. The old guy . . . Bjorgstad?"

"Listen, my friend. You've been plenty straight with me, and I with you, except for my 'forgetting' to mention that old fart. I'll take care of *him*, too, gratis, just like I gave you the free information about him. See, I ain't so bad! Just keep me in mind for future work, in the event I decide *not* to retire! That AIDS crap doesn't affect *me*, so wiping out the formula and leaving it for science to rediscover is no big deal. I have every faith that they'll get it, eventually." He laughed. "Just make sure you get the money to the right account."

"I'll take care of your deposit as soon as I get some news. Keep me posted. Good by." Luis hung up.

Sal took a small black book from his pocket. He ran his finger down the list, then dialed a New York City number, humming as he waited for an answer. The phone booth door caught his finger as he went to close it. *"Damn!"* Someone answered the phone. "Er, no, not you . . . the phone booth door. Is this Charlie?"

"Sal? Is that *you?"* Charlie laughed. *"How the hell are you?* I haven't heard from you in years!"

"Yeah, Charlie, it's been a long time. Are you still dodging that racketeering charge?" Sal chided.

"Which one? The one *you* ditched when you chicken-shitted out of here and went to Palermo? No, no. That was three or four attempts ago. They can't get me!" he bragged.

"Yeah, that's *good*, Charlie. You're just too smart for 'em." Sal laughed. "Say, are you interested in a little *action* work, like the *old* days? None of that bookkeeping garbage. I mean *fun* stuff, intrigue, danger, *you* remember!"

"What's up? Sounds terrific!"

"It's too long to talk about on the phone. Will you be around there for a couple of days?" Sal leaned against the glass booth.

"Sure, yeah. I'm not goin' anywhere."

"Great. I'll fly over there in a day or two and explain. Meanwhile, put together a few guys that you can trust. They need to be tight-lipped and reliable, and *gutsy*. I'll call you again when I get there."

"Sure, Sal. Now you've got me *excited*. It's been real boring around here for too long. Since about the time *you* left! Call when you get in. I'll have you picked up at the airport. See 'ya then."

"Sure, Charlie. I'm looking forward to seeing you." He hung up, threw the phone booth door open, and grinned.

• • •

Sal's plane landed at 10:57 a.m. He'd called ahead to give Charlie his flight number, and arrangements were made to pick him up. He walked briskly to the baggage area and retrieved his suit bag, then went to the departure area to wait near the door.

"Sal?" The short fat bald man said. "Is that you?" He hurried up to Sal and gave him a jovial bear hug.

"Tommy! Long time no see! What's it been, fifteen years? Wow! Shh-h-h-h-h, though," he toned down, pressing his finger to his lips. "My passport says Phillip Ash."

"Gotcha. You've got your bag already, good. Let's get outa here so we can talk." They left through the automatic doors and jumped in the back seat of the occupied blue Mercedes sedan waiting at the curbside. The driver, whom Sal didn't know, pulled away under the scrutiny of the traffic cop.

"Sal, meet K.J. and Jimmy," said Tommy, glancing at the men in the front seat.

"Nice to meet you gentlemen." Sal looked at them with a grin. The two twenty year olds acknowledged with nods and smiles. The driver, Joey, was mean looking and well built, but smiled easily. Sal sensed that he wasn't too bright.

K.J., the passenger, leaned over the seat and shook hands, smacking his bubble gum as he spoke. "I'm *honored* to meet you, Salvadore. I've known about you since I was just a boy. You've been kind of a *role model* for me." He spoke with a slow, Bronx accent. The others laughed.

"Well, *thank you*, K.J. One request, though. Will you guys call me Phil? The cops here would *still* like to find Salvadore Danella, I think, after all these years!"

"Sure, *Phil*, sure," replied K.J. with a barking laugh.

They sped along the freeway. "Nothin's changed around *here*, I see," Sal said, looking out the window at the passing heavy traffic.

"Nope," K.J. chimed. "Same shit, different day!"

"That's *good*, K.J., that's good!" Joey, the dumb one, laughed like a hyena.

They chatted idly during the hour's drive, arriving at Charlie Tanzini's house in the early afternoon. Charlie waited in the yard as the car pulled into the arced driveway of the magnificent old home.

"Charlie! *Damn* it's good to see you," cried Sal as he jumped from the car. They hugged.

"Let me look at you, ya big jerk!" Charlie backed off a step and scanned Sal head to toe. "Just as good looking as ever! How 'bout a drink? Dewar's over, isn't it?"

"Yeah, what a memory! The only difference I see in *you* is a little graying at the temples. More *distinguished!*" Sal slapped him on the shoulder. They lumbered up to the house.

They reveled in their old one-liners as Charlie finished fixing the drinks and handed the scotch to Sal. "So, sit down, sit down. I can't stand it. Tell me about your big plans."

"Sure Charlie, but I'd like to lay it on you in *private* first."

"Boys?" Charlie motioned to K.J. and Joey. They obediently left the room.

"O.K., Charlie, you're not going to believe *this* one. The Cubans have contracted me to devise a way to take down a *U.S. Air Force bomber.* The cargo is some high tech electronics that they don't want to arrive here in the States." He lied.

"The *Cubans?* As in *Fidel Castro? No shit,* huh? They want you to take out an Air Force *bomber?"* Charlie was awestruck. His rotund, fifty-year-old body shook with delight.

"Yeah. Me and Fidel are *buddies,"* Sal gloated, reverting to his New York grammar. "I met him in Havana a month ago, and he bought some information from me. I'm not going to go into all of that. It's a long story, and it ain't important here. Anyway, they hired me to take this plane down so the cargo can never be recovered, *never.* Now, I been thinkin' about this a lot over the past few days, and I can't seem to come up with a plan. I'd like your ideas. Oh, yeah, you'd better know that the CIA's watching it, too." Sal watched for a reaction.

"A United States Air Force *bomber?* The *CIA?* Shit, Sal, you must be *losin'* it! This'll be *great!* Now, let's see . . . I'd just guess it would be a B1-B, if, as you say, it's a long range model. It'd be real tough."

"That's why I came to *you,* Charlie, my friend. Your aviation knowledge. You still got friends in the military you can buy?"

"Sure, they're *always* around. And I've still got some markers out with a *colonel.* What d'ya want to know? *I* still know a lot about military procedures too, ya know." Charlie stirred the ice in his glass with his finger.

"O.K., then, open up! The plane will be landing at the civilian airport in Rome to pick up the merchandise, then most likely go to the Aviano base for refueling. How do we blow it up and ditch the cargo? We've got a half million bucks to play with. If there's anything left after expenses, we'll split it."

"O.K., O.K." He rubbed his hands together, thinking out loud. "If it refuels at Aviano . . . Wait a minute . . . What the hell's the destination in the U.S.?"

"Damn, I don't even know!" Sal thought a couple of minutes. "Say, let me use your phone to call my man in Rome." He stepped to the phone on the bar. "Er, Charlie, would you excuse me for a minute?"

"Uh, sure, Sal, yeah." He blushed, then put his drink down and went out on the patio with the two thugs. He overheard Sal's muffled voice for a few minutes.

"Charlie, come on back in here," Sal yelled. "Bingo!" he said when Charlie returned. "It's headed for the Homestead Base, in Miami."

"All right, all right. That means they'll probably put down in the Azores on the way. Hmmm . . . " He filled his glass again as he thought. "Sal, want another?"

"You bet!" Sal handed his tumbler to Charlie.

"Do you know anything about plastic explosives, Sal?"

"Not much, but I'm a quick study!" Sal admired the way Charlie's brain churned problems into solutions.

"Here's what we do. I'll get the name of a flight line NCO at Aviano. One that has access to the aircraft, so he wouldn't raise suspicions if he was out working on a plane." He paused to think. "We'll get a sergeant, maybe, who has a family here in the States, then we can hold his family to force him to help us. He could plant some timed plastic explosives in the engines to blow them in flight, out over the ocean. Yeah, digital clock timers, they'd do nicely."

"Damn, you're good, Charlie!" Sal beamed.

"Quiet, I'm thinking. If I remember right, there's a wide, deep valley in the ocean floor northeast of the Azores, the direction they'd be flying from. I can't remember the name of it . . . the . . . uh . . . "

Sal was going crazy. This was Charlie's singular fault in plotting, trying to remember details of irrelevant minutia. An idiosyncracy that could be overlooked, Sal thought, for a master planner of his ability. After all, paying attention to detail was why Charlie had continually moved up in the organization. He was just too damned smart! "That's O.K., Charlie, it'll come to you later. What about the ocean valley, how do we use it?"

"Simple! We just figure out the time lapse between Aviano and the valley, and set the timers accordingly. *BLOOIE!*" He slapped his hands together. "The plane goes quickly to the bowels of the ocean, too deep to recover it *or* the cargo!"

"Brilliant, you son of a bitch!" Sal declared.

"Piece of cake, nothing more." Charlie wallowed.

"That's absolute dynamite! A toast! To you, Charlie, may your brilliance shine forever!" He thrust his glass upward in delight.

"Here, here!" Charlie joined in, raising his tumbler.

Sal put his glass on the bar. "Now, there's another thing." He became serious. "There's a scientist in Stockholm who knows about this equipment, and could duplicate it. A real old geezer, named Bjorgstad. Fidel wants him taken out, too."

"No sweat, *that'll* be easy. We'll ship K.J. and Joey over to take care of him the same day the plane blows. It might raise some eyebrows if he got killed before the plane goes. The CIA'd be all over that cargo like stink on shit, if it's all as important as it seems." He looked at Sal.

"Yeah, Charlie, it's *real* important. I'm not even sure what the equipment *is*, to be honest. Maybe the Russians are ultimately behind this, I don't know."

"Oh, so *now* maybe we have a little KGB action, huh? *Super!* When you do something, Sal, my boy, you do it big!"

"Another toast! Just like the old days, huh, Charlie, in the neighborhood? But on a *much* grander scale than scamming beer off the backs of trucks in the alley!"

Charlie laughed and choked into his upturned drink. "You got *that* right!" He heaved a sigh, "Yeah, to the *old* days!" He raised his glass again.

"Yeah . . . " Sal joined in. "Well, anyway. So lay out the steps."

"O.K. I'll get you the name of a non-com in Aviano. That might take me a few days, so lay around the house here and relax. You'll be responsible for taking care of him, then, when this comes down, so start surveillance on him right away when you go back to Italy."

"No problem, I'll go straight to Aviano when I leave here, just to check the guy out before I go back to Rome to watch the cargo."

"Yeah, good. When you call me with the *go* sign, I'll ship you the plastics pronto, with the instructions for proper care and feeding." They both laughed. "I'll put my boys Tommy and Richard onto picking up the NCO's family. We'll keep 'em in the basement down at my office. I'll have everybody talk Italian so the family won't know where in the hell they are. If we do it just right, and there aren't any screw ups, the family will be returned. I *promise.* I really hate to mash nice people." He hesitated. "But on the other hand, oh, how I *love* to mash assholes!" He laughed.

1993

NEW YORK CITY, FEBRUARY

"Hey, Charlie, the phone's for you!" K.J. yelled into the living room. "It's Sal!"

Charlie threw the newspaper to the side and grunted while he heaved his large body out of the Lazy Boy recliner. "Who took the phone from my chair again?" he yelled. *Damn* those guys, anyway. He'd told them to leave the phone where he could reach it from his chair fifty times! He lumbered over to the phone at the bar. "Hello, Sal, how 'ya doin'?"

"Mighty fine, mighty fine . . . Every day's a holiday and every meal's a picnic! How're you?"

"What're you on, anyway? I want some!" Charlie laughed.

"Charlie, you got everything set up?"

"Sure, smooth as can be. Just been waiting for your call."

"Well, *this* is it! The Air Force plane, and you're right, it's a B-1B, will be putting down in Rome on the morning of February tenth to pick up the goods, so start things rolling!"

"Good enough, I'll take care of things. I'll get the explosives delivered to Mazzone's for you on your side of the big water. Did you get a good handle on Sergeant Judson at Aviano?" Charlie asked.

"That's affirmative. I think he's a good choice. I guess he's got a real chip on his shoulder since he quit the marines and joined the Air Force a few years back. But he's supposed to be a real strong family man, and he'd put *them* above anything else in his life. He's supposed to be a real tough cookie, and he's been in trouble for bar brawling in the past."

"See? Can I pick 'em or what?"

"Yeah, Charlie, good job." Sal felt obliged to feed his ego.

"When this is done, why don't you come back here and relax for a while? We'll have a little fun, like the old days!" Charlie said. "I haven't had such fun in years! This has been a gas, this little project of yours. All we have to do now is keep an eye on the news. Oh, yeah, about the money. If there's any left, after expenses, *you* keep it! Hell, I don't need it."

"Shit, Charlie, you're a sweet guy! Now, I've got some work to do. Maybe I'll get over there in a couple of weeks. See ya." Click.

BILOXI, FEBRUARY

The big gray Oldsmobile slowly cruised down Brent Street. It was a quiet, tree lined residential area, with older homes that military personnel could afford. "There it is, the yellow two story," Tommy said, his rotund belly shaking with the potholes in the old street.

"I see it." The driver, Richard, pulled the car into the driveway and parked in front of the garage alongside the house. Unnecessary attention was to be avoided. "Ready?"

"Yeah, let's go." The men got out and closed the car doors quietly. Monday morning had been chosen because most of the neighborhood residents would be at work. They walked around to the front of the house and climbed the stairs to the porch. Tommy rang the bell.

The whine of a vacuum cleaner stopped, and a rather plain looking woman, in her late twenties, opened the door. "Yes?" she questioned apprehensively, looking at the strangers.

"Pamela Judson?" Tommy asked.

"Yes, I'm Mrs. Judson. Who are you men, anyway?"

Richard reached into his coat pocket, then flashed a wallet bearing a gold badge. He quickly flipped it shut again and returned it to his pocket. "Air Force Intelligence, ma'am. Nothing seriously wrong. We need you to come with us to headquarters. We have news from your husband."

"*Rusty?* Is he all right?" Pam tensed.

"Oh, sure," Tommy replied. "But he's on classified duty and can't communicate directly with you. He has something of a personal nature that he needs to speak with you about, so we've arranged a special communication. I believe he's in Italy still. We're just the messengers."

"Oh . . . All right." She was confused. "Katy, come down here," she called upstairs. "And bring your jacket." Pam took her coat from the peg next to the door.

The men looked at each other. Katy, a pretty little girl of about seven, hopped down the stairs toward the front door. "Who are those men, Mommy?" She hugged her doll.

"They work with your father, and we're going with them so we can talk to him."

"Oh boy, *Daddy? Let's go*!" She ran out of the house.

They walked around the house to the car. "Why did you park way back here?" Pam asked. Now her suspicion was aroused. "Who are you, really?"

"Please, ma'am, get in the car quietly," Tommy said. He showed her the butt of the pistol in his pocket, then opened the rear door for her. The color faded from her face as she slid in after Katy. Tommy closed the door, then climbed into the front passenger seat. Pam tried to open her door, then the window, but both were jammed.

Careful not to alarm Katy, she asked, "Where are we going?"

The men ignored her. The car backed from the driveway and turned down the street. After several direction changes, she knew they were headed for the airport.

The car pulled onto the main airport boulevard and went to the far end of the commercial airline terminal, passing several rental car areas before finally stopping next to the door of a large hangar. Richard got out and went inside for a few minutes, then came back and started the car. The large door opened and the car pulled inside. Pam saw a medium sized jet, with a single engine on the tail. Tommy got out and opened Pam's door as the large hangar door closed again. "Get out, please," he politely commanded.

Pam and Katy were ushered into a small office in the corner of the building. Another man closed the door behind them as they sat on a bench. There was a roaring din outside in the hangar, and then the whine of the jet engine. Men's voices grew ever louder, and more excited, to compensate for the noise. Pam thought she heard them speaking in a foreign language, then she was sure when the office door opened again. It was Italian. From this angle she could read '24 HOUR EXPRESS' on the side of the jet, an overnight delivery company, she assumed. Now, her self discipline wearing thin, she became overcome by fright.

Tommy opened the office door and said, "Come with me, please," then motioned them to follow. They followed him to a large crate sitting on the platform of a hydraulic lift next to the jet. "I'm sorry for the discomfort, but you must follow all instructions *explicitly*. You'll be treated courteously, and won't be harmed in any way. Now, do either of you wish to use the rest room before departure?"

"No," Pam replied. "*Where* are you taking us, and *why*?" She tried to maintain her composure for Katy's sake. The man didn't answer. "Don't be afraid, Katy, I'm sure this is some kind of mistake, and we'll be home soon." Katy began to whimper.

"This crate isn't very large, but you'll only be in it briefly, maybe two hours. Actually, there's plenty of room to sit and stretch, and it's lighted for reading. There are also snacks and drinks. "Please . . . " Tommy gestured them inside the box. The bottom was lined with a thin mattress and pillows. He reached inside and clicked on a battery operated lantern which provided sufficient light. They climbed inside, Pam now fighting sheer panic. Katy was crying, sensing her mother's fear. A panel was placed on the side of the crate and hammered shut.

Again they heard the drone of foreign speech.

The hydraulic lift started, and Pam felt the crate move upward. More muffled, high-pitched speech, and the crate was shoved sideways through the door in the side of the plane. The door slammed, and the voices disappeared completely. The only sound now was that of the idling jet engine. All was still for a while, then the jet engine wound up and the plane moved slowly forward. They taxied a short distance, then stopped, turned, and accelerated down the runway. The surface was bumpy until Pam felt an abrupt upthrust. She knew they were airborne.

"Mommy, who are those men, and where are they taking us? To Daddy?" Katy cried.

"I'm not sure, honey, but see how nice they treat us? Pretend we're on a secret mission. Here," she handed her a candy bar, "Eat this candy, then we'll take a nap." Pam knew sleep would be long in coming.

Two hours passed, and the plane began dropping in altitude. Twenty minutes later they bounced as they hit the runway, with the roar of the flaps and shuddering of the plane suggesting either a short runway, or the pilot's misjudging the length of the landing strip. More taxiing, then an abrupt stop. The engine shut down, and Pam heard the freight door of the plane being opened. The crate was shoved again, and again the sound of a hydraulic lift. She heard a large motor approaching, like that of a heavy truck with low gears. Now, in the quiet, she could once again hear people speaking excitedly in Italian. She heard the voice of the fat man, speaking mostly English, and using occasional Italian. If nothing else, she could tell he was more comfortable with English.

The crate moved downward, turned hard to the left, then slid again. More speech, and then she heard truck doors slamming. There was a slight lurch, then they were moved again. Pam checked her watch. It was 12:30 p.m . . . or was it a.m.? She must get control! Yes, they had left home just a couple of hours ago, in the morning. It must be just after noon.

The truck stopped and started frequently, and Pam heard the muffled roar of heavy traffic. They must be in a congested area, in whatever city they were in. The truck finally made a hard slow turn and rolled to a stop. It was 1:17 p.m. The rear doors opened. More voices and sliding, then the box suddenly tipped forty-five degrees. Pam and Katy were thrown to the downward side as the box dropped to the ground with a thud, landing on its side. They heard loud speech, probably cursing, in Italian. "Are you all right, Katy?" Pam asked.

Katy cried and clung to Pam. "I'm *scared*, Mommy. I'm really *scared.*"

"We'll be O.K., little one. I'll take care of you."

The box was righted and lifted slightly off the ground, then set back down. Smooth motion then, as if rolling on some kind of cart. More doors opened and closed with strange new voices in English and Italian, both male and female now. And always the voice of the fat man. It was quieter; they must have been moved inside somewhere. She heard two more doors open and close, and the motion stopped.

The side of the crate suddenly fell away, and the fat man stood before them. "Are you both all right? That last little jolt, when we dropped the crate, must have shaken you." He laughed a little. "You're in your temporary home now. *How* temporary depends on how you behave, and how your husband handles his assignment. We're holding you for your own safety, but I can't tell you anything more than that."

"What do you want—" Pam started.

Tommy cut her off. "You'll have all the comforts here, and you're free to move about these three rooms. But don't attempt to open the door at any time. It's guarded on the outside. Someone will see to your hygiene and food needs. You'll have television, radio, reading material, and games. I leave you now to settle in." He left through what must be the main door, and Pam heard him mutter something to someone on the outside. Then she heard shuffling footsteps, as if climbing stairs. She examined their quarters.

There were three rooms, probably totaling four hundred square feet. The walls were plain, mortared stone. It was a very old building, and smelled musty. No windows, and the walls were cool and clammy. A basement, sure. There were beds in one room, and the larger area had a bathroom to one side. It appeared that they were once small guest rooms.

The accommodations were comfortable enough. In the corner of the larger room there was a refrigerator which had been stocked with cold cuts, vegetables, and drinks. A note hanging from the top rack read, "To avoid the dangers in letting you use heating sources, hot meals will be served to you three times daily."

"Mommy, how long will we be here?" Katy asked, seeming now to have accepted their situation.

"I'm not sure, but it looks as though we'll be treated decently, so let's try to make the best of things. You use the bed against the wall." Pam tried her best to make sense of what was happening.

There was a matronly woman, who spoke only Italian, who obligingly delivered their meals. Pam wasn't sure that she didn't understand English, and asked her repeatedly why they were holding them. The woman's sole response was a blank stare.

"Why are you doing this to us? We are just common people. *Please* let us go home." She still tried not to show her fear in front of Katy. "If you think that you can get Rusty to do anything against his country by holding *us*, forget it. *Never!*"

The next morning Tommy came in. "We'll keep you until your husband finishes his assigned mission, then release you, unharmed, and see you safely home. If all goes well, you'll be released within the next three days."

"What's this all about? What are you trying to make Rusty do?" Pam became obstinate.

"Nothing major, I assure you. It involves national security, and he won't have to harm anyone, either, so don't worry about that." Tommy smiled.

"What if a neighbor, or my family, calls my house? They'll be alarmed if no one answers."

"Taken care of. The woman we have watching your home will tell people that you're away for a couple of days and she's a friend, house sitting in your absence. Everything has been well thought out, believe me. Now, I want you to pay strict attention to this. You'll be released in the same fashion you arrived, being flown in that crate back to your home town. You'll never know where you have been held. You must never, *never* report this to the police. For the sake of your family's future safety, just forget the entire episode. Your husband has been instructed to do the same. You are *not* to discuss this with your husband, either. This has been a classified mission in Air Force intelligence. Just as your husband can't tell *you* things under his security oath, neither can you tell *him* anything. You saw my partner's badge when we first came to your house, so you know we're real."

"So you're really intelligence people, *really*? And you're really going to let us go home?" Pam's usually skeptical judgment was swayed by this pleasant man. She needed to keep her sanity.

"I *promise* you. Always remember what I just said. *No police*, and don't expect your husband to talk to you about this, and vice versa, agreed?"

"Oh, yes, I *promise*!" Pam was elated. They *must* be legitimate agents after all! So she and Katy had to go through a few difficult days, big deal! It involved the security of her country.

AVIANO, ITALY

Tech Sergeant Judson was busy preparing the aircraft maintenance program for the upcoming week when he was paged to pick up line six on the phone. He dropped his pencil and reached over to punch the blinking button. "Judson."

"Is this Sergeant Judson, on the flight line?" Sal asked.

"Uh, yes, it is. Who's calling, please?"

"That's not important. I have some extremely important news for you, and I can't tell you my name. It concerns your wife and daughter. I need to call you privately at home, but I couldn't get your number except by talking with you. Give me your home number, and I'll call you this evening, say, seven thirty."

"Wait a minute, who *is* this?" he demanded.

"Like I said, I can't tell you my name. It's imperative that I call you tonight so we can speak privately . . . A *must.* And be advised that you are to tell absolutely *no* one of this call, *no one.* It concerns the safety of your family, and I have ways of immediately discovering any breach of confidence, so *don't break it,* got it? If you must, make a call to your home in Biloxi. There'll be no answer until tomorrow, at which time our house sitter will be there. But do it on a private line, got it? You're only *protecting your family* by following my instructions. Again, tell no one. Now, what's your number?"

Judson was numbed, off balance. "Uh, yeah, O.K. What do you want again?" His thinking was muddled.

"Give me your home phone number so I can call you tonight. Make sure you are alone when I call, and tell no one of this in the interim. I'm going to hang up in fifteen seconds, and you'll never hear from me again, so you'd better do what I ask. If I don't have your number, I can't call."

"Wait, wait.. Uh, it's uh . . . it's uh . . . " He couldn't recall the number he'd had for the past two years. "875-6548, yeah, that's it. 875-6548. Please call me, *please*!" The phone went dead and the dial tone resumed.

Judson was a short, stocky man, and not a man given to panic. He was self righteous by nature, a disgruntled sergeant who felt he'd been unfairly treated by the military. He'd quit the Marines and joined the Air Force three years earlier. He thought promotions would come faster, but he was passed over several times because of his 'attitude problem.' "It's probably a spiteful vengeance call from one of the idiot airmen I transferred to guard duty last week for playing cards on tour," he mumbled aloud.

He picked up the phone and dialed his home number in Biloxi, with instructions to reverse the charges. He checked his watch. It would be three or four in the morning their time. He tapped his pencil impatiently while the phone rang, whistling a nervous little ditty like he always did under stress. He let the phone ring fifteen, twenty times, and then he became alarmed. Pam would *surely* be home at that hour. It was Sunday. Maybe they'd gone to her mother's house for the weekend, eighty miles away. He hung up the phone and retrieved his mother-in-law's number from his directory in the desk. He called the number collect, then listened to the ringing.

After the fourth ring a sleepy woman's voice answered, "Hullo."

The operator said, "This is a collect call from Russell Judson in Aviano, Italy. Will you pay for the call?"

A yawn. "Um, yes, operator."

"Hello, Mom? This is your son-in-law, in case you've forgotten," he nervously chuckled.

She didn't appreciate the humor. "What time is it? Why are you calling during the middle of the night?"

"Listen, I got a crank call, probably from one of the goofballs I transferred last week. I just wanted to know if my girls are there."

"Well, no, I haven't seen them for three or four weeks. Why, what's wrong?"

"Uh, oh nothing, really. I guess I just got a premonition or something. You know how a person gets a sense of something being wrong once in a while? I think I just got one of those. Not to worry. I'll call them in a few hours to say hello. You go back to sleep and pretend this was all a bad dream. At least until you get your phone bill." He laughed again.

"Is there something wrong, really? Why didn't you call *them*?"

He was stuck for a rational answer. "Uh . . . I didn't want to wake little Katy, I guess. You go back to sleep now. I'll call them later."

"Are you sure everything's all right?"

His realized that his explanation hadn't made sense. "Yeah, Mom, really. I'm just having a little anxiety attack. I guess I miss being at home too much."

"Yes, I can understand that. They miss you, too. It won't be long before you're done over there and can come home. You take care of yourself, now."

He sensed the concern in her voice. "Sure will. Sorry to bother you. Good night." He hung up the phone and his anxiety began to crescendo. Where in the hell *are* they? He tried to console himself. Pam had probably partied too much the night before and stayed over somewhere. She was a strictly loyal woman, but she *did* like to have a good time. Probably went to some girlfriend's house and had a bit too much. Then she wouldn't have wanted to drive home with Katy in the car late at night. *Sure.* He didn't feel good about this one. Distressing thoughts kept tumbling in his head. *Was* she loyal, or had he been away too long? There *is* a breaking point in the human animal. He knew that all too well. *He'd* broken before. So what next?

He attempted to isolate the possibilities. He glanced at his schedule sheet, having accomplished nothing in the past hour. Should have been done by now. He started to develop a dull ache from his neck upward to his temples. He hadn't had a tension head ache like this since he flunked out of his sophomore year in college, ten years ago. There was no way he could concentrate on work. He lifted the phone and dialed operations. "This is Sergeant Judson. Put me through to Captain Ogelvie, please."

"Captain Ogelvie speaking," the Texan drawled.

"Sir, this is Sergeant Judson in maintenance. I think I've come down with a bad flu." He *was* nauseated. "I'd like to request permission to be relieved of duty for the rest of my tour today. I have most of next week's scheduling done. It just needs to be finalized, and Sergeant Rawlings can finish for me. May I leave my post, sir?"

"Certainly, Sergeant. I'll have Rawlings notified immediately. You go home and get well. If you're still feeling ill in the morning, call early enough so we can arrange coverage."

"Thank you, sir." Rusty cradled the phone, hurriedly straightened his desk, and headed home to face a day of headache and anxiety.

He stopped at the base hospital on his way home, hoping to get some relief for his mounting headache. The medic on duty gave him a dozen butalbital pills, specifically for tension headaches. Then he proceeded homeward to somehow endure the emotional drain and headache.

The three room apartment provided by the military was cramped, with awful yellow wallpaper and worn diamond-patterned linoleum in the kitchen. The living room was dark and even smaller than the kitchen, with cheap, uncomfortable furniture.

The hours dragged by as he sat in front of the television, watching Italian soaps and game shows, sometimes flipping to the U.S. sponsored news station to see if there happened to be anything worldly going on that could be related. Nothing. Maybe a mid eastern crisis again, and there were terrorists involved in something clandestine. Maybe whatever it was just hadn't made the news yet.

He tried to avoid taking the pills, knowing that they might make him drowsy when the phone call arrived at the proscribed time of seven thirty. He needed to be fully alert to handle this precarious situation. His family . . . *Were they really in the hands of some kidnapper? What for?* What had he ever done to anyone that would warrant anything so monstrous? His family had barely enough money to live a lower middle class military lifestyle, so a ransom motive was out.

He hadn't had an appetite since he'd received the first call. It was approaching seven thirty, time for the next contact. He hadn't taken any of the pills, saving them in case the message he was to receive precipitated a more severe head ache. He sat at the small chrome legged kitchen dinette, rolling the pill bottle back and forth, with only a dull awareness of his surroundings. Realizing that he was too numb to remember anything unless he wrote it down, he had a pencil and paper ready to take notes. The hard ring of the phone made him jump, and he sprang from the chair and snatched it from the wall.

"Hello, Russell Judson speaking."

"Yes, Sergeant. It's me again," said Sal, the mysterious caller. "I'm going to be very brief to avoid the possibility of a trace, even though I know you haven't told anyone. That's good. Listen *carefully*, and don't interrupt. We're holding Pam and Katy. They're both safe, and will be returned to you unharmed after you complete this mission. The mission involves your sabotage of a B-1B bomber. We know that you have free access to the planes on the flight line. This will be a special flight, carrying a secret cargo and destined for the Homestead Air Force Base in Miami. This is *important*. You must monitor the flight plans, because this flight will have stopped at the civilian airport in Rome to pick up the load just before flying to Aviano for refueling. I don't know the flight number, but *you* can get it. And if you fail, *you* are responsible for the future welfare of your family. That's all for now. You think about everything I've just told you. I'll call back again soon. And, I repeat, tell *no* one. Good by."

Rusty replaced the phone with his left hand while he wrote notes with the right. Sabotage . . . B-1B . . . secret cargo . . . from Rome . . . maintenance here . . . bound for Miami. So *that* was why his family had been kidnapped, he finally realized. Someone trying to down the cargo for some reason. They must have some good intelligence connections to know all this intricate information, and have planned so well. *What to do?* Can't tell anyone. His mind again became boggled out of desperation. Common sense was minimal, and analytical thought processes were impossible.

He concluded that all he could do was wait for the next call. Perhaps something would come to light and give him some direction to pursue, some way in which to resolve this crisis, with harm to none. He poured himself a cup of coffee.

How were they treating Pam and Katy? Where were they holding them? In the States, or a foreign country? Had they been *tortured?* He couldn't dwell on that. Were they being cared for properly, at the least? Were they scared? Did they know why they'd been kidnapped? Were they threatened with harm if they didn't cooperate? *Pam* would be all right. She'd get a handle on things quickly. That was one of the reasons he had married her . . . She handled things well, had a high level of common sense, made the best of bad situations. All much like himself.

If they *hurt* either one of them, in any way, mentally or physically . . . He vowed he would kill as many of the bastards as were involved, regardless of their legal 'civil rights' protection as criminals.

"Rusty, you home?" Rusty's neighbor, Jerry, had cracked opened the front door and was peering in.

"Yeah, come on in," Rusty called from the kitchen.

Jerry entered the small kitchen. "Hey guy, what's up? What're you doing home? You kinda look like shit . . . Are You all right?"

"Sure, well, sort of . . . I've got this *ferocious* headache, so I came home early. I was *supposed* to work until eleven."

Jerry sat down. "How about a cup of coffee?"

Rusty stood up and went to the coffee pot on the counter. "Hey, what's this stuff?" Jerry asked, pointing to the notes on the table.

"Oh, uh, nothing . . . "Rusty had to think fast. "It's, uh, some info on a flight next week, and it's *classified*, Jerry." He jerked the notes from the table and stuffed them in his pocket.

"Oh, *sorry*," the embarrassed Jerry responded. "So, why the head ache? Are you all stressed out again?"

"I guess I am, sure. My, uh, brother called and his house got ripped off yesterday," Rusty lied. "Goddamn crooks, they all ought to be shot! How much money do we spend, fifty thousand a year to house each one? So they can lift weights and play basketball and live for free . . . disgusting."

"Whoa!" Jerry said. "What about the sociologists' claim that they turned to crime because they were victims of society, growing up in bad neighborhoods, deprived of opportunity."

"I grew up in an inner city neighborhood, too, but I am a *human*, not a Goddamned animal." Rusty seethed. "The U.S. criminal justice system, what a joke! Protecting the 'rights' of the criminal in preference to the satisfaction of the victim. It's *bullshit.* A rapist rapes and murders a child, then gets a few years in prison and is paroled because the prison is full, just to go do it again, then repeat the bullshit process."

"Pretty strong stuff, my friend." Jerry sipped his coffee.

"And it costs the conscientious working people literally thousands of dollars to support the sick animal while he plays through the courts and then lives a good life in prison. Demanding and striking for better food, health care, and *color television,* no less, living off us taxpayers! And most of the time, they enjoy a much better lifestyle! It's *bullshit!*"

"Calm down. Remember your head ache!" Jerry laughed.

"Shoot the bastards! Rid society of the dung, the cancer. Don't *reward* that type of subhuman life! I like the middle eastern 'eye for an eye' justice. You steal, you get your hand hacked off, no screwing around with appeals and demanding your rights as a criminal. You kill, you hang . . . as simple as that. I remember when I traveled to Iraq. I could leave this expensive camera on a bus station seat and return for it two hours later. It'd still be there! No one would *dare* touch it."

"Yeah, I see what you mean." Jerry looked at his watch, trying to get out of this one-sided, bent conversation. "Well, I guess I'd better get home. Big day tomorrow." He stood up and walked to the door. "Good night, Rusty. Hope you get over your head ache."

"Yeah, sure thing, thanks. Good night." Jerry stepped out the door.

Rusty started thinking again. Whoever was behind this kidnapping was sinister and calculating, and had the backing of some kind of governmental network. An alarming combination of evil at worst, a well planned solution to a world problem at best.

What could the cargo be that would warrant the sabotage of a multimillion dollar plane, yet alone the sacrifice of the four crewmen? "Wait a minute," he said to himself, "burn the crew?" He thought hard for a moment. He had been skirting that issue, he realized, thinking earlier that he was simply to make the plane inoperable, maybe just for a short period of time, a delay tactic. "What if they *do* expect me to destroy it in flight? Shit, man."

"What *is* the cargo?" Nuclear components? Secret high tech components, maybe computer parts for the space defense program, communications satellites? Biological weapons?

The first step, he reasoned, was to try to determine who was behind it. That may answer the cargo and the motive questions. Then he could narrow down the possible kidnappers, and maybe the location of Pam and Katy. He resolved to listen intently to voice inflection during the next call. Maybe a subtle foreign dialect. He'd been too wired to think about that in the earlier calls. *Yeah, tape record the next one and play it back. Listen for background noise, that's the way the cops do it on TV.* He went to the bedroom and found his cassette recorder, then took it to the kitchen and taped the microphone to the side of the phone's ear piece.

His head began pounding unbearably. He had the recorder in place now. There was nothing more to do but wait. He could afford to take a pain pill now. He picked up the bottle, unscrewed the cap, and removed one of the small blue pills. He looked at it. Should I or shouldn't I? He walked to the kitchen sink, tapped a glass of water, and chased the pill down his throat. "I can't take the damn headache. Maybe I can think more clearly, even with the drug, if the pain is gone."

He returned to watching Italian television in the living room, picking up a few words now and then. His interest in the program waxed and waned with concern for his family. He'd dealt with the sudden death of his father better than this, he recalled. At least that had left nothing to chance. It was a cold fact that he was *dead*, not suffering at the hands of some unknown.

Two long hours later the phone rang. He looked at the wall clock. It was eleven p.m. He was thinking now. He went to the kitchen, turned on the tape recorder, and picked up the phone. The drug hadn't seemed to affect his thinking. Good.

"Hello, Sergeant Judson speaking."

"Yeah, Rusty. This is Rawlings. The captain said I might have to cover for you again tomorrow, and I'd like to know, because I had plans. It's my day off. How're you doing?"

Rusty heaved a sigh of relief. "Not worth a shit. My head's killing me. I hate to cut in on your off time, but there's no way I can come in. *Please*, if I never ask you for anything again, can you do it?"

Silence. "What the hell's wrong with you, guy? I've never known you to get so worked up. Always the cool one on the entire crew. Are you O.K.?"

"Well, not really. I'm undergoing a major crisis that I can't talk about. And I've got to get off the phone right away. I'm expecting an important call. Can you do it, Joe?"

"Umm, sure, Rusty. Count on me. Just do the same for me sometime. I hope everything works out."

"Thanks, pal. You'll never know how much I appreciate this. I've got to go, see you later." Rusty hung up the phone, then in frustration he slammed his fist into the wall, denting the gypsum. "Shit!" he yelled.

Back to the rotten, meaningless TV. He dozed. The phone rang again. He jolted upright and looked at the clock. It was eleven forty-five p.m.

"Hello, Sergeant Judson speaking."

"Sergeant Judson, it's me again. Did you understand the information from the earlier call?"

"Er, yes, I did." He switched on the recorder.

"Good. To continue, then. I assure you that your family is being well cared for. They're safe and secure. We're *not* criminals. We have an interest in preventing the B-1B flight from reaching the United States for political reasons. The sabotage of the flight will not compromise the security of your country in any way, but the *failure* to do so could affect the security of your *family*. You must trust me. Now tomorrow you'll stay home from work. A private delivery service will deliver a package to your address. In it you'll find two packages of plastic explosives, each wrapped securely in the same kind of tool bag you carry at work on the flight line. You'll also find two battery powered digital alarm clocks—"

"Not so fast . . . I'm trying to take notes," Rusty interrupted.

"*Don't* interrupt me! The plane will arrive at your base sometime the day after tomorrow during your shift. You will set the alarms, according to the following instructions. One should be set for three hours fifteen minutes after departure, and the other fifteen minutes after that. You'll then wire the leads from the clocks into the explosives, one clock on each explosive. Pretend to be checking the rotors on the jet engines on each wing, then pack the explosives into the cowl at the anterior intakes of each engine, and *leave* them there. Clear the plane for take off only then. Do you have any questions whatsoever?"

"Who are you, anyway?" He was frantic.

"Sergeant, control yourself. I repeat, do you have any questions?"

"No, no, I've got it, O.K. Just don't hurt my family. O.K.?" He begged. He wanted to threaten the caller, but couldn't out of fear for his family.

"I promise you we won't. They have no idea what this is about. Once confirmation is received of the plane going down, your family will reappear in the U.S. Please be assured of that. I repeat, we aren't criminals."

"But what about the crew on the plane?"

"After the second engine blows and the plane begins to falter, they'll jump to safety. But that's up to their discretion, whether to jump or fly the crippled plane to it's demise. I know your American pilots are well trained, and so we're forced to rely on their judgement."

"What about my wife and daughter? How do I get them back?"

"They'll be found, unharmed, after the mission is completed. That's all I can say. I won't call again. I am hanging up now. I have twenty seconds to do so without a trace. Any more questions?"

"No, I guess not." He felt an emptiness enveloping his body. The phone went dead.

Rusty re-wound the tape, then replayed it several times. There weren't any background noises for clues to the origin of the call. The caller had a medium-pitched, mature voice, but not old. Maybe in his forties. There was a dialect with certain words, he noticed, even though it was obvious the man was trying to disguise it. The vowels were hard and evenly pronounced.

The speech pattern was *formal* English, not the commoner, slang type in use in the states. The speaker had been formally trained in English, most likely overseas. He used a subtle 'th' sound with the letter 'd,' but the most noticeable trait was the pronunciation of soft 'c' sounds like a 'th,' as in the word 'receive.' He listened carefully through the tape again. That was the only time, with a 'c.' All the letters 's' were pronounced properly, so it wasn't a lisp, it was an underlying language trait.

The tone of the conversation was strange, too, like the guy wasn't entirely relaxed. He was trying to force the naturalness of having a dialect in a language in which he wasn't comfortable.

Rusty was perplexed. He dialed Jerry next door. "Hi, Jerry. Me, Rusty. Say, listen. I'm trying to get a handle on a language trait for something I'm working on."

"Sure, but that doesn't mean I'm a language expert!" Jerry laughed.

"I know. But you've been exposed to languages around Europe for a long time, and maybe you can help. Give it a try. What language pronounces the letter 'c' like 'th,' like in the word 'with?'"

"That's a good one. In fact, I have a story about that very thing! It's funny. I was at a restaurant in Southern Germany right after I came over here. The men at the table next to me all talked that way, and I thought they were *gay*. It turned into a great laugh, because one of the friends I was with straightened me out, informing me that that's the way proper *Spanish* is spoken!"

"Oh, that *is* funny. But the guy I've heard say it makes it sound forced, awkward." Rusty replied.

"Then he's not Spanish, or he's really *gay!*"

"O.K., Jerry, thanks," Rusty laughed, "That helps."

"How's your headache?"

"Much better, thanks. See ya later." Rusty hung up and began to think . . . *Wait a minute . . . The Italian accent was there, too, slightly. Oh, shit, he's just playing with me so I can't figure it out.*

Still nowhere. What countries speak formal Spanish? Spain, of course. But then there were all the Latin American countries, South American countries, and a multitude of islands scattered all over the world. But what about the smattering of forced Italian accent? His moment of glory deflated as quickly as it had inflated. So what? The guy *maybe* speaks Spanish. Where would that lead him? No where. His options were exhausted. He'd *have* to down the plane, regardless.

The caller was right, the crew should know to get the hell out, so he shouldn't have to worry about them. Could he blow up a three hundred million dollar piece of United States property to save his family? If he *had* to, damn right. The government wasted millions all the time on absolute crap. What's one plane? Have to blow the sucker up!

With the timing instructions for the explosives, where would that put the plane down? If the crew was in a hurry to get to Florida, they'd refuel traveling that direction. Probably at Lajes, in the Azores Islands. He went to his bedroom desk and took out a world atlas to get a geographical perspective. That timing would put them on the east side of the ocean's Atlantic Ridge, about five hundred miles off the coast of Portugal, halfway from the coast to the Azores. There was a deep trench in the ocean floor there called the Cape Finisterre Basin, one of the deepest ocean valleys on the planet. Somebody wanted that cargo, whatever it was, lost forever. He went to bed.

• • •

"Good morning, Captain Ogelvie's office," the receptionist answered.

"Yes, good morning. This is Sergeant Judson calling. Would you please tell the captain that I won't be in today? I'm still not feeling well."

"I certainly will, Sergeant. He told me to expect your call. I hope you get to feeling better. We'll call Rawlings in."

"Thank you. Bye." Rusty was still upset with himself for his failure to devise some kind of plan. He stayed in the house all morning, nervously awaiting the delivery truck. He felt jittery, from a low blood sugar, he decided, but he couldn't eat. He'd been taking pain pills occasionally, adding a guilt complex to his already compromised mental state.

The truck finally arrived just after noon. The driver handed him a clipboard to sign for the delivery, then handed him a corrugated box weighing about fifteen pounds.

He took the box in the kitchen and laid it on the dinette table, then opened it and retrieved the contents. There were two tool belts, heavily wrapped in packing paper, and two cheap digital clocks, still in their original boxes, with fresh batteries taped to the sides. There was nothing else in the package, no clues. He examined a tool belt and found a malleable, grayish-colored, doughy glob packed inside. He assumed that it was the explosive, as he had never seen plastic explosives before. He placed the items in the box, then walked away from the table.

"It'll be another long, sleepless day and night," he said to himself. His anxieties had numbed somewhat since he'd first been contacted. He'd concluded that there was *nothing* he could do about his family. Not right now, anyway. He planted himself on the couch and spent the afternoon and evening inanely watching the television, gloomily anticipating another long night of sleepless tossing and turning. He finally dozed in the late evening from mental exhaustion.

Hours later the phone rang and wrested him from his first deep sleep. He sprang for the kitchen to grab the phone, still half asleep.

"Hello?"

"Sergeant Judson?" It was a woman's voice.

"Uh . . . Speaking."

"Yes, Sergeant. This is Susan, from flight operations, calling for Captain Ogelvie. Are you coming in today?"

"Yes, ma'am. I feel much better. I'll be in." He hung up and looked at the clock. It was five thirty a.m., an hour and a half before report time.

He splashed cold water on his face, then shaved carefully, still a little buzzed from the pills he'd been taking. It felt kind of like a booze hangover, only more in the head rather than the gut. Not so much an ache, either . . . more of a dizzy feeling. He stood in the shower, slowly turning up the cold water. It was refreshing, and seemed to abate the dizziness a little.

By now the acute, frenzied emotions of his unalterable circumstances had passed, leaving the feeling that all he could do was to follow orders, hanging on the hope that his family would be safely returned. There was a kind of bargaining phase, thinking to himself that he'd try to be a better father and husband in the future, if only God would see his family safely through this ordeal. "Please, just make everything like it was three days ago."

He finished up in the bathroom and decided he'd better try to eat something. Nothing appealed to him, so he quickly prepared his standard breakfast of cold cereal and coffee. After staring blankly at it for a few minutes, he shoved it away and went to the bedroom.

He dressed in his fatigues and boots, failing to check himself in the mirror to be certain he could pass the always possible, impromptu military inspection. He brushed his hair as he quickly checked through the house to make sure everything was in order.

The tool belts from the box were laid on the table, and he set the clocks to the current time. All he'd later need to do would be to set the alarms. The instructions were simple enough. A clock was placed in each tool bag.

He locked the front door behind him, then picked up the morning newspaper in the driveway to read on his lunch hour as usual. *Today*, of all days, he wanted to do *nothing* out of the ordinary that may draw any attention, no matter how trivial it seemed. The tool bags were placed in his car, one on the seat, the other stuffed underneath, in case the gate sentry might notice *two* bags as he entered the secured flight line area.

"Good morning, Sergeant." The sentry snapped a salute and flagged him on. Rusty waved and smiled and proceeded to the flight line.

He parked in his reserved spot near the flight operations building and pulled the tool belt from under the seat. Carrying one openly in view, he kept the other wrapped in his coat and draped it over his arm, then entered the building. The usual biddings of good morning to the staff seemed natural enough, fending off inquisitive statements and questions. "How are you feeling, glad to see you back . . . "

He tried hard to act his normal, outgoing self, in spite of the dual fears of being caught and his family's safety.

The incoming flight board indicated another mundane day, with no mention of a flight from Rome. This flight must be *really* secret, he thought. Then the thought occurred that possibly there wouldn't be a special flight at all!

That's strange. There had *never* been a completely unscheduled flight before, even if it was unexpected. It was necessary for him to know the flights enough in advance to plan the crews for the day. It was *his* job. There should be *some* indication, at the very latest on the morning of a plane's arrival.

Other irregular flights had scurried through before on classified missions, but they'd appeared on the morning roster. *Do I dare ask about it?* His logical reasoning, luckily, was still intact, and he decided against it. *Somebody* must know about it, and he'd blow his cover if he acted inquisitive. He'd be patient and go about his business as usual, trying not to exhibit too much anxiety.

He walked to his desk in the little cubby hole the military referred to as an office and placed the tool belts in a file drawer.

It was all he could do to restrain himself from asking about the special flight. It ate at him as he sat at his desk, preparing the notes for the known arrivals that day, assigning crews to each plane based on the need. Technicians were designated for repairs and refueling stopovers. The men were assigned according to their individual abilities and training.

Then an agonizing thought occurred to him. *How in hell do I legitimize my being on the lift, examining the engines of a bomber?* He needed a plan, *now.* He couldn't believe that during this entire past two days he hadn't planned his strategy! Attempts at clear thinking were obtunded for the next ninety minutes.

Aha! He contrived a reasonable plan, and was putting the final polish on pat answers to conceivable questions, when his phone rang.

"Judson speaking."

"Yes, Sgt. Judson. Captain Ogelvie here. I've just gotten word that a nonscheduled, classified flight will be coming through here in two hours. It's a B-1B, flight number AF 1414. It needs prompt attention, refueling and an interflight check. Apparently it put down at the civilian airport in Rome to pick up a classified cargo. That's the first time I've ever heard of that. Something's going on. Maybe a dignitary or something. Anyway, it's first priority and *classified.* Make sure the crewmen on it have a recent security clearance. I want *you* to handle it personally."

What a stroke of luck! He silently thanked God. "Um, yes, sir, I'll take care of it. Do you know the exact ETA and departure time?" Rusty radiated with anticipation.

"Estimated time of arrival is 1417 hours. It's scheduled for take off an hour later."

"Will the crew take a break?"

"I don't know, but I'd think so, if they're on the ground for an hour."

Another fortunate break. No one to watch his activity. "Yes sir. I'll get right on it."

"Thank you, Sergeant. Oh, say, are you feeling better? I hate to work a sick man." The captain's patronizing attitude wasn't very convincing.

"Yes sir, much better. Thank you." *The bastard.* He didn't care if a guy was sick or not. Rusty's friend, Rawlings, had told him that most of the 'little people' didn't dare ask Ogelvie for sick time, so if they *did* ask, the bastard felt obligated to let them go. It wasn't a matter of compassion, it was because the captain had once forced a lieutenant with pneumonia to work. The poor stricken man nearly died as a result of being out in the cold blowing wind, and the captain had been severely reprimanded. It took him three years to get his old duty back.

Rusty remembered the last time the old man caught someone goofing off. He couldn't recall the guy's name, but he remembered he was busted to airman real fast and then was transferred to Alaska.

The next hour crawled by at a near standstill. "Hey, Judson, would you stop tapping that pencil on your desk?" called Alex, the sergeant in the next cubby hole. Rusty had accomplished a minimum amount of scheduling and a maximum amount of clock watching.

"Sorry, I wasn't thinking," Rusty called back.

"Then try a little more thinking and a lot less tapping. It's driving me up a wall," Alex said wryly. "If you get too bored you can always go to the basement and drag your fingernails across the chalk board."

"Real funny, Alex." Rusty could catch up on the paper work tomorrow, blaming his lack of productivity today on the incoming flight he'd suddenly been asked to take care of.

It was time . . . The flight would be on the ground in thirty minutes. Rusty opened the drawer containing the tool belts, again wrapping one in his coat and draping it over his arm, and carrying the other openly in view.

He descended the stairs and strode nervously toward the hangars next to the tarmac where AF 1414 was to park. Entering the colossal "A" hangar, he traversed the fifty yards to the desk and picked up the microphone. Screw the "recent security clearance" that Ogelvie ordered. Two imbeciles were required for this job.

"Jimmy, Roger, report to the desk *now*," he barked into the microphone. Seconds later the airmen were jogging toward the desk.

Both were dolts. They got all the crap jobs because of incompetence, an inability to think on their feet. Rusty used to joke about how he'd like to plant them in his garden to see what came up in the spring.

They arrived simultaneously and stood erect. "Yes, Sir," they spoke and saluted in unison, with four arched eyebrows the most striking trait of the pair of statues. The scene humorously reminded Rusty of the Wrigley's gum commercials, with identical twins enacting identical body and speech patterns.

"Boys, today's your big chance to show me what you can do. We've got an unscheduled B-1B arriving in thirty minutes that'll need prompt servicing. You're the only men available, so you've been 'elect-ed.' *Good teamwork* is the word. I want you to stick together like hot glue and ready the equipment, but *I'll* do the mechanical check myself. If I give you an order, just *do* it. *No questions.* Got it?"

"Yes sir," again in unison. Their eyes were wide with excitement.

"If you don't screw this up, I'll get you off hangar maintenance and back on the line, all right?" Rusty smiled manipulatively.

"Yes, sir," Jimmy snapped, smiling. "Sir, if I may, why so seri-ous?"

"No, you may not!" Rusty growled. "Now, one of you get the huffy, and the other the fuel truck and extinguishers. Oh, yeah, we'll need the hydraulic lift, too."

Roger asked, "What for, sir, trouble?"

"I told you just *do* it, remember? No questions!"

Roger looked at him sheepishly. Rusty looked at the floor then back at Roger. "All right, I guess the only way you'll ever learn is by asking questions. The crew is going to break for an hour. They report-ed some engine vibration and want the rotors and turbines checked, so that's why I'm here. I'll be in here until the aircraft arrives, so holler at me when you see it coming. The 'follow me' truck's been alerted." He'd seen to that before he left the office. "Now, move out, on the double!"

They saluted and darted off for the equipment. He was alone now, behind the counter, with the tool bags on the desk. "O.K.," his chest heaved. "Departure at 1517, so one alarm sets at 1847, and the other at 1902." He set the alarms as he talked to himself.

Enough time had passed to where he was now emotionally calloused to what he must do. All those books and TV shows he grew up watching were right on in their depictions. Even *honorable* men were capable of repealing their deepest beliefs and ingrained loyalties when a threat to their loved ones arose. There were no more pangs of guilt to overcome.

One belt was again hidden in his coat and slung over his arm, and the other openly carried. He nervously strutted toward the front of the building.

Just as he exited the small doorway the giant plane touched down with a dull screech as the rubber hit the runway. It rumbled past him at a high speed out on the landing strip, then abruptly slowed and turned inward toward the hangar. The truck waited to guide it to the proper hangar, pulling in front when the plane was sufficiently slowed to taxiing speed. Within a few minutes the plane was stopped in front of the hangar. The engines shut down and the 'follow me' truck pulled away. The airmen were busy placing equipment around the base of the plane.

Rusty looked through the jet's windshield and saw the crew stand and stretch in the small cockpit. All were young, possibly in their late twenties. They stretched and yawned and joked as they descended the stairway. Rusty didn't want to confront them face to face; there was no way he could handle that, so he stayed at the doorway and watched them walk toward the main building. "I hope you guys know when to get the hell out," he muttered, shaking his head. He walked out to the plane and looked it over. It appeared to be fairly new.

"Jimmy, get that lift under engine one." Rusty watched as the airman quickly obeyed, pushing the hydraulic platform lift under the wing.

Rusty boarded the lift, still carrying the tool bags, and held the 'up' lever until he was waist high with the intake of the huge engine. "Now, go over and help Roger with the fuel," he yelled down. His actions were deliberate, keeping himself on the opposite side of the plane from the men at all times. As he reached into the tool belt he quickly glanced around to make certain no one was watching.

He pulled out the malleable material and molded it into the engine's lower lip, in front of the rotor, packing it tightly. Then he took out a clock and deftly inserted the ends of the wires protruding from its case into the receptacle holes on the explosive, rechecking the alarm set. He rolled up the empty belt and quickly stuffed it into the pocket of his coat, then revealed the other belt. After spending a few more minutes feigning an examination, he loudly proclaimed, "This one's O.K." He released the lift and slowly sunk to the ground.

"Boys, help me get the lift to engine two on the other side," he called out. They came under the plane's belly and scooted the heavy machine to the other engine. "Now, go check on the huffy," he ordered as he raised himself once more. The men disappeared to the other side. Rusty could see only their legs. Again he checked around for observers before repeating the process with the second belt's contents.

He waited a few minutes, then called out, "This one looks good, too." The lift sunk as he crammed the second empty belt in his other coat pocket. "Whew," he softly moaned to himself, "It's done."

He climbed off the platform and approached the men. "Any problems?"

"No, sir," Jimmy said. "Everything's under control. How can you be out here, in the freezing cold, and not be *wearing* that coat instead of carrying it?"

"Uh, it's not *that* cold, I guess." Rusty realized his vulnerability. "Er, I'm going back to the office." He walked away.

"Sir?"

"Yes, Jimmy?" Rusty looked back over his shoulder.

"Did you leave your tool belt on the lift? I noticed you don't have it with you."

Shit, he thought . . . "Uh, no," he grinned with embarrassment as he pulled it from his coat pocket. "I . . . I, er, I got all the way out here and realized I'd left my tools in the hangar, but I thought I'd go get 'em only if I needed to use 'em. You know, instead of walking all the way the hell back to the desk at the other end of the hangar before I checked the engines. If I found anything wrong, *then* I'd have to go get 'em. But thanks for reminding me to go grab 'em before I went back to my office. You guys are doing a *great* job! Keep it up."

He knew he was babbling, and he realized that the men knew it, too, the way they stared at him. He turned to his right and walked toward the hangar instead of the main building. The intensely cold, humid air made his teeth chatter, and his voice cracked a little when he made that poor attempt at an explanation.

He could feel the men's eyes piercing the back of his head as he walked away. "Shit!" The small hangar door slammed behind him as he crossed the distance to the desk again, just for appearance's sake. Behind the cover of the raised counter, he puffed out the pocket and closed the flap on one belt to make it appear full, then flung the other, empty one the thirty feet skyward to land in the eave at the top of the wall. No one will *ever* find it there, unless they happen to tear the building down someday . . . *And then, who cares?*

The shiny concrete floor reflected the overhead floodlights into his eyes as he crossed the giant floor again on the way to the small exit doorway. A blast of cold air hit him when he opened the door, making him realize how truly *stupid* it really had looked to the other men when he was out without his coat on the lift.

He passed the men outside again, waving and smiling, the full-appearing tool belt now dangling over his shoulder. The goofballs smiled and waved back, still a little suspiciously, Rusty decided.

It was time to wait, to do nothing but wait . . . nothing but wait. How would he be notified of his family's release? *That* was something that had been overlooked. Nothing to do but wait . . . .

The warm air rushing from his office building felt good as he opened the door, starting up the stairs. Turning around on the midlevel landing, he ran face-first into the flight crew of AF 1414! "Uh, hello, sirs," Rusty saluted weakly.

They acknowledged him flippantly, then carried on with their light-hearted banter as they continued down the stairs. "Yeah, my wife expects me home in three weeks," the captain said.

Rusty heard the voice and the other's laughter trail off below him. He leaned backward against the railing on the landing for a moment to recompose himself. "Oh, God, how I didn't want *that* to happen." *Everything had gone so perfectly,* in spite of his blunder with the tool belt.

They looked like nice young men; probably had families of their own. He'd felt an instant urge to blurt out a warning to jump if anything inordinate happened during their flight, but luckily nothing came out of his parched mouth. The laughing died away as the crew hit the level below.

1510 came too quickly, and the crew approached the plane again. Rusty stood and watched from his office window, a perceptible tremor in his knees, a lump in his throat. He wiped a bead of sweat from his forehead.

The crewmen lumbered up the stairs and entered the aircraft, and in another minute the engines whined. The plane reversed until it had a clear pathway to turn around, then just sat, motionless.

Rusty could clearly picture the crew in his mind, imagining their conversation in progress with flight operations.

"This is AF 1414 calling Aviano Clearance Delivery."

"Clearance Delivery, go ahead AF 1414."

"AF 1414 requesting clearance to Lajes AFB, Azores."

"AF 1414 cleared as filed to Lajes AFB. Maintain flight level one six thousand. Expect flight level three one zero five minutes after departure."

"10-4, Clearance Delivery. Aviano Ground, this is AF 1414 ready to taxi."

"AF 1414 cleared to taxi runway 8."

Rusty watched as the plane began to taxi down the tarmac, *exactly* on his imagined cue. The voice transmissions continued as he watched the giant metal hulk roll to the end of runway 8 and sit, motionless, again.

"Aviano Tower . . . AF 1414 ready for take-off."

It was the typical pilot-to-control-tower's monotonic vocal quality that he could hear so *vividly* now. Was he really imagining, or *could* he hear it? He covered his ears and closed his eyes. There it was again . . . The final line he so desperately hated to hear . . .

"AF 1414 clear to take off runway 8." The final order from the controller was inevitable.

He opened his eyes again. The big plane roared to life, picked up speed, and thrusted ahead down the runway. First the nose, then the aft wheels, lifted effortlessly off the concrete. The plane suddenly disappeared behind a row of huge gray hangars at the end of the field.

"Good luck . . . *Please* jump, you young fools!" he begged. Maybe they *could* hear him, like he'd heard them. He'd hoped they would have been older, more experienced, wiser, less cocky, less *bold.* It was time for another agonizing wait . . .

HAVANA, FEBRUARY

"Good evening, and welcome to the evening news this tenth day of February, nineteen hundred ninety-three. I'm Tom Danlau," the newscaster in the navy blue blazer and red silk tie half smiled. "Tonight in the top news stories, we have an update on the AIDS crisis and the move to establish quarantine colonies in sparsely populated areas in the United States. On a related topic, we'll discuss the CDC's concentrated effort in combatting the spread of the disease in Miami. But first, these messages from our sponsors."

Fidel muted the volume again while the commercials aired. He secretly envied some of the products available to American consumers and openly laughed at the stupidity of others. "Look, they sell a talking cloth rag! And *specialized* talking rags, no less! *Whipits*, or something like that. One to clean the toilet, one to clean the furniture, one to clean the windows! I *never!*" he laughed with delight.

Luis grinned from the chair opposite him. "How *funny*! You'd think they would be embarrassed to use such a thing! Maybe you should rethink your stance on allowing American TV to be broadcast into our country, General. Let the Americanos embarrass themselves with their laziness and stupidity in front of our people! Maybe set up another satellite dish out on the Plaza de la Revolucion and let the people watch only the commercials!" Luis turned the revolving leather chair back and forth as he spoke. He became serious. "Maybe we'll hear some news tonight about the move to set up sanitariums in the U.S. for the AIDS sufferers."

Fidel asked, "It's about time the Americanos got smart and established AIDS quarantine colonies, like we did years ago, no, Colonel? The infection rate stabilized here immediately, and, fortunately, involved only our undesirables to begin with. We don't even consider AIDS a *problem*, much less a threat to national security like the Americanos do." He changed the mood. "Are you sure today was the day?" Fidel raised a bushy eyebrow and his outer upper lip twisted upward.

"Yes, General, and I've taken care of everything very handily." Luis returned his attention to Fidel from gazing out the window into the early winter darkness. "The vaccine, by now, is lying in one of the deepest valleys in the floor of the Atlantic Ocean, and no one is the wiser. Except, of course, for a few people from the CIA and the CDC. I hope they report something about the crash in this broadcast."

They laughed with delight, relishing their victory, as the still silent TV aired a beer commercial.

Fidel was elated. "Imagine how *frustrated* they must be! To think they had the vaccine within their grasp, only to be outsmarted by such a small and insignificant enemy as we! The elephant is brought down by the ant!" Castro was beside himself with laughter with his head rolled back, looking at the ceiling.

"Yes, incredible, General. It seems our long range planning over the past fifteen years is blossoming before our eyes." Luis's eyes glossed with the satisfaction of vengeance gained.

"Sh-h-h, our Mr. Danlau is back." Fidel hit the volume switch again.

"Welcome back." There was a close-up of the self-assured

reporter, but occasional static lines from the poor satellite reception blurred his screen image. "As reported often in the news of late, the surgeon general and top level advisors in the health service have been proponents of a move to establish quarantine communities throughout the country. Their goal, of course, is to try and halt the spread of the AIDS virus."

Fidel cut in. "They want to put them in sparsely populated areas such as the western deserts. Imagine how strongly the local people in those areas will fight against it."

"Yes . . . *I* would fight it, too," Luis remarked. "There have been large-scale demonstrations against this stratagem by liberal dissidents who're claiming it's a violation of civil rights. The majority of the dissenters reportedly have the disease *themselves*, according to what I've seen from their health department publications. Let's listen."

Danlau's picture was clear again. "Until the recent Supreme Court decision, which allows the records of persons testing HIV positive to be made public for the protection of the public domain, the Surgeon General couldn't use the testing results to substantiate this urgent request for quarantine communities. We now take you, live, to the mall in Washington, D.C., where correspondent Charles Malloy is covering the mass demonstration against this proposal. Charles?"

The scene changed to a close-up of the nattily dressed field reporter, with one of the omnipresent symbols of the nation's capital, the Washington Monument, in the background.

"I'm Charles Malloy. The opponents of the quarantine plan, those infected, according to the health service, have deemed this approach as medieval, with a liking to the tuberculosis and leprosy colonies of earlier history. I have with me Mr. Alfred Redding, the spokesman for the activist group fighting the proposal. Mr. Redding, what is your position regarding the proposed quarantine?"

Redding grabbed the microphone. He was frail, with sunken features and bony hands, and wore poorly fitted clothing. "This plan is *barbaric*, medieval! The quarantine proponents are encroaching on our very right to call ourselves human!" He turned and spoke to the applauding crowd.

"What ever happened to the concepts of human intellectual enlightenment and a progressive civilization?" he cried out. "We *call* ourselves a civilized society. We supposedly threw out archaic concepts of health and disease long ago. There has been *nothing* even close to this proposal for dealing with disease since the turn of the century!"

There was more en masse outrage and screaming from the field below. The camera slowly panned the placard-laden sea of human faces.

Redding continued, "We, as citizens of this country, predicated on personal rights and freedoms, demand our right to come and go as we choose." He emphatically slapped the makeshift podium. "We've lost one battle at the Supreme Court already, that which has denied our right to privacy by exposing our test results for public use, in whatever way the government sees fit. We've been denied jobs, or fired from our existing jobs, even in professional capacities. See my clothes?" he indicated his ill fitting, outmoded sport jacket and mismatched pants. "I am a lawyer, or, *was* a lawyer, with a very successful practice. I worked hard to be a success. But, now, my own *country* has allowed that to be taken away from me, not my *disease!* I must fight, daily, to pay for my medicine. I've had to *steal* to pay for my medication!"

The crowd gasped and applauded at the same time. Redding continued, "We've been persecuted in the schools and the health care system. And now we're denied even the most basic freedom of this country's founding, the freedom of religious choice! Our families and friends have abandoned us. We have *nothing* left, with the exception, *today* anyway, of the right of freedom of movement. We *will*, therefore, fight this proposal until we are physically carried off to these desolate prison camps!"

The camera once again panned over the thousands of screaming supporters gathered on the mall. Redding took the microphone in both hands in a dramatic gesture. His mood changed to one of defiance as he turned back directly at the TV camera. "And, let the record show, that I, like thousands more of the unfortunate afflicted before you," he turned from the TV audience and motioned over the crowd, then faced the camera again, "do not, and never have, engaged in homosexual activity or intravenous drug abuse. We're not all whores and whoremongers. We're *people*, like *you*, who've unfortunately contracted this God forsaken plague. We *implore* you. *Help* us, don't *shun* us. Until you do, we must act for ourselves, for our constitutional rights. We will fight on!" He raised a closed fist as the din crescendoed.

The crowd's volume swelled to a deafening roar, with people waving banners and chanting, "We shall overcome!"

The camera's focus quickly returned to the field reporter, Malloy. "The senate debates over this issue are still in progress. Meanwhile, at the Department of Health and Human Services, federal attorneys are seeking a legal instrument whereby the constitutional right to personal freedom may be overridden in the wake of a national health and security threat. Health Department authorities could then begin the initiation of the quarantine program immediately. This is Charles Malloy, reporting live from Washington."

"Thank you, Charles." Tom Danlau reappeared. "The latest statistics show that there are over two point seven million Americans with AIDS. Estimates run as high as possibly twelve million more persons that have either not been tested, or are avoiding testing. To date, over one million have died. The current epicenters of the disease include all of the major metropolitan areas, with Miami as the area hardest hit. When we return from our commercial break, we'll take you to Ted Killian, on the outskirts of Miami."

Fidel cut the volume again and looked at Luis. "Tsk, tsk, tsk, what a terrible thing to happen," he sneered. He extended his hand in a congratulatory handshake to his cohort.

"The sweetness of success, General, is to be savored," smiled Luis. "Have you any brandy?"

"Certainly!" Castro ambled to the cabinet which hid the bar and retrieved two snifters and a favored old bottle of cognac, poured them a third full, and returned to Luis.

Luis raised his glass, "To *us*, and the crash of America as we used to know it!" Castro lifted his drink, and they both pulled them dry with large gulps before setting their snifters on the desk. "Ah," Luis quipped, wiping the spillage from his lower lip. "Fidel, have you heard any new developments on the vaccine that the famous Dr. Jonas Salk has been working on?"

"No, nothing. My intelligence sources tell me they're still far from any real breakthroughs, and that some of the test volunteers have quietly and suspiciously perished."

"I *do* feel something for the men and women of God who've sacrificed themselves in the name of Christian humanitarianism, even though I don't personally share their religious beliefs," Luis said.

"It's war, my friend," Castro responded. He turned the volume up again as Danlau reappeared, mumbling about Miami.

The studio camera cut out and the Miami skyline appeared on the screen, then zoomed to Mr. Killian. "Thank you, Tom," the dark-suited reporter started. "Miami, Florida, today is a city under siege." The camera panned the skyline. "As you can see, the city appears normal in appearance, from this distance, anyway."

Then the camera zoomed in on a freeway interchange that was void of the usual heavy traffic, and a roadblock came into view.

"It has been a week since the commencement of this police action, ordered by the mayor, John Dalton. The AIDS virus has become so widespread, throughout the entire city, that these special roadblocks have been placed by the health and police departments to attempt a slowing of the transmission by warning the traveling public of the dangers. Known prostitutes and drug abusers have been cordoned off in the downtown barrio, and police are letting no one in or out of the area. Food and medical aid are being provided by the U.S. Department of Health and Human Services."

The camera returned to the reporter. "Miami is the major epicenter for this contagious disease, now known commonly as the 'white plague.' The disease has severely affected other urban areas, but not to this extent. At the onset there was no explanation for the major occurrence here, but health department officials theorize that the fulminant nature of the problem is due to the influx, thirteen years ago, of the Cuban prison population during the Mariel Boatlift." He looked at his notes.

"In 1980, Fidel Castro dumped thousands of Cuban prisoners on the Florida coast, intermixed with other Cubans seeking political freedom. U.S. immigration officials realized too late that virtually all of those prisoners who were not later returned to Cuba tested HIV positive. That discovery still confounds the scientific community. That question, however, has now been tabled in favor of all available health care dollars being funnelled into the plague." A chart reflecting dollar amounts projected on the TV screen.

Killian continued, "Billions have been spent on research, health care of the afflicted, welfare payments for those who can no longer work, and, last but not least, hugely expensive attempts by federal and local governments to curb further spread by means such as the roadblocks you see here in Miami. The dollar amount of this campaign has far exceeded the wildest expectations of just three years ago. The national budget has been changed dramatically in the past year, with health care funding outpacing the national defense budget three-to-one for the first time in the nation's history."

A U.S. map appeared with many of the central prairie states blocked out. "Despite this all-out attempt, the disease is progressively spreading into the heartland of the country. Researchers again, however, predict that the natural occurrence of this disease will peak at some point, and the disease will burn itself out. From Miami, I'm Ted Killian reporting."

The New York studio aired. "We'll be right back," a somber Tom Danlau said. Another commercial played about a foot soaking tub called 'Happy Feet,' accompanied by a lighthearted little jingle and caricatures of smiling feet.

"I find it so incredible!" Fidel exclaimed. "Their country is falling apart, crumbling under the black cloud of an incurable disease, and those imbeciles are more concerned with their poor aching feet!" He laughed. "Colonel, thanks to you I've met a personal goal of many year's duration. The giant imperialistic country of the world will be brought down by an invisible little bug. And the reporter in Miami said they didn't know why our prisoners were all infected. Shall we *tell* them?"

Luis couldn't tell whether Castro was serious. "I *don't* think it would be so wise, General." He returned to the main topic. "Thank you for your compliments, but it took *your* determination and power to make it happen. Now we can—"

Luis was interrupted by Danlau's return. "A U.S. Air Force B-1B bomber crashed today midway between Portugal and the Azores Islands," a map of the Azores area flashed behind Danlau, "in calm seas and perfect flying conditions. The four man crew reportedly ejected to safety after both engines mysteriously exploded. Two of the crew were unharmed, and the others are hospitalized with internal injuries but are expected to live. They were picked up by a passing Greek freighter. Air Force officials report that it was a routine flight, returning from the Aviano base in Italy to the Homestead Air Force Base in Miami. Other sources, however, suggest that the flight was of an unknown nature, and possibly carried a secret cargo. Air Force officials refused further comment, saying they are investigating the incident at this time. The plane sunk into one of the deepest known valleys in the Atlantic Ocean floor, with the Air Force reporting that there is no hope of recovering the plane's flight recorders to assist in determining the cause of the crash. If, indeed, there *was* a secret cargo, that too is lost."

A rendering of the plane replaced the Azores map. "The B-1B has come under attack often as being unreliable, with frequent inspection groundings ordered since it was first placed in service by the Air Force in late 1984. To date, there have been eight crashes involving this long-range, multi-role strategic bomber, many of which were due to engine problems."

The plane on the back screen was replaced by a stock market

chart. "In the business news, Wall Street today reports no change in the slumping market, with the Dow Jones Industrial Average closing down a half point in light trading."

Luis turned to Fidel. "I'm glad they chose to broadcast the news of the plane crash today. Now the Italians can reunite a very worried family."

"Yes, and again, congratulations on a difficult but well executed plan, Colonel!" Fidel exclaimed. "You really did it! You, and the bastard Danella, brought down the only hope the Americanos had. It's too bad that we were forced to lose the vaccine that way, but at least the Americanos didn't get to use it to try to curtail the epidemic . . . It would have been sweet if *we* could have retrieved it from the Vatican before they did and sold it to them for some outrageous fortune! They would've paid *anything* for it, even knowing that it may not work effectively because of the viruses' mutations over the years. They don't have the luxury of waiting on Dr. Salk."

Luis looked at him. "Yes, General, a well-executed plan, in spite of our loss of the vaccine. Oh, well . . . All's fair in love and etcetera . . . " he smiled.

"You know, Colonel, I think that very soon you'll share the title of General with me," Fidel mused aloud, his hands folded across his gut. "You're the best man in my entire revolutionary state, my friend. Yes, I'll see to it tomorrow. You'll enjoy the rank of *General!* There's no stopping the economic crash of the United States, now, because of this spectacular plan."

"But, General, you give me too much credit. Without your commitment and wise decision to endorse this strategy, we'd be nowhere. *I* feel we should enjoy the moment as equals." Luis smiled at the general.

Fidel squirmed. "No, no, my friend, you go too far with your interpretation here! I strongly disagree with your use of the word *equals*. As you say, we both contributed to this plan. However, as you say, without *my* decision to proceed, the mission would have failed. You're too strong in your language. Remember, *I* am still the overseer of this country."

"I'm very sorry, General, I didn't mean to put myself in *total* equality with you, I simply meant . . . " Luis tempered his ire.

"Certainly, Colonel, I understand. Enough said."

The broadcast continued in the background. They returned their focus to the television, trying to gracefully ease out of the uncomfortable conversation.

"And, finally in the news tonight," Danlau turned to Camera 2 and continued, "Nobel Science Award nominee, Dr. Hans Bjorgstad, was gunned down this morning in a drive-by, gangland style shooting as he left his home in Stockholm for work at the university. He had been nominated several times for the prestigious award, most recently in 1987 for his work in anti-cancer drugs. He was eighty-three years old. No motive has been established for the brutal slaying. We will follow that story as more developments occur.

"And so, for this tenth day of February, 1993, we bid you farewell, and wish a pleasant evening for all. I'm Tom Danlau. Good night." A swell of symphony music suddenly overpowered the screen image of Danlau behind the list of scrolling credits.

Fidel remotely turned off the television. "Colonel, you took care of *that* loose end too, no? You amaze me, you simply amaze me. A thousand pardons, I meant to call you General!" He looked over at Luis.

"Yes General. The timing was perfect. I authorized Danella to take out the old Doctor Bjorgstad. I wanted a clean sweep, to remove the only existing source for the molecular structure of the vaccine. It had to be done at the same time that the plane went down, because I feared that Dr. Bjorgstad could hear of the loss of the vaccine and come forward to spill his guts. There was also the chance that the *CIA* may have been watching him. He was still a man of limited scruples, you know, and he might've divulged the conspiracy if he thought he was the only man alive that could help. There was no other choice."

"Yes, Colonel, er, I forgot . . . I mean *General*! You did the proper thing. Well, why don't you remain in Cuba now that the mission is accomplished? There's no need for you in Hungary anymore, not since they've stupidly rescinded communism in favor of putrid capitalism and democracy a few years ago."

"I'm not too sure, I consider it my home now."

Castro cleared his throat, then leaned forward and poured the snifters full of cognac again. "I wouldn't want you to be tempted by the black markets that have formed over there since the idiots joined the European Common Market last year." He again gave Luis a cold look, watching for contrary body language.

Luis laughed awkwardly. "It's not that, General . . . It's just that I've formed many fast friendships over the years." He gave Fidel a sideways look, not wanting to expose his inner feelings. *I'm ten steps ahead of you, you dumb flunkie.* He had grown accustomed to free choice was the real truth. He *couldn't* live under this dictator anymore.

"Let's both give it some thought, my friend," Fidel replied. He smiled uneasily and quickly changed the subject. "So, the world has unwittingly been subjected to another historical drama. A maniacal cardinal starts a plague to wipe out immorality, but his grandiose plan is exploited by a handful of brilliant men," he smiled boastfully, "and used as a political weapon with great success."

"Here, here!" Luis toasted the summation.

"By the way, whatever became of the old crazy cardinal, anyway?"

"I'm not sure . . . The intelligence I have is that he was in trouble with the church for suspicion of embezzlement. I wouldn't worry too much about him, though . . . He *definitely* won't talk."

"And what of the creep, Danella?"

"People like him are a dime a dozen . . . *He'll* never talk to a soul about what his part has been. He's probably lying on a beach somewhere, still blowing money extravagantly and promising himself he'll retire after the next job."

Fidel wiped a spot from his spit-shined black military boot. "And so . . . The world will continue turning, but without the knowledge or the benefit of where this disease came from, possibly for all eternity!

That's mind boggling! And a vaccine . . . The only hope now is Dr. Jonas Salk. Good luck, Doctor!" Fidel raised his glass in a pretentious salute. He turned to Luis. "Luis, I've suddenly decided that I want you *here*, beside me, in Havana. You're such a capable man!"

Luis slumped in his chair, thanking Fidel for the ill-gotten praise. *You don't know well, yet, what I'm capable of, my General.* He eyed the large solid teak desk and opulent office. It was a simple matter of time, he thought to himself. He'd have to replace the leather chair occupied by Fidel, because the current one squeaked loudly and had become misshapen under the large weight over the years. It still reeked of sour cigar smoke even though "El Presidente" had quit years earlier. Other than the chair, the office suited him just fine.

VATICAN, JUNE
1993

It's so peaceful here, so serene, mused the young, impressionable priest, Roland Dorwick, as he sauntered along the ancient stone pathway through the gardens. The youthful priest was caught up in the elation that befell most young priests on their first trip to the Holy See.

He was in his mid-thirties, with an easy, unassuming manner, the result of an overly protected childhood. He flashed large, white, straight teeth when he smiled, which provided a contrast to his jet black hair and close-cropped beard.

The lilacs were in full bloom, marvelously stimulating his olfactory sense. The rolling lawns were emerald green now, and would stay that way for months. Late Spring was always his favorite time of year, and to spend it at the Vatican! The morning air refreshed his palate, and he took several deep cleansing breaths. "Ah, yes, it's wonderful here! I think I'm going to like this place a lot."

The young Englishman had just arrived at the Holy See late the night before. The Vatican was his choice for sabbatical leave after completing seven years at the parish in London. After eight care-free month's worth of studying his passion, theology, he'd finish his

Master's thesis and return to London to a much desired teaching post at the University of Notre Dame. This was a dream he'd aspired to since he was ordained at the age of twenty-six. Roland stooped and picked a small but lovely yellow flower from a rock-lined garden and put it to his nostrils.

"Hey, Father, what are you doing?" called another priest from under a large straw hat working in the next flower bed. "Do you know how much the bulbs cost for those, and how hard they are to grow?"

Roland looked at him in embarrassment. "Uh, no . . . I'm very sorry."

The old priest waved his hand downward. "Eh, don't worry about it. Just don't pick any more." He took off his gloves and approached Roland. "Who are you, anyway?"

"Roland Dorwick, here on sabbatical. And who are you?"

"I'm Monsignor Peter Matusek." They shook hands. "I'm retired, and live in the apartments. I tend the gardens."

"Are *you* responsible for all of this loveliness? Incredible! Look at those huge cypress trees." Roland looked all around him at the elliptical towers.

"Some of them are hundreds of years old, Father. Beautiful, aren't they?"

Roland stared, starry-eyed. "Yes, so stately and magnificent. Hundreds of years, huh? Just think of all the world history these trees have witnessed."

"That's for sure." The monsignor joined Roland's inspired mentum. He laughed curtly, "And, you know, my naive young priest, that not *all* of the events that've occurred over history in these gardens have been so noble. The Romans, the Inquisition, and so on . . . And, if these trees could talk, I'm sure they could tell us of even more recent human tribulations that were devised in this place, but on more surreptitious terms, and possibly not so grand in scale." He laughed oddly, "Yes . . . the great mystery trees."

Roland stood and looked from tree to tree, then back at the gardener. "It's overwhelming, huh? Well, I'd better move on so you can do your beautiful work. Good day to you, Monsignor."

"Good day to you, Father. If you need assistance settling in, please call on me."

"Thank you . . . And I'm sorry about the flower."

"Ah, forget it. Have a nice day." The old gardener wandered off.

Roland continued walking through the gardens, rounding a row of cypress, then entered a small clearing dotted with stone tables and benches. Even these cold stone fixtures probably concealed unknown twists of world history. There was a handful of men seated in the area, each indifferent to the presence of the others, each consumed in his own personal undertaking.

Most of them were cassocked men, some reading, some pensive in meditation. Roland couldn't know whether they were priests, monsignors, or whatever rank by their dress alone. There was a bishop at one table, evidenced by the red pinstriping on his cassock. He was reading a thick, leather bound volume. *What an idyllic place this is!*

He was attracted to an old man in his peripheral vision, a very old man, seated by himself sixty paces away. The man was gaunt, weathered. Steel gray eyes penetrated thick glasses, fixed blankly on the evergreen shrub opposite him. His face was highlighted by the linear furrows of too many years in the sun. He wasn't wearing a cassock, as were the rest of the men, but worn, woolen trousers and a heavy, faded flannel shirt. He had an unkempt look about him, with a white stubbly beard of several days growth, and scraggly white, thin hair.

Roland detected an aura of something unique about this man, a charisma of sorts. The old man sat with his hands folded in front of him, his elbows resting on the table. He appeared sad, disturbed. Roland thought him to be seeking consolation, or possibly forgiveness.

Roland felt a compelling urge to speak with this troubled man. The old retch interfered with Roland's perception of the tranquility of the garden; he needed help. He slowly approached the man, not wanting to barge forth and cause disruption in the serenity.

The man's eyes were dull, flat in their affect. He didn't look up.

Roland was too close now for the old man to not have seen him coming. Maybe he was mentally ill, and had somehow, inadvertently, found his way to the garden. Maybe he was just an old, lost bum.

"Good morning, sir," Roland opened. "A very nice time to be in the garden, don't you think?"

As expected, there was no response. He tried once again; after all, mental illness can cause impediments in a person's ability to communicate. Roland sat down directly opposite him. There was no way the pathetic old man could continue to refuse acknowledging Roland's presence.

"My old friend, is something wrong? Can I do anything to help you?" Roland tilted his head to the side, trying to exude empathy. Still no response. The old man's fixed gaze was unyielding, now dead centered on Roland's chest.

Roland saw another cassocked man deliberately approach from over the old man's shoulder. The priest motioned from behind the old man for Roland to follow him.

"Excuse me, sir, but I'll leave now," Roland said. "Perhaps we can talk in a little while." He stood and hurriedly walked the forty feet behind the old man to where the beckoner had seated himself at another table.

The cassocked man spoke first. "You're new here. I'm Monsignor Salerno." He extended his hand.

"A pleasure to meet you, Monsignor. I'm Roland Dorwick. I'm here on sabbatical to continue my study of theology, and yes, I arrived only last night."

"Oh, yes, I've heard of you. The Vatican is known for its ability to spread news quickly by word of mouth. I believe anywhere else, in a less 'pious' atmosphere, this form of communication is referred to as *gossip*! I daresay it'd be impossible to keep a little *secret* here, let alone any furtive activity of greater importance!" He laughed.

Roland liked him. "That gives me a great sense of security, then," Roland laughed sarcastically. "I love it here already. It's just as I imagined. Monsignor, what's the problem with that troubled old man you called me away from? Is he ill or something?"

"No, Father, he's not ill, not in a *physical* sense. You wouldn't know it now, but he was once a powerful man, a *very* powerful man. His name is Cardinal Desmond Wentworth, at least, he *was* a cardinal. He was the prefect for the Congregation of the Doctrine of the Faith until four months ago."

"*That* old man is Cardinal Desmond Wentworth? That's hard to believe!"

"Yes, the same man. His mental function began deteriorating at about that time. He became severely depressed and entered into his own little world. The doctors first thought it was Alzheimer's disease, but decided no, that it was more a condition of self-imposed burnout and depression. Desmond refused to accept psychiatric help, and kept getting worse over time. One evening in February, during the news on television, he stood up abruptly and left the room. Something on TV, it seemed, disturbed him greatly. Those present in the room tried to figure it out but couldn't. There was just the usual update on the AIDS situation in the U.S., and news of a plane that went down somewhere near the Azores Islands. One thing, though, the only thing that was even seemingly connected . . . An old doctor friend from his past was shot to death that day, in Stockholm."

"Well, *that* would be a reasonable explanation for his behavior," mused the young priest.

"Yes, it would seem so . . . But apparently he'd left the room before the newscast ever got to the story about the doctor's murder. It appeared coincidental to those in the room."

"I see . . . strange behavior, yes." Roland paused.

"Then one day, soon after that, he suddenly resigned his position, then renounced his affiliation with the church. He moved into a dingy little apartment, not too far from here. No one's ever known why, but there has always been a lot of speculation . . . loss of faith, unresolved guilt over past deeds, that kind of thing."

"Yes, it's coming back to me now," Roland replied. "I remember what a fervor his leaving caused a few months ago. Wasn't there some kind of financial audit or something?"

"Yes, there was. He insisted that it was his right to do what he saw fit with the money in that discretionary account, and it truly was. But to have spent *that* kind of money, and with no substantiation, was a bit too much. That was about the same time he starting not speaking to anyone and entered this cold shell, like you see him now."

"Why won't he speak? Surely there must be *someone* he'll speak to about his problems . . . family, trusted friend, surely *someone*."

"No, Father, I'm afraid not. Shortly thereafter he took a vow of silence, and hasn't spoken a word in the past four months to anyone. He spends most days sitting on that very bench where you see him now, with the same, exact expression on his face. Maybe deep in prayer, or possibly horror, no one will ever know. I've noticed his physical condition deteriorating over time. He looks worse now than ever, and refuses medical care. Apparently he wants his life to end. Sometimes, people say, before he took his solemn vow, he'd be sitting right there and start mumbling repetitiously about how the only thing left for mankind is hope. Nothing more than that . . . I think something traumatic shook his faith to its very foundation, if you ask me. Oh, well," Salerno sighed. "Another of the great mysteries of this garden. No one will ever know . . . "

Please Feel Free to Make a Copy of This Order Form

Yes, I want to order _____ Collector's Edition hardcover copies of *The Pandora* Factor @ $29.95 each. New Mexico residents please add state sales tax. Shipping & handling, $3.00 (first book) $1.50 each additional book (shipped to the same address).

Yes, I want to order _____ quality trade paperback copies of *The Pandora Factor* @ $13.95 each. New Mexico residents please add state sales tax. Shipping & handling, $3.00 (first book) $1.50 each additional book (shipped to the same address).

Send check or money order to:

Western Publishers Consortium
PO Box 35819
Albuquerque, New Mexico 87176-5819

or call the WPC VISA & MasterCard Order Line
1-800-U READ ME • 1-800-873-2363

Quantity x Cover Price	______________
New Mexico State Tax (5.75%)	______________
Shipping & Handling	______________
Total	______________

This book was produced, manufactured, and marketed with the support of Western Publishers' Consortium, located in Albuquerque, New Mexico, U.S.A. This organization provides full-service publishing capabilities nationwide, from editing, typesetting, layout, cover design, and proofreading, to printing, binding, free book storage, nation-wide marketing, and fulfillment services (including toll-free ordering honoring VISA & MasterCard).

WPC

For information from Western Publishers Consortium about author/publisher services, write to Western Publishers' Consortium, Box 35819, Albuquerque, New Mexico 87176-5819, call 505-243-5333, or FAX 505-242-4327.

Western Publishers' Consortium
Full Service Support